THE
GREAT
GATSBY

F. SCOTT FITZGERALD

THE GREAT GATSBY

AND RELATED STORIES

THE LIBRARY OF AMERICA CORRECTED TEXT

Edited by James L. W. West III

LIBRARY OF AMERICA

The Great Gatsby and Related Stories

Published in the United States by Library of America.
Visit our website at www.loa.org.

Distributed to the trade in the United States by Penguin Random House Inc. and in Canada by Penguin Random House Canada Ltd.

Library of Congress Control Number: 2022951281
ISBN 978-1-59853-756-7

1 3 5 7 9 10 8 6 4 2

Printed in the United States of America

CONTENTS

PREFACE

This volume brings together F. Scott Fitzgerald's classic novel *The Great Gatsby* (1925) and four related stories that share the novel's themes and preoccupations, all in newly edited, corrected texts prepared for Library of America. This edition also includes a selection of correspondence between Fitzgerald and his editor, Maxwell Perkins, concerning the composition and revision of the novel.

In preparing this new text of *The Great Gatsby*, I have consulted Fitzgerald's manuscript, his working galleys, and his personal reading copy of the novel. This volume presents the first printing of the 1925 Scribner's edition, lightly emended in various ways, with the majority of the alterations made on Fitzgerald's authority. Control of the text has been given to Fitzgerald. The treatment of the text for this edition is similar to the cleaning and restoration of a work of art that has deteriorated, ever so slightly, over time. The goal of these labors is to capture accurately the author's intentions for the novel, as nearly as those intentions can be recovered from the evidence that survives. Readers interested in a more detailed understanding of the textual work undertaken for *The Great Gatsby* and the other selections in this volume should consult the Note on the Texts.

The Great Gatsby is probably the most widely read American novel of the twentieth century. It is a fast-moving story told by a narrator,

Nick Carraway, whom we like and trust. Its characters are indelibly drawn: Jay Gatsby, with his mysterious origins and air of danger; Daisy Buchanan, with her voice full of money; Tom Buchanan, rich, over-bearing, and belligerent; Jordan Baker, wan and faintly arrogant. The minor characters are memorable. Fitzgerald has given us George and Myrtle Wilson, desperate to escape their marginal lives; Myrtle's sister Catherine, with her "sticky bob of red hair"; Chester McKee, show-ing Nick his murky "photographic studies"; Chester's wife, Lucille, "languid, handsome, and horrible"; Meyer Wolfshiem, exhibiting his peculiar cufflinks to Nick; Ewing Klipspringer, performing his "liver exercises" on the floor; Owl Eyes, peering at the unopened books in Gatsby's library. And there is Gatsby's aquaplane, his medal from "Lit-tle Montenegro," his piles of beautiful shirts, his pink suit, the parties on his blue lawn, the stylish dancing and hot jazz, the glamorous and dissipated guests—all of this stays in the mind.

The four stories included in this volume are closely related to *The Great Gatsby*. Fitzgerald often used short stories as trial grounds for characters, settings, themes, and narrative approaches that he would later employ in his novels. This is particularly true for *The Great Gatsby*. "Winter Dreams"—which Fitzgerald, in an undated letter of June 1925 to Perkins, called a "1st draft of the Gatsby idea"—is a poignant rich girl/poor boy narrative that the author wrote almost three years before publication of the novel. Judy Jones, the golden girl of "Winter Dreams," becomes a much desired ideal for Dexter Green. He achieves conven-tional success but cannot win her heart. By the end of the story he is disillusioned, unable to accept the passage of time and the inevitability of change. "Absolution," a tense story about an adolescent boy and a priest, was salvaged from the original ur-text of *The Great Gatsby*, a first attempt at the novel set by Fitzgerald in the upper Midwest. Rudolph

Miller, the youthful hero, yearns to escape from the limitations of his upbringing and the suffocating influence of the Catholic church, much as Jay Gatsby desires to move beyond his own humble origins in North Dakota. "Rags Martin-Jones and the Pr-nce of W-les" is a work of light fiction, a romantic fantasy in which the stalwart hero, John M. Chestnut, eventually captures the impossible Rags Martin-Jones. He creates a glittering, illusory world in order to attract her, much as Jay Gatsby stages his glamorous parties in hopes of luring Daisy Buchanan, the object of his dreams, to his ersatz mansion. "The Rich Boy," the longest of the stories in this volume, was written just *after* publication of *The Great Gatsby*. The action of the story is seen through the eyes of a character who resembles Nick Carraway. This nameless narrator has observed the "very rich" and found them to be "different from you and me." He is a keen observer who recognizes the differences between old and new money. He comes to understand that his friend, a rich boy named Anson Hunter, nourishes a sense of superiority and privilege that takes precedence over all else, even emotional commitment and love.

Fitzgerald had a close relationship with Maxwell Perkins. The correspondence between the two men reveals a great deal about the inception, composition, revision, and publication of *The Great Gatsby*. Fitzgerald relied on Perkins for professional advice; he also valued the editor's critiques of his manuscripts, especially in matters of structure and characterization. In the letters written during the composition and revision of *The Great Gatsby*, we can see Perkins's influence on the novel, especially on the manner in which Jay Gatsby's past is revealed. Particularly important here is the November 20, 1924, letter from Perkins to Fitzgerald. In this letter Perkins confesses to Fitzgerald that, for him, "Gatsby is somewhat vague." Perkins continues: "The reader's eyes can never quite focus upon him, his outlines are dim." Part of the problem for Perkins was that, in the early version of the novel he was reading, the details of Gatsby's past were not revealed until very nearly the end of the book. Perkins urged Fitzgerald to drop hints about Gatsby's past life earlier in the narrative, with "phrases, and possibly incidents, little touches of various kinds, that would suggest that he was in some active way mysteriously engaged." Fitzgerald took this advice, along with other suggestions in the letter, and put his novel through a major revision in galley proofs, giving us the text that we know today. In this revised version we learn much earlier about Jay Gatsby's past, with further details revealed as the narrative unfolds.

The Great Gatsby is Fitzgerald's masterpiece. The period of its composition was his finest hour: inspiration, talent, self-discipline, and luck came together magically to create a novel that has an enduring hold on the popular imagination and continues to win new readers. Fitzgerald had a pitch-perfect ear for language and a gift for dialogue. Many of the passages in the novel are unforgettable: Daisy and Jordan dressed in white, floating on the sofa in Daisy's sunroom; Nick woozy with drink in Tom and Myrtle's love nest; Gatsby smiling down on his departing guests from the steps of his mansion; Nick riding with Gatsby in his gorgeous yellow car, whirling through the Valley of Ashes on the way to the glamorous streets of Manhattan. At the end of the novel Fitzgerald leaves us gazing at the green light on Daisy's dock. It shines through the night from across the bay. Readers know what the green light signifies, even if they cannot put it into words. *The Great Gatsby* captures something uniquely American: our hopes and fantasies, our sense of infinite possibility, our disappointment when our dreams are not fulfilled. That's quite a lot for one short novel.

J. L. W. W. III

THE
GREAT
GATSBY

Then wear the gold hat, if that will move her;
If you can bounce high, bounce for her too,
Till she cry "Lover, gold-hatted, high-bouncing lover,
I must have you!"

—THOMAS PARKE D'INVILLIERS.

ONCE AGAIN
TO
ZELDA

CHAPTER I

In my younger and more vulnerable years my father gave me some advice that I've been turning over in my mind ever since.

"Whenever you feel like criticizing anyone," he told me, "just remember that all the people in this world haven't had the advantages that you've had."

He didn't say any more, but we've always been unusually communicative in a reserved way, and I understood that he meant a great deal more than that. In consequence, I'm inclined to reserve all judgments, a habit that has opened up many curious natures to me and also made me the victim of not a few veteran bores. The abnormal mind is quick to detect and attach itself to this quality when it appears in a normal person, and so it came about that in college I was unjustly accused of being a politician, because I was privy to the secret griefs of wild, unknown men. Most of the confidences were unsought—frequently I have feigned sleep, preoccupation, or a hostile levity when I realized by some unmistakable sign that an intimate revelation was quivering on the horizon; for the intimate revelations of young men, or at least the terms in which they express them, are usually plagiaristic and marred by obvious suppressions. Reserving judgments is a matter of infinite hope. I am still a little afraid of missing something if I forget that, as my father snobbishly suggested, and

I snobbishly repeat, a sense of the fundamental decencies is parcelled out unequally at birth.

And, after boasting this way of my tolerance, I come to the admission that it has a limit. Conduct may be founded on the hard rock or the wet marshes, but after a certain point I don't care what it's founded on. When I came back from the East last autumn I felt that I wanted the world to be in uniform and at a sort of moral attention forever; I wanted no more riotous excursions with privileged glimpses into the human heart. Only Gatsby, the man who gives his name to this book, was exempt from my reaction—Gatsby, who represented everything for which I have an unaffected scorn. If personality is an unbroken series of successful gestures, then there was something gorgeous about him, some heightened sensitivity to the promises of life, as if he were related to one of those intricate machines that register earthquakes ten thousand miles away. This responsiveness had nothing to do with that flabby impressionability which is dignified under the name of the "creative temperament"—it was an extraordinary gift for hope, a romantic readiness such as I have never found in any other person and which it is not likely I shall ever find again. No—Gatsby turned out all right at the end; it is what preyed on Gatsby, what foul dust floated in the wake of his dreams that temporarily closed out my interest in the abortive sorrows and short-winded elations of men.

◆

My family have been prominent, well-to-do people in this Middle Western city for three generations. The Carraways are something of a clan, and we have a tradition that we're descended from the Dukes of Buccleuch, but the actual founder of my line was my grandfather's brother, who came here in fifty-one, sent a substitute to the Civil War, and started the wholesale hardware business that my father carries on today.

I never saw this great-uncle, but I'm supposed to look like him—with special reference to the rather hard-boiled painting that hangs in father's office. I graduated from New Haven in 1915, just a quarter of a century after my father, and a little later I participated in that delayed Teutonic migration known as the Great War. I enjoyed the counter-raid so thoroughly that I came back restless. Instead of being the warm center of the world, the Middle West now seemed like the ragged edge of the universe—so I decided to go East and learn the bond business. Everybody I knew was in the bond business, so I supposed it could support one more single man. All my aunts and uncles talked it over as if they were choosing a prep school for me, and finally said, "Why—ye-es," with very grave, hesitant faces. Father agreed to finance me for a year, and after various delays I came East, permanently, I thought, in the spring of twenty-two.

The practical thing was to find rooms in the city, but it was a warm season, and I had just left a country of wide lawns and friendly trees, so when a young man at the office suggested that we take a house together in a commuting town, it sounded like a great idea. He found the house, a weather-beaten cardboard bungalow at eighty a month, but at the last minute the firm ordered him to Washington, and I went out to the country alone. I had a dog—at least I had him for a few days until he ran away—and an old Dodge and a Finnish woman, who made my bed and cooked breakfast and muttered Finnish wisdom to herself over the electric stove.

It was lonely for a day or so until one morning some man, more recently arrived than I, stopped me on the road.

"How do you get to West Egg Village?" he asked helplessly.

I told him. And as I walked on I was lonely no longer. I was a guide, a pathfinder, an original settler. He had casually conferred on me the freedom of the neighborhood.

And so with the sunshine and the great bursts of leaves growing on the trees, just as things grow in fast movies, I had that familiar conviction that life was beginning over again with the summer.

There was so much to read, for one thing, and so much fine health to be pulled down out of the young breath-giving air. I bought a dozen volumes on banking and credit and investment securities, and they stood on my shelf in red and gold like new money from the mint, promising to unfold the shining secrets that only Midas and Morgan and Mæcenas knew. And I had the high intention of reading many other books besides. I was rather literary in college—one year I wrote a series of very solemn and obvious editorials for the Yale News—and now I was going to bring back all such things into my life and become again that most limited of all specialists, the "well-rounded man." This isn't just an epigram—life is much more successfully looked at from a single window, after all.

It was a matter of chance that I should have rented a house in one of the strangest communities in North America. It was on that slender riotous island which extends itself due east of New York—and where there are, among other natural curiosities, two unusual formations of land. Twenty miles from the city a pair of enormous eggs, identical in contour and separated only by a courtesy bay, jut out into the most domesticated body of salt water in the Western hemisphere, the great wet barnyard of Long Island Sound. They are not perfect ovals—like the egg in the Columbus story, they are both crushed flat at the contact end—but their physical resemblance must be a source of perpetual confusion to the gulls that fly overhead. To the wingless a more arresting phenomenon is their dissimilarity in every particular except shape and size.

I lived at West Egg, the—well, the less fashionable of the two, though this is a most superficial tag to express the bizarre and not a little sinister contrast between them. My house was at the very tip of the egg, only fifty yards from the Sound, and squeezed between two huge places that rented for twelve or fifteen thousand a season. The one on my right was a colossal affair by any standard—it was a factual imitation of some Hôtel de Ville in Normandy, with a tower on one side, spanking new under a thin beard of raw ivy, and a marble swimming pool, and more than forty acres of lawn and garden. It was Gatsby's mansion. Or, rather, as I didn't know Mr. Gatsby, it was a mansion inhabited by a gentleman of that name. My own house was an eyesore, but it was a small eyesore, and it had been overlooked, so I had a view of the water, a partial view of my neighbor's lawn, and the consoling proximity of millionaires—all for eighty dollars a month.

Across the courtesy bay the white palaces of fashionable East Egg glittered along the water, and the history of the summer really begins on the evening I drove over there to have dinner with the Tom Buchanans. Daisy was my second cousin once removed, and I'd known Tom in college. And just after the war I spent two days with them in Chicago.

Her husband, among various physical accomplishments, had been one of the most powerful ends that ever played football at New Haven—a national figure in a way, one of those men who reach such an acute limited excellence at twenty-one that everything afterward savors of anti-climax. His family were enormously wealthy—even in college his freedom with money was a matter for reproach—but now he'd left Chicago and come East in a fashion that rather took your breath away: for instance, he'd brought down a string of polo ponies from

Lake Forest. It was hard to realize that a man in my own generation was wealthy enough to do that.

Why they came East I don't know. They had spent a year in France for no particular reason, and then drifted here and there unrestfully wherever people played polo and were rich together. This was a permanent move, said Daisy over the telephone, but I didn't believe it—I had no sight into Daisy's heart, but I felt that Tom would drift on forever seeking, a little wistfully, for the dramatic turbulence of some irrecoverable football game.

And so it happened that on a warm windy evening I drove over to East Egg to see two old friends whom I scarcely knew at all. Their house was even more elaborate than I expected, a cheerful red-and-white Georgian Colonial mansion, overlooking the bay. The lawn started at the beach and ran toward the front door for a quarter of a mile, jumping over sun-dials and brick walks and burning gardens—finally when it reached the house drifting up the side in bright vines as though from the momentum of its run. The front was broken by a line of French windows, glowing now with reflected gold and wide open to the warm windy afternoon, and Tom Buchanan in riding clothes was standing with his legs apart on the front porch.

He had changed since his New Haven years. Now he was a sturdy straw-haired man of thirty with a rather hard mouth and a supercilious manner. Two shining arrogant eyes had established dominance over his face and gave him the appearance of always leaning aggressively forward. Not even the effeminate swank of his riding clothes could hide the enormous power of that body—he seemed to fill those glistening boots until he strained the top lacing, and you could see a great pack of muscle shifting when his shoulder moved under his thin coat. It was a body capable of enormous leverage—a cruel body.

His speaking voice, a gruff husky tenor, added to the impression of fractiousness he conveyed. There was a touch of paternal contempt in it, even toward people he liked—and there were men at New Haven who had hated his guts.

"Now, don't think my opinion on these matters is final," he seemed to say, "just because I'm stronger and more of a man than you are." We were in the same senior society, and while we were never intimate I always had the impression that he approved of me and wanted me to like him with some harsh, defiant wistfulness of his own.

We talked for a few minutes on the sunny porch.

"I've got a nice place here," he said, his eyes flashing about restlessly.

Turning me around by one arm, he moved a broad flat hand along the front vista, including in its sweep a sunken Italian garden, a half acre of deep, pungent roses, and a snub-nosed motor-boat that bumped the tide offshore.

"It belonged to Demaine, the oil man." He turned me around again, politely and abruptly. "We'll go inside."

We walked through a high hallway into a bright rosy-colored space, fragilely bound into the house by French windows at either end. The windows were ajar and gleaming white against the fresh grass outside that seemed to grow a little way into the house. A breeze blew through the room, blew curtains in at one end and out the other like pale flags, twisting them up toward the frosted wedding-cake of the ceiling, and then rippled over the wine-colored rug, making a shadow on it as wind does on the sea.

The only completely stationary object in the room was an enormous couch on which two young women were buoyed up as though upon an anchored balloon. They were both in white, and their dresses were rippling and fluttering as if they had just been blown back in after a short flight around the house. I must have stood for a few moments listening to the whip and snap of the curtains and the groan of a picture on the wall. Then there was a boom as Tom Buchanan shut the rear windows and the caught wind died out about the room, and the curtains and the rugs and the two young women ballooned slowly to the floor.

The younger of the two was a stranger to me. She was extended full length at her end of the divan, completely motionless, and with her chin raised a little, as if she were balancing something on it which was quite likely to fall. If she saw me out of the corner of her eyes she gave no hint of it—indeed, I was almost surprised into murmuring an apology for having disturbed her by coming in.

The other girl, Daisy, made an attempt to rise—she leaned slightly forward with a conscientious expression—then she laughed, an absurd, charming little laugh, and I laughed too and came forward into the room.

"I'm p-paralyzed with happiness."

She laughed again, as if she said something very witty, and held my hand for a moment, looking up into my face, promising that there was no one in the world she so much wanted to see. That was a way she had. She hinted in a murmur that the surname of the balancing girl was Baker. (I've heard it said that Daisy's murmur was only to make people lean toward her; an irrelevant criticism that made it no less charming.)

At any rate, Miss Baker's lips fluttered, she nodded at me almost imperceptibly, and then quickly tipped her head back again—the object she was balancing had obviously tottered a little and given her something of a fright. Again a sort of apology arose to my lips. Almost any exhibition of complete self-sufficiency draws a stunned tribute from me.

I looked back at my cousin, who began to ask me questions in her low, thrilling voice. It was the kind of voice that the ear follows up and down, as if each speech is an arrangement of notes that will never be played again. Her face was sad and lovely with bright things in it, bright eyes and a bright passionate mouth, but there was an excitement in her voice that men who had cared for her found difficult to forget: a singing compulsion, a whispered "Listen," a promise that she had done gay, exciting things just a while since and that there were gay, exciting things hovering in the next hour.

I told her how I had stopped off in Chicago for a day on my way East, and how a dozen people had sent their love through me.

"Do they miss me?" she cried ecstatically.

"The whole town is desolate. All the cars have the left rear wheel painted black as a mourning wreath, and there's a persistent wail all night along the North Shore."

"How gorgeous! Let's go back, Tom. Tomorrow!" Then she added irrelevantly: "You ought to see the baby."

"I'd like to."

"She's asleep. She's three years old. Haven't you ever seen her?"

"Never."

"Well, you ought to see her. She's——"

Tom Buchanan, who had been hovering restlessly about the room, stopped and rested his hand on my shoulder.

"What you doing, Nick?"

"I'm a bond man."

"Who with?"

I told him.

"Never heard of them," he remarked decisively.

This annoyed me.

"You will," I answered shortly. "You will if you stay in the East."

"Oh, I'll stay in the East, don't you worry," he said, glancing at Daisy and then back at me, as if he were alert for something more. "I'd be a God Damn fool to live anywhere else."

At this point Miss Baker said: "Absolutely!" with such suddenness that I started—it was the first word she had uttered since I came into the room. Evidently it surprised her as much as it did me, for she yawned and with a series of rapid, deft movements stood up into the room.

"I'm stiff," she complained. "I've been lying on that sofa for as long as I can remember."

"Don't look at me," Daisy retorted. "I've been trying to get you to New York all afternoon."

"No, thanks," said Miss Baker to the four cocktails just in from the pantry. "I'm absolutely in training."

Her host looked at her incredulously.

"You are!" He took down his drink as if it were a drop in the bottom of a glass. "How you ever get anything done is beyond me."

I looked at Miss Baker, wondering what it was she "got done." I enjoyed looking at her. She was a slender, small-breasted girl, with an erect carriage, which she accentuated by throwing her body backward at the shoulders like a young cadet. Her gray sun-strained eyes looked back at me with polite reciprocal curiosity out of a wan, charming, discontented face. It occurred to me now that I had seen her, or a picture of her, somewhere before.

"You live in West Egg," she remarked contemptuously. "I know somebody there."

"I don't know a single——"

"You must know Gatsby."

"Gatsby?" demanded Daisy. "What Gatsby?"

Before I could reply that he was my neighbor dinner was announced; wedging his tense arm imperatively under mine, Tom Buchanan compelled me from the room as though he were moving a checker to another square.

Slenderly, languidly, their hands set lightly on their hips, the two young women preceded us out onto a rosy-colored porch, open toward the sunset, where four candles flickered on the table in the diminished wind.

"Why *candles*?" objected Daisy, frowning. She snapped them out with her fingers. "In two weeks it'll be the longest day in the year." She looked at us all radiantly. "Do you always watch for the longest day of the year and then miss it? I always watch for the longest day in the year and then miss it."

"We ought to plan something," yawned Miss Baker, sitting down at the table as if she were getting into bed.

"All right," said Daisy. "What'll we plan?" She turned to me helplessly: "What do people plan?"

Before I could answer her eyes fastened with an awed expression on her little finger.

"Look!" she complained. "I hurt it."

We all looked——the knuckle was black and blue.

"You did it, Tom," she said accusingly. "I know you didn't mean to, but you *did* do it. That's what I get for marrying a brute of a man, a great, big, hulking physical specimen of a——"

"I hate that word hulking," objected Tom crossly, "even in kidding."

"Hulking," insisted Daisy.

Sometimes she and Miss Baker talked at once, unobtrusively and with a bantering inconsequence that was never quite chatter, that was as cool as their white dresses and their impersonal eyes in the absence of all desire. They were here, and they accepted Tom and me, making only a polite pleasant effort to entertain or to be entertained. They knew that presently dinner would be over and a little later the evening too would be over and casually put away. It was sharply different from the West, where an evening was hurried from phase to phase toward its close, in a continually disappointed anticipation or else in sheer nervous dread of the moment itself.

"You make me feel uncivilized, Daisy," I confessed on my second glass of corky but rather impressive claret. "Can't you talk about crops or something?"

I meant nothing in particular by this remark, but it was taken up in an unexpected way.

"Civilization's going to pieces," broke out Tom violently. "I've gotten to be a terrible pessimist about things. Have you read 'The Rise of the Colored Empires' by this man Goddard?"

"Why, no," I answered, rather surprised by his tone.

"Well, it's a fine book, and everybody ought to read it. The idea is if we don't look out the white race will be—will be utterly submerged. It's all scientific stuff; it's been proved."

"Tom's getting very profound," said Daisy, with an expression of unthoughtful sadness. "He reads deep books with long words in them. What was that word we——"

"Well, these books are all scientific," insisted Tom, glancing at her impatiently. "This fellow has worked out the whole thing. It's up to us, who are the dominant race, to watch out or these other races will have control of things."

"We've got to beat them down," whispered Daisy, winking ferociously toward the fervent sun.

"You ought to live in California——" began Miss Baker, but Tom interrupted her by shifting heavily in his chair.

"This idea is that we're Nordics. I am, and you are, and you are, and——" After an infinitesimal hesitation he included Daisy with a slight nod, and she winked at me again. "——And we've produced all the things that go to make civilization——oh, science and art, and all that. Do you see?"

There was something pathetic in his concentration, as if his complacency, more acute than of old, was not enough to him any more. When, almost immediately, the telephone rang inside and the butler left the porch Daisy seized upon the momentary interruption and leaned toward me.

"I'll tell you a family secret," she whispered enthusiastically. "It's about the butler's nose. Do you want to hear about the butler's nose?"

"That's why I came over tonight."

"Well, he wasn't always a butler; he used to be the silver polisher for some people in New York that had a silver service for two hundred people. He had to polish it from morning till night, until finally it began to affect his nose——"

"Things went from bad to worse," suggested Miss Baker.

"Yes. Things went from bad to worse, until finally he had to give up his position."

For a moment the last sunshine fell with romantic affection upon her glowing face; her voice compelled me forward breathlessly as I listened—then the glow faded, each light deserting her with lingering regret, like children leaving a pleasant street at dusk.

The butler came back and murmured something close to Tom's ear, whereupon Tom frowned, pushed back his chair, and without a word went inside. As if his absence quickened something within her, Daisy leaned forward again, her voice glowing and singing.

"I love to see you at my table, Nick. You remind me of a—of a rose, an absolute rose. Doesn't he?" She turned to Miss Baker for confirmation: "An absolute rose?"

This was untrue. I am not even faintly like a rose. She was only extemporizing, but a stirring warmth flowed from her, as if her heart was trying to come out to you concealed in one of those breathless, thrilling words. Then suddenly she threw her napkin on the table and excused herself and went into the house.

Miss Baker and I exchanged a short glance consciously devoid of meaning. I was about to speak when she sat up alertly and said "Sh!" in a warning voice. A subdued impassioned murmur was audible in the room beyond, and Miss Baker leaned forward unashamed, trying to hear. The murmur trembled on the verge of coherence, sank down, mounted excitedly, and then ceased altogether.

"This Mr. Gatsby you spoke of is my neighbor——" I said.

"Don't talk. I want to hear what happens."

"Is something happening?" I inquired innocently.

"You mean to say you don't know?" said Miss Baker, honestly surprised. "I thought everybody knew."

"I don't."

"Why——" she said hesitantly, "Tom's got some woman in New York."

"Got some woman?" I repeated blankly.

Miss Baker nodded.

"She might have the decency not to telephone him at dinner-time. Don't you think?"

Almost before I had grasped her meaning there was the flutter of a dress and the crunch of leather boots, and Tom and Daisy were back at the table.

"It couldn't be helped!" cried Daisy with tense gayety.

She sat down, glanced searchingly at Miss Baker and then at me, and continued: "I looked outdoors for a minute, and it's very romantic outdoors. There's a bird on the lawn that I think must be a nightingale come over on the Cunard or White Star Line. He's singing away——" Her voice sang: "It's romantic, isn't it, Tom?"

"Very romantic," he said, and then miserably to me: "If it's light enough after dinner, I want to take you down to the stables."

The telephone rang inside, startlingly, and as Daisy shook her head decisively at Tom the subject of the stables, in fact all subjects, vanished into air. Among the broken fragments of the last five minutes at table I remember the candles being lit again, pointlessly, and I was conscious of wanting to look squarely at everyone, and yet to avoid all eyes. I couldn't guess what Daisy and Tom were thinking, but I doubt if even Miss Baker, who seemed to have mastered a certain hardy skepticism, was able utterly to put this fifth guest's shrill metallic urgency out of mind. To a certain temperament the situation might have seemed intriguing—my own instinct was to telephone immediately for the police.

The horses, needless to say, were not mentioned again. Tom and Miss Baker, with several feet of twilight between them, strolled back into the library, as if to a vigil beside a perfectly tangible body, while, trying to look pleasantly interested and a little deaf, I followed Daisy around a chain of connecting verandas to the porch in front. In its deep gloom we sat down side by side on a wicker settee.

Daisy took her face in her hands as if feeling its lovely shape, and her eyes moved gradually out into the velvet dusk. I saw that turbulent emotions possessed her, so I asked what I thought would be some sedative questions about her little girl.

"We don't know each other very well, Nick," she said suddenly. "Even if we are cousins. You didn't come to my wedding."

"I wasn't back from the war."

"That's true." She hesitated. "Well, I've had a very bad time, Nick, and I'm pretty cynical about everything."

Evidently she had reason to be. I waited but she didn't say any more, and after a moment I returned rather feebly to the subject of her daughter.

"I suppose she talks, and—eats, and everything."

"Oh, yes." She looked at me absently. "Listen, Nick; let me tell you what I said when she was born. Would you like to hear?"

"Very much."

"It'll show you how I've gotten to feel about—things. Well, she was less than an hour old and Tom was God knows where. I woke up out of the ether with an utterly abandoned feeling, and asked the nurse right away if it was a boy or a girl. She told me it was a girl, and so I turned my head away and wept. 'All right,' I said, 'I'm glad it's a girl. And I hope she'll be a fool—that's the best thing a girl can be in this world, a beautiful little fool.'

"You see I think everything's terrible anyhow," she went on in a convinced way. "Everybody thinks so—the most advanced people. And I *know*. I've been everywhere and seen everything and done everything." Her eyes flashed around her in a defiant way, rather like Tom's, and she laughed with thrilling scorn. "Sophisticated—God, I'm sophisticated!"

The instant her voice broke off, ceasing to compel my attention, my belief, I felt the basic insincerity of what she had said. It made me uneasy, as though the whole evening had been a trick of some sort to exact a contributary emotion from me. I waited, and sure enough, in a moment she looked at me with an absolute smirk on her lovely face, as if she had asserted her membership in a rather distinguished secret society to which she and Tom belonged.

◆

Inside, the crimson room bloomed with light. Tom and Miss Baker sat at either end of the long couch and she read aloud to him from the Saturday Evening Post—the words, murmurous and uninflected, running together in a soothing tune. The lamp-light, bright on his boots and dull on the autumn-leaf yellow of her hair, glinted along the paper as she turned a page with a flutter of slender muscles in her arms.

When we came in she held us silent for a moment with a lifted hand.

"To be continued," she said, tossing the magazine on the table, "in our very next issue."

Her body asserted itself with a restless movement of her knee, and she stood up.

"Ten o'clock," she remarked, apparently finding the time on the ceiling. "Time for this good girl to go to bed."

"Jordan's going to play in the tournament tomorrow," explained Daisy, "over at Westchester."

"Oh—you're *Jor*dan Baker."

I knew now why her face was familiar—its pleasing contemptuous expression had looked out at me from many rotogravure pictures of the sporting life at Asheville and Hot Springs and Palm Beach. I had heard some story of her too, a critical, unpleasant story, but what it was I had forgotten long ago.

"Good night," she said softly. "Wake me at eight, won't you."

"If you'll get up."

"I will. Good night, Mr. Carraway. See you anon."

"Of course you will," confirmed Daisy. "In fact I think I'll arrange a marriage. Come over often, Nick, and I'll sort of—oh—fling you together. You know—lock you up accidentally in linen closets and push you out to sea in a boat, and all that sort of thing——"

"Good night," called Miss Baker from the stairs. "I haven't heard a word."

"She's a nice girl," said Tom after a moment. "They oughtn't to let her run around the country this way."

"Who oughtn't to?" inquired Daisy coldly.

"Her family."

"Her family is one aunt about a thousand years old. Besides, Nick's going to look after her, aren't you, Nick? She's going to spend lots of weekends out here this summer. I think the home influence will be very good for her."

Daisy and Tom looked at each other for a moment in silence.

"Is she from New York?" I asked quickly.

"From Louisville. Our white girlhood was passed together there. Our beautiful white——"

"Did you give Nick a little heart-to-heart talk on the veranda?" demanded Tom suddenly.

"Did I?" She looked at me. "I can't seem to remember, but I think we talked about the Nordic race. Yes, I'm sure we did. It sort of crept up on us and first thing you know——"

"Don't believe everything you hear, Nick," he advised me.

I said lightly that I had heard nothing at all, and a few minutes later I got up to go home. They came to the door with me and stood side by side in a cheerful square of light. As I started my motor Daisy peremptorily called: "Wait!

"I forgot to ask you something, and it's important. We heard you were engaged to a girl out West."

"That's right," corroborated Tom kindly. "We heard that you were engaged."

"It's a libel. I'm too poor."

"But we heard it," insisted Daisy, surprising me by opening up again in a flower-like way. "We heard it from three people, so it must be true."

Of course I knew what they were referring to, but I wasn't even vaguely engaged. The fact that gossip had published the banns was one of the reasons I had come East. You can't stop going with an old friend on account of rumors, and on the other hand I had no intention of being rumored into marriage.

Their interest rather touched me and made them less remotely rich—nevertheless, I was confused and a little disgusted as I drove away. It seemed to me that the thing for Daisy to do was to rush out of the house, child in arms—but apparently there were no such intentions in her head. As for Tom, the fact that he "had some woman in New York" was really less surprising than that he had been depressed by a book. Something was making him nibble at the edge of stale ideas as if his sturdy physical egotism no longer nourished his peremptory heart.

Already it was deep summer on roadhouse roofs and in front of wayside garages, where new red gas-pumps sat out in pools of light, and when I reached my estate at West Egg I ran the car under its shed and sat for a while on an abandoned grass roller in the yard. The wind had blown off, leaving a loud, bright night, with wings beating in the trees and a persistent organ sound as the full bellows of the earth blew the frogs full of life. The silhouette of a moving cat wavered across the moonlight, and turning my head to watch it, I saw that I was not alone—fifty feet away a figure had emerged from the shadow of my neighbor's mansion and was standing with his hands in his pockets regarding the silver pepper of the stars. Something in his leisurely movements and the secure position of his feet upon the lawn suggested that it was Mr. Gatsby himself, come out to determine what share was his of our local heavens.

I decided to call to him. Miss Baker had mentioned him at dinner, and that would do for an introduction. But I didn't call to him, for he gave a sudden intimation that he was content to be alone—he stretched out his arms toward the dark water in a curious way, and, far as I was from him, I could have sworn he was trembling. Involuntarily I glanced seaward—and distinguished nothing except a single green light, minute and far away, that might have been at the end of a dock. When I looked once more for Gatsby he had vanished, and I was alone again in the unquiet darkness.

CHAPTER II

About half way between West Egg and New York the motor-road hastily joins the railroad and runs beside it for a quarter of a mile, so as to shrink away from a certain desolate area of land. This is a valley of ashes—a fantastic farm where ashes grow like wheat into ridges and hills and grotesque gardens; where ashes take the forms of houses and chimneys and rising smoke and, finally, with a transcendent effort, of men who move dimly and already crumbling through the powdery air. Occasionally a line of gray cars crawls along an invisible track, gives out a ghastly creak, and comes to rest, and immediately the ash-gray men swarm up with leaden spades and stir up an impenetrable cloud, which screens their obscure operations from your sight.

But above the gray land and the spasms of bleak dust which drift endlessly over it, you perceive, after a moment, the eyes of Doctor T. J. Eckleburg. The eyes of Doctor T. J. Eckleburg are blue and gigantic—their retinas are one yard high. They look out of no face, but, instead, from a pair of enormous yellow spectacles which pass over a non-existent nose. Evidently some wild wag of an oculist set them there to fatten his practice in the borough of Queens, and then sank down himself into eternal blindness, or forgot them and moved away. But his eyes, dimmed a little by many paintless days under sun and rain, brood on over the solemn dumping ground.

The valley of ashes is bounded on one side by a small foul river, and, when the drawbridge is up to let barges through, the passengers on waiting trains can stare at the dismal scene for as long as half an hour. There is always a halt there of at least a minute, and it was because of this that I first met Tom Buchanan's mistress.

The fact that he had one was insisted upon wherever he was known. His acquaintances resented the fact that he turned up in popular restaurants with her and, leaving her at a table, sauntered about, chatting with whomsoever he knew. Though I was curious to see her, I had no desire to meet her—but I did. I went up to New York with Tom on the train one afternoon, and when we stopped by the ashheaps he jumped to his feet and, taking hold of my elbow, literally forced me from the car.

"We're getting off," he insisted. "I want you to meet my girl."

I think he'd tanked up a good deal at luncheon, and his determination to have my company bordered on violence. The supercilious assumption was that on Sunday afternoon I had nothing better to do.

I followed him over a low whitewashed railroad fence, and we walked back a hundred yards along the road under Doctor Eckleburg's persistent stare. The only building in sight was a small block of yellow brick sitting on the edge of the waste land, a sort of compact Main Street ministering to it, and contiguous to absolutely nothing. One of the three shops it contained was for rent and another was an all-night restaurant, approached by a trail of ashes; the third was a garage—*Repairs*. GEORGE B. WILSON. *Cars bought and sold.*—and I followed Tom inside.

The interior was unprosperous and bare; the only car visible was the dust-covered wreck of a Ford which crouched in a dim corner. It had occurred to me that this shadow of a garage must be a blind, and that sumptuous and romantic apartments were concealed overhead, when the proprietor himself appeared in the door of an office, wiping his hands on a piece of waste. He was a blond, spiritless man, anæmic, and faintly handsome. When he saw us a damp gleam of hope sprang into his light blue eyes.

"Hello, Wilson, old man," said Tom, slapping him jovially on the shoulder. "How's business?"

"I can't complain," answered Wilson unconvincingly. "When are you going to sell me that car?"

"Next week; I've got my man working on it now."

"Works pretty slow, don't he?"

"No, he doesn't," said Tom coldly. "And if you feel that way about it, maybe I'd better sell it somewhere else after all."

"I don't mean that," explained Wilson quickly. "I just meant——"

His voice faded off and Tom glanced impatiently around the garage. Then I heard footsteps on a stairs, and in a moment the thickish figure of a woman blocked out the light from the office door. She was in the middle thirties, and faintly stout, but she carried her surplus flesh sensuously as some women can. Her face, above a spotted dress of dark blue crêpe-de-chine, contained no facet or gleam of beauty, but there was an immediately perceptible vitality about her as if the nerves of her body were continually smouldering. She smiled slowly and, walking through her husband as if he were a ghost, shook hands with Tom, looking him flush in the eye. Then she wet her lips, and without turning around spoke to her husband in a soft, coarse voice:

"Get some chairs, why don't you, so somebody can sit down."

"Oh, sure," agreed Wilson hurriedly, and went toward the little office, mingling immediately with the cement color of the walls. A white ashen dust veiled his dark suit and his pale hair as it veiled everything in the vicinity—except his wife, who moved close to Tom.

"I want to see you," said Tom intently. "Get on the next train."

"All right."

"I'll meet you by the newsstand on the lower level."

She nodded and moved away from him just as George Wilson emerged with two chairs from his office door.

We waited for her down the road and out of sight. It was a few days before the Fourth of July, and a gray, scrawny Italian child was setting torpedoes in a row along the railroad track.

"Terrible place, isn't it," said Tom, exchanging a frown with Doctor Eckleburg.

"Awful."

"It does her good to get away."

"Doesn't her husband object?"

"Wilson? He thinks she goes to see her sister in New York. He's so dumb he doesn't know he's alive."

So Tom Buchanan and his girl and I went up together to New York—or not quite together, for Mrs. Wilson sat discreetly in another car. Tom deferred that much to the sensibilities of those East Eggers who might be on the train.

She had changed her dress to a brown figured muslin, which stretched tight over her rather wide hips as Tom helped her to the platform in New York. At the newsstand she bought a copy of Town Tattle and a moving-picture magazine, and in the station drug-store some cold cream and a small flask of perfume. Upstairs in the solemn echoing drive she let four taxi cabs drive away before she selected a new one, lavender-colored with gray upholstery, and in this we slid out from the mass of the station into the glowing sunshine. But immediately she turned sharply from the window and, leaning forward, tapped on the front glass.

"I want to get one of those dogs," she said earnestly. "I want to get one for the apartment. They're nice to have—a dog."

We backed up to a gray old man who bore an absurd resemblance to John D. Rockefeller. In a basket swung from his neck cowered a dozen very recent puppies of an indeterminate breed.

"What kind are they?" asked Mrs. Wilson eagerly, as he came to the taxi window.

"All kinds. What kind do you want, lady?"

"I'd like to get one of those police dogs; I don't suppose you got that kind?"

The man peered doubtfully into the basket, plunged in his hand and drew one up, wriggling, by the back of the neck.

"That's no police dog," said Tom.

"No, it's not exactly a po*lice* dog," said the man with disappointment in his voice. "It's more of an Airedale." He passed his hand over the brown wash-rag of a back. "Look at that coat. Some coat. That's a dog that'll never bother you with catching cold."

"I think it's cute," said Mrs. Wilson enthusiastically. "How much is it?"

"That dog?" He looked at it admiringly. "That dog will cost you ten dollars."

The Airedale—undoubtedly there was an Airedale concerned in it somewhere, though its feet were startlingly white—changed hands and settled down into Mrs. Wilson's lap, where she fondled the weather-proof coat with rapture.

"Is it a boy or a girl?" she asked delicately.

"That dog? That dog's a boy."

"It's a bitch," said Tom decisively. "Here's your money. Go and buy ten more dogs with it."

We drove over to Fifth Avenue, so warm and soft, almost pastoral, on the summer Sunday afternoon that I wouldn't have been surprised to see a great flock of white sheep turn the corner.

"Hold on," I said. "I have to leave you here."

"No, you don't," interposed Tom quickly. "Myrtle'll be hurt if you don't come up to the apartment. Won't you, Myrtle?"

"Come on," she urged. "I'll telephone my sister Catherine. She's said to be very beautiful by people who ought to know."

"Well, I'd like to, but——"

We went on, cutting back again over the Park toward the West Hundreds. At 158th Street the cab stopped at one slice in a long white cake of apartment-houses. Throwing a regal homecoming glance around the neighborhood, Mrs. Wilson gathered up her dog and her other purchases, and went haughtily in.

"I'm going to have the McKees come up," she announced as we rose in the elevator. "And, of course, I got to call up my sister, too."

The apartment was on the top floor—a small living-room, a small dining-room, a small bedroom, and a bath. The living-room was crowded to the doors with a set of tapestried furniture entirely too large for it, so that to move about was to stumble continually over scenes of ladies swinging in the gardens of Versailles. The only picture was an over-enlarged photograph, apparently a hen sitting on a blurred rock. Looked at from a distance, however, the hen resolved itself into a bonnet, and the countenance of a stout old lady beamed down into the room. Several old copies of Town Tattle lay on the table together with a copy of "Simon Called Peter," and some of the small scandal magazines of Broadway. Mrs. Wilson was first concerned with the dog. A reluctant elevator-boy went for a box full of straw and some milk, to which he added on his own initiative a tin of large, hard dog-biscuits—one of which decomposed apathetically in the saucer of milk all afternoon. Meanwhile Tom brought out a bottle of whiskey from a locked bureau door.

I have been drunk just twice in my life, and the second time was that afternoon; so everything that happened has a dim, hazy cast over it, although until after eight o'clock the apartment was full of cheerful sun. Sitting on Tom's lap Mrs. Wilson called up several people on the telephone; then there were no cigarettes, and I went out to buy some at the drug-store on the corner. When I came back they had disappeared, so I sat down discreetly in the living-room and read a chapter of "Simon Called Peter"—either it was terrible stuff or the whiskey distorted things, because it didn't make any sense to me.

Just as Tom and Myrtle (after the first drink Mrs. Wilson and I called each other by our first names) reappeared, company commenced to arrive at the apartment-door.

The sister, Catherine, was a slender, worldly girl of about thirty, with a solid, sticky bob of red hair, and a complexion powdered milky white. Her eyebrows had been plucked and then drawn on again at a more rakish angle, but the efforts of nature toward the restoration of the old alignment gave a blurred air to her face. When she moved about there was an incessant clicking as innumerable pottery bracelets jingled up and down upon her arms. She came in with such a proprietary haste and looked around so possessively at the furniture that I wondered if she lived here. But when I asked her she laughed immoderately, repeated my question aloud, and told me she lived with a girl friend at a hotel.

Mr. McKee was a pale, feminine man from the flat below. He had just shaved, for there was a white spot of lather on his cheekbone, and he was most respectful in his greeting to everyone in the room. He informed me that he was in the "artistic game," and I gathered later that he was a photographer and had made the dim enlargement of Mrs. Wilson's mother which hovered like an ectoplasm on the wall. His wife was shrill, languid, handsome, and horrible. She told me with pride that her husband had photographed her a hundred and twenty-seven times since they had been married.

Mrs. Wilson had changed her costume sometime before, and was now attired in an elaborate afternoon dress of cream-colored chiffon, which gave out a continual rustle as she swept about the room. With the influence of the dress her personality had also undergone a change. The intense vitality that had been so remarkable in the garage was converted into impressive hauteur. Her laughter, her gestures, her assertions became more violently affected moment by moment, and as she expanded the room grew smaller around her, until she seemed to be revolving on a noisy, creaking pivot through the smoky air.

"My dear," she told her sister in a high, mincing shout, "most of these fellas will cheat you every time. All they think of is money. I had a woman up here last week to look at my feet, and when she gave me the bill you'd of thought she had my appendicitus out."

"What was the name of the woman?" asked Mrs. McKee.

"Mrs. Eberhardt. She goes around looking at people's feet in their own homes."

"I like your dress," remarked Mrs. McKee. "I think it's adorable."

Mrs. Wilson rejected the compliment by raising her eyebrow in disdain.

"It's just a crazy old thing," she said. "I just slip it on sometimes when I don't care what I look like."

"But it looks wonderful on you, if you know what I mean," pursued Mrs. McKee. "If Chester could only get you in that pose I think he could make something of it."

We all looked in silence at Mrs. Wilson, who removed a strand of hair from over her eyes and looked back at us with a brilliant smile. Mr. McKee regarded her intently with his head on one side, and then moved his hand back and forth slowly in front of his face.

"I should change the light," he said after a moment. "I'd like to bring out the modelling of the features. And I'd try to get hold of all the back hair."

"I wouldn't think of changing the light," cried Mrs. McKee. "I think it's——"

Her husband said "*Sh!*" and we all looked at the subject again, whereupon Tom Buchanan yawned audibly and got to his feet.

"You McKees have something to drink," he said. "Get some more ice and mineral water, Myrtle, before everybody goes to sleep."

"I told that boy about the ice." Myrtle raised her eyebrows in despair at the shiftlessness of the lower orders. "These people! You have to keep after them all the time."

She looked at me and laughed pointlessly. Then she flounced over to the dog, kissed it with ecstasy, and swept into the kitchen, implying that a dozen chefs awaited her orders there.

"I've done some nice things out on Long Island," asserted Mr. McKee.

Tom looked at him blankly.

"Two of them we have framed downstairs."

"Two what?" demanded Tom.

"Two studies. One of them I call 'Montauk Point—The Gulls,' and the other I call 'Montauk Point—The Sea.'"

The sister Catherine sat down beside me on the couch.

"Do you live down on Long Island, too," she inquired.

"I live at West Egg."

"Really? I was down there at a party about a month ago. At a man named Gatsby's. Do you know him?"

"I live next door to him."

"Well, they say he's a nephew or a cousin of Kaiser Wilhelm's. That's where all his money comes from."

"Really?"

She nodded.

"I'm scared of him. I'd hate to have him get anything on me."

This absorbing information about my neighbor was interrupted by Mrs. McKee's pointing suddenly at Catherine:

"Chester, I think you could do something with *her*," she broke out, but Mr. McKee only nodded in a bored way, and turned his attention to Tom.

"I'd like to do more work on Long Island, if I could get the entry. All I ask is that they should give me a start."

"Ask Myrtle," said Tom, breaking into a short shout of laughter as Mrs. Wilson entered with a tray. "She'll give you a letter of introduction, won't you, Myrtle?"

"Do what?" she asked, startled.

"You'll give McKee a letter of introduction to your husband, so he can do some studies of him." His lips moved silently for a moment as he invented. "'George B. Wilson at the Gasoline Pump,' or something like that."

Catherine leaned close to me and whispered in my ear:

"Neither of them can stand the person they're married to."

"Can't they?"

"Can't *stand* them." She looked at Myrtle and then at Tom. "What I say is, why go on living with them if they can't stand them? If I was them I'd get a divorce and get married to each other right away."

"Doesn't she like Wilson either?"

The answer to this was unexpected. It came from Myrtle, who had overheard the question, and it was violent and obscene.

"You see?" cried Catherine triumphantly. She lowered her voice again. "It's really his wife that's keeping them apart. She's a Catholic, and they don't believe in divorce."

Daisy was not a Catholic, and I was a little shocked at the elaborateness of the lie.

"When they do get married," continued Catherine, "they're going West to live for a while until it blows over."

"It'd be more discreet to go to Europe."

"Oh, do you like Europe?" she exclaimed surprisingly. "I just got back from Monte Carlo."

"Really."

"Just last year. I went over there with another girl."

"Stay long?"

"No, we just went to Monte Carlo and back. We went by way of Marseilles. We had over twelve hundred dollars when we started, but we got gypped out of it all in two days in the private rooms. We had an awful time getting back, I can tell you. God, how I hated that town!"

The late afternoon sky bloomed in the window for a moment like the blue honey of the Mediterranean—then the shrill voice of Mrs. McKee called me back into the room.

"I almost made a mistake, too," she declared vigorously. "I almost married a little kyke who'd been after me for years. I knew he was below me. Everybody kept saying to me: 'Lucille, that man's way below you!' But if I hadn't met Chester, he'd of got me sure."

"Yes, but listen," said Myrtle Wilson, nodding her head up and down. "At least you didn't marry him."

"I know I didn't."

"Well, I married him," said Myrtle, ambiguously. "And that's the difference between your case and mine."

"Why did you, Myrtle?" demanded Catherine. "Nobody forced you to."

Myrtle considered.

"I married him because I thought he was a gentleman," she said finally. "I thought he knew something about breeding, but he wasn't fit to lick my shoe."

"You were crazy about him for a while," said Catherine.

"Crazy about him!" cried Myrtle incredulously. "Who said I was crazy about him? I never was any more crazy about him than I was about that man there."

She pointed suddenly at me, and everyone looked at me accusingly. I tried to show by my expression that I had played no part in her past.

"The only *crazy* I was was when I married him. I knew right away I made a mistake. He borrowed somebody's best suit to get married in, and never even told me about it, and the man came after it one day when he was out." She looked to see who was listening. "'Oh, is that your suit?' I said. 'This is the first I ever heard about it.' But I gave it to him and then I lay down and cried to beat the band all afternoon."

"She really ought to get away from him," resumed Catherine to me. "They've been living over that garage for eleven years. And Tom's the first sweetie she ever had."

The bottle of whiskey—a second one—was now in constant demand by all present, excepting Catherine, who "felt just as good on nothing at all." Tom rang for the janitor and sent him for some celebrated sandwiches which were a complete supper in themselves. I wanted to get out and walk eastward toward the Park through the soft twilight, but each time I tried to go I became entangled in some wild, strident argument which pulled me back, as if with ropes, into my chair. Yet high over the city our line of yellow windows must have contributed their share of human secrecy to the casual watcher in the darkening streets, and I was him too, looking up and wondering. I was within and without, simultaneously enchanted and repelled by the inexhaustible variety of life.

Myrtle pulled her chair close to mine, and suddenly her warm breath poured over me the story of her first meeting with Tom.

"It was on the two little seats facing each other that are always the last ones left on the train. I was going up to New York to see my sister and spend the night. He had on a dress suit and patent leather shoes, and I couldn't keep my eyes off him, but every time he looked at me I had to pretend to be looking at the advertisement over his head. When we came into the station he was next to me, and his white shirt front pressed against my arm, and so I told him I'd have to call a policeman, but he knew I lied. I was so excited that when I got into a taxi with him I didn't hardly know I wasn't getting into a subway train. All I kept thinking about, over and over, was 'You can't live forever, you can't live forever.'"

She turned to Mrs. McKee and the room rang full of her artificial laughter.

"My dear," she cried, "I'm going to give you this dress as soon as I'm through with it. I've got to get another one tomorrow. I'm going to make a list of all the things I've got to get. A massage and a wave, and a collar for the dog, and one of those cute little ash trays where you touch a spring, and a wreath with a black silk bow for mother's grave that'll last all summer. I got to write down a list so I won't forget all the things I got to do."

It was nine o'clock—almost immediately afterward I looked at my watch and found it was ten. Mr. McKee was asleep on a chair with his fists clenched in his lap, like a photograph of a man of action. Taking out my handkerchief I wiped from his cheek the spot of dried lather that had worried me all the afternoon.

The little dog was sitting on the table looking with blind eyes through the smoke, and from time to time groaning faintly. People disappeared, reappeared, made plans to go somewhere, and then lost each other, searched for each other, found each other a few feet away. Some time toward midnight Tom Buchanan and Mrs. Wilson stood face to face discussing, in impassioned voices, whether Mrs. Wilson had any right to mention Daisy's name.

"Daisy! Daisy! Daisy!" shouted Mrs. Wilson. "I'll say it whenever I want to! Daisy! Dai——"

Making a short deft movement, Tom Buchanan broke her nose with his open hand.

Then there were bloody towels upon the bathroom floor, and women's voices scolding, and high over the confusion a long broken wail of pain. Mr. McKee awoke from his doze and started in a daze toward the door. When he had gone half way he turned around and stared at the scene—his wife and Catherine scolding and consoling as they stumbled here and there among the crowded furniture with articles of aid, and the despairing figure on the couch, bleeding fluently, and trying to spread a copy of Town Tattle over the tapestry scenes of Versailles. Then Mr. McKee turned and continued on out the door. Taking my hat from the chandelier, I followed.

"Come to lunch some day," he suggested, as we groaned down in the elevator.

"Where?"

"Anywhere."

"Keep your hands off the lever," snapped the elevator boy.

"I beg your pardon," said Mr. McKee with dignity. "I didn't know I was touching it."

"All right," I agreed, "I'll be glad to."

. . . I was standing beside his bed and he was sitting up between the sheets, clad in his underwear, with a great portfolio in his hands.

"Beauty and the Beast . . . Loneliness . . . Old Grocery Horse . . . Brook'n Bridge . . ."

Then I was lying half asleep in the cold lower level of the Pennsylvania Station, staring at the morning Tribune, and waiting for the four o'clock train.

CHAPTER III

There was music from my neighbor's house through the summer nights. In his blue gardens men and girls came and went like moths among the whisperings and the champagne and the stars. At high tide in the afternoon I watched his guests diving from the tower of his raft, or taking the sun on the hot sand of his beach while his two motor-boats slit the waters of the Sound, drawing aquaplanes over cataracts of foam. On weekends his Rolls-Royce became an omnibus, bearing parties to and from the city between nine in the morning and long past midnight, while his station wagon scampered like a brisk yellow bug to meet all trains. And on Mondays eight servants, including an extra gardener, toiled all day with mops and scrubbing-brushes and hammers and garden shears, repairing the ravages of the night before.

Every Friday five crates of oranges and lemons arrived from a fruiterer in New York—every Monday these same oranges and lemons left his back door in a pyramid of pulpless halves. There was a machine in the kitchen which could extract the juice of two hundred oranges in half an hour if a little button was pressed two hundred times by a butler's thumb.

At least once a fortnight a corps of caterers came down with several hundred feet of canvas and enough colored lights to make a Christmas tree of Gatsby's enormous garden. On buffet tables, garnished with glistening hors-d'œuvre, spiced baked hams crowded against salads of harlequin designs and pastry pigs and turkeys bewitched to a dark gold. In the main hall a bar with a real brass rail was set up, and stocked with gins and liquors and with cordials so long forgotten that most of his female guests were too young to know one from another.

By seven o'clock the orchestra has arrived, no thin five-piece affair, but a whole pitful of oboes and trombones and saxophones and viols and cornets and piccolos, and low and high drums. The last swimmers have come in from the beach now and are dressing upstairs; the cars from New York are parked five deep in the drive, and already the halls and salons and verandas are gaudy with primary colors, and hair shorn in strange new ways, and shawls beyond the dreams of Castile. The bar is in full swing, and floating rounds of cocktails permeate the garden outside, until the air is alive with chatter and laughter, and casual innuendo and introductions forgotten on the spot, and enthusiastic meetings between women who never knew each other's names.

The lights grow brighter as the earth lurches away from the sun, and now the orchestra is playing yellow cocktail music, and the opera of voices pitches a key higher. Laughter is easier minute by minute, spilled with prodigality, tipped out at a cheerful word. The groups change more swiftly, swell with new arrivals, dissolve and form in the same breath; already there are wanderers, confident girls who weave here and there among the stouter and more stable, become for a sharp, joyous moment the center of a group, and then, excited with triumph, glide on through the sea-change of faces and voices and color under the constantly changing light.

Suddenly one of these gypsies, in trembling opal, seizes a cocktail out of the air, dumps it down for courage and, moving her hands like Frisco, dances out alone on the canvas platform. A momentary hush;

the orchestra leader varies his rhythm obligingly for her, and there is a burst of chatter as the erroneous news goes around that she is Gilda Gray's understudy from the Follies. The party has begun.

I believe that on the first night I went to Gatsby's house I was one of the few guests who had actually been invited. People were not invited—they went there. They got into automobiles which bore them out to Long Island, and somehow they ended up at Gatsby's door. Once there they were introduced by somebody who knew Gatsby, and after that they conducted themselves according to the rules of behavior associated with amusement parks. Sometimes they came and went without having met Gatsby at all, came for the party with a simplicity of heart that was its own ticket of admission.

I had been actually invited. A chauffeur in a uniform of robin's-egg blue crossed my lawn early that Saturday morning with a surprisingly formal note from his employer: the honor would be entirely Gatsby's, it said, if I would attend his "little party" that night. He had seen me several times, and had intended to call on me long before, but a peculiar combination of circumstances had prevented it—signed Jay Gatsby, in a majestic hand.

Dressed up in white flannels I went over to his lawn a little after seven, and wandered around rather ill at ease among swirls and eddies of people I didn't know—though here and there was a face I had noticed on the commuting train. I was immediately struck by the number of young Englishmen dotted about; all well-dressed, all looking a little hungry, and all talking in low, earnest voices to solid and prosperous Americans. I was sure that they were selling something: bonds or insurance or automobiles. They were at least agonizingly aware of the easy money in the vicinity and convinced that it was theirs for a few words in the right key.

As soon as I arrived I made an attempt to find my host, but the two or three people of whom I asked his whereabouts stared at me in such an amazed way, and denied so vehemently any knowledge of his movements, that I slunk off in the direction of the cocktail table—the only place in the garden where a single man could linger without looking purposeless and alone.

I was on my way to get roaring drunk from sheer embarrassment when Jordan Baker came out of the house and stood at the head of the marble steps, leaning a little backward and looking with contemptuous interest down into the garden.

Welcome or not, I found it necessary to attach myself to someone before I should begin to address cordial remarks to the passers-by.

"Hello!" I roared, advancing toward her. My voice seemed unnaturally loud across the garden.

"I thought you might be here," she responded absently as I came up. "I remembered you lived next door to——"

She held my hand impersonally, as a promise that she'd take care of me in a minute, and gave ear to two girls in twin yellow dresses, who stopped at the foot of the steps.

"Hello!" they cried together. "Sorry you didn't win."

That was for the golf tournament. She had lost in the finals the week before.

"You don't know who we are," said one of the girls in yellow, "but we met you here about a month ago."

"You've dyed your hair since then," remarked Jordan, and I started, but the girls had moved casually on and her remark was addressed to the premature moon, produced like the supper, no doubt, out of a caterer's basket. With Jordan's slender golden arm resting in mine, we descended the steps and sauntered about the garden. A tray of cocktails floated at us through the twilight, and we sat down at a table with the two girls in yellow and three men, each one introduced to us as Mr. Mumble.

"Do you come to these parties often?" inquired Jordan of the girl beside her.

"The last one was the one I met you at," answered the girl, in an alert confident voice. She turned to her companion: "Wasn't it for you, Lucille?"

It was for Lucille, too.

"I like to come," Lucille said. "I never care what I do, so I always have a good time. When I was here last I tore my gown on a chair, and he asked me my name and address—inside of a week I got a package from Croirier's with a new evening gown in it."

"Did you keep it?" asked Jordan.

"Sure I did. I was going to wear it tonight, but it was too big in the bust and had to be altered. It was gas blue with lavender beads. Two hundred and sixty-five dollars."

"There's something funny about a fellow that'll do a thing like that," said the other girl eagerly. "He doesn't want any trouble with *any*body."

"Who doesn't?" I inquired.

"Gatsby. Somebody told me——"

The two girls and Jordan leaned together confidentially.

"Somebody told me they thought he killed a man once."

A thrill passed over all of us. The three Mr. Mumbles bent forward and listened eagerly.

"I don't think it's so much *that*," argued Lucille skeptically; "it's more that he was a German spy during the war."

One of the men nodded in confirmation.

"I heard that from a man who knew all about him, grew up with him in Germany," he assured us positively.

"Oh, no," said the first girl, "it couldn't be that, because he was in the American army during the war." As our credulity switched back to her she leaned forward with enthusiasm. "You look at him sometime when he thinks nobody's looking at him. I'll bet he killed a man."

She narrowed her eyes and shivered. Lucille shivered. We all turned and looked around for Gatsby. It was testimony to the romantic speculation he inspired that there were whispers about him from those who had found little that it was necessary to whisper about in this world.

The first supper—there would be another one after midnight— was now being served, and Jordan invited me to join her own party, who were spread around a table on the other side of the garden. There were three married couples and Jordan's escort, a persistent undergraduate given to violent innuendo, and obviously under the impression that sooner or later Jordan was going to yield him up her person to a greater or lesser degree. Instead of rambling this party had preserved a dignified homogeneity, and assumed to itself the function of representing the staid nobility of the country-side—East Egg condescending to West Egg, and carefully on guard against its spectroscopic gayety.

"Let's get out," whispered Jordan, after a somehow wasteful and inappropriate half hour; "this is much too polite for me."

We got up, and she explained that we were going to find the host: I had never met him, she said, and it was making me uneasy. The undergraduate nodded in a cynical, melancholy way.

The bar, where we glanced first, was crowded, but Gatsby was not there. She couldn't find him from the top of the steps, and he wasn't on the veranda. On a chance we tried an important-looking door, and walked into a high Gothic library, panelled with carved English oak, and probably transported complete from some ruin overseas.

A stout, middle-aged man, with enormous owl-eyed spectacles, was sitting somewhat drunk on the edge of a great table, staring with unsteady concentration at the shelves of books. As we entered he wheeled excitedly around and examined Jordan from head to foot.

"What do you think?" he demanded impetuously.

"About what?"

He waved his hand toward the bookshelves.

"About that. As a matter of fact you needn't bother to ascertain. I ascertained. They're real."

"The books?"

He nodded.

"Absolutely real—have pages and everything. I thought they'd be a nice durable cardboard. Matter of fact, they're absolutely real. Pages and— Here! Lemme show you."

Taking our skepticism for granted, he rushed to the bookcases and returned with Volume One of the "Stoddard Lectures."

"See!" he cried triumphantly. "It's a bona-fide piece of printed matter. It fooled me. This fella's a regular Belasco. It's a triumph. What thoroughness! What realism! Knew when to stop, too—didn't cut the pages. But what do you want? What do you expect?"

He snatched the book from me and replaced it hastily on its shelf, muttering that if one brick was removed the whole library was liable to collapse.

"Who brought you?" he demanded. "Or did you just come? I was brought. Most people were brought."

Jordan looked at him alertly, cheerfully, without answering.

"I was brought by a woman named Roosevelt," he continued. "Mrs. Claud Roosevelt. Do you know her? I met her somewhere last night.

I've been drunk for about a week now, and I thought it might sober me up to sit in a library."

"Has it?"

"A little bit, I think. I can't tell yet. I've only been here an hour. Did I tell you about the books? They're real. They're———"

"You told us."

We shook hands with him gravely and went back outdoors.

There was dancing now on the canvas in the garden; old men pushing young girls backward in eternal graceless circles, superior couples holding each other tortuously, fashionably, and keeping in the corners—and a great number of single girls dancing individualistically or relieving the orchestra for a moment of the burden of the banjo or the traps. By midnight the hilarity had increased. A celebrated tenor had sung in Italian, and a notorious contralto had sung in jazz, and between the numbers people were doing "stunts" all over the garden, while happy, vacuous bursts of laughter rose toward the summer sky. A pair of stage twins, who turned out to be the girls in yellow, did a baby act in costume, and champagne was served in glasses bigger than finger-bowls. The moon had risen higher, and floating in the Sound was a triangle of silver scales, trembling a little to the stiff, tinny drip of the banjoes on the lawn.

I was still with Jordan Baker. We were sitting at a table with a man of about my age and a rowdy little girl, who gave way upon the slightest provocation to uncontrollable laughter. I was enjoying myself now. I had taken two finger-bowls of champagne, and the scene had changed before my eyes into something significant, elemental, and profound.

At a lull in the entertainment the man looked at me and smiled.

"Your face is familiar," he said, politely. "Weren't you in the Third Division during the war?"

"Why, yes. I was in the Ninth Machine-Gun Battalion."

"I was in the Seventh Infantry until June nineteen-eighteen. I knew I'd seen you somewhere before."

We talked for a moment about some wet, gray little villages in France. Evidently he lived in this vicinity, for he told me that he had just bought a hydroplane, and was going to try it out in the morning.

"Want to go with me, old sport? Just near the shore along the Sound."

"What time?"

"Any time that suits you best."

It was on the tip of my tongue to ask his name when Jordan looked around and smiled.

"Having a gay time now?" she inquired.

"Much better." I turned again to my new acquaintance. "This is an unusual party for me. I haven't even seen the host. I live over there—" I waved my hand at the invisible hedge in the distance, "and this man Gatsby sent over his chauffeur with an invitation."

For a moment he looked at me as if he failed to understand.

"I'm Gatsby," he said suddenly.

"What!" I exclaimed. "Oh, I beg your pardon."

"I thought you knew, old sport. I'm afraid I'm not a very good host."

He smiled understandingly—much more than understandingly. It was one of those rare smiles with a quality of eternal reassurance in it, that you may come across four or five times in life. It faced—or seemed to face—the whole external world for an instant, and then concentrated on *you* with an irresistible prejudice in your favor. It understood you just so far as you wanted to be understood, believed in you as you would like to believe in yourself, and assured you that it had precisely the impression of you that, at your best, you hoped to convey. Precisely at that point it vanished—and I was looking at an elegant young rough-neck, a year or two over thirty, whose elaborate formality of speech just missed being absurd. Sometime before he introduced himself I'd got a strong impression that he was picking his words with care.

Almost at the moment when Mr. Gatsby identified himself a butler hurried toward him with the information that Chicago was calling him on the wire. He excused himself with a small bow that included each of us in turn.

"If you want anything just ask for it, old sport," he urged me. "Excuse me. I will rejoin you later."

When he was gone I turned immediately to Jordan—constrained to assure her of my surprise. I had expected that Mr. Gatsby would be a florid and corpulent person in his middle years.

"Who is he?" I demanded. "Do you know?"

"He's just a man named Gatsby."

"Where is he from, I mean? And what does he do?"

"Now *you*'re started on the subject," she answered with a wan smile. "Well, he told me once he was an Oxford man."

A dim background started to take shape behind him, but at her next remark it faded away.

"However, I don't believe it."

"Why not?"

"I don't know," she insisted. "I just don't think he went there."

Something in her tone reminded me of the other girl's "I think he killed a man," and had the effect of stimulating my curiosity. I would have accepted without question the information that Gatsby sprang from the swamps of Louisiana or from the Lower East Side of New York. That was comprehensible. But young men didn't—at least in my provincial inexperience I believed they didn't—drift coolly out of nowhere and buy a palace on Long Island Sound.

"Anyhow, he gives large parties," said Jordan, changing the subject with an urban distaste for the concrete. "And I like large parties. They're so intimate. At small parties there isn't any privacy."

There was the boom of a bass drum, and the voice of the orchestra leader rang out suddenly above the echolalia of the garden.

"Ladies and gentlemen," he cried. "At the request of Mr. Gatsby we are going to play for you Mr. Vladimir Tostoff's latest work, which attracted so much attention at Carnegie Hall last May. If you read the papers you know there was a big sensation." He smiled with jovial condescension, and added: "Some sensation!" Whereupon everybody laughed.

"The piece is known," he concluded lustily, "as 'Vladimir Tostoff's Jazz History of the World.'"

The nature of Mr. Tostoff's composition eluded me, because just as it began my eyes fell on Gatsby, standing alone on the marble steps and looking from one group to another with approving eyes. His tanned skin was drawn attractively tight on his face and his short hair looked as though it were trimmed every day. I could see nothing sinister about him. I wondered if the fact that he was not drinking helped to set him off from his guests, for it seemed to me that he grew more correct as the fraternal hilarity increased. When the "Jazz History of the World" was over, girls were putting their heads on men's shoulders in a puppyish, convivial way, girls were swooning backward playfully into men's arms, even into groups, knowing that someone would arrest their falls—but no one swooned backward on Gatsby, and no French bob touched Gatsby's shoulder, and no singing quartets were formed with Gatsby's head for one link.

"I beg your pardon."

Gatsby's butler was suddenly standing beside us.

"Miss Baker?" he inquired. "I beg your pardon, but Mr. Gatsby would like to speak to you alone."

"With me?" she exclaimed in surprise.

"Yes, madame."

She got up slowly, raising her eyebrows at me in astonishment, and followed the butler toward the house. I noticed that she wore her evening-dress, all her dresses, like sports clothes—there was a jauntiness about her movements as if she had first learned to walk upon golf courses on clean, crisp mornings.

I was alone and it was almost two. For some time confused and intriguing sounds had issued from a long, many-windowed room which overhung the terrace. Eluding Jordan's undergraduate, who was now engaged in an obstetrical conversation with two chorus girls, and who implored me to join him, I went inside.

The large room was full of people. One of the girls in yellow was playing the piano, and beside her stood a tall, red-haired young lady from a famous chorus, engaged in song. She had drunk a quantity of champagne, and during the course of her song she had decided, ineptly, that everything was very, very sad—she was not only singing, she was weeping too. Whenever there was a pause in the song she filled it with gasping, broken sobs, and then took up the lyric again in a quavering soprano. The tears coursed down her cheeks—not freely, however, for when they came into contact with her heavily beaded eyelashes they assumed an inky color, and pursued the rest of their way in slow black rivulets. A humorous suggestion was made that she sing the notes on her face, whereupon she threw up her hands, sank into a chair, and went off into a deep vinous sleep.

"She had a fight with a man who says he's her husband," explained a girl at my elbow.

I looked around. Most of the remaining women were now having fights with men said to be their husbands. Even Jordan's party, the quartet from East Egg, were rent asunder by dissension. One of the men was talking with curious intensity to a young actress, and his wife, after attempting to laugh at the situation in a dignified and indifferent way, broke down entirely and resorted to flank attacks—at intervals she appeared suddenly at his side like an angry diamond, and hissed: "You promised!" into his ear.

The reluctance to go home was not confined to wayward men. The hall was at present occupied by two deplorably sober men and their highly indignant wives. The wives were sympathizing with each other in slightly raised voices.

"Whenever he sees I'm having a good time he wants to go home."

"Never heard anything so selfish in my life."

"We're always the first ones to leave."

"So are we."

"Well, we're almost the last tonight," said one of the men sheepishly. "The orchestra left half an hour ago."

In spite of the wives' agreement that such malevolence was beyond credibility, the dispute ended in a short struggle, and both wives were lifted, kicking, into the night.

As I waited for my hat in the hall the door of the library opened and Jordan Baker and Gatsby came out together. He was saying some last word to her, but the eagerness in his manner tightened abruptly into formality as several people approached him to say good-by.

Jordan's party were calling impatiently to her from the porch, but she lingered for a moment to shake hands.

"I've just heard the most amazing thing," she whispered. "How long were we in there?"

"Why, about an hour."

"It was . . . simply amazing," she repeated abstractedly. "But I swore I wouldn't tell it and here I am tantalizing you." She yawned gracefully in my face. "Please come and see me. . . . Phone book. . . . Under the name of Mrs. Sigourney Howard. . . . My aunt. . . ." She was hurrying off as she talked—her brown hand waved a jaunty salute as she melted into her party at the door.

Rather ashamed that on my first appearance I had stayed so late, I joined the last of Gatsby's guests, who were clustered around him. I wanted to explain that I'd hunted for him early in the evening and to apologize for not having known him in the garden.

"Don't mention it," he enjoined me eagerly. "Don't give it another thought, old sport." The familiar expression held no more familiarity than the hand which reassuringly brushed my shoulder. "And don't forget we're going up in the hydroplane tomorrow morning, at nine o'clock."

Then the butler, behind his shoulder:

"Philadelphia wants you on the phone, sir."

"All right, in a minute. Tell them I'll be right there. . . . Good night."

"Good night."

"Good night." He smiled—and suddenly there seemed to be a pleasant significance in having been among the last to go, as if he had desired it all the time. "Good night, old sport. . . . Good night."

But as I walked down the steps I saw that the evening was not quite over. Fifty feet from the door a dozen headlights illuminated a bizarre and tumultuous scene. In the ditch beside the road, right side up, but violently shorn of one wheel, rested a new coupé which had left Gatsby's drive not two minutes before. The sharp jut of a wall accounted for the detachment of the wheel, which was now getting considerable attention from half a dozen curious chauffeurs. However, as they had left their cars blocking the road, a harsh, discordant din from those in the rear had been audible for some time, and added to the already violent confusion of the scene.

A man in a long duster had dismounted from the wreck and now stood in the middle of the road, looking from the car to the tire and from the tire to the observers in a pleasant, puzzled way.

"See!" he explained. "It went in the ditch."

The fact was infinitely astonishing to him, and I recognized first the unusual quality of wonder, and then the man—it was the late patron of Gatsby's library.

"How'd it happen?"

He shrugged his shoulders.

"I know nothing whatever about mechanics," he said decisively.

"But how did it happen? Did you run into the wall?"

"Don't ask me," said Owl Eyes, washing his hands of the whole matter. "I know very little about driving—next to nothing. It happened, and that's all I know."

"Well, if you're a poor driver you oughtn't to try driving at night."

"But I wasn't even trying," he explained indignantly. "I wasn't even trying."

An awed hush fell upon the bystanders.

"Do you want to commit suicide?"

"You're lucky it was just a wheel! A bad driver and not even *try*ing!"

"You don't understand," explained the criminal. "I wasn't driving. There's another man in the car."

The shock that followed this declaration found voice in a sustained "Ah-h-h!" as the door of the coupé swung slowly open. The crowd—it was now a crowd—stepped back involuntarily, and when the door had opened wide there was a ghostly pause. Then, very gradually, part by part, a pale, dangling individual stepped out of the wreck, pawing tentatively at the ground with a large uncertain dancing shoe.

Blinded by the glare of the headlights and confused by the incessant groaning of the horns, the apparition stood swaying for a moment before he perceived the man in the duster.

"Wha's matter?" he inquired calmly. "Did we run outa gas?"

"Look!"

Half a dozen fingers pointed at the amputated wheel—he stared at it for a moment, and then looked upward as though he suspected that it had dropped from the sky.

"It came off," someone explained.

He nodded.

"At first I din' notice we'd stopped."

A pause. Then, taking a long breath and straightening his shoulders, he remarked in a determined voice:

"Wonder'ff tell me where there's a gas'line station?"

At least a dozen men, some of them little better off than he was, explained to him that wheel and car were no longer joined by any physical bond.

"Back out," he suggested after a moment. "Put her in reverse."

"But the *wheel's* off!"

He hesitated.

"No harm in trying," he said.

The caterwauling horns had reached a crescendo and I turned away and cut across the lawn toward home. I glanced back once. A wafer of a moon was shining over Gatsby's house, making the night fine as before, and surviving the laughter and the sound of his still glowing garden.

A sudden emptiness seemed to flow now from the windows and the great doors, endowing with complete isolation the figure of the host, who stood on the porch, his hand up in a formal gesture of farewell.

◆

Reading over what I have written so far, I see I have given the impression that the events of three nights several weeks apart were all that absorbed me. On the contrary, they were merely casual events in a crowded summer, and, until much later, they absorbed me infinitely less than my personal affairs.

Most of the time I worked. In the early morning the sun threw my shadow westward as I hurried down the white chasms of lower New York to the Probity Trust. I knew the other clerks and young bond-salesmen by their first names, and lunched with them in dark, crowded restaurants on little pig sausages and mashed potatoes and coffee. I even had a short affair with a girl who lived in Jersey City and worked in the accounting department, but her brother began throwing mean looks in my direction, so when she went on her vacation in July I let it blow quietly away.

I took dinner usually at the Yale Club—for some reason it was the gloomiest event of my day—and then I went upstairs to the library and studied investments and securities for a conscientious hour. There were generally a few rioters around, but they never came into the library, so it was a good place to work. After that, if the night was mellow, I strolled down Madison Avenue past the old Murray Hill Hotel, and over Thirty-third Street to the Pennsylvania Station.

I began to like New York, the racy, adventurous feel of it at night, and the satisfaction that the constant flicker of men and women and machines gives to the restless eye. I liked to walk up Fifth Avenue and pick out romantic women from the crowd and imagine that in a few minutes I was going to enter into their lives, and no one would ever know or disapprove. Sometimes, in my mind, I followed them to their apartments on the corners of hidden streets, and they turned and smiled back at me before they faded through a door into warm darkness. At the enchanted metropolitan twilight I felt a haunting loneliness sometimes, and felt it in others—poor young clerks who loitered in front of windows waiting until it was time for a solitary restaurant dinner—young clerks in the dusk, wasting the most poignant moments of night and life.

Again at eight o'clock, when the dark lanes of the Forties were five deep with throbbing taxi cabs, bound for the theatre district, I felt a sinking in my heart. Forms leaned together in the taxis as they waited, and voices sang, and there was laughter from unheard jokes, and lighted cigarettes outlined unintelligible gestures inside. Imagining that I, too, was hurrying toward gayety and sharing their intimate excitement, I wished them well.

For a while I lost sight of Jordan Baker, and then in midsummer I found her again. At first I was flattered to go places with her, because she was a golf champion, and everyone knew her name. Then it was something more. I wasn't actually in love, but I felt a sort of tender curiosity. The bored haughty face that she turned to the world concealed something—most affectations conceal something eventually, even though they don't in the beginning—and one day I found what it was. When we were on a house-party together up in Warwick, she left a borrowed car out in the rain with the top down, and then lied about it—and suddenly I remembered the story about her that had eluded me that night at Daisy's. At her first big golf tournament there was a row that nearly reached the newspapers—a suggestion that she had moved her ball from a bad lie in the semi-final round. The thing approached the proportions of a scandal—then died away. A caddy retracted his statement, and the only other witness admitted that he might have been mistaken. The incident and the name had remained together in my mind.

Jordan Baker instinctively avoided clever, shrewd men, and now I saw that this was because she felt safer on a plane where any divergence from a code would be thought impossible. She was incurably dishonest. She wasn't able to endure being at a disadvantage and, given this unwillingness, I suppose she had begun dealing in subterfuges when she was very young in order to keep that cool, insolent smile turned to the world and yet satisfy the demands of her hard, jaunty body.

It made no difference to me. Dishonesty in a woman is a thing you never blame deeply—I was casually sorry, and then I forgot. It was on that same house-party that we had a curious conversation about driving a car. It started because she passed so close to some workmen that our fender flicked a button on one man's coat.

"You're a rotten driver," I protested. "Either you ought to be more careful, or you oughtn't to drive at all."

"I am careful."

"No, you're not."

"Well, other people are," she said lightly.

"What's that got to do with it?"

"They'll keep out of my way," she insisted. "It takes two to make an accident."

"Suppose you met somebody just as careless as yourself."

"I hope I never will," she answered. "I hate careless people. That's why I like you."

Her gray, sun-strained eyes stared straight ahead, but she had deliberately shifted our relations, and for a moment I thought I loved her. But I am slow-thinking and full of interior rules that act as brakes on my desires, and I knew that first I had to get myself definitely out of that tangle back home. I'd been writing letters once a week and signing them: "Love, Nick," and all I could think of was how, when that certain girl played tennis, a faint mustache of perspiration appeared on her upper lip. Nevertheless there was a vague understanding that had to be tactfully broken off before I was free.

Everyone suspects himself of at least one of the cardinal virtues, and this is mine: I am one of the few honest people that I have ever known.

CHAPTER IV

O
n Sunday morning while church bells rang in the villages along-shore, the world and its mistress returned to Gatsby's house and twinkled hilariously on his lawn.

"He's a bootlegger," said the young ladies, moving somewhere between his cocktails and his flowers. "One time he killed a man who had found out that he was nephew to Von Hindenburg and second cousin to the devil. Reach me a rose, honey, and pour me a last drop into that there crystal glass."

Once I wrote down on the empty spaces of a time-table the names of those who came to Gatsby's house that summer. It is an old time-table now, disintegrating at its folds, and headed "This schedule in effect July 5th, 1922." But I can still read the gray names, and they will give you a better impression than my generalities of those who accepted Gatsby's hospitality and paid him the subtle tribute of knowing nothing whatever about him.

From East Egg, then, came the Chester Beckers and the Leeches, and a man named Bunsen, whom I knew at Yale, and Doctor Webster Civet, who was drowned last summer up in Maine. And the Hornbeams and the Willie Voltaires, and a whole clan named Blackbuck, who always gathered in a corner and flipped up their noses like goats at whosoever came near. And the Ismays and the Chrysties (or rather

Hubert Auerbach and Mr. Chrystie's wife), and Edgar Beaver, whose hair, they say, turned cotton-white one winter afternoon for no good reason at all.

Clarence Endive was from East Egg, as I remember. He came only once, in white knickerbockers, and had a fight with a bum named Etty in the garden. From farther out on the Island came the Cheadles and the O. R. P. Schraeders, and the Stonewall Jackson Abrams of Georgia, and the Fishguards and the Ripley Snells. Snell was there three days before he went to the penitentiary, so drunk out on the gravel drive that Mrs. Ulysses Swett's automobile ran over his right hand. The Dancies came, too, and S. B. Whitebait, who was well over sixty, and Maurice A. Flink, and the Hammerheads, and Beluga the tobacco importer, and Beluga's girls.

From West Egg came the Poles and the Mulreadys and Cecil Roebuck and Cecil Schoen and Gulick the state senator and New-ton Orchid, who controlled Films Par Excellence, and Eckhaust and Clyde Cohen and Don S. Schwartze (the son) and Arthur McCarty, all connected with the movies in one way or another. And the Catlips and the Bembergs and G. Earl Muldoon, brother to that Muldoon who afterward strangled his wife. Da Fontano the promoter came there, and Ed Legros and James B. ("Rot-Gut") Ferret and the De Jongs and Ernest Lilly—they came to gamble, and when Ferret wandered into the garden it meant he was cleaned out and Associated Traction would have to fluctuate profitably next day.

A man named Klipspringer was there so often and so long that he became known as "the boarder"—I doubt if he had any other home. Of theatrical people there were Gus Waize and Horace O'Donavan and Lester Myer and George Duckweed and Francis Bull. Also from New York were the Chromes and the Backhyssons and the Dennickers and Russel Betty and the Corrigans and the Kellehers and the Dewars and the Scullys and S. W. Belcher and the Smirkes and the young Quinns, divorced now, and Henry L. Palmetto, who killed himself by jumping in front of a subway train in Times Square.

Benny McClenahan arrived always with four girls. They were never quite the same ones in physical person, but they were so identical one with another that it inevitably seemed they had been there before. I have forgotten their names—Jaqueline, I think, or else Consuela, or Gloria or Judy or June, and their last names were either the melodious names of flowers and months or the sterner ones of the great American capitalists whose cousins, if pressed, they would confess themselves to be.

In addition to all these I can remember that Faustina O'Brien came there at least once and the Baedeker girls and young Brewer, who had his nose shot off in the war, and Mr. Albrucksburger and Miss Haag, his fiancée, and Ardita Fitz-Peters and Mr. P. Jewett, once head of the American Legion, and Miss Claudia Hip, with a man reputed to be her chauffeur, and a prince of something, whom we called Duke, and whose name, if I ever knew it, I have forgotten.

All these people came to Gatsby's house in the summer.

◆

At nine o'clock, one morning late in July, Gatsby's gorgeous car lurched up the rocky drive to my door and gave out a burst of melody from its three-noted horn. It was the first time he had called on me, though I had gone to two of his parties, mounted in his hydroplane, and, at his urgent invitation, made frequent use of his beach.

"Good morning, old sport. You're having lunch with me today and I thought we'd ride up together."

He was balancing himself on the dashboard of his car with that resourcefulness of movement that is so peculiarly American—that comes, I suppose, with the absence of lifting work or rigid sitting in youth and, even more, with the formless grace of our nervous, sporadic games. This quality was continually breaking through his punctilious manner in the shape of restlessness. He was never quite still; there was always a tapping foot somewhere or the impatient opening and closing of a hand.

He saw me looking with admiration at his car.

"It's pretty, isn't it, old sport?" He jumped off to give me a better view. "Haven't you ever seen it before?"

I'd seen it. Everybody had seen it. It was a rich cream color, bright with nickel, swollen here and there in its monstrous length with triumphant hat-boxes and supper-boxes and tool-boxes, and terraced with a labyrinth of wind-shields that mirrored a dozen suns. Sitting down behind many layers of glass in a sort of green leather conservatory, we started to town.

I had talked with him perhaps half a dozen times in the past month and found, to my disappointment, that he had little to say. So my first impression, that he was a person of some undefined consequence, had gradually faded and he had become simply the proprietor of an elaborate roadhouse next door.

And then came that disconcerting ride. We hadn't reached West Egg Village before Gatsby began leaving his elegant sentences unfinished and slapping himself indecisively on the knee of his caramel-colored suit.

"Look here, old sport," he broke out surprisingly. "What's your opinion of me, anyhow?"

A little overwhelmed, I began the generalized evasions which that question deserves.

"Well, I'm going to tell you something about my life," he interrupted. "I don't want you to get a wrong idea of me from all these stories you hear."

So he was aware of the bizarre accusations that flavored conversation in his halls.

"I'll tell you God's truth." His right hand suddenly ordered divine retribution to stand by. "I am the son of some wealthy people in the Middle West—all dead now. I was brought up in America but educated at Oxford, because all my ancestors have been educated there for many years. It is a family tradition."

He looked at me sideways—and I knew why Jordan Baker had believed he was lying. He hurried the phrase "educated at Oxford," or swallowed it, or choked on it, as though it had bothered him before. And with this doubt, his whole statement fell to pieces, and I wondered if there wasn't something a little sinister about him, after all.

"What part of the Middle West?" I inquired casually.

"San Francisco."

"I see."

"My family all died and I came into a good deal of money."

His voice was solemn, as if the memory of that sudden extinction of a clan still haunted him. For a moment I suspected that he was pulling my leg, but a glance at him convinced me otherwise.

"After that I lived like a young rajah in all the capitals of Europe— Paris, Venice, Rome—collecting jewels, chiefly rubies, hunting big game, painting a little, things for myself only, and trying to forget something very sad that had happened to me long ago."

With an effort I managed to restrain my incredulous laughter. The very phrases were worn so threadbare that they evoked no image except that of a turbaned "character" leaking sawdust at every pore as he pursued a tiger through the Bois de Boulogne.

"Then came the war, old sport. It was a great relief, and I tried very hard to die, but I seemed to bear an enchanted life. I accepted a commission as first lieutenant when it began. In the Argonne Forest I took two machine-gun detachments so far forward that there was a half mile gap on either side of us where the infantry couldn't advance. We stayed there two days and two nights, a hundred and thirty men with sixteen Lewis guns, and when the infantry came up at last they found the insignia of three German divisions among the piles of dead. I was promoted to be a major, and every Allied government gave me a decoration—even Montenegro, little Montenegro down on the Adriatic Sea!"

Little Montenegro! He lifted up the words and nodded at them— with his smile. The smile comprehended Montenegro's troubled history and sympathized with the brave struggles of the Montenegrin people. It appreciated fully the chain of national circumstances which had elicited this tribute from Montenegro's warm little heart. My incredulity was submerged in fascination now; it was like skimming hastily through a dozen magazines.

He reached in his pocket, and a piece of metal, slung on a ribbon, fell into my palm.

"That's the one from Montenegro."

To my astonishment, the thing had an authentic look. "Orderi di Danilo," ran the circular legend, "Montenegro, Nicolas Rex."

"Turn it."

"Major Jay Gatsby," I read. "For Valour Extraordinary."

"Here's another thing I always carry. A souvenir of Oxford days. It was taken in Trinity Quad—the man on my left is now the Earl of Doncaster."

It was a photograph of half a dozen young men in blazers loafing in an archway through which were visible a host of spires. There was Gatsby, looking a little, not much, younger—with a cricket bat in his hand.

Then it was all true. I saw the skins of tigers flaming in his palace on the Grand Canal; I saw him opening a chest of rubies to ease, with their crimson-lighted depths, the gnawings of his broken heart.

"I'm going to make a big request of you today," he said, pocketing his souvenirs with satisfaction, "so I thought you ought to know something about me. I didn't want you to think I was just some nobody. You see, I usually find myself among strangers because I drift here and there trying to forget the sad thing that happened to me." He hesitated. "You'll hear about it this afternoon."

"At lunch?"

"No, this afternoon. I happened to find out that you're taking Miss Baker to tea."

"Do you mean you're in love with Miss Baker?"

"No, old sport, I'm not. But Miss Baker has kindly consented to speak to you about this matter."

I hadn't the faintest idea what "this matter" was, but I was more annoyed than interested. I hadn't asked Jordan to tea in order to discuss Mr. Jay Gatsby. I was sure the request would be something utterly fantastic, and for a moment I was sorry I'd ever set foot upon his over-populated lawn.

He wouldn't say another word. His correctness grew on him as we neared the city. We passed Port Roosevelt, where there was a glimpse of red-belted ocean-going ships, and sped along a cobbled slum lined with the dark, undeserted saloons of the faded-gilt nineteen-hundreds. Then the valley of ashes opened out on both sides of us, and I had a glimpse of Mrs. Wilson straining at the garage pump with panting vitality as we went by.

With fenders spread like wings we scattered light through half Astoria—only half, for as we twisted among the pillars of the elevated I heard the familiar "jug-jug-*spat!*" of a motorcycle, and a frantic policeman rode alongside.

"All right, old sport," called Gatsby. We slowed down. Taking a white card from his wallet, he waved it before the man's eyes.

"Right you are," agreed the policeman, tipping his cap. "Know you next time, Mr. Gatsby. Excuse *me!*"

"What was that?" I inquired. "The picture of Oxford?"

"I was able to do the commissioner a favor once, and he sends me a Christmas card every year."

Over the great bridge, with the sunlight through the girders making a constant flicker upon the moving cars, with the city rising up across the river in white heaps and sugar lumps all built with a wish out of non-olfactory money. The city seen from the Queensboro Bridge is always the city seen for the first time, in its first wild promise of all the mystery and the beauty in the world.

A dead man passed us in a hearse heaped with blooms, followed by two carriages with drawn blinds, and by more cheerful carriages for friends. The friends looked out at us with the tragic eyes and short upper lips of southeastern Europe, and I was glad that the sight of Gatsby's splendid car was included in their somber holiday. As we crossed Blackwell's Island a limousine passed us, driven by a white chauffeur, in which sat three modish negroes, two bucks and a girl. I laughed aloud as the yolks of their eyeballs rolled toward us in haughty rivalry.

"Anything can happen now that we've slid over this bridge," I thought; "anything at all. . . ."

Even Gatsby could happen, without any particular wonder.

◆

Roaring noon. In a well-fanned Forty-second Street cellar I met Gatsby for lunch. Blinking away the brightness of the street outside, my eyes picked him out obscurely in the anteroom, talking to another man.

"Mr. Carraway, this is my friend Mr. Wolfshiem."

A small, flat-nosed Jew raised his large head and regarded me with two fine growths of hair which luxuriated in either nostril. After a moment I discovered his tiny eyes in the half darkness.

"—So I took one look at him," said Mr. Wolfshiem, shaking my hand earnestly, "and what do you think I did?"

"What?" I inquired politely.

But evidently he was not addressing me, for he dropped my hand and covered Gatsby with his expressive nose.

"I handed the money to Katspaugh and I sid: 'All right, Katspaugh, don't pay him a penny till he shuts his mouth.' He shut it then and there."

Gatsby took an arm of each of us and moved forward into the restaurant, whereupon Mr. Wolfshiem swallowed a new sentence he was starting and lapsed into a somnambulatory abstraction.

"Highballs?" asked the head waiter.

"This is a nice restaurant here," said Mr. Wolfshiem, looking at the Presbyterian nymphs on the ceiling. "But I like across the street better!"

"Yes, highballs," agreed Gatsby, and then to Mr. Wolfshiem: "It's too hot over there."

"Hot and small—yes," said Mr. Wolfshiem, "but full of memories."

"What place is that?" I asked Gatsby.

"The old Metropole."

"The old Metropole," brooded Mr. Wolfshiem gloomily. "Filled with faces dead and gone. Filled with friends gone now forever. I can't forget so long as I live the night they shot Rosy Rosenthal there. It was six of us at the table, and Rosy had eat and drunk a lot all evening. When it was almost morning the waiter came up to him with a funny look and says somebody wants to speak to him outside. 'All right,' says Rosy, and begins to get up, and I pulled him down in his chair.

"'Let the bastards come in here if they want you, Rosy, but don't you, so help me, move outside this room.'

"It was four o'clock in the morning then, and if we'd of raised the blinds we'd of seen daylight."

"Did he go?" I asked innocently.

"Sure he went." Mr. Wolfshiem's nose flashed at me indignantly. "He turned around in the door and says: 'Don't let that waiter take away my coffee!' Then he went out on the sidewalk, and they shot him three times in his full belly and drove away."

"Four of them were electrocuted," I said, remembering.

"Five, with Becker." His nostrils turned to me in an interested way. "I understand you're looking for a business gonnegtion."

The juxtaposition of these two remarks was startling. Gatsby answered for me:

"Oh, no," he exclaimed, "this isn't the man."

"No?" Mr. Wolfshiem seemed disappointed.

"This is just a friend. I told you we'd talk about that some other time."

"I beg your pardon," said Mr. Wolfshiem. "I had a wrong man."

A succulent hash arrived, and Mr. Wolfshiem, forgetting the more sentimental atmosphere of the old Metropole, began to eat with ferocious delicacy. His eyes, meanwhile, roved very slowly all around the

THE GREAT GATSBY

room—he completed the arc by turning to inspect the people directly behind. I think that, except for my presence, he would have taken one short glance beneath our own table.

"Look here, old sport," said Gatsby, leaning toward me, "I'm afraid I made you a little angry this morning in the car."

There was the smile again, but this time I held out against it.

"I don't like mysteries," I answered, "and I don't understand why you won't come out frankly and tell me what you want. Why has it all got to come through Miss Baker?"

"Oh, it's nothing underhand," he assured me. "Miss Baker's a great sportswoman, you know, and she'd never do anything that wasn't all right."

Suddenly he looked at his watch, jumped up, and hurried from the room, leaving me with Mr. Wolfshiem at the table.

"He has to telephone," said Mr. Wolfshiem, following him with his eyes. "Fine fellow, isn't he? Handsome to look at and a perfect gentleman."

"Yes."

"He's an Oggsford man."

"Oh!"

"He went to Oggsford College in England. You know Oggsford College?"

"I've heard of it."

"It's one of the most famous colleges in the world."

"Have you known Gatsby for a long time?" I inquired.

"Several years," he answered in a gratified way. "I made the pleasure of his acquaintance just after the war. But I knew I had discovered a man of fine breeding after I talked with him an hour. I said to myself: 'There's the kind of man you'd like to take home and introduce to your mother and sister.'" He paused. "I see you're looking at my cuff buttons."

I hadn't been looking at them, but I did now. They were composed of oddly familiar pieces of ivory.

"Finest specimens of human molars," he informed me.

"Well!" I inspected them. "That's a very interesting idea."

"Yeah." He flipped his sleeves up under his coat. "Yeah, Gatsby's very careful about women. He would never so much as look at a friend's wife."

When the subject of this instinctive trust returned to the table and sat down Mr. Wolfshiem drank his coffee with a jerk and got to his feet.

"I have enjoyed my lunch," he said, "and I'm going to run off from you two young men before I outstay my welcome."

"Don't hurry, Meyer," said Gatsby, without enthusiasm. Mr. Wolfshiem raised his hand in a sort of benediction.

"You're very polite, but I belong to another generation," he announced solemnly. "You sit here and discuss your sports and your young ladies and your——" He supplied an imaginary noun with another wave of his hand. "As for me, I am fifty years old, and I won't impose myself on you any longer."

As he shook hands and turned away his tragic nose was trembling. I wondered if I had said anything to offend him.

"He becomes very sentimental sometimes," explained Gatsby. "This is one of his sentimental days. He's quite a character around New York—a denizen of Broadway."

"Who is he, anyhow, an actor?"

"No."

"A dentist?"

"Meyer Wolfshiem? No, he's a gambler." Gatsby hesitated, then added coolly: "He's the man who fixed the World's Series back in 1919."

"Fixed the World's Series?" I repeated.

The idea staggered me. I remembered, of course, that the World's Series had been fixed in 1919, but if I had thought of it at all I would have thought of it as a thing that merely *happened*, the end of some inevitable chain. It never occurred to me that one man could start to play with the faith of fifty million people—with the single-mindedness of a burglar blowing a safe.

"How did he happen to do that?" I asked after a minute.

"He just saw the opportunity."

"Why isn't he in jail?"

"They can't get him, old sport. He's a smart man."

I insisted on paying the check. As the waiter brought my change I caught sight of Tom Buchanan across the crowded room.

"Come along with me for a minute," I said; "I've got to say hello to someone."

When he saw us Tom jumped up and took half a dozen steps in our direction.

"Where've you been?" he demanded eagerly. "Daisy's furious because you haven't called up."

"This is Mr. Gatsby, Mr. Buchanan."

They shook hands briefly, and a strained, unfamiliar look of embarrassment came over Gatsby's face.

"How've you been, anyhow?" demanded Tom of me. "How'd you happen to come up this far to eat?"

"I've been having lunch with Mr. Gatsby."

I turned toward Mr. Gatsby, but he was no longer there.

◆

One October day in nineteen-seventeen——

(said Jordan Baker that afternoon, sitting up very straight on a straight chair in the tea-garden at the Plaza Hotel)

—I was walking along from one place to another, half on the sidewalks and half on the lawns. I was happier on the lawns because I had on shoes from England with rubber nobs on the soles that bit into the soft ground. I had on a new plaid skirt also that blew a little in the wind, and whenever this happened the red, white, and blue banners in front of all the houses stretched out stiff and said *tut-tut-tut-tut,* in a disapproving way.

The largest of the banners and the largest of the lawns belonged to Daisy Fay's house. She was just eighteen, two years older than me, and by far the most popular of all the young girls in Louisville. She dressed in white, and had a little white roadster, and all day long the telephone rang in her house and excited young officers from Camp Taylor demanded the privilege of monopolizing her that night. "Anyways, for an hour!"

When I came opposite her house that morning her white roadster was beside the curb, and she was sitting in it with a lieutenant I had never seen before. They were so engrossed in each other that she didn't see me until I was five feet away.

"Hello, Jordan," she called unexpectedly. "Please come here."

I was flattered that she wanted to speak to me, because of all the older girls I admired her most. She asked me if I was going to the Red Cross and make bandages. I was. Well, then, would I tell them that she couldn't come that day? The officer looked at Daisy while she was speaking, in a way that every young girl wants to be looked at sometime, and because it seemed romantic to me I have remembered the incident ever since. His name was Jay Gatsby, and I didn't lay eyes on him again for over four years—even after I'd met him on Long Island I didn't realize it was the same man.

That was nineteen-seventeen. By the next year I had a few beaux myself, and I began to play in tournaments, so I didn't see Daisy very often. She went with a slightly older crowd—when she went with any-one at all. Wild rumors were circulating about her—how her mother had found her packing her bag one winter night to go to New York and say good-by to a soldier who was going overseas. She was effectually prevented, but she wasn't on speaking terms with her family for several weeks. After that she didn't play around with the soldiers any more, but only with a few flat-footed, short-sighted young men in town, who couldn't get into the army at all.

By the next autumn she was gay again, gay as ever. She had a début after the armistice, and in February she was presumably engaged to a man from New Orleans. In June she married Tom Buchanan of Chicago, with more pomp and circumstance than Louisville ever knew before. He came down with a hundred people in four private cars, and hired a whole floor of the Seelbach Hotel, and the day before the wedding he gave her a string of pearls valued at three hundred and fifty thousand dollars.

I was a bridesmaid. I came into her room half an hour before the bridal dinner, and found her lying on her bed as lovely as the June night in her flowered dress—and as drunk as a monkey. She had a bottle of Sauterne in one hand and a letter in the other.

"'Gratulate me," she muttered. "Never had a drink before, but oh how I do enjoy it."

"What's the matter, Daisy?"

I was scared, I can tell you; I'd never seen a girl like that before.

"Here, deares'." She groped around in a wastebasket she had with her on the bed and pulled out the string of pearls. "Take 'em downstairs and give 'em back to whoever they belong to. Tell 'em all Daisy's change' her mine. Say: 'Daisy's change' her mine!'"

She began to cry—she cried and cried. I rushed out and found her mother's maid, and we locked the door and got her into a cold bath. She wouldn't let go of the letter. She took it into the tub with her and squeezed it up into a wet ball, and only let me leave it in the soap dish when she saw that it was coming to pieces like snow.

But she didn't say another word. We gave her spirits of ammonia and put ice on her forehead and hooked her back into her dress, and half an hour later, when we walked out of the room, the pearls were around her neck and the incident was over. Next day at five o'clock she married Tom Buchanan without so much as a shiver, and started off on a three months' trip to the South Seas.

I saw them in Santa Barbara when they came back, and I thought I'd never seen a girl so mad about her husband. If he left the room for a minute she'd look around uneasily, and say: "Where's Tom gone?" and wear the most abstracted expression until she saw him coming in the door. She used to sit on the sand with his head in her lap by the hour, rubbing her fingers over his eyes and looking at him with unfathomable delight. It was touching to see them together—it made you laugh in a hushed, fascinated way. That was in August. A week after I left Santa Barbara Tom ran into a wagon on the Ventura road one night, and ripped a front wheel off his car. The girl who was with him got into the papers, too, because her arm was broken—she was one of the chambermaids in the Santa Barbara Hotel.

The next April Daisy had her little girl, and they went to France for a year. I saw them one spring in Cannes, and later in Deauville, and then they came back to Chicago to settle down. Daisy was popular in Chicago, as you know. They moved with a fast crowd, all of them young and rich and wild, but she came out with an absolutely perfect reputation. Perhaps because she doesn't drink. It's a great advantage not to drink among hard-drinking people. You can hold your tongue, and, moreover, you can time any little irregularity of your own so that everybody else is so blind that they don't see or care. Perhaps Daisy never went in for amour at all—and yet there's something in that voice of hers. . . .

Well, about six weeks ago, she heard the name Gatsby for the first time in years. It was when I asked you—do you remember?—if you knew Gatsby in West Egg. After you had gone home she came into my room and woke me up, and said: "What Gatsby?" and when I described him—I was half asleep—she said in the strangest voice that it must be the man she used to know. It wasn't until then that I connected this Gatsby with the officer in her white car.

◆

When Jordan Baker had finished telling all this we had left the Plaza for half an hour and were driving in a Victoria through Central Park. The sun had gone down behind the tall apartments of the movie stars in the West Fifties, and the clear voices of children, already gathered like crickets on the grass, rose through the hot twilight:

> "I'm the Sheik of Araby.
> Your love belongs to me.
> At night when you're asleep
> Into your tent I'll creep——"

"It was a strange coincidence," I said.

"But it wasn't a coincidence at all."

"Why not?"

"Gatsby bought that house so that Daisy would be just across the bay."

Then it had not been merely the stars to which he had aspired on that June night. He came alive to me, delivered suddenly from the womb of his purposeless splendor.

"He wants to know," continued Jordan, "if you'll invite Daisy to your house some afternoon and then let him come over."

The modesty of the demand shook me. He had waited five years and bought a mansion where he dispensed starlight to casual moths—so that he could "come over" some afternoon to a stranger's garden.

"Did I have to know all this before he could ask such a little thing?"

"He's afraid. He's waited so long. He thought you might be offended. You see, he's a regular tough underneath it all."

Something worried me.

"Why didn't he ask you to arrange a meeting?"

"He wants her to see his house," she explained. "And your house is right next door."

"Oh!"

"I think he half expected her to wander into one of his parties, some night," went on Jordan, "but she never did. Then he began asking people casually if they knew her, and I was the first one he found. It was that night he sent for me at his dance, and you should have heard the elaborate way he worked up to it. Of course, I immediately suggested a luncheon in New York—and I thought he'd go mad:

"'I don't want to do anything out of the way!' he kept saying. 'I want to see her right next door.'

"When I said you were a particular friend of Tom's, he started to abandon the whole idea. He doesn't know very much about Tom, though he says he's read a Chicago paper for years just on the chance of catching a glimpse of Daisy's name."

It was dark now, and as we dipped under a little bridge I put my arm around Jordan's golden shoulder and drew her toward me and asked her to dinner. Suddenly I wasn't thinking of Daisy and Gatsby any more, but of this clean, hard, limited person, who dealt in universal skepticism, and who leaned back jauntily just within the circle of my arm. A phrase began to beat in my ears with a sort of heady excitement: "There are only the pursued, the pursuing, the busy and the tired."

"And Daisy ought to have something in her life," murmured Jordan to me.

"Does she want to see Gatsby?"

"She's not to know about it. Gatsby doesn't want her to know. You're just supposed to invite her to tea."

We passed a barrier of dark trees, and then the façade of Fifty-ninth Street, a block of delicate pale light, beamed down into the Park. Unlike Gatsby and Tom Buchanan, I had no girl whose disembodied face floated along the dark cornices and blinding signs, and so I drew up the girl beside me, tightening my arms. Her wan, scornful mouth smiled, and so I drew her up again closer, this time to my face.

CHAPTER V

When I came home to West Egg that night I was afraid for a moment that my house was on fire. Two o'clock and the whole corner of the peninsula was blazing with light, which fell unreal on the shrubbery and made thin elongating glints upon the roadside wires. Turning a corner, I saw that it was Gatsby's house, lit from tower to cellar.

At first I thought it was another party, a wild rout that had resolved itself into "hide-and-go-seek" or "sardines-in-the-box" with all the house thrown open to the game. But there wasn't a sound. Only wind in the trees, which blew the wires and made the lights go off and on again as if the house had winked into the darkness. As my taxi groaned away I saw Gatsby walking toward me across his lawn.

"Your place looks like the World's Fair," I said.

"Does it?" He turned his eyes toward it absently. "I have been glancing into some of the rooms. Let's go to Coney Island, old sport. In my car."

"It's too late."

"Well, suppose we take a plunge in the swimming pool? I haven't made use of it all summer."

"I've got to go to bed."

"All right."

He waited, looking at me with suppressed eagerness.

"I talked with Miss Baker," I said after a moment. "I'm going to call up Daisy tomorrow and invite her over here to tea."

"Oh, that's all right," he said carelessly. "I don't want to put you to any trouble."

"What day would suit you?"

"What day would suit *you*?" he corrected me quickly. "I don't want to put you to any trouble, you see."

"How about the day after tomorrow?"

He considered for a moment. Then, with reluctance:

"I want to get the grass cut," he said.

We both looked at the grass—there was a sharp line where my ragged lawn ended and the darker, well-kept expanse of his began. I suspected that he meant my grass.

"There's another little thing," he said uncertainly, and hesitated.

"Would you rather put it off for a few days?" I asked.

"Oh, it isn't about that. At least—" He fumbled with a series of beginnings. "Why, I thought—why, look here, old sport, you don't make much money, do you?"

"Not very much."

This seemed to reassure him and he continued more confidently.

"I thought you didn't, if you'll pardon my—you see, I carry on a little business on the side, a sort of sideline, you understand. And I thought that if you don't make very much—You're selling bonds, aren't you, old sport?"

"Trying to."

"Well, this would interest you. It wouldn't take up much of your time and you might pick up a nice bit of money. It happens to be a rather confidential sort of thing."

I realize now that under different circumstances that conversation might have been one of the crises of my life. But, because the offer was obviously and tactlessly for a service to be rendered, I had no choice except to cut him off there.

"I've got my hands full," I said. "I'm much obliged but I couldn't take on any more work."

"You wouldn't have to do any business with Wolfshiem." Evidently he thought that I was shying away from the "gonnegtion" mentioned at lunch, but I assured him he was wrong. He waited a moment longer, hoping I'd begin a conversation, but I was too absorbed to be responsive, so he went unwillingly home.

The evening had made me light-headed and happy; I think I walked into a deep sleep as I entered my front door. So I don't know whether or not Gatsby went to Coney Island, or for how many hours he "glanced into rooms" while his house blazed gaudily on. I called up Daisy from the office next morning, and invited her to come to tea.

"Don't bring Tom," I warned her.

"What?"

"Don't bring Tom."

"Who is 'Tom'?" she asked innocently.

The day agreed upon was pouring rain. At eleven o'clock a man in a raincoat, dragging a lawn-mower, tapped at my front door and said that Mr. Gatsby had sent him over to cut my grass. This reminded me that I had forgotten to tell my Finn to come back, so I drove into West Egg Village to search for her among soggy whitewashed alleys and to buy some cups and lemons and flowers.

The flowers were unnecessary, for at two o'clock a greenhouse arrived from Gatsby's, with innumerable receptacles to contain it. An hour later the front door opened nervously, and Gatsby, in a white flannel suit, silver shirt, and gold-colored tie, hurried in. He was pale, and there were dark signs of sleeplessness beneath his eyes.

"Is everything all right?" he asked immediately.

"The grass looks fine, if that's what you mean."

"What grass?" he inquired blankly. "Oh, the grass in the yard." He looked out the window at it, but, judging from his expression, I don't believe he saw a thing.

"Looks very good," he remarked vaguely. "One of the papers said they thought the rain would stop about four. I think it was The Journal. Have you got everything you need in the shape of—of tea?"

I took him into the pantry, where he looked a little reproachfully at the Finn. Together we scrutinized the twelve lemon cakes from the delicatessen shop.

"Will they do?" I asked.

"Of course, of course! They're fine!" and he added hollowly, ". . . old sport."

The rain cooled about half-past three to a damp mist, through which occasional thin drops swam like dew. Gatsby looked with vacant eyes through a copy of Clay's "Economics," starting at the Finnish tread that shook the kitchen floor, and peering toward the bleared windows from time to time as if a series of invisible but alarming happenings were taking place outside. Finally he got up and informed me, in an uncertain voice, that he was going home.

"Why's that?"

"Nobody's coming to tea. It's too late!" He looked at his watch as if there was some pressing demand on his time elsewhere. "I can't wait all day."

"Don't be silly; it's just two minutes to four."

He sat down miserably, as if I had pushed him, and simultaneously there was the sound of a motor turning into my lane. We both jumped up, and, a little harrowed myself, I went out into the yard.

Under the dripping bare lilac trees a large open car was coming up the drive. It stopped. Daisy's face, tipped sideways beneath a three-cornered lavender hat, looked out at me with a bright ecstatic smile.

"Is this absolutely where you live, my dearest one?"

The exhilarating ripple of her voice was a wild tonic in the rain. I had to follow the sound of it for a moment, up and down, with my ear alone, before any words came through. A damp streak of hair lay like a dash of blue paint across her cheek, and her hand was wet with glistening drops as I took it to help her from the car.

"Are you in love with me," she said low in my ear, "or why did I have to come alone?"

"That's the secret of Castle Rackrent. Tell your chauffeur to go far away and spend an hour."

"Come back in an hour, Ferdie." Then in a grave murmur: "His name is Ferdie."

"Does the gasoline affect his nose?"

"I don't think so," she said innocently. "Why?"

We went in. To my overwhelming surprise the living-room was deserted.

"Well, that's funny!" I exclaimed.

"What's funny?"

She turned her head as there was a light dignified knocking at the front door. I went out and opened it. Gatsby, pale as death, with his hands plunged like weights in his coat pockets, was standing in a puddle of water glaring tragically into my eyes.

With his hands still in his coat pockets he stalked by me into the hall, turned sharply as if he were on a wire, and disappeared into the living-room. It wasn't a bit funny. Aware of the loud beating of my own heart I pulled the door to against the increasing rain.

For half a minute there wasn't a sound. Then from the living-room I heard a sort of choking murmur and part of a laugh, followed by Daisy's voice on a clear artificial note:

"I certainly am awfully glad to see you again."

A pause; it endured horribly. I had nothing to do in the hall, so I went into the room.

Gatsby, his hands still in his pockets, was reclining against the mantelpiece in a strained counterfeit of perfect ease, even of boredom. His head leaned back so far that it rested against the face of a defunct mantelpiece clock, and from this position his distraught eyes stared down at Daisy, who was sitting, frightened but graceful, on the edge of a stiff chair.

"We've met before," muttered Gatsby. His eyes glanced momentarily at me, and his lips parted with an abortive attempt at a laugh. Luckily the clock took this moment to tilt dangerously at the pressure of his head, whereupon he turned and caught it with trembling fingers and set it back in place. Then he sat down, rigidly, his elbow on the arm of the sofa and his chin in his hand.

"I'm sorry about the clock," he said.

My own face had now assumed a deep tropical burn. I couldn't muster up a single commonplace out of the thousand in my head.

"It's an old clock," I told them idiotically.

I think we all believed for a moment that it had smashed in pieces on the floor.

"We haven't met for many years," said Daisy, her voice as matter-of-fact as it could ever be.

"Five years next November."

The automatic quality of Gatsby's answer set us all back at least another minute. I had them both on their feet with the desperate suggestion that they help me make tea in the kitchen when the demoniac Finn brought it in on a tray.

Amid the welcome confusion of cups and cakes a certain physical decency established itself. Gatsby got himself into a shadow and, while Daisy and I talked, looked conscientiously from one to the other of us with tense, unhappy eyes. However, as calmness wasn't an end in itself, I made an excuse at the first possible moment, and got to my feet.

"Where are you going?" demanded Gatsby in immediate alarm.

"I'll be back."

"I've got to speak to you about something before you go."

He followed me wildly into the kitchen, closed the door, and whispered: "Oh, God!" in a miserable way.

"What's the matter?"

"This is a terrible mistake," he said, shaking his head from side to side, "a terrible, terrible mistake."

"You're just embarrassed, that's all," and luckily I added: "Daisy's embarrassed too."

"She's embarrassed?" he repeated incredulously.

"Just as much as you are."

"Don't talk so loud."

"You're acting like a little boy," I broke out impatiently. "Not only that, but you're rude. Daisy's sitting in there all alone."

He raised his hand to stop my words, looked at me with unforgettable reproach, and, opening the door cautiously, went back into the other room.

I walked out the back way—just as Gatsby had when he had made his nervous circuit of the house half an hour before—and ran for a huge black knotted tree, whose massed leaves made a fabric against the rain. Once more it was pouring, and my irregular lawn, well-shaved by Gatsby's gardener, abounded in small muddy swamps and prehistoric marshes. There was nothing to look at from under the tree except Gatsby's enormous house, so I stared at it, like Kant at his church steeple, for half an hour. A brewer had built it early in the "period" craze, a decade before, and there was a story that he'd agreed to pay five years' taxes on all the neighboring cottages if the owners would have their roofs thatched with straw. Perhaps their refusal took the heart out of his plan to Found a Family—he went into an immediate decline. His children sold his house with the black wreath still on the door. Americans, while occasionally willing to be serfs, have always been obstinate about being peasantry.

After half an hour, the sun shone again, and the grocer's automobile rounded Gatsby's drive with the raw material for his servants' dinner—I felt sure he wouldn't eat a spoonful. A maid began opening the upper windows of his house, appeared momentarily in each, and, leaning from a large central bay, spat meditatively into the garden. It was time I went back. While the rain continued it had seemed like the murmur of their voices, rising and swelling a little now and then with gusts of emotion. But in the new silence I felt that silence had fallen within the house too.

I went in—after making every possible noise in the kitchen, short of pushing over the stove—but I don't believe they heard a sound.

They were sitting at either end of the couch, looking at each other as if some question had been asked, or was in the air, and every vestige of embarrassment was gone.

Daisy's face was smeared with tears, and when I came in she jumped up and began wiping at it with her handkerchief before a mirror. But there was a change in Gatsby that was simply confounding. He literally glowed; without a word or a gesture of exultation a new well-being radiated from him and filled the little room.

"Oh, hello, old sport," he said, as if he hadn't seen me for years. I thought for a moment he was going to shake hands.

"It's stopped raining."

"Has it?" When he realized what I was talking about, that there were twinkle-bells of sunshine in the room, he smiled like a weather man, like an ecstatic patron of recurrent light, and repeated the news to Daisy. "What do you think of that? It's stopped raining."

"I'm glad, Jay." Her throat, full of aching, grieving beauty, told only of her unexpected joy.

"I want you and Daisy to come over to my house," he said. "I'd like to show her around."

"You're sure you want me to come?"

"Absolutely, old sport."

Daisy went upstairs to wash her face—too late I thought with humiliation of my towels—while Gatsby and I waited on the lawn.

"My house looks well, doesn't it?" he demanded. "See how the whole front of it catches the light."

I agreed that it was splendid.

"Yes." His eyes went over it, every arched door and square tower. "It took me just three years to earn the money that bought it."

"I thought you inherited your money."

"I did, old sport," he said automatically, "but I lost most of it in the big panic—the panic of the war."

I think he hardly knew what he was saying, for when I asked him what business he was in he answered: "That's my affair," before he realized that it wasn't an appropriate reply.

"Oh, I've been in several things," he corrected himself. "I was in the drug business and then I was in the oil business. But I'm not in either one now." He looked at me with more attention. "Do you mean you've been thinking over what I proposed the other night?"

Before I could answer, Daisy came out of the house and two rows of brass buttons on her dress gleamed in the sunlight.

"That huge place *there*?" she cried pointing.

"Do you like it?"

"I love it, but I don't see how you live there all alone."

"I keep it always full of interesting people, night and day. People who do interesting things. Celebrated people."

Instead of taking the short-cut along the Sound we went down to the road and entered by the big postern. With enchanting murmurs Daisy admired this aspect or that of the feudal silhouette against the sky, admired the gardens, the sparkling odor of jonquils and the frothy odor of hawthorn and plum blossoms and the pale gold odor of kiss-me-at-the-gate. It was strange to reach the marble steps and find no stir of bright dresses in and out the door, and hear no sound but bird voices in the trees.

And inside, as we wandered through Marie Antoinette music-rooms and Restoration salons, I felt that there were guests concealed behind every couch and table, under orders to be breathlessly silent until we had passed through. As Gatsby closed the door of "the Merton College

Library" I could have sworn I heard the owl-eyed man break into ghostly laughter.

We went upstairs, through period bedrooms swathed in rose and lavender silk and vivid with new flowers, through dressing-rooms and poolrooms, and bathrooms with sunken baths—intruding into one chamber where a dishevelled man in pajamas was doing liver exercises on the floor. It was Mr. Klipspringer, the "boarder." I had seen him wandering hungrily about the beach that morning. Finally we came to Gatsby's own apartment, a bedroom and a bath, and an Adam study, where we sat down and drank a glass of some Chartreuse he took from a cupboard in the wall.

He hadn't once ceased looking at Daisy, and I think he revalued everything in his house according to the measure of response it drew from her well-loved eyes. Sometimes, too, he stared around at his possessions in a dazed way, as though in her actual and astounding presence none of it was any longer real. Once he nearly toppled down a flight of stairs.

His bedroom was the simplest room of all—except where the dresser was garnished with a toilet set of pure dull gold. Daisy took the brush with delight, and smoothed her hair, whereupon Gatsby sat down and shaded his eyes and began to laugh.

"It's the funniest thing, old sport," he said hilariously. "I can't— When I try to———"

He had passed visibly through two states and was entering upon a third. After his embarrassment and his unreasoning joy he was consumed with wonder at her presence. He had been full of the idea so long, dreamed it right through to the end, waited with his teeth set, so to speak, at an inconceivable pitch of intensity. Now, in the reaction, he was running down like an overwound clock.

Recovering himself in a minute he opened for us two hulking patent cabinets which held his massed suits and dressing gowns and ties, and his shirts, piled like bricks in stacks a dozen high.

"I've got a man in England who buys me clothes. He sends over a selection of things at the beginning of each season, spring and fall."

He took out a pile of shirts and began throwing them, one by one, before us, shirts of sheer linen and thick silk and fine flannel, which lost their folds as they fell and covered the table in many-colored disarray. While we admired he brought more and the soft rich heap mounted higher—shirts with stripes and scrolls and plaids in coral and apple-green and lavender and faint orange, with monograms of Indian blue. Suddenly, with a strained sound, Daisy bent her head into the shirts and began to cry stormily.

"They're such beautiful shirts," she sobbed, her voice muffled in the thick folds. "It makes me sad because I've never seen such—such beautiful shirts before."

◆

After the house, we were to see the grounds and the swimming pool, and the hydroplane and the midsummer flowers—but outside Gatsby's window it began to rain again, so we stood in a row looking at the corrugated surface of the Sound.

"If it wasn't for the mist we could see your home across the bay," said Gatsby. "You always have a green light that burns all night at the end of your dock."

Daisy put her arm through his abruptly, but he seemed absorbed in what he had just said. Possibly it had occurred to him that the colossal significance of that light had now vanished forever. Compared to the great distance that had separated him from Daisy it had seemed very near to her, almost touching her. It had seemed as close as a star to the moon. Now it was again a green light on a dock. His count of enchanted objects had diminished by one.

I began to walk about the room, examining various indefinite objects in the half darkness. A large photograph of an elderly man in yachting costume attracted me, hung on the wall over his desk.

"Who's this?"

"That? That's Mr. Dan Cody, old sport."

The name sounded faintly familiar.

"He's dead now. He used to be my best friend years ago."

There was a small picture of Gatsby, also in yachting costume, on the bureau—Gatsby with his head thrown back defiantly—taken apparently when he was about eighteen.

"I adore it," exclaimed Daisy. "The pompadour! You never told me you had a pompadour—or a yacht."

"Look at this," said Gatsby quickly. "Here's a lot of clippings—about you."

They stood side by side examining it. I was going to ask to see the rubies when the phone rang, and Gatsby took up the receiver.

"Yes. . . . Well, I can't talk now. . . . I can't talk now, old sport. . . . I said a *small* town. . . . He must know what a small town is. . . . Well, he's no use to us if Detroit is his idea of a small town. . . ."

He rang off.

"Come here *quick!*" cried Daisy at the window.

The rain was still falling, but the darkness had parted in the west, and there was a pink and golden billow of foamy clouds above the sea.

"Look at that," she whispered, and then after a moment: "I'd like to just get one of those pink clouds and put you in it and push you around."

I tried to go then, but they wouldn't hear of it; perhaps my presence made them feel more satisfactorily alone.

"I know what we'll do," said Gatsby. "We'll have Klipspringer play the piano."

He went out of the room calling "Ewing!" and returned in a few minutes accompanied by an embarrassed, slightly worn young man, with shell-rimmed glasses and scanty blond hair. He was now decently clothed in a "sport-shirt," open at the neck, sneakers, and duck trousers of a nebulous hue.

"Did we interrupt your exercises?" inquired Daisy politely.

"I was asleep," cried Mr. Klipspringer, in a spasm of embarrassment. "That is, I'd *been* asleep. Then I got up . . ."

"Klipspringer plays the piano," said Gatsby, cutting him off. "Don't you, Ewing, old sport?"

"I don't play well. I don't—I hardly play at all. I'm all out of prac——"

"We'll go downstairs," interrupted Gatsby. He flipped a switch. The gray windows disappeared as the house glowed full of light.

In the music-room Gatsby turned on a solitary lamp beside the piano. He lit Daisy's cigarette from a trembling match, and sat down with her on a couch far across the room, where there was no light save what the gleaming floor bounced in from the hall.

When Klipspringer had played "The Love Nest" he turned around on the bench and searched unhappily for Gatsby in the gloom.

"I'm all out of practice, you see. I told you I couldn't play. I'm all out of prac——"

"Don't talk so much, old sport," commanded Gatsby. "Play!"

> "In the morning,
>   In the evening,
>   Ain't we got fun———"

Outside the wind was loud and there was a faint flow of thunder along the Sound. All the lights were going on in West Egg now; the electric trains, men-carrying, were plunging home through the rain from New York. It was the hour of a profound human change, and excitement was generating on the air.

> "One thing's sure and nothing's surer
>   The rich get richer and the poor get——children.
>   In the meantime,
>   In between time———"

As I went over to say good-by I saw that the expression of bewilderment had come back into Gatsby's face, as though a faint doubt had occurred to him as to the quality of his present happiness. Almost five years! There must have been moments even that afternoon when Daisy tumbled short of his dreams—not through her own fault, but because of the colossal vitality of his illusion. It had gone beyond her, beyond everything. He had thrown himself into it with a creative passion, adding to it all the time, decking it out with every bright feather that drifted his way. No amount of fire or freshness can challenge what a man will store up in his ghostly heart.

As I watched him he adjusted himself a little, visibly. His hand took hold of hers, and as she said something low in his ear he turned toward her with a rush of emotion. I think that voice held him most, with its fluctuating, feverish warmth, because it couldn't be over-dreamed— that voice was a deathless song.

They had forgotten me, but Daisy glanced up and held out her hand; Gatsby didn't know me now at all. I looked once more at them and they looked back at me, remotely, possessed by intense life. Then I went out of the room and down the marble steps into the rain, leaving them there together.

CHAPTER VI

bout this time an ambitious young reporter from New York arrived one morning at Gatsby's door and asked him if he had anything to say.

"Anything to say about what?" inquired Gatsby politely.

"Why—any statement to give out."

It transpired after a confused five minutes that the man had heard
Gatsby's name around his office in a connection which he either
wouldn't reveal or didn't fully understand. This was his day off and
with laudable initiative he had hurried out "to see."

It was a random shot, and yet the reporter's instinct was right.
Gatsby's notoriety, spread about by the hundreds who had accepted
his hospitality and so become authorities upon his past, had increased
all summer until he fell just short of being news. Contemporary leg-
ends such as the "underground pipe-line to Canada" attached themselves to him, and there was one persistent story that he didn't live
in a house at all, but in a boat that looked like a house and was moved
secretly up and down the Long Island shore. Just why these inven-
tions were a source of satisfaction to James Gatz of North Dakota
isn't easy to say.

James Gatz—that was really, or at least legally, his name. He had
changed it at the age of seventeen and at the specific moment that

witnessed the beginning of his career—when he saw Dan Cody's yacht drop anchor over the most insidious flat on Lake Superior. It was James Gatz who had been loafing along the beach that afternoon in a torn green jersey and a pair of canvas pants, but it was already Jay Gatsby who borrowed a rowboat, pulled out to the *Tuolomee*, and informed Cody that a wind might catch him and break him up in half an hour.

I suppose he'd had the name ready for a long time, even then. His parents were shiftless and unsuccessful farm people—his imagination had never really accepted them as his parents at all. The truth was that Jay Gatsby of West Egg, Long Island, sprang from his Platonic conception of himself. He was a son of God—a phrase which, if it means anything, means just that—and he must be about His Father's business, the service of a vast, vulgar, and meretricious beauty. So he invented just the sort of Jay Gatsby that a seventeen-year-old boy would be likely to invent, and to this conception he was faithful to the end.

For over a year he had been beating his way along the south shore of Lake Superior as a clam-digger and a salmon-fisher or in any other capacity that brought him food and bed. His brown, hardening body lived naturally through the half fierce, half lazy work of the bracing days. He knew women early, and since they spoiled him he became contemptuous of them, of young virgins because they were ignorant, of the others because they were hysterical about things which in his overwhelming self-absorption he took for granted.

But his heart was in a constant, turbulent riot. The most grotesque and fantastic conceits haunted him in his bed at night. A universe of ineffable gaudiness spun itself out in his brain while the clock ticked on the wash-stand and the moon soaked with wet light his tangled clothes upon the floor. Each night he added to the pattern of his fancies until drowsiness closed down upon some vivid scene with an oblivious embrace. For a while these reveries provided an outlet for his imagination; they were a satisfactory hint of the unreality of reality, a promise that the rock of the world was founded securely on a fairy's wing.

An instinct toward his future glory had led him, some months before, to the small Lutheran college of St. Olaf's in southern Minnesota. He stayed there two weeks, dismayed at its ferocious indifference to the drums of his destiny, to destiny itself, and despising the janitor's work with which he was to pay his way through. Then he drifted back to Lake Superior, and he was still searching for something to do on the day that Dan Cody's yacht dropped anchor in the shallows alongshore.

Cody was fifty years old then, a product of the Nevada silver fields, of the Yukon, of every rush for metal since seventy-five. The transactions in Montana copper that made him many times a millionaire found him physically robust but on the verge of soft-mindedness, and, suspecting this, an infinite number of women tried to separate him from his money. The none too savory ramifications by which Ella Kaye, the newspaper woman, played Madame de Maintenon to his weakness and sent him to sea in a yacht, were common property of the turgid journalism of 1902. He had been coasting along all too hospitable shores for five years when he turned up as James Gatz's destiny in Little Girl Bay.

To young Gatz, resting on his oars and looking up at the railed deck, that yacht represented all the beauty and glamour in the world. I suppose he smiled at Cody—he had probably discovered that people liked him when he smiled. At any rate Cody asked him a few questions (one of them elicited the brand new name) and found that he was quick and extravagantly ambitious. A few days later he took him to Duluth and bought him a blue coat, six pair of white duck trousers, and a yachting cap. And when the *Tuolomee* left for the West Indies and the Barbary Coast, Gatsby left too.

He was employed in a vague personal capacity—while he remained with Cody he was in turn steward, mate, skipper, secretary, and even jailor, for Dan Cody sober knew what lavish doings Dan Cody drunk might soon be about, and he provided for such contingencies by reposing more and more trust in Gatsby. The arrangement lasted five years, during which the boat went three times around the Continent. It might have lasted indefinitely except for the fact that Ella Kaye came on board one night in Boston and a week later Dan Cody inhospitably died.

I remember the portrait of him up in Gatsby's bedroom, a gray, florid man with a hard, empty face—the pioneer debauchee, who during one phase of American life brought back to the Eastern seaboard the savage violence of the frontier brothel and saloon. It was indirectly due to Cody that Gatsby drank so little. Sometimes in the course of gay parties women used to rub champagne into his hair; for himself he formed the habit of letting liquor alone.

And it was from Cody that he inherited money—a legacy of twenty-five thousand dollars. He didn't get it. He never understood the legal device that was used against him, but what remained of the millions went intact to Ella Kaye. He was left with his singularly appropriate education; the vague contour of Jay Gatsby had filled out to the substantiality of a man.

◆

He told me all this very much later, but I've put it down here with the idea of exploding those first wild rumors about his antecedents, which weren't even faintly true. Moreover he told it to me at a time of confusion, when I had reached the point of believing everything and nothing about him. So I take advantage of this short halt, while Gatsby, so to speak, caught his breath, to clear this set of misconceptions away.

It was a halt, too, in my association with his affairs. For several weeks I didn't see him or hear his voice on the phone—mostly I was in New York, trotting around with Jordan and trying to ingratiate myself with her senile aunt—but finally I went over to his house one Sunday afternoon. I hadn't been there two minutes when somebody brought Tom Buchanan in for a drink. I was startled, naturally, but the really surprising thing was that it hadn't happened before.

They were a party of three on horseback—Tom and a man named Sloane and a pretty woman in a brown riding habit, who had been there previously.

"I'm delighted to see you," said Gatsby, standing on his porch. "I'm delighted that you dropped in."

As though they cared!

"Sit right down. Have a cigarette or a cigar." He walked around the room quickly, ringing bells. "I'll have something to drink for you in just a minute."

He was profoundly affected by the fact that Tom was there. But he would be uneasy anyhow until he had given them something, realizing in a vague way that that was all they came for. Mr. Sloane wanted nothing. A lemonade? No, thanks. A little champagne? Nothing at all, thanks. . . . I'm sorry——

"Did you have a nice ride?"

"Very good roads around here."

"I suppose the automobiles——"

"Yeah."

Moved by an irresistible impulse, Gatsby turned to Tom, who had accepted the introduction as a stranger.

"I believe we've met somewhere before, Mr. Buchanan."

"Oh, yes," said Tom, gruffly polite, but obviously not remembering. "So we did. I remember very well."

"About two weeks ago."

"That's right. You were with Nick here."

"I know your wife," continued Gatsby, almost aggressively.

"That so?"

Tom turned to me.

"You live near here, Nick?"

"Next door."

"That so?"

Mr. Sloane didn't enter into the conversation, but lounged back haughtily in his chair; the woman said nothing either—until unexpectedly, after two highballs, she became cordial.

"We'll all come over to your next party, Mr. Gatsby," she suggested. "What do you say?"

"Certainly. I'd be delighted to have you."

"Be ver' nice," said Mr. Sloane, without gratitude. "Well—think ought to be starting home."

"Please don't hurry," Gatsby urged them. He had control of himself now, and he wanted to see more of Tom. "Why don't you—why don't you stay for supper? I wouldn't be surprised if some other people dropped in from New York."

"You come to supper with *me*," said the lady enthusiastically. "Both of you."

This included me. Mr. Sloane got to his feet.

"Come along," he said—but to her only.

"I mean it," she insisted. "I'd love to have you. Lots of room."

Gatsby looked at me questioningly. He wanted to go, and he didn't see that Mr. Sloane had determined he shouldn't.

"I'm afraid I won't be able to," I said.

"Well, you come," she urged, concentrating on Gatsby.

Mr. Sloane murmured something close to her ear.

"We won't be late if we start now," she insisted aloud.

"I haven't got a horse," said Gatsby. "I used to ride in the army, but I've never bought a horse. I'll have to follow you in my car. Excuse me for just a minute."

The rest of us walked out on the porch, where Sloane and the lady began an impassioned conversation aside.

"My God, I believe the man's coming," said Tom. "Doesn't he know she doesn't want him?"

"She says she does want him."

"She has a big dinner party and he won't know a soul there." He frowned. "I wonder where in the devil he met Daisy. By God, I may be old-fashioned in my ideas, but women run around too much these days to suit me. They meet all kinds of crazy fish."

Suddenly Mr. Sloane and the lady walked down the steps and mounted their horses.

"Come on," said Mr. Sloane to Tom. "We're late. We've got to go." And then to me: "Tell him we couldn't wait, will you?"

Tom and I shook hands, the rest of us exchanged a cool nod, and they trotted quickly down the drive, disappearing under the August foliage just as Gatsby, with hat and light overcoat in hand, came out the front door.

Tom was evidently perturbed at Daisy's running around alone, for on the following Saturday night he came with her to Gatsby's party. Perhaps his presence gave the evening its peculiar quality of oppressiveness—it stands out in my memory from Gatsby's other parties that summer. There were the same people, or at least the same sort of people, the same profusion of champagne, the same many-colored, many-keyed commotion, but I felt an unpleasantness in the air, a pervading harshness that hadn't been there before. Or perhaps I had merely grown used to it, grown to accept West Egg as a world complete in itself, with its own standards and its own great figures, second to nothing because it had no consciousness of being so, and now I was looking at it again, through Daisy's eyes. It is invariably saddening to look through new eyes at things upon which you have expended your own powers of adjustment.

They arrived at twilight, and, as we strolled out among the sparkling hundreds, Daisy's voice was playing murmurous tricks in her throat.

"These things excite me *so*," she whispered. "If you want to kiss me any time during the evening, Nick, just let me know and I'll be glad to arrange it for you. Just mention my name. Or present a green card. I'm giving out green——"

"Look around," suggested Gatsby.

"I'm looking around. I'm having a marvellous——"

"You must see the faces of many people you've heard about."

Tom's arrogant eyes roamed the crowd.

"We don't go around very much," he said. "In fact, I was just think-ing I don't know a soul here."

"Perhaps you know that lady." Gatsby indicated a gorgeous, scarcely human orchid of a woman who sat in state under a white-plum tree. Tom and Daisy stared, with that peculiarly unreal feeling that accompanies the recognition of a hitherto ghostly celeb-rity of the movies.

"She's lovely," said Daisy.

"The man bending over her is her director."

He took them ceremoniously from group to group:

"Mrs. Buchanan . . . and Mr. Buchanan——" After an instant's hesi-tation he added: "the polo player."

"Oh no," objected Tom quickly, "not me."

But evidently the sound of it pleased Gatsby for Tom remained "the polo player" for the rest of the evening.

"I've never met so many celebrities," Daisy exclaimed. "I liked that man—what was his name?—with the sort of blue nose."

Gatsby identified him, adding that he was a small producer.

"Well, I liked him anyhow."

"I'd a little rather not be the polo player," said Tom pleasantly. "I'd rather look at all these famous people in—in oblivion."

Daisy and Gatsby danced. I remember being surprised by his grace-ful, conservative fox-trot—I had never seen him dance before. Then they sauntered over to my house and sat on the steps for half an hour, while at her request I remained watchfully in the garden. "In case there's a fire or a flood," she explained, "or any act of God."

Tom appeared from his oblivion as we were sitting down to supper together. "Do you mind if I eat with some people over here?" he said. "A fellow's getting off some funny stuff."

"Go ahead," answered Daisy genially, "and if you want to take down any addresses here's my little gold pencil." . . . She looked around after a moment and told me the girl was "common but pretty," and I knew that except for the half hour she'd been alone with Gatsby she wasn't having a good time.

We were at a particularly tipsy table. That was my fault—Gatsby had been called to the phone, and I'd enjoyed these same people only two weeks before. But what had amused me then turned septic on the air now.

"How do you feel, Miss Baedeker?"

The girl addressed was trying, unsuccessfully, to slump against my shoulder. At this inquiry she sat up and opened her eyes.

"Wha'?"

A massive and lethargic woman, who had been urging Daisy to play golf with her at the local club tomorrow, spoke in Miss Baedeker's defense:

"Oh, she's all right now. When she's had five or six cocktails she always starts screaming like that. I tell her she ought to leave it alone."

"I do leave it alone," affirmed the accused hollowly.

"We heard you yelling, so I said to Doc Civet here: 'There's somebody that needs your help, Doc.'"

"She's much obliged, I'm sure," said another friend, without gratitude, "but you got her dress all wet when you stuck her head in the pool."

"Anything I hate is to get my head stuck in a pool," mumbled Miss Baedeker. "They almost drowned me once over in New Jersey."

"Then you ought to leave it alone," countered Doctor Civet.

"Speak for yourself!" cried Miss Baedeker violently. "Your hand shakes. I wouldn't let you operate on me!"

It was like that. Almost the last thing I remember was standing with Daisy and watching the moving-picture director and his Star. They were still under the white-plum tree and their faces were touching except for a pale, thin ray of moonlight between. It occurred to me that he had been very slowly bending toward her all evening to attain this proximity, and even while I watched I saw him stoop one ultimate degree and kiss at her cheek.

"I like her," said Daisy. "I think she's lovely."

But the rest offended her—and inarguably, because it wasn't a gesture but an emotion. She was appalled by West Egg, this unprecedented "place" that Broadway had begotten upon a Long Island fishing village—appalled by its raw vigor that chafed under the old euphemisms and by the too obtrusive fate that herded its inhabitants along a short-cut from nothing to nothing. She saw something awful in the very simplicity she failed to understand.

I sat on the front steps with them while they waited for their car. It was dark here in front; only the bright door sent ten square feet of light volleying out into the soft black morning. Sometimes a shadow moved against a dressing-room blind above, gave way to another shadow, an indefinite procession of shadows, who rouged and powdered in an invisible glass.

"Who is this Gatsby anyhow?" demanded Tom suddenly. "Some big bootlegger?"

"Where'd you hear that?" I inquired.

"I didn't hear it. I imagined it. A lot of these newly rich people are just big bootleggers, you know."

"Not Gatsby," I said shortly.

He was silent for a moment. The pebbles of the drive crunched under his feet.

"Well, he certainly must have strained himself to get this menagerie together."

A breeze stirred the gray haze of Daisy's fur collar.

"At least they are more interesting than the people we know," she said with an effort.

"You didn't look so interested."

"Well, I was."

Tom laughed and turned to me.

"Did you notice Daisy's face when that girl asked her to put her under a cold shower?"

Daisy began to sing with the music in a husky, rhythmic whisper, bringing out a meaning in each word that it had never had before and would never have again. When the melody rose her voice broke up sweetly, following it, in a way contralto voices have, and each change tipped out a little of her warm human magic upon the air.

"Lots of people come who haven't been invited," she said suddenly. "That girl hadn't been invited. They simply force their way in and he's too polite to object."

"I'd like to know who he is and what he does," insisted Tom. "And I think I'll make a point of finding out."

"I can tell you right now," she answered. "He owned some drug-stores, a lot of drug-stores. He built them up himself."

The dilatory limousine came rolling up the drive.

"Good night, Nick," said Daisy.

Her glance left me and sought the lighted top of the steps, where "Three o'Clock in the Morning," a neat, sad little waltz of that year, was drifting out the open door. After all, in the very casualness of Gatsby's party there were romantic possibilities totally absent from her world. What was it up there in the song that seemed to be calling her back inside? What would happen now in the dim, incalculable hours? Perhaps some unbelievable guest would arrive, a person infinitely rare and to be marvelled at, some authentically radiant young girl who with one fresh glance at Gatsby, one moment of magical encounter, would blot out those five years of unwavering devotion.

I stayed late that night. Gatsby asked me to wait until he was free, and I lingered in the garden until the inevitable swimming party had run up, chilled and exalted, from the black beach, until the lights were extinguished in the guest-rooms overhead. When he came down the steps at last the tanned skin was drawn unusually tight on his face, and his eyes were bright and tired.

"She didn't like it," he said immediately.

"Of course she did."

"She didn't like it," he insisted. "She didn't have a good time."

He was silent, and I guessed at his unutterable depression.

"I feel far away from her," he said. "It's hard to make her understand."

"You mean about the dance?"

"The dance?" He dismissed all the dances he had given with a snap of his fingers. "Old sport, the dance is unimportant."

He wanted nothing less of Daisy than that she should go to Tom and say: "I never loved you." After she had obliterated four years with that sentence they could decide upon the more practical measures to be taken. One of them was that, after she was free, they were to go back to Louisville and be married from her house—just as if it were five years ago.

"And she doesn't understand," he said. "She used to be able to understand. We'd sit for hours——"

He broke off and began to walk up and down a desolate path of fruit rinds and discarded favors and crushed flowers.

"I wouldn't ask too much of her," I ventured. "You can't repeat the past."

"Can't repeat the past?" he cried incredulously. "Why of course you can!"

He looked around him wildly, as if the past were lurking here in the shadow of his house, just out of reach of his hand.

"I'm going to fix everything just the way it was before," he said, nodding determinedly. "She'll see."

He talked a lot about the past, and I gathered that he wanted to recover something, some idea of himself perhaps, that had gone into loving Daisy. His life had been confused and disordered since then, but if he could once return to a certain starting place and go over it all slowly, he could find out what that thing was. . . .

. . . One autumn night, five years before, they had been walking down the street when the leaves were falling, and they came to a place where there were no trees and the sidewalk was white with moonlight. They stopped here and turned toward each other. Now it was a cool night with that mysterious excitement in it which comes at the two changes of the year. The quiet lights in the houses were humming out into the darkness and there was a stir and bustle among the stars. Out of the corner of his eye Gatsby saw that the blocks of the sidewalks really formed a ladder and mounted to a secret place above the trees—he could climb to it, if he climbed alone, and once there he could suck on the pap of life, gulp down the incomparable milk of wonder.

His heart beat faster and faster as Daisy's white face came up to his own. He knew that when he kissed this girl, and forever wed his unutterable visions to her perishable breath, his mind would never romp again like the mind of God. So he waited, listening for a moment longer to the tuning-fork that had been struck upon a star. Then he kissed her. At his lips' touch she blossomed for him like a flower and the incarnation was complete.

Through all he said, even through his appalling sentimentality, I was reminded of something—an elusive rhythm, a fragment of lost words, that I had heard somewhere a long time ago. For a moment a phrase tried to take shape in my mouth and my lips parted like a dumb man's, as though there was more struggling upon them than a wisp of startled air. But they made no sound, and what I had almost remembered was uncommunicable forever.

CHAPTER VII

It was when curiosity about Gatsby was at its highest that the lights in his house failed to go on one Saturday night—and, as obscurely as it had begun, his career as Trimalchio was over. Only gradually did I become aware that the automobiles which turned expectantly into his drive stayed for just a minute and then drove sulkily away. Wondering if he were sick I went over to find out—an unfamiliar butler with a villainous face squinted at me suspiciously from the door.

"Is Mr. Gatsby sick?"

"Nope." After a pause he added "sir" in a dilatory, grudging way.

"I hadn't seen him around, and I was rather worried. Tell him Mr. Carraway came over."

"Who?" he demanded rudely.

"Carraway."

"Carraway. All right, I'll tell him."

Abruptly he slammed the door.

My Finn informed me that Gatsby had dismissed every servant in his house a week ago and replaced them with half a dozen others, who never went into West Egg Village to be bribed by the tradesmen, but ordered moderate supplies over the telephone.

The grocery boy reported that the kitchen looked like a pigsty, and the general opinion in the village was that the new people weren't servants at all.

Next day Gatsby called me on the phone.

"Going away?" I inquired.

"No, old sport."

"I hear you fired all your servants."

"I wanted somebody who wouldn't gossip. Daisy comes over quite often—in the afternoons."

So the whole caravansary had fallen in like a card house at the disapproval in her eyes.

"They're some people Wolfshiem wanted to do something for. They're all brothers and sisters. They used to run a small hotel."

"I see."

He was calling up at Daisy's request—would I come to lunch at her house tomorrow? Miss Baker would be there. Half an hour later Daisy herself telephoned and seemed relieved to find that I was coming. Something was up. And yet I couldn't believe that they would choose this occasion for a scene—especially for the rather harrowing scene that Gatsby had outlined in the garden.

The next day was broiling, almost the last, certainly the warmest, of the summer. As my train emerged from the tunnel into sunlight, only the hot whistles of the National Biscuit Company broke the simmering hush at noon. The straw seats of the car hovered on the edge of combustion; the woman next to me perspired delicately for a while into her white shirtwaist, and then, as her newspaper dampened under her fingers, lapsed despairingly into deep heat with a desolate cry. Her pocket-book slapped to the floor.

"Oh, my!" she gasped.

I picked it up with a weary bend and handed it back to her, holding it at arm's length and by the extreme tip of the corners to indicate that I had no designs upon it—but everyone nearby, including the woman, suspected me just the same.

"Hot!" said the conductor to familiar faces. "Some weather! . . . Hot! . . . Hot! . . . Hot! . . . Is it hot enough for you? Is it hot? Is it . . . ?"

My commutation ticket came back to me with a dark stain from his hand. That anyone should care in this heat whose flushed lips he kissed, whose head made damp the pajama pocket over his heart!

. . . Through the hall of the Buchanans' house blew a faint wind, carrying the sound of the telephone bell out to Gatsby and me as we waited at the door.

"The master's body!" roared the butler into the mouthpiece. "I'm sorry, madame, but we can't furnish it—it's far too hot to touch this noon!"

What he really said was: "Yes . . . Yes . . . I'll see."

He set down the receiver and came toward us, glistening slightly, to take our stiff straw hats.

"Madame expects you in the salon!" he cried, needlessly indicating the direction. In this heat every extra gesture was an affront to the common store of life.

The room, shadowed well with awnings, was dark and cool. Daisy and Jordan lay upon an enormous couch, like silver idols weighing down their own white dresses against the singing breeze of the fans.

"We can't move," they said together.

Jordan's fingers, powdered white over their tan, rested for a moment in mine.

"And Mr. Thomas Buchanan, the athlete?" I inquired.

Simultaneously I heard his voice, gruff, muffled, husky, at the hall telephone.

Gatsby stood in the center of the crimson carpet and gazed around with fascinated eyes. Daisy watched him and laughed, her sweet, exciting laugh; a tiny gust of powder rose from her bosom into the air.

"The rumor is," whispered Jordan, "that that's Tom's girl on the telephone."

We were silent. The voice in the hall rose high with annoyance: "Very well, then, I won't sell you the car at all. . . . I'm under no obligations to you at all . . . and as for your bothering me about it at lunch-time, I won't stand that at all!"

"Holding down the receiver," said Daisy cynically.

"No, he's not," I assured her. "It's a bona-fide deal. I happen to know about it."

Tom flung open the door, blocked out its space for a moment with his thick body, and hurried into the room.

"Mr. Gatsby!" He put out his broad, flat hand with well-concealed dislike. "I'm glad to see you, sir . . . Nick. . . ."

"Make us a cold drink," cried Daisy.

As he left the room again she got up and went over to Gatsby and pulled his face down, kissing him on the mouth.

"You know I love you," she murmured.

"You forget there's a lady present," said Jordan.

Daisy looked around doubtfully.

"You kiss Nick too."

"What a low, vulgar girl!"

"I don't care!" cried Daisy, and began to clog on the brick fireplace. Then she remembered the heat and sat down guiltily on the couch just as a freshly laundered nurse leading a little girl came into the room.

"Bles-sed pre-cious," she crooned, holding out her arms. "Come to your own mother that loves you."

The child, relinquished by the nurse, rushed across the room and rooted shyly into her mother's dress.

"The bles-sed pre-cious! Did mother get powder on your old yel-lowy hair? Stand up now, and say—How-de-do."

Gatsby and I in turn leaned down and took the small reluctant hand. Afterward he kept looking at the child with surprise. I don't think he had ever really believed in its existence before.

"I got dressed before luncheon," said the child, turning eagerly to Daisy.

"That's because your mother wanted to show you off." Her face bent into the single wrinkle of the small white neck. "You dream, you. You absolute little dream."

"Yes," admitted the child calmly. "Aunt Jordan's got on a white dress too."

"How do you like mother's friends?" Daisy turned her around so that she faced Gatsby. "Do you think they're pretty?"

"Where's Daddy?"

"She doesn't look like her father," explained Daisy. "She looks like me. She's got my hair and shape of the face."

Daisy sat back upon the couch. The nurse took a step forward and held out her hand.

"Come, Pammy."

"Good-by, sweetheart!"

With a reluctant backward glance the well-disciplined child held to her nurse's hand and was pulled out the door, just as Tom came back, preceding four gin rickeys that clicked full of ice.

Gatsby took up his drink.

"They certainly look cool," he said, with visible tension.

We drank in long, greedy swallows.

"I read somewhere that the sun's getting hotter every year," said Tom genially. "It seems that pretty soon the earth's going to fall into the sun—or wait a minute—it's just the opposite—the sun's getting colder every year.

"Come outside," he suggested to Gatsby. "I'd like you to have a look at the place."

I went with them out to the veranda. On the green Sound, stagnant in the heat, one small sail crawled slowly toward the fresher sea. Gatsby's eyes followed it momentarily; he raised his hand and pointed across the bay.

"I'm right across from you."

"So you are."

Our eyes lifted over the rose-beds and the hot lawn and the weedy refuse of the dog-days alongshore. Slowly the white wings of the boat moved against the blue cool limit of the sky. Ahead lay the scalloped ocean and the abounding blessed isles.

"There's sport for you," said Tom, nodding. "I'd like to be out there with him for about an hour."

We had luncheon in the dining-room, darkened too against the heat, and drank down nervous gayety with the cold ale.

"What'll we do with ourselves this afternoon?" cried Daisy. "And the day after that, and the next thirty years?"

"Don't be morbid," Jordan said. "Life starts all over again when it gets crisp in the fall."

"But it's so hot," insisted Daisy, on the verge of tears, "and everything's so confused. Let's all go to town!"

Her voice struggled on through the heat, beating against it, molding its senselessness into forms.

"I've heard of making a garage out of a stable," Tom was saying to Gatsby, "but I'm the first man who ever made a stable out of a garage."

"Who wants to go to town?" demanded Daisy insistently. Gatsby's eyes floated toward her. "Ah," she cried, "you look so cool."

Their eyes met, and they stared together at each other, alone in space. With an effort she glanced down at the table.

"You always look so cool," she repeated.

She had told him that she loved him, and Tom Buchanan saw. He was astounded. His mouth opened a little, and he looked at Gatsby, and then back at Daisy as if he had just recognized her as someone he knew a long time ago.

"You resemble the advertisement of the man," she went on innocently. "You know the advertisement of the man———"

"All right," broke in Tom quickly, "I'm perfectly willing to go to town. Come on—we're all going to town."

He got up, his eyes still flashing between Gatsby and his wife. No one moved.

"Come on!" His temper cracked a little. "What's the matter, anyhow? If we're going to town, let's start."

His hand, trembling with his effort at self-control, bore to his lips the last of his glass of ale. Daisy's voice got us to our feet and out on to the blazing gravel drive.

"Are we just going to go?" she objected. "Like this? Aren't we going to let anyone smoke a cigarette first?"

"Everybody smoked all through lunch."

"Oh, let's have fun," she begged him. "It's too hot to fuss."

He didn't answer.

"Have it your own way," she said. "Come on, Jordan."

They went upstairs to get ready while we three men stood there shuffling the hot pebbles with our feet. A silver curve of the moon hovered already in the western sky. Gatsby started to speak, changed his mind, but not before Tom wheeled and faced him expectantly.

"Pardon me?"

"Have you got your stables here?" asked Gatsby with an effort.

"About a quarter of a mile down the road."

"Oh."

A pause.

"I don't see the idea of going to town," broke out Tom savagely. "Women get these notions in their heads——"

"Shall we take anything to drink?" called Daisy from an upper window.

"I'll get some whiskey," answered Tom. He went inside.

Gatsby turned to me rigidly:

"I can't say anything in his house, old sport."

"She's got an indiscreet voice," I remarked. "It's full of——" I hesitated.

"Her voice is full of money," he said suddenly.

That was it. I'd never understood before. It was full of money—that was the inexhaustible charm that rose and fell in it, the jingle of it, the cymbals' song of it. . . . High in a white palace the king's daughter, the golden girl. . . .

Tom came out of the house wrapping a quart bottle in a towel, followed by Daisy and Jordan wearing small tight hats of metallic cloth and carrying light capes over their arms.

"Shall we all go in my car?" suggested Gatsby. He felt the hot, green leather of the seat. "I ought to have left it in the shade."

"Is it standard shift?" demanded Tom.

"Yes."

"Well, you take my coupé and let me drive your car to town."

The suggestion was distasteful to Gatsby.

"I don't think there's much gas," he objected.

"Plenty of gas," said Tom boisterously. He looked at the gauge. "And if it runs out I can stop at a drug-store. You can buy anything at a drug-store nowadays."

A pause followed this apparently pointless remark. Daisy looked at Tom frowning, and an indefinable expression, at once definitely unfamiliar and vaguely recognizable, as if I had only heard it described in words, passed over Gatsby's face.

"Come on, Daisy," said Tom, pressing her with his hand toward Gatsby's car. "I'll take you in this circus wagon."

He opened the door, but she moved out from the circle of his arm.

"You take Nick and Jordan. We'll follow you in the coupé."

She walked close to Gatsby, touching his coat with her hand. Jordan and Tom and I got into the front seat of Gatsby's car, Tom pushed the unfamiliar gears tentatively, and we shot off into the oppressive heat, leaving them out of sight behind.

"Did you see that?" demanded Tom.

"See what?"

He looked at me keenly, realizing that Jordan and I must have known all along.

"You think I'm pretty dumb, don't you?" he suggested. "Perhaps I am, but I have a—almost a second sight, sometimes, that tells me what to do. Maybe you don't believe that, but science———"

He paused. The immediate contingency overtook him, pulled him back from the edge of the theoretical abyss.

"I've made a small investigation of this fellow," he continued. "I could have gone deeper if I'd known———"

"Do you mean you've been to a medium?" inquired Jordan humorously.

"What?" Confused, he stared at us as we laughed. "A medium?"

"About Gatsby."

"About Gatsby! No, I haven't. I said I'd been making a small investigation of his past."

"And you found he was an Oxford man," said Jordan helpfully.

"An Oxford man!" He was incredulous. "Like hell he is! He wears a pink suit."

"Nevertheless he's an Oxford man."

"Oxford, New Mexico," snorted Tom contemptuously, "or something like that."

"Listen, Tom. If you're such a snob, why did you invite him to lunch?" demanded Jordan crossly.

"Daisy invited him; she knew him before we were married—God knows where!"

We were all irritable now with the fading ale, and aware of it we drove for a while in silence. Then as Doctor T. J. Eckleburg's faded eyes came into sight down the road, I remembered Gatsby's caution about gasoline.

"We've got enough to get us to town," said Tom.

"But there's a garage right here," objected Jordan. "I don't want to get stalled in this baking heat."

Tom threw on both brakes impatiently, and we slid to an abrupt dusty stop under Wilson's sign. After a moment the proprietor emerged from the interior of his establishment and gazed hollow-eyed at the car.

"Let's have some gas!" cried Tom roughly. "What do you think we stopped for—to admire the view?"

"I'm sick," said Wilson without moving. "Been sick all day."

"What's the matter?"

"I'm all run down."

"Well, shall I help myself?" Tom demanded. "You sounded well enough on the phone."

With an effort Wilson left the shade and support of the doorway and, breathing hard, unscrewed the cap of the tank. In the sunlight his face was green.

"I didn't mean to interrupt your lunch," he said. "But I need money pretty bad, and I was wondering what you were going to do with your old car."

"How do you like this one?" inquired Tom. "I bought it last week."

"It's a nice yellow one," said Wilson, as he strained at the handle.

"Like to buy it?"

"Big chance," Wilson smiled faintly. "No, but I could make some money on the other."

"What do you want money for, all of a sudden?"

"I've been here too long. I want to get away. My wife and I want to go West."

"Your wife does!" exclaimed Tom, startled.

"She's been talking about it for ten years." He rested for a moment against the pump, shading his eyes. "And now she's going whether she wants to or not. I'm going to get her away."

The coupé flashed by us with a flurry of dust and the flash of a waving hand.

"What do I owe you?" demanded Tom harshly.

"I just got wised up to something funny the last two days," remarked Wilson. "That's why I want to get away. That's why I been bothering you about the car."

"What do I owe you?"

"Dollar twenty."

The relentless beating heat was beginning to confuse me and I had a bad moment there before I realized that so far his suspicions hadn't alighted on Tom. He had discovered that Myrtle had some sort of life apart from him in another world, and the shock had made him physically sick. I stared at him and then at Tom, who had made a parallel discovery less than an hour before—and it occurred to me that there was no difference between men, in intelligence or race, so profound as the difference between the sick and the well. Wilson was so sick that he looked guilty, unforgivably guilty—as if he had just got some poor girl with child.

"I'll let you have that car," said Tom. "I'll send it over tomorrow afternoon."

That locality was always vaguely disquieting, even in the broad glare of afternoon, and now I turned my head as though I had been warned of something behind. Over the ashheaps the giant eyes of Doctor T. J. Eckleburg kept their vigil, but I perceived, after a moment, that other eyes were regarding us with peculiar intensity from less than twenty feet away.

In one of the windows over the garage the curtains had been moved aside a little, and Myrtle Wilson was peering down at the car. So engrossed was she that she had no consciousness of being observed, and one emotion after another crept into her face like objects into a slowly developing picture. Her expression was curiously familiar—it was an expression I had often seen on women's faces, but on Myrtle Wilson's face it seemed purposeless and inexplicable until I realized that her eyes, wide with jealous terror, were fixed not on Tom, but on Jordan Baker, whom she took to be his wife.

◆

There is no confusion like the confusion of a simple mind, and as we drove away Tom was feeling the hot whips of panic. His wife and his mistress, until an hour ago secure and inviolate, were slipping precipitately from his control. Instinct made him step on the accelerator with the double purpose of overtaking Daisy and leaving Wilson behind, and we sped along toward Astoria at fifty miles an hour, until, among the spidery girders of the elevated, we came in sight of the easygoing blue coupé.

"Those big movies around Fiftieth Street are cool," suggested Jordan. "I love New York on summer afternoons when everyone's away. There's something very sensuous about it—overripe, as if all sorts of funny fruits were going to fall into your hands."

The word "sensuous" had the effect of further disquieting Tom, but before he could invent a protest the coupé came to a stop, and Daisy signalled us to draw up alongside.

"Where are we going?" she cried.

"How about the movies?"

"It's so hot," she complained. "You go. We'll ride around and meet you after." With an effort her wit rose faintly. "We'll meet you on some corner. I'll be the man smoking two cigarettes."

"We can't argue about it here," Tom said impatiently, as a truck gave out a cursing whistle behind us. "You follow me to the south side of Central Park, in front of the Plaza."

Several times he turned his head and looked back for their car, and if the traffic delayed them he slowed up until they came into sight. I think he was afraid they would dart down a side street and out of his life forever.

But they didn't. And we all took the less explicable step of engaging the parlor of a suite in the Plaza Hotel.

The prolonged and tumultuous argument that ended by herding us into that room eludes me, though I have a sharp physical memory that, in the course of it, my underwear kept climbing like a damp snake around my legs and intermittent beads of sweat raced cool across my back. The notion originated with Daisy's suggestion that we hire five bathrooms and take cold baths, and then assumed more tangible form as "a place to have a mint julep." Each of us said over and over that it was a "crazy idea"—we all talked at once to a baffled clerk and thought, or pretended to think, that we were being very funny . . .

The room was large and stifling, and, though it was already four o'clock, opening the windows admitted only a gust of hot shrubbery from the Park. Daisy went to the mirror and stood with her back to us, fixing her hair.

"It's a swell suite," whispered Jordan respectfully, and everyone laughed.

"Open another window," commanded Daisy, without turning around.

"There aren't any more."

"Well, we'd better telephone for an axe———"

"The thing to do is to forget about the heat," said Tom impatiently. "You make it ten times worse by crabbing about it."

He unrolled the bottle of whiskey from the towel and put it on the table.

"Why not let her alone, old sport?" remarked Gatsby. "You're the one that wanted to come to town."

There was a moment of silence. The telephone book slipped from its nail and splashed to the floor, whereupon Jordan whispered, "Excuse me"—but this time no one laughed.

"I'll pick it up," I offered.

"I've got it." Gatsby examined the parted string, muttered "Hum!" in an interested way, and tossed the book on a chair.

"That's a great expression of yours, isn't it?" said Tom sharply.

"What is?"

"All this 'old sport' business. Where'd you pick that up?"

"Now see here, Tom," said Daisy, turning around from the mirror, "if you're going to make personal remarks I won't stay here a minute. Call up and order some ice for the mint julep."

As Tom took up the receiver the compressed heat exploded into sound and we were listening to the portentous chords of Mendelssohn's Wedding March from the ballroom below.

"Imagine marrying anybody in this heat!" cried Jordan dismally.

"Still—I was married in the middle of June," Daisy remembered. "Louisville in June! Somebody fainted. Who was it fainted, Tom?"

"Biloxi," he answered shortly.

"A man named Biloxi. 'Blocks' Biloxi, and he made boxes—that's a fact—and he was from Biloxi, Tennessee."

"They carried him into my house," appended Jordan, "because we lived just two doors from the church. And he stayed three weeks, until

Daddy told him he had to get out. The day after he left Daddy died." After a moment she added, as if she might have sounded irreverent, "There wasn't any connection."

"I used to know a Bill Biloxi from Memphis," I remarked.

"That was his cousin. I knew his whole family history before he left. He gave me an aluminum putter that I use today."

The music had died down as the ceremony began and now a long cheer floated in at the window, followed by intermittent cries of "Yea—ea—ea!" and finally by a burst of jazz as the dancing began.

"We're getting old," said Daisy. "If we were young we'd rise and dance."

"Remember Biloxi," Jordan warned her. "Where'd you know him, Tom?"

"Biloxi?" He concentrated with an effort. "I didn't know him. He was a friend of Daisy's."

"He was not," she denied. "I'd never seen him before. He came down in the private car."

"Well, he said he knew you. He said he was raised in Louisville. Asa Bird brought him around at the last minute and asked if we had room for him."

Jordan smiled.

"He was probably bumming his way home. He told me he was president of your class at Yale."

Tom and I looked at each other blankly.

"Biloxi?"

"First place, we didn't have any president——"

Gatsby's foot beat a short, restless tattoo and Tom eyed him suddenly.

"By the way, Mr. Gatsby, I understand you're an Oxford man."

"Not exactly."

"Oh, yes, I understand you went to Oxford."

"Yes—I went there."

A pause. Then Tom's voice, incredulous and insulting:

"You must have gone there about the time Biloxi went to New Haven."

Another pause. A waiter knocked and came in with crushed mint and ice but the silence was unbroken by his "thank you" and the soft closing of the door. This tremendous detail was to be cleared up at last.

"I told you I went there," said Gatsby.

"I heard you, but I'd like to know when."

"It was in nineteen-nineteen, I only stayed five months. That's why I can't really call myself an Oxford man."

Tom glanced around to see if we mirrored his unbelief. But we were all looking at Gatsby.

"It was an opportunity they gave to some of the officers after the armistice," he continued. "We could go to any of the universities in England or France."

I wanted to get up and slap him on the back. I had one of those renewals of complete faith in him that I'd experienced before.

Daisy rose, smiling faintly, and went to the table.

"Open the whiskey, Tom," she ordered, "and I'll make you a mint julep. Then you won't seem so stupid to yourself. . . . Look at the mint!"

"Wait a minute," snapped Tom. "I want to ask Mr. Gatsby one more question."

"Go on," Gatsby said politely.

"What kind of a row are you trying to cause in my house anyhow?"

They were out in the open at last and Gatsby was content.

"He isn't causing a row." Daisy looked desperately from one to the other. "You're causing a row. Please have a little self-control."

"Self-control!" repeated Tom incredulously. "I suppose the latest thing is to sit back and let Mr. Nobody from Nowhere make love to your wife. Well, if that's the idea you can count me out. . . . Nowadays people begin by sneering at family life and family institutions, and next they'll throw everything overboard and have intermarriage between black and white."

Flushed with his impassioned gibberish, he saw himself standing alone on the last barrier of civilization.

"We're all white here," murmured Jordan.

"I know I'm not very popular. I don't give big parties. I suppose you've got to make your house into a pigsty in order to have any friends—in the modern world."

Angry as I was, as we all were, I was tempted to laugh whenever he opened his mouth. The transition from libertine to prig was so complete.

"I've got something to tell *you*, old sport—" began Gatsby. But Daisy guessed at his intention.

"Please don't!" she interrupted helplessly. "Please let's all go home. Why don't we all go home?"

"That's a good idea." I got up. "Come on, Tom. Nobody wants a drink."

"I want to know what Mr. Gatsby has to tell me."

"Your wife doesn't love you," said Gatsby. "She's never loved you. She loves me."

"You must be crazy!" exclaimed Tom automatically.

Gatsby sprang to his feet, vivid with excitement.

"She never loved you, do you hear?" he cried. "She only married you because I was poor and she was tired of waiting for me. It was a terrible mistake, but in her heart she never loved anyone except me!"

At this point Jordan and I tried to go, but Tom and Gatsby insisted with competitive firmness that we remain—as though neither of them had anything to conceal and it would be a privilege to partake vicariously of their emotions.

"Sit down, Daisy." Tom's voice groped unsuccessfully for the paternal note. "What's been going on? I want to hear all about it."

"I told you what's been going on," said Gatsby. "Going on for five years—and you didn't know."

Tom turned to Daisy sharply.

"You've been seeing this fellow for five years?"

"Not seeing," said Gatsby. "No, we couldn't meet. But both of us loved each other all that time, old sport, and you didn't know. I used to laugh sometimes"—but there was no laughter in his eyes—"to think that you didn't know."

"Oh—that's all." Tom tapped his thick fingers together like a clergyman and leaned back in his chair.

"You're crazy!" he exploded. "I can't speak about what happened five years ago, because I didn't know Daisy then—and I'll be damned if I see how you got within a mile of her unless you brought the groceries to the back door. But all the rest of that's a God Damned lie. Daisy loved me when she married me and she loves me now."

"No," said Gatsby, shaking his head.

"She does, though. The trouble is that sometimes she gets foolish ideas in her head and doesn't know what she's doing." He nodded sagely. "And what's more, I love Daisy too. Once in a while I go off on a spree and make a fool of myself, but I always come back, and in my heart I love her all the time."

"You're revolting," said Daisy. She turned to me, and her voice, dropping an octave lower, filled the room with thrilling scorn: "Do you know why we left Chicago? I'm surprised that they didn't treat you to the story of that little spree."

Gatsby walked over and stood beside her.

"Daisy, that's all over now," he said earnestly. "It doesn't matter any more. Just tell him the truth—that you never loved him—and it's all wiped out forever."

She looked at him blindly. "Why—how could I love him—possibly?"

"You never loved him."

She hesitated. Her eyes fell on Jordan and me with a sort of appeal, as though she realized at last what she was doing—and as though she had never, all along, intended doing anything at all. But it was done now. It was too late.

"I never loved him," she said, with perceptible reluctance.

"Not at Kapiolani?" demanded Tom suddenly.

"No."

From the ballroom beneath, muffled and suffocating chords were drifting up on hot waves of air.

"Not that day I carried you down from the Punch Bowl to keep your shoes dry?" There was a husky tenderness in his tone. . . . "Daisy?"

"Please don't." Her voice was cold, but the rancor was gone from it. She looked at Gatsby. "There, Jay," she said—but her hand as she tried to light a cigarette was trembling. Suddenly she threw the cigarette and the burning match on the carpet.

"Oh, you want too much!" she cried to Gatsby. "I love you now—isn't that enough? I can't help what's past." She began to sob helplessly. "I did love him once—but I loved you too."

Gatsby's eyes opened and closed.

"You loved me *too?*" he repeated.

"Even that's a lie," said Tom savagely. "She didn't know you were alive. Why—there're things between Daisy and me that you'll never know, things that neither of us can ever forget."

The words seemed to bite physically into Gatsby.

"I want to speak to Daisy alone," he insisted. "She's all excited now——"

"Even alone I can't say I never loved Tom," she admitted in a pitiful voice. "It wouldn't be true."

"Of course it wouldn't," agreed Tom.

She turned to her husband.

"As if it mattered to you," she said.

"Of course it matters. I'm going to take better care of you from now on."

"You don't understand," said Gatsby, with a touch of panic. "You're not going to take care of her any more."

"I'm not?" Tom opened his eyes wide and laughed. He could afford to control himself now. "Why's that?"

"Daisy's leaving you."

"Nonsense."

"I am, though," she said with a visible effort.

"She's not leaving me!" Tom's words suddenly leaned down over Gatsby. "Certainly not for a common swindler who'd have to steal the ring he put on her finger."

"I won't stand this!" cried Daisy. "Oh, please let's get out."

"Who are you, anyhow?" broke out Tom. "You're one of that bunch that hangs around with Meyer Wolfshiem—that much I happen to know. I've made a little investigation into your affairs—and I'll carry it further tomorrow."

"You can suit yourself about that, old sport," said Gatsby steadily.

"I found out what your 'drug-stores' were." He turned to us and spoke rapidly. "He and this Wolfshiem bought up a lot of side-street drug-stores here and in Chicago and sold grain alcohol over the counter. That's one of his little stunts. I picked him for a bootlegger the first time I saw him, and I wasn't far wrong."

"What about it?" said Gatsby politely. "I guess your friend Walter Chase wasn't too proud to come in on it."

"And you left him in the lurch, didn't you? You let him go to jail for a month over in New Jersey. God! You ought to hear Walter on the subject of *you*."

"He came to us dead broke. He was very glad to pick up some money, old sport."

"Don't you call me 'old sport'!" cried Tom. Gatsby said nothing. "Walter could have you up on the betting laws too, but Wolfshiem scared him into shutting his mouth."

That unfamiliar yet recognizable look was back again in Gatsby's face.

"That drug-store business was just small change," continued Tom slowly, "but you've got something on now that Walter's afraid to tell me about."

I glanced at Daisy, who was staring terrified between Gatsby and her husband, and at Jordan, who had begun to balance an invisible but absorbing object on the tip of her chin. Then I turned back to Gatsby— and was startled at his expression. He looked—and this is said in all contempt for the babbled slander of his garden—as if he had "killed a man." For a moment the set of his face could be described in just that fantastic way.

It passed, and he began to talk excitedly to Daisy, denying everything, defending his name against accusations that had not been made. But with every word she was drawing further and further into herself, so he gave that up, and only the dead dream fought on as the afternoon slipped away, trying to touch what was no longer tangible, struggling unhappily, undespairingly, toward that lost voice across the room.

The voice begged again to go.

"*Please*, Tom! I can't stand this any more."

Her frightened eyes told that whatever intentions, whatever courage she had had, were definitely gone.

"You two start on home, Daisy," said Tom. "In Mr. Gatsby's car."

She looked at Tom, alarmed now, but he insisted with magnanimous scorn.

"Go on. He won't annoy you. I think he realizes that his presumptuous little flirtation is over."

They were gone, without a word, snapped out, made accidental, isolated, like ghosts, even from our pity.

After a moment Tom got up and began wrapping the unopened bottle of whiskey in the towel.

"Want any of this stuff? Jordan? . . . Nick?"

I didn't answer.

"Nick?" He asked again.

"What?"

"Want any?"

"No . . . I just remembered that today's my birthday."

I was thirty. Before me stretched the portentous, menacing road of a new decade.

It was seven o'clock when we got into the coupé with him and started for Long Island. Tom talked incessantly, exulting and laughing, but his voice was as remote from Jordan and me as the foreign clamor on the sidewalk or the tumult of the elevated overhead. Human sympathy has its limits, and we were content to let all their tragic arguments fade with the city lights behind. Thirty—the promise of a decade of loneliness, a thinning list of single men to know, a thinning brief-case of enthusiasm, thinning hair. But there was Jordan beside me, who, unlike Daisy, was too wise ever to carry well-forgotten dreams from age to age. As we passed over the dark bridge her wan face fell lazily against my coat's shoulder and the formidable stroke of thirty died away with the reassuring pressure of her hand.

So we drove on toward death through the cooling twilight.

◆

The young Greek, Michaelis, who ran the coffee joint beside the ash-heaps was the principal witness at the inquest. He had slept through the heat until after five, when he strolled over to the garage, and found George Wilson sick in his office—really sick, pale as his own pale hair and shaking all over. Michaelis advised him to go to bed, but Wilson refused, saying that he'd miss a lot of business if he did. While his neighbor was trying to persuade him a violent racket broke out overhead.

"I've got my wife locked in up there," explained Wilson calmly. "She's going to stay there till the day after tomorrow, and then we're going to move away."

Michaelis was astonished; they had been neighbors for four years, and Wilson had never seemed faintly capable of such a statement. Generally he was one of these worn-out men: when he wasn't working, he sat on a chair in the doorway and stared at the people and the cars that passed along the road. When anyone spoke to him he invariably laughed in an agreeable, colorless way. He was his wife's man and not his own.

So naturally Michaelis tried to find out what had happened, but Wilson wouldn't say a word—instead he began to throw curious, suspicious glances at his visitor and ask him what he'd been doing at certain times on certain days. Just as the latter was getting uneasy, some workmen came past the door bound for his restaurant, and Michaelis took the opportunity to get away, intending to come back later. But he didn't. He supposed he forgot to, that's all. When he came outside again, a little after seven, he was reminded of the conversation because he heard Mrs. Wilson's voice, loud and scolding, downstairs in the garage.

"Beat me!" he heard her cry. "Throw me down and beat me, you dirty little coward!"

A moment later she rushed out into the dusk, waving her hands and shouting—before he could move from his door the business was over.

The "death car," as the newspapers called it, didn't stop; it came out of the gathering darkness, wavered tragically for a moment, and then disappeared around the next bend. Michaelis wasn't even sure of its color—he told the first policeman that it was light green. The other car, the one going toward New York, came to rest a hundred yards beyond, and its driver hurried back to where Myrtle Wilson, her life violently extinguished, knelt in the road and mingled her thick dark blood with the dust.

Michaelis and this man reached her first, but when they had torn open her shirtwaist, still damp with perspiration, they saw that her left breast was swinging loose like a flap, and there was no need to listen for the heart beneath. The mouth was wide open and ripped at the corners, as though she had choked a little in giving up the tremendous vitality she had stored so long.

◆

We saw the three or four automobiles and the crowd when we were still some distance away.

"Wreck!" said Tom. "That's good. Wilson'll have a little business at last."

He slowed down, but still without any intention of stopping, until, as we came nearer, the hushed, intent faces of the people at the garage door made him automatically put on the brakes.

"We'll take a look," he said doubtfully, "just a look."

I became aware now of a hollow, wailing sound which issued incessantly from the garage, a sound which as we got out of the coupé and walked toward the door resolved itself into the words "Oh, my God!" uttered over and over in a gasping moan.

"There's some bad trouble here," said Tom excitedly.

He reached up on tiptoes and peered over a circle of heads into the garage, which was lit only by a yellow light in a swinging wire basket overhead. Then he made a harsh sound in his throat, and with a violent thrusting movement of his powerful arms pushed his way through.

The circle closed up again with a running murmur of expostulation; it was a minute before I could see anything at all. Then new arrivals disarranged the line, and Jordan and I were pushed suddenly inside.

Myrtle Wilson's body, wrapped in a blanket, and then in another blanket, as though she suffered from a chill in the hot night, lay on a work table by the wall, and Tom, with his back to us, was bending over it, motionless. Next to him stood a motorcycle policeman taking down names with much sweat and correction in a little book. At first I couldn't find the source of the high, groaning words that echoed clamorously through the bare garage—then I saw Wilson standing on the raised threshold of his office, swaying back and forth and holding to the doorposts with both hands. Some man was talking to him in a low voice and attempting, from time to time, to lay a hand on his shoulder, but Wilson neither heard nor saw. His eyes would drop slowly from the swinging light to the laden table by the wall, and then jerk back to the light again, and he gave out incessantly his high, horrible call:

"Oh, my Ga-od! Oh, my Ga-od! Oh, Ga-od! Oh, my Ga-od!"

Presently Tom lifted his head with a jerk and, after staring around the garage with glazed eyes, addressed a mumbled incoherent remark to the policeman.

"M-a-v——" the policeman was saying, "——o———"

"No, r——" corrected the man, "M-a-v-r-o———"

"Listen to me!" muttered Tom fiercely.

"r——" said the policeman, "o———"

"g———"

"g——" He looked up as Tom's broad hand fell sharply on his shoulder. "What you want, fella?"

"What happened?—that's what I want to know."

"Auto hit her. Ins'antly killed."

"Instantly killed," repeated Tom, staring.

"She ran out ina road. Son-of-a-bitch didn't even stopus car."

"There was two cars," said Michaelis, "one comin', one goin', see?"

"Going where?" asked the policeman keenly.

"One goin' each way. Well, she"—his hand rose toward the blankets but stopped half way and fell to his side—"she ran out there an' the one comin' from N'York knock right into her, goin' thirty or forty miles an hour."

"What's the name of this place here?" demanded the officer.

"Hasn't got any name."

A pale well-dressed negro stepped near.

"It was a yellow car," he said, "big yellow car. New."

"See the accident?" asked the policeman.

"No, but the car passed me down the road, going faster'n forty. Going fifty, sixty."

"Come here and let's have your name. Look out now. I want to get his name."

Some words of this conversation must have reached Wilson, swaying in the office door, for suddenly a new theme found voice among his gasping cries:

"You don't have to tell me what kind of car it was! I know what kind of car it was!"

Watching Tom, I saw the wad of muscle back of his shoulder tighten under his coat. He walked quickly over to Wilson and, standing in front of him, seized him firmly by the upper arms.

"You've got to pull yourself together," he said with soothing gruffness.

Wilson's eyes fell upon Tom; he started up on his tiptoes and then would have collapsed to his knees had not Tom held him upright.

"Listen," said Tom, shaking him a little. "I just got here a minute ago, from New York. I was bringing you that coupé we've been talking about. That yellow car I was driving this afternoon wasn't mine—do you hear? I haven't seen it all afternoon."

Only the negro and I were near enough to hear what he said, but the policeman caught something in the tone and looked over with truculent eyes.

"What's all that?" he demanded.

"I'm a friend of his." Tom turned his head but kept his hands firm on Wilson's body. "He says he knows the car that did it. . . . It was a yellow car."

Some dim impulse moved the policeman to look suspiciously at Tom.

"And what color's your car?"

"It's a blue car, a coupé."

"We've come straight from New York," I said.

Someone who had been driving a little behind us confirmed this, and the policeman turned away.

"Now, if you'll let me have that name again correct———"

Picking up Wilson like a doll, Tom carried him into the office, set him down in a chair, and came back.

"If somebody'll come here and sit with him," he snapped authoritatively. He watched while the two men standing closest glanced at each other and went unwillingly into the room. Then Tom shut the door on them and came down the single step, his eyes avoiding the table. As he passed close to me he whispered: "Let's get out."

Self-consciously, with his authoritative arms breaking the way, we pushed through the still gathering crowd, passing a hurried doctor, case in hand, who had been sent for in wild hope half an hour ago.

Tom drove slowly until we were beyond the bend—then his foot came down hard, and the coupé raced along through the night. In a little while I heard a low husky sob, and saw that the tears were overflowing down his face.

"The God Damn coward!" he whimpered. "He didn't even stop his car."

◆

The Buchanans' house floated suddenly toward us through the dark rustling trees. Tom stopped beside the porch and looked up at the second floor, where two windows bloomed with light among the vines.

"Daisy's home," he said. As we got out of the car he glanced at me and frowned slightly.

"I ought to have dropped you in West Egg, Nick. There's nothing we can do tonight."

A change had come over him, and he spoke gravely, and with decision. As we walked across the moonlit gravel to the porch he disposed of the situation in a few brisk phrases.

"I'll telephone for a taxi to take you home, and while you're waiting you and Jordan better go in the kitchen and have them get you some supper—if you want any." He opened the door. "Come in."

"No, thanks. But I'd be glad if you'd order me the taxi. I'll wait outside."

Jordan put her hand on my arm.

"Won't you come in, Nick?"

"No, thanks."

I was feeling a little sick and I wanted to be alone. But Jordan lingered for a moment more.

"It's only half past nine," she said.

I'd be damned if I'd go in; I'd had enough of all of them for one day, and suddenly that included Jordan too. She must have seen something of this in my expression, for she turned abruptly away and ran up the porch steps into the house. I sat down for a few minutes with my head in my hands, until I heard the phone taken up inside and the butler's voice calling a taxi. Then I walked slowly down the drive away from the house, intending to wait by the gate.

I hadn't gone twenty yards when I heard my name and Gatsby stepped from between two bushes into the path. I must have felt pretty weird by that time, because I could think of nothing except the luminosity of his pink suit under the moon.

"What are you doing?" I inquired.

"Just standing here, old sport."

Somehow, that seemed a despicable occupation. For all I knew he was going to rob the house in a moment; I wouldn't have been surprised to see sinister faces, the faces of "Wolfshiem's people," behind him in the dark shrubbery.

"Did you see any trouble on the road?" he asked after a minute.

"Yes."

He hesitated.

"Was she killed?"

"Yes."

"I thought so; I told Daisy I thought so. It's better that the shock should all come at once. She stood it pretty well."

He spoke as if Daisy's reaction was the only thing that mattered.

"I got to West Egg by a side road," he went on, "and left the car in my garage. I don't think anybody saw us, but of course I can't be sure."

I disliked him so much by this time that I didn't find it necessary to tell him he was wrong.

"Who was the woman?" he inquired.

"Her name was Wilson. Her husband owns the garage. How the devil did it happen?"

"Well, I tried to swing the wheel—" He broke off, and suddenly I guessed at the truth.

"Was Daisy driving?"

"Yes," he said after a moment, "but of course I'll say I was. You see, when we left New York she was very nervous and she thought it would steady her to drive—and this woman rushed out at us just as we were passing a car coming the other way. It all happened in a minute, but it seemed to me that she wanted to speak to us, thought we were somebody she knew. Well, first Daisy turned away from the woman toward the other car, and then she lost her nerve and turned back. The second my hand reached the wheel I felt the shock—it must have killed her instantly."

"It ripped her open——"

"Don't tell me, old sport." He winced. "Anyhow—Daisy stepped on it. I tried to make her stop, but she couldn't, so I pulled on the emergency brake. Then she fell over into my lap and I drove on.

"She'll be all right tomorrow," he said presently. "I'm just going to wait here and see if he tries to bother her about that unpleasantness this afternoon. She's locked herself into her room, and if he tries any brutality she's going to turn the light out and on again."

"He won't touch her," I said. "He's not thinking about her."

"I don't trust him, old sport."

"How long are you going to wait?"

"All night, if necessary. Anyhow, till they all go to bed."

A new point of view occurred to me. Suppose Tom found out that Daisy had been driving. He might think he saw a connection in it—he might think anything. I looked at the house; there were two or three bright windows downstairs and the pink glow from Daisy's room on the second floor.

"You wait here," I said. "I'll see if there's any sign of a commotion."

I walked back along the border of the lawn, traversed the gravel softly, and tiptoed up the veranda steps. The drawing-room curtains were open, and I saw that the room was empty. Crossing the porch where we had dined that June night three months before, I came to a small rectangle of light which I guessed was the pantry window. The blind was drawn, but I found a rift at the sill.

Daisy and Tom were sitting opposite each other at the kitchen table, with a plate of cold fried chicken between them, and two bottles of ale. He was talking intently across the table at her, and in his earnestness his hand had fallen upon and covered her own. Once in a while she looked up at him and nodded in agreement.

They weren't happy, and neither of them had touched the chicken or the ale—and yet they weren't unhappy either. There was an unmistakable air of natural intimacy about the picture, and anybody would have said that they were conspiring together.

As I tiptoed from the porch I heard my taxi feeling its way along the dark road toward the house. Gatsby was waiting where I had left him in the drive.

"Is it all quiet up there?" he asked anxiously.

"Yes, it's all quiet." I hesitated. "You'd better come home and get some sleep."

He shook his head.

"I want to wait here till Daisy goes to bed. Good night, old sport."

He put his hands in his coat pockets and turned back eagerly to his scrutiny of the house, as though my presence marred the sacredness of the vigil. So I walked away and left him standing there in the moonlight—watching over nothing.

CHAPTER VIII

I couldn't sleep all night; a fog-horn was groaning incessantly on the Sound, and I tossed half sick between grotesque reality and savage, frightening dreams. Toward dawn I heard a taxi go up Gatsby's drive, and immediately I jumped out of bed and began to dress—I felt that I had something to tell him, something to warn him about, and morning would be too late.

Crossing his lawn, I saw that his front door was still open and he was leaning against a table in the hall, heavy with dejection or sleep.

"Nothing happened," he said wanly. "I waited, and about four o'clock she came to the window and stood there for a minute and then turned out the light."

His house had never seemed so enormous to me as it did that night when we hunted through the great rooms for cigarettes. We pushed aside curtains that were like pavilions, and felt over innumerable feet of dark wall for electric light switches—once I tumbled with a sort of splash upon the keys of a ghostly piano. There was an inexplicable amount of dust everywhere, and the rooms were musty, as though they hadn't been aired for many days. I found the humidor on an unfamiliar table, with two stale, dry cigarettes inside. Throwing open the French windows of the drawing-room, we sat smoking out into the darkness.

"You ought to go away," I said. "It's pretty certain they'll trace your car."

"Go away *now*, old sport?"

"Go to Atlantic City for a week, or up to Montreal."

He wouldn't consider it. He couldn't possibly leave Daisy until he knew what she was going to do. He was clutching at some last hope and I couldn't bear to shake him free.

It was this night that he told me the strange story of his youth with Dan Cody—told it to me because "Jay Gatsby" had broken up like glass against Tom's hard malice, and the long secret extravaganza was played out. I think that he would have acknowledged anything now, without reserve, but he wanted to talk about Daisy.

She was the first "nice" girl he had ever known. In various unrevealed capacities he had come in contact with such people, but always with indiscernible barbed wire between. He found her excitingly desirable. He went to her house, at first with other officers from Camp Taylor, then alone. It amazed him—he had never been in such a beautiful house before. But what gave it an air of breathless intensity was that Daisy lived there—it was as casual a thing to her as his tent out at camp was to him. There was a ripe mystery about it, a hint of bedrooms upstairs more beautiful and cool than other bedrooms, of gay and radiant activities taking place through its corridors, and of romances that were not musty and laid away already in lavender but fresh and breathing and redolent of this year's shining motor-cars and of dances whose flowers were scarcely withered. It excited him, too, that many men had already loved Daisy—it increased her value in his eyes. He felt their presence all about the house, pervading the air with the shades and echoes of still vibrant emotions.

But he knew that he was in Daisy's house by a colossal accident. However glorious might be his future as Jay Gatsby, he was at present a penniless young man without a past, and at any moment the invisible cloak of his uniform might slip from his shoulders. So he made the most of his time. He took what he could get, ravenously and unscrupulously—eventually he took Daisy one still October night, took her because he had no real right to touch her hand.

He might have despised himself, for he had certainly taken her under false pretenses. I don't mean that he had traded on his phantom millions, but he had deliberately given Daisy a sense of security; he let her believe that he was a person from much the same strata as herself—that he was fully able to take care of her. As a matter of fact, he had no such facilities—he had no comfortable family standing behind him, and he was liable at the whim of an impersonal government to be blown anywhere about the world.

But he didn't despise himself and it didn't turn out as he had imagined. He had intended, probably, to take what he could and go—but now he found that he had committed himself to the following of a grail. He knew that Daisy was extraordinary, but he didn't realize just how extraordinary a "nice" girl could be. She vanished into her rich house, into her rich, full life, leaving Gatsby—nothing. He felt married to her, that was all.

When they met again, two days later, it was Gatsby who was breathless, who was, somehow, betrayed. Her porch was bright with the bought luxury of star-shine; the wicker of the settee squeaked fashionably as she turned toward him and he kissed her curious and lovely mouth. She had caught a cold, and it made her voice huskier and more charming than ever, and Gatsby was overwhelmingly aware of the youth and mystery that wealth imprisons and preserves, of the freshness of many clothes, and of Daisy, gleaming like silver, safe and proud above the hot struggles of the poor.

◆

"I can't describe to you how surprised I was to find out I loved her, old sport. I even hoped for a while that she'd throw me over, but she didn't, because she was in love with me too. She thought I knew a lot because I knew different things from her . . . Well, there I was, way off my ambitions, getting deeper in love every minute, and all of a sudden I didn't care. What was the use of doing great things if I could have a better time telling her what I was going to do?"

On the last afternoon before he went abroad, he sat with Daisy in his arms for a long, silent time. It was a cold fall day, with fire in the room and her cheeks flushed. Now and then she moved and he changed his arm a little, and once he kissed her dark shining hair. The afternoon had made them tranquil for a while, as if to give them a deep memory for the long parting the next day promised. They had never been closer in their month of love, nor communicated more profoundly one with another, than when she brushed silent lips against his coat's shoulder or when he touched the end of her finger, gently, as though she were asleep.

◆

He did extraordinarily well in the war. He was a captain before he went to the front, and following the Argonne battles he got his majority and the command of the divisional machine-guns. After the armistice he tried frantically to get home, but some complication or

misunderstanding sent him to Oxford instead. He was worried now—
there was a quality of nervous despair in Daisy's letters. She didn't
see why he couldn't come. She was feeling the pressure of the world
outside, and she wanted to see him and feel his presence beside her and
be reassured that she was doing the right thing after all.

For Daisy was young and her artificial world was redolent of orchids
and pleasant, cheerful snobbery and orchestras which set the rhythm of
the year, summing up the sadness and suggestiveness of life in new tunes.
All night the saxophones wailed the hopeless comment of the "Beale
Street Blues" while a hundred pairs of golden and silver slippers shuf-
fled the shining dust. At the gray tea hour there were always rooms that
throbbed incessantly with this low, sweet fever, while fresh faces drifted
here and there like rose petals blown by the sad horns around the floor.

Through this twilight universe Daisy began to move again with the
season; suddenly she was again keeping half a dozen dates a day with
half a dozen men, and drowsing asleep at dawn with the beads and
chiffon of an evening dress tangled among dying orchids on the floor
beside her bed. And all the time something within her was crying for
a decision. She wanted her life shaped now, immediately—and the
decision must be made by some force—of love, of money, of unques-
tionable practicality—that was close at hand.

That force took shape in the middle of spring with the arrival of
Tom Buchanan. There was a wholesome bulkiness about his person
and his position, and Daisy was flattered. Doubtless there was a certain
struggle and a certain relief. The letter reached Gatsby while he was
still at Oxford.

◆

It was dawn now on Long Island and we went about opening the rest of the windows downstairs, filling the house with gray-turning, gold-turning light. The shadow of a tree fell abruptly across the dew and ghostly birds began to sing among the blue leaves. There was a slow, pleasant movement in the air, scarcely a wind, promising a cool, lovely day.

"I don't think she ever loved him." Gatsby turned around from a window and looked at me challengingly. "You must remember, old sport, she was very excited this afternoon. He told her those things in a way that frightened her—that made it look as if I was some kind of cheap sharper. And the result was she hardly knew what she was saying."

He sat down gloomily.

"Of course she might have loved him just for a minute, when they were first married—and loved me more even then, do you see?"

Suddenly he came out with a curious remark.

"In any case," he said, "it was just personal."

What could you make of that, except to suspect some intensity in his conception of the affair that couldn't be measured?

He came back from France when Tom and Daisy were still on their wedding trip, and made a miserable but irresistible journey to Louisville on the last of his army pay. He stayed there a week, walking the streets where their footsteps had clicked together through the November night and revisiting the out-of-the-way places to which they had driven in her white car. Just as Daisy's house had always seemed to him more mysterious and gay than other houses, so his idea of the city itself, even though she was gone from it, was pervaded with a melancholy beauty.

He left feeling that if he had searched harder, he might have found her—that he was leaving her behind. The day-coach—he was penniless now—was hot. He went out to the open vestibule and sat down on a folding chair, and the station slid away and the backs of unfamiliar buildings moved by. Then out into the spring fields, where a yellow trolley raced them for a minute with people in it who might once have seen the pale magic of her face along the casual street.

The track curved and now it was going away from the sun, which, as it sank lower, seemed to spread itself in benediction over the vanishing city where she had drawn her breath. He stretched out his hand desperately as if to snatch only a wisp of air, to save a fragment of the spot that she had made lovely for him. But it was all going by too fast now for his blurred eyes and he knew that he had lost that part of it, the freshest and the best, forever.

◆

It was nine o'clock when we finished breakfast and went out on the porch. The night had made a sharp difference in the weather and there was an autumn flavor in the air. The gardener, the last one of Gatsby's former servants, came to the foot of the steps.

"I'm going to drain the pool today, Mr. Gatsby. Leaves'll start falling pretty soon, and then there's always trouble with the pipes."

"Don't do it today," Gatsby answered. He turned to me apologetically. "You know, old sport, I've never used that pool all summer?"

I looked at my watch and stood up.

"Twelve minutes to my train."

I didn't want to go to the city. I wasn't worth a decent stroke of work, but it was more than that—I didn't want to leave Gatsby. I missed that train, and then another, before I could get myself away.

"I'll call you up," I said finally.

"Do, old sport."

"I'll call you about noon."

We walked slowly down the steps.

"I suppose Daisy'll call too." He looked at me anxiously, as if he hoped I'd corroborate this.

"I suppose so."

"Well, good-by."

We shook hands and I started away. Just before I reached the hedge I remembered something and turned around.

"They're a rotten crowd," I shouted across the lawn. "You're worth the whole damn bunch put together."

I've always been glad I said that. It was the only compliment I ever gave him, because I disapproved of him from beginning to end. First he nodded politely, and then his face broke into that radiant and under-standing smile, as if we'd been in ecstatic cahoots on that fact all the time. His gorgeous pink rag of a suit made a bright spot of color against the white steps, and I thought of the night when I first came to his ancestral home, three months before. The lawn and drive had been crowded with the faces of those who guessed at his corruption—and he had stood on those steps, concealing his incorruptible dream, as he waved them good-by.

I thanked him for his hospitality. We were always thanking him for that—I and the others.

"Good-by," I called. "I enjoyed breakfast, Gatsby."

◆

Up in the city, I tried for a while to list the quotations on an interminable amount of stock, then I fell asleep in my swivel chair. Just before
noon the phone woke me, and I started up with sweat breaking out on
my forehead. It was Jordan Baker; she often called me up at this hour
because the uncertainty of her own movements between hotels and
clubs and private houses made her hard to find in any other way. Usually
her voice came over the wire as something fresh and cool, as if a divot
from a green golf-links had come sailing in at the office window, but
this morning it seemed harsh and dry.

"I've left Daisy's house," she said. "I'm at Hempstead, and I'm going
down to Southampton this afternoon."

Probably it had been tactful to leave Daisy's house, but the act
annoyed me, and her next remark made me rigid.

"You weren't so nice to me last night."

"How could it have mattered then?"

Silence for a moment. Then:

"However—I want to see you."

"I want to see you, too."

"Suppose I don't go to Southampton, and come into town this
afternoon?"

"No—I don't think this afternoon."

"Very well."

"It's impossible this afternoon. Various——"

We talked like that for a while, and then abruptly we weren't talking
any longer. I don't know which of us hung up with a sharp click, but I
know I didn't care. I couldn't have talked to her across a tea-table that
day if I never talked to her again in this world.

I called Gatsby's house a few minutes later, but the line was busy. I tried four times; finally an exasperated Central told me the wire was being kept open for Long Distance from Detroit. Taking out my time-table, I drew a small circle around the three-fifty train. Then I leaned back in my chair and tried to think. It was just noon.

◆

When I passed the ashheaps on the train that morning I had crossed deliberately to the other side of the car. I supposed there'd be a curious crowd around there all day with little boys searching for dark spots in the dust, and some garrulous man telling over and over what had happened, until it became less and less real even to him and he could tell it no longer, and Myrtle Wilson's tragic achievement was forgotten. Now I want to go back a little and tell what happened at the garage after we left there the night before.

They had difficulty in locating the sister, Catherine. She must have broken her rule against drinking that night, for when she arrived she was stupid with liquor and unable to understand that the ambulance had already gone to Flushing. When they convinced her of this, she immediately fainted, as if that was the intolerable part of the affair. Someone, kind or curious, took her in his car and drove her in the wake of her sister's body.

Until long after midnight a changing crowd lapped up against the front of the garage, while George Wilson rocked himself back and forth on the couch inside. For a while the door of the office was open, and everyone who came into the garage glanced irresistibly through it. Finally someone said it was a shame, and closed the door. Michaelis and several other men were with him; first, four or five men, later two or three men. Still later Michaelis had to ask the last stranger to wait there fifteen minutes longer, while he went back to his own place and made a pot of coffee. After that, he stayed there alone with Wilson until dawn.

About three o'clock the quality of Wilson's incoherent muttering changed—he grew quieter and began to talk about the yellow car. He announced that he had a way of finding out whom the yellow car belonged to, and then he blurted out that a couple of months ago his wife had come from the city with her face bruised and her nose swollen.

But when he heard himself say this, he flinched and began to cry "Oh, my God!" again in his groaning voice. Michaelis made a clumsy attempt to distract him.

"How long have you been married, George? Come on there, try and sit still a minute and answer my question. How long have you been married?"

"Twelve years."

"Ever had any children? Come on, George, sit still—I asked you a question. Did you ever have any children?"

The hard brown beetles kept thudding against the dull light, and whenever Michaelis heard a car go tearing along the road outside it sounded to him like the car that hadn't stopped a few hours before. He didn't like to go into the garage, because the work bench was stained where the body had been lying, so he moved uncomfortably around the office—he knew every object in it before morning—and from time to time sat down beside Wilson trying to keep him more quiet.

"Have you got a church you go to sometimes, George? Maybe even if you haven't been there for a long time? Maybe I could call up the church and get a priest to come over and he could talk to you, see?"

"Don't belong to any."

"You ought to have a church, George, for times like this. You must have gone to church once. Didn't you get married in a church? Listen, George, listen to me. Didn't you get married in a church?"

"That was a long time ago."

The effort of answering broke the rhythm of his rocking—for a moment he was silent. Then the same half knowing, half bewildered look came back into his faded eyes.

"Look in the drawer there," he said, pointing at the desk.

"Which drawer?"

"That drawer—that one."

Michaelis opened the drawer nearest his hand. There was nothing in it but a small, expensive dog-leash, made of leather and braided silver. It was apparently new.

"This?" he inquired, holding it up.

Wilson stared and nodded.

"I found it yesterday afternoon. She tried to tell me about it, but I knew it was something funny."

"You mean your wife bought it?"

"She had it wrapped in tissue paper on her bureau."

Michaelis didn't see anything odd in that, and he gave Wilson a dozen reasons why his wife might have bought the dog-leash. But conceivably Wilson had heard some of these same explanations before, from Myrtle, because he began saying "Oh, my God!" again in a whisper—his comforter left several explanations in the air.

"Then he killed her," said Wilson. His mouth dropped open suddenly.

"Who did?"

"I have a way of finding out."

"You're morbid, George," said his friend. "This has been a strain to you and you don't know what you're saying. You'd better try and sit quiet till morning."

"He murdered her."

"It was an accident, George."

Wilson shook his head. His eyes narrowed and his mouth widened slightly with the ghost of a superior "Hm!"

"I know," he said definitely. "I'm one of these trusting fellas and I don't think any harm to nobody, but when I get to know a thing I know it. It was the man in that car. She ran out to speak to him and he wouldn't stop."

Michaelis had seen this too, but it hadn't occurred to him that there was any special significance in it. He believed that Mrs. Wilson had been running away from her husband, rather than trying to stop any particular car.

"How could she of been like that?"

"She's a deep one," said Wilson, as if that answered the question. "Ah-h-h———"

He began to rock again, and Michaelis stood twisting the leash in his hand.

"Maybe you got some friend that I could telephone for, George?"

This was a forlorn hope—he was almost sure that Wilson had no friend: there was not enough of him for his wife. He was glad a little later when he noticed a change in the room, a blue quickening by the window, and realized that dawn wasn't far off. About five o'clock it was blue enough outside to snap off the light.

Wilson's glazed eyes turned out to the ashheaps, where small gray clouds took on fantastic shapes and scurried here and there in the faint dawn wind.

"I spoke to her," he muttered, after a long silence. "I told her she might fool me but she couldn't fool God. I took her to the window"—with an effort he got up and walked to the rear window and leaned with his face pressed against it—"and I said 'God knows what you've been doing, everything you've been doing. You may fool me, but you can't fool God!'"

Standing behind him, Michaelis saw with a shock that he was looking at the eyes of Doctor T. J. Eckleburg, which had just emerged, pale and enormous, from the dissolving night.

"God sees everything," repeated Wilson.

"That's an advertisement," Michaelis assured him. Something made him turn away from the window and look back into the room. But Wilson stood there a long time, his face close to the window pane, nodding into the twilight.

◆

By six o'clock Michaelis was worn out, and grateful for the sound of a car stopping outside. It was one of the watchers of the night before who had promised to come back, so he cooked breakfast for three, which he and the other man ate together. Wilson was quieter now, and Michaelis went home to sleep; when he awoke four hours later and hurried back to the garage, Wilson was gone.

His movements—he was on foot all the time—were afterward traced to Port Roosevelt and then to Gad's Hill, where he bought a sandwich that he didn't eat, and a cup of coffee. He must have been tired and walking slowly, for he didn't reach Gad's Hill until noon. Thus far there was no difficulty in accounting for his time—there were boys who had seen a man "acting sort of crazy," and motorists at whom he stared oddly from the side of the road. Then for three hours he disappeared from view. The police, on the strength of what he said to Michaelis, that he "had a way of finding out," supposed that he spent that time going from garage to garage thereabouts, inquiring for a yellow car. On the other hand, no garage man who had seen him ever came forward, and perhaps he had an easier, surer way of finding out what he wanted to know. By half past two he was in West Egg, where he asked someone the way to Gatsby's house. So by that time he knew Gatsby's name.

◆

At two o'clock Gatsby put on his bathing suit and left word with the butler that if anyone phoned word was to be brought to him at the pool. He stopped at the garage for a pneumatic mattress that had amused his guests during the summer, and the chauffeur helped him pump it up. Then he gave instructions that the open car wasn't to be taken out under any circumstances—and this was strange, because the front right fender needed repair.

Gatsby shouldered the mattress and started for the pool. Once he stopped and shifted it a little, and the chauffeur asked him if he needed help, but he shook his head and in a moment disappeared among the yellowing trees.

No telephone message arrived, but the butler went without his sleep and waited for it until four o'clock—until long after there was anyone to give it to if it came. I have an idea that Gatsby himself didn't believe it would come, and perhaps he no longer cared. If that was true he must have felt that he had lost the old warm world, paid a high price for living too long with a single dream. He must have looked up at an unfamiliar sky through frightening leaves and shivered as he found what a grotesque thing a rose is and how raw the sunlight was upon the scarcely created grass. A new world, material without being real, where poor ghosts, breathing dreams like air, drifted fortuitously about . . . like that ashen, fantastic figure gliding toward him through the amorphous trees.

The chauffeur—he was one of Wolfshiem's protégés—heard the shots—afterward he could only say that he hadn't thought anything much about them. I drove from the station directly to Gatsby's house and my rushing anxiously up the front steps was the first thing that alarmed anyone. But they knew then, I firmly believe. With scarcely a word said, four of us, the chauffeur, butler, gardener, and I, hurried down to the pool.

There was a faint, barely perceptible movement of the water as the fresh flow from one end urged its way toward the drain at the other. With little ripples that were hardly the shadows of waves, the laden mattress moved irregularly down the pool. A small gust of wind that scarcely corrugated the surface was enough to disturb its accidental course with its accidental burden. The touch of a cluster of leaves revolved it slowly, tracing, like the leg of a compass, a thin red circle in the water.

It was after we started with Gatsby toward the house that the gardener saw Wilson's body a little way off in the grass, and the holocaust was complete.

CHAPTER IX

fter two years I remember the rest of that day, and that night and the next day, only as an endless drill of police and photographers and newspaper men in and out of Gatsby's front door. A rope stretched across the main gate and a policeman by it kept out the curious, but little boys soon discovered that they could enter through my yard, and there were always a few of them clustered open-mouthed about the pool. Someone with a positive manner, perhaps a detective, used the expression "madman" as he bent over Wilson's body that afternoon, and the adventitious authority of his voice set the key for the newspaper reports next morning.

Most of those reports were a nightmare—grotesque, circumstantial, eager, and untrue. When Michaelis's testimony at the inquest brought to light Wilson's suspicions of his wife I thought the whole tale would shortly be served up in racy pasquinade—but Catherine, who might have said anything, didn't say a word. She showed a surprising amount of character about it too—looked at the coroner with determined eyes under that corrected brow of hers, and swore that her sister had never seen Gatsby, that her sister was completely happy with her husband, that her sister had been into no mischief whatever. She convinced herself of it, and cried into her handkerchief, as if the very suggestion was more than she could endure. So Wilson was reduced to a man "deranged by grief" in order that the case might remain in its simplest form. And it rested there.

But all this part of it seemed remote and unessential. I found myself on Gatsby's side, and alone. From the moment I telephoned news of the catastrophe to West Egg Village, every surmise about him, and every practical question, was referred to me. At first I was surprised and confused; then, as he lay in his house and didn't move or breathe or speak, hour upon hour, it grew upon me that I was responsible, because no one else was interested—interested, I mean, with that intense personal interest to which everyone has some vague right at the end.

I called up Daisy half an hour after we found him, called her instinctively and without hesitation. But she and Tom had gone away early that afternoon, and taken baggage with them.

"Left no address?"

"No."

"Say when they'd be back?"

"No."

"Any idea where they are? How I could reach them?"

"I don't know. Can't say."

I wanted to get somebody for him. I wanted to go into the room where he lay and reassure him: "I'll get somebody for you, Gatsby. Don't worry. Just trust me and I'll get somebody for you——"

Meyer Wolfshiem's name wasn't in the phone book. The butler gave me his office address on Broadway, and I called Information, but by the time I had the number it was long after five, and no one answered the phone.

"Will you ring again?"

"I've rung them three times."

"It's very important."

"Sorry. I'm afraid no one's there."

I went back to the drawing-room and thought for an instant that they were chance visitors, all these official people who suddenly filled it. But, as they drew back the sheet and looked at Gatsby with unmoved eyes, his protest continued in my brain:

"Look here, old sport, you've got to get somebody for me. You've got to try hard. I can't go through this alone."

Someone started to ask me questions, but I broke away and going upstairs looked hastily through the unlocked parts of his desk—he'd never told me definitely that his parents were dead. But there was nothing—only the picture of Dan Cody, a token of forgotten violence, staring down from the wall.

Next morning I sent the butler to New York with a letter to Wolfshiem, which asked for information and urged him to come out on the next train. That request seemed superfluous when I wrote it. I was sure he'd start when he saw the newspapers, just as I was sure there'd be a wire from Daisy before noon—but neither a wire nor Mr. Wolfshiem arrived; no one arrived except more police and photographers and newspaper men. When the butler brought back Wolfshiem's answer I began to have a feeling of defiance, of scornful solidarity between Gatsby and me against them all.

Dear Mr. Carraway. This has been one of the most terrible shocks of my life to me I hardly can believe it that it is true at all. Such a mad act as that man did should make us all think. I cannot come down now as I am tied up in some very important business and cannot get mixed up in this thing now. If there is anything I can do a little later let me know in a letter by Edgar. I hardly know where I am when I hear about a thing like this and am completely knocked down and out.

Yours truly

Meyer Wolfshiem

and then hasty addenda beneath:

Let me know about the funeral etc do not know his family at all.

When the phone rang that afternoon and Long Distance said Chicago was calling I thought this would be Daisy at last. But the connection came through as a man's voice, very thin and far away.

"This is Slagle speaking . . ."

"Yes?" The name was unfamiliar.

"Hell of a note, isn't it? Get my wire?"

"There haven't been any wires."

"Young Parke's in trouble," he said rapidly. "They picked him up when he handed the bonds over the counter. They got a circular from New York giving 'em the numbers just five minutes before. What d'you know about that, hey? You never can tell in these hick towns——"

"Hello!" I interrupted breathlessly. "Look here—this isn't Mr. Gatsby. Mr. Gatsby's dead."

There was a long silence on the other end of the wire, followed by an exclamation . . . then a quick squawk as the connection was broken.

◆

I think it was on the third day that a telegram signed Henry C. Gatz arrived from a town in Minnesota. It said only that the sender was leaving immediately and to postpone the funeral until he came.

It was Gatsby's father, a solemn old man, very helpless and dismayed, bundled up in a long cheap ulster against the warm September day. His eyes leaked continuously with excitement, and when I took the bag and umbrella from his hands he began to pull so incessantly at his sparse gray beard that I had difficulty in getting off his coat. He was on the point of collapse, so I took him into the music-room and made him sit down while I sent for something to eat. But he wouldn't eat, and the glass of milk spilled from his trembling hand.

"I saw it in the Chicago newspaper," he said. "It was all in the Chicago newspaper. I started right away."

"I didn't know how to reach you."

His eyes, seeing nothing, moved ceaselessly about the room.

"It was a madman," he said. "He must have been mad."

"Wouldn't you like some coffee?" I urged him.

"I don't want anything. I'm all right now, Mr.———"

"Carraway."

"Well, I'm all right now. Where have they got Jimmy?"

I took him into the drawing-room, where his son lay, and left him there. Some little boys had come up on the steps and were looking into the hall; when I told them who had arrived, they went reluctantly away.

After a little while Mr. Gatz opened the door and came out, his mouth ajar, his face flushed slightly, his eyes leaking isolated and unpunctual tears. He had reached an age where death no longer has the quality of ghastly surprise, and when he looked around him now for the first time and saw the height and splendor of the hall and the great rooms opening out from it into other rooms, his grief began to be mixed with an awed pride. I helped him to a bedroom upstairs; while he took off his coat and vest I told him that all arrangements had been deferred until he came.

"I didn't know what you'd want, Mr. Gatsby——"

"Gatz is my name."

"——Mr. Gatz. I thought you might want to take the body West."

He shook his head.

"Jimmy always liked it better down East. He rose up to his position in the East. Were you a friend of my boy's, Mr.——?"

"We were close friends."

"He had a big future before him, you know. He was only a young man, but he had a lot of brain power here."

He touched his head impressively, and I nodded.

"If he'd of lived, he'd of been a great man. A man like James J. Hill. He'd of helped build up the country."

"That's true," I said, uncomfortably.

He fumbled at the embroidered coverlet, trying to take it from the bed, and lay down stiffly—was instantly asleep.

That night an obviously frightened person called up, and demanded to know who I was before he would give his name.

"This is Mr. Carraway," I said.

"Oh!" He sounded relieved. "This is Klipspringer."

I was relieved too, for that seemed to promise another friend at Gatsby's grave. I didn't want it to be in the papers and draw a sightseeing crowd, so I'd been calling up a few people myself. They were hard to find.

"The funeral's tomorrow," I said. "Three o'clock, here at the house. I wish you'd tell anybody who'd be interested."

"Oh, I will," he broke out hastily. "Of course I'm not likely to see anybody, but if I do."

His tone made me suspicious.

"Of course you'll be there yourself."

"Well, I'll certainly try. What I called up about is———"

"Wait a minute," I interrupted. "How about saying you'll come?"

"Well, the fact is—the truth of the matter is that I'm staying with some people up here in Greenwich, and they rather expect me to be with them tomorrow. In fact, there's a sort of picnic or something. Of course I'll do my very best to get away."

I ejaculated an unrestrained "Huh!" and he must have heard me, for he went on nervously:

"What I called up about was a pair of shoes I left there. I wonder if it'd be too much trouble to have the butler send them on. You see, they're tennis shoes, and I'm sort of helpless without them. My address is care of B. F.———"

I didn't hear the rest of the name, because I hung up the receiver.

After that I felt a certain shame for Gatsby—one gentleman to whom I telephoned implied that he had got what he deserved. However, that was my fault, for he was one of those who used to sneer most bitterly at Gatsby on the courage of Gatsby's liquor, and I should have known better than to call him.

The morning of the funeral I went up to New York to see Meyer Wolfshiem; I couldn't seem to reach him any other way. The door that I pushed open, on the advice of an elevator boy, was marked "The Swastika Holding Company," and at first there didn't seem to be anyone inside. But when I'd shouted "hello" several times in vain, an argument broke out behind a partition, and presently a lovely Jewess appeared at an interior door and scrutinized me with black hostile eyes.

"Nobody's in," she said. "Mr. Wolfshiem's gone to Chicago."

The first part of this was obviously untrue, for someone had begun to whistle "The Rosary," tunelessly, inside.

"Please say that Mr. Carraway wants to see him."

"I can't get him back from Chicago, can I?"

At this moment a voice, unmistakably Wolfshiem's, called "Stella!" from the other side of the door.

"Leave your name on the desk," she said quickly. "I'll give it to him when he gets back."

"But I know he's there."

She took a step toward me and began to slide her hands indignantly up and down her hips.

"You young men think you can force your way in here any time," she scolded. "We're getting sickantired of it. When I say he's in Chicago, he's in Chicago."

I mentioned Gatsby.

"Oh-h!" She looked at me all over again. "Will you just— What was your name?"

She vanished. In a moment Meyer Wolfshiem stood solemnly in the doorway, holding out both hands. He drew me into his office, remarking in a reverent voice that it was a sad time for all of us, and offered me a cigar.

"My memory goes back to when first I met him," he said. "A young major just out of the army and covered over with medals he got in the war. He was so hard up he had to keep on wearing his uniform because he couldn't buy some regular clothes. First time I saw him was when he come into Winebrenner's poolroom at Forty-third Street and asked for a job. He hadn't eat anything for a couple of days. 'Come on have some lunch with me,' I sid. He ate more than four dollars' worth of food in half an hour."

"Did you start him in business?" I inquired.

"Start him! I made him."

"Oh."

"I raised him up out of nothing, right out of the gutter. I saw right away he was a fine-appearing, gentlemanly young man, and when he told me he was an Oggsford I knew I could use him good. I got him to join up in the American Legion and he used to stand high there. Right off he did some work for a client of mine up to Albany. We were so thick like that in everything"—he held up two bulbous fingers— "always together."

I wondered if this partnership had included the World's Series transaction in 1919.

"Now he's dead," I said after a moment. "You were his closest friend, so I know you'll want to come to his funeral this afternoon."

"I'd like to come."

"Well, come then."

The hair in his nostrils quivered slightly, and as he shook his head his eyes filled with tears.

"I can't do it—I can't get mixed up in it," he said.

"There's nothing to get mixed up in. It's all over now."

"When a man gets killed I never like to get mixed up in it in any way. I keep out. When I was a young man it was different—if a friend of mine died, no matter how, I stuck with them to the end. You may think that's sentimental, but I mean it—to the bitter end."

I saw that for some reason of his own he was determined not to come, so I stood up.

"Are you a college man?" he inquired suddenly.

For a moment I thought he was going to suggest a "gonnegtion," but he only nodded and shook my hand.

"Let us learn to show our friendship for a man when he is alive and not after he is dead," he suggested. "After that my own rule is to let everything alone."

When I left his office the sky had turned dark and I got back to West Egg in a drizzle. After changing my clothes I went next door and found Mr. Gatz walking up and down excitedly in the hall. His pride in his son and in his son's possessions was continually increasing and now he had something to show me.

"Jimmy sent me this picture." He took out his wallet with trembling fingers. "Look there."

It was a photograph of the house, cracked in the corners and dirty with many hands. He pointed out every detail to me eagerly. "Look there!" and then sought admiration from my eyes. He had shown it so often that I think it was more real to him now than the house itself.

"Jimmy sent it to me. I think it's a very pretty picture. It shows up well."

"Very well. Had you seen him lately?"

"He come out to see me two years ago and bought me the house I live in now. Of course we was broke up when he run off from home, but I see now there was a reason for it. He knew he had a big future in front of him. And ever since he made a success he was very generous with me."

He seemed reluctant to put away the picture, held it for another minute, lingeringly, before my eyes. Then he returned the wallet and pulled from his pocket a ragged old copy of a book called "Hopalong Cassidy."

"Look here, this is a book he had when he was a boy. It just shows you."

He opened it at the back cover and turned it around for me to see. On the last fly-leaf was printed the word SCHEDULE, and the date September 1 2, 1 906. And underneath:

Rise from bed	6.00	A.M.
Dumbbell exercise and wall-scaling	6.15–6.30	"
Study electricity, etc.	7.15–8.15	"
Work	8.30–4.30	P.M.
Baseball and sports	4.30–5.00	"
Practice elocution, poise and how to attain it	5.00–6.00	"
Study needed inventions	7.00–9.00	"

GENERAL RESOLVES

No wasting time at Shafters or [a name, indecipherable]
No more smoking or chewing.
Bath every other day
Read one improving book or magazine per week
Save $5.00 [crossed out] $3.00 per week
Be better to parents

"I come across this book by accident," said the old man. "It just shows you, don't it?"

"It just shows you."

"Jimmy was bound to get ahead. He always had some resolves like this or something. Do you notice what he's got about improving his mind? He was always great for that. He told me I et like a hog once, and I beat him for it."

He was reluctant to close the book, reading each item aloud and then looking eagerly at me. I think he rather expected me to copy down the list for my own use.

A little before three the Lutheran minister arrived from Flushing, and I began to look involuntarily out the windows for other cars. So did Gatsby's father. And as the time passed and the servants came in and stood waiting in the hall, his eyes began to blink anxiously, and he spoke of the rain in a worried, uncertain way. The minister glanced several times at his watch, so I took him aside and asked him to wait for half an hour. But it wasn't any use. Nobody came.

◆

About five o'clock our procession of three cars reached the cemetery and stopped in a thick drizzle beside the gate—first a motor-hearse, horribly black and wet, then Mr. Gatz and the minister and I in the limousine, and a little later four or five servants and the postman from West Egg, in Gatsby's station wagon, all wet to the skin. As we started through the gate into the cemetery I heard a car stop and then the sound of someone splashing after us over the soggy ground. I looked around. It was the man with owl-eyed glasses whom I had found marvelling over Gatsby's books in the library one night three months before.

I'd never seen him since then. I don't know how he knew about the funeral, or even his name. The rain poured down his thick glasses, and he took them off and wiped them to see the protecting canvas unrolled from Gatsby's grave.

I tried to think about Gatsby then for a moment, but he was already too far away, and I could only remember, without resentment, that Daisy hadn't sent a message or a flower. Dimly I heard someone murmur "Blessed are the dead that the rain falls on," and then the owl-eyed man said "Amen to that," in a brave voice.

We straggled down quickly through the rain to the cars. Owl Eyes spoke to me by the gate.

"I couldn't get to the house," he remarked.

"Neither could anybody else."

"Go on!" He started. "Why, my God! they used to go there by the hundreds."

He took off his glasses and wiped them again, outside and in.

"The poor son-of-a-bitch," he said.

◆

One of my most vivid memories is of coming back West from prep school and later from college at Christmas time. Those who went farther than Chicago would gather in the old dim Union Station at six o'clock of a December evening, with a few Chicago friends, already caught up into their own holiday gayeties, to bid them a hasty good-by. I remember the fur coats of the girls returning from Miss This-or-That's and the chatter of frozen breath and the hands waving overhead as we caught sight of old acquaintances, and the matchings of invitations: "Are you going to the Ordways'? the Herseys'? the Schultzes'?" and the long green tickets clasped tight in our gloved hands. And last the murky yellow cars of the Chicago, Milwaukee & St. Paul railroad looking cheerful as Christmas itself on the tracks beside the gate.

When we pulled out into the winter night and the real snow, our snow, began to stretch out beside us and twinkle against the windows, and the dim lights of small Wisconsin stations moved by, a sharp wild brace came suddenly into the air. We drew in deep breaths of it as we walked back from dinner through the cold vestibules, unutterably aware of our identity with this country for one strange hour, before we melted indistinguishably into it again.

That's my Middle West—not the wheat or the prairies or the lost Swede towns, but the thrilling returning trains of my youth, and the street lamps and sleigh bells in the frosty dark and the shadows of holly wreaths thrown by lighted windows on the snow. I am part of that, a little solemn with the feel of those long winters, a little complacent from growing up in the Carraway house in a city where dwellings are still called through decades by a family's name. I see now that this has been a story of the West, after all—Tom and Gatsby, Daisy and Jordan and I, were all Westerners, and perhaps we possessed some deficiency in common which made us subtly unadaptable to Eastern life.

Even when the East excited me most, even when I was most keenly aware of its superiority to the bored, sprawling, swollen towns beyond the Ohio, with their interminable inquisitions which spared only the children and the very old—even then it had always for me a quality of distortion. West Egg, especially, still figures in my more fantastic dreams. I see it as a night scene by El Greco: a hundred houses, at once conventional and grotesque, crouching under a sullen, overhanging sky and a lustreless moon. In the foreground four solemn men in dress suits are walking along the sidewalk with a stretcher on which lies a drunken woman in a white evening dress. Her hand, which dangles over the side, sparkles cold with jewels. Gravely the men turn in at a house—the wrong house. But no one knows the woman's name, and no one cares.

After Gatsby's death the East was haunted for me like that, distorted beyond my eyes' power of correction. So when the blue smoke of brittle leaves was in the air and the wind blew the wet laundry stiff on the line I decided to come back home.

There was one thing to be done before I left, an awkward, unpleasant thing that perhaps had better have been let alone. But I wanted to leave things in order and not just trust that obliging and indifferent sea to sweep my refuse away. I saw Jordan Baker and talked over and around what had happened to us together, and what had happened afterward to me, and she lay perfectly still, listening, in a big chair.

She was dressed to play golf, and I remember thinking she looked like a good illustration, her chin raised a little jauntily, her hair the color of an autumn leaf, her face the same brown tint as the fingerless glove on her knee. When I had finished she told me without comment that she was engaged to another man. I doubted that, though there were several she could have married at a nod of her head, but I pretended to be surprised. For just a minute I wondered if I wasn't making a mistake, then I thought it all over again quickly and got up to say good-by.

"Nevertheless you did throw me over," said Jordan suddenly. "You threw me over on the telephone. I don't give a damn about you now, but it was a new experience for me, and I felt a little dizzy for a while."

We shook hands.

"Oh, and do you remember"—she added—"a conversation we had once about driving a car?"

"Why—not exactly."

"You said a bad driver was only safe until she met another bad driver? Well, I met another bad driver, didn't I? I mean it was careless of me to make such a wrong guess. I thought you were rather an honest, straightforward person. I thought it was your secret pride."

"I'm thirty," I said. "I'm five years too old to lie to myself and call it honor."

She didn't answer. Angry, and half in love with her, and tremendously sorry, I turned away.

◆

One afternoon late in October I saw Tom Buchanan. He was walking ahead of me along Fifth Avenue in his alert, aggressive way, his hands out a little from his body as if to fight off interference, his head moving sharply here and there, adapting itself to his restless eyes. Just as I slowed up to avoid overtaking him he stopped and began frowning into the windows of a jewelry store. Suddenly he saw me and walked back, holding out his hand.

"What's the matter, Nick? Do you object to shaking hands with me?"

"Yes. You know what I think of you."

"You're crazy, Nick," he said quickly. "Crazy as hell. I don't know what's the matter with you."

"Tom," I inquired, "what did you say to Wilson that afternoon?"

He stared at me without a word, and I knew I had guessed right about those missing hours. I started to turn away, but he took a step after me and grabbed my arm.

"I told him the truth," he said. "He came to the door while we were getting ready to leave, and when I sent down word that we weren't in he tried to force his way upstairs. He was crazy enough to kill me if I hadn't told him who owned the car. His hand was on a revolver in his pocket every minute he was in the house—" He broke off defiantly. "What if I did tell him? That fellow had it coming to him. He threw dust into your eyes just like he did in Daisy's, but he was a tough one. He ran over Myrtle like you'd run over a dog and never even stopped his car."

There was nothing I could say, except the one unutterable fact that it wasn't true.

"And if you think I didn't have my share of suffering—look here, when I went to give up that flat and saw that damn box of dog biscuits sitting there on the sideboard, I sat down and cried like a baby. By God it was awful———"

I couldn't forgive him or like him, but I saw that what he had done was, to him, entirely justified. It was all very careless and confused. They were careless people, Tom and Daisy—they smashed up things and creatures and then retreated back into their money or their vast carelessness, or whatever it was that kept them together, and let other people clean up the mess they had made. . . .

I shook hands with him; it seemed silly not to, for I felt suddenly as though I were talking to a child. Then he went into the jewelry store to buy a pearl necklace—or perhaps only a pair of cuff buttons—rid of my provincial squeamishness forever.

◆

Gatsby's house was still empty when I left—the grass on his lawn had grown as long as mine. One of the taxi drivers in the village never took a fare past the entrance gate without stopping for a minute and pointing inside; perhaps it was he who drove Daisy and Gatsby over to East Egg the night of the accident, and perhaps he had made a story about it all his own. I didn't want to hear it and I avoided him when I got off the train.

I spent my Saturday nights in New York because those gleaming, dazzling parties of his were with me so vividly that I could still hear the music and the laughter, faint and incessant, from his garden, and the cars going up and down his drive. One night I did hear a material car there, and saw its lights stop at his front steps. But I didn't investigate. Probably it was some final guest who had been away at the ends of the earth and didn't know that the party was over.

On the last night, with my trunk packed and my car sold to the grocer, I went over and looked at that huge incoherent failure of a house once more. On the white steps an obscene word, scrawled by some boy with a piece of brick, stood out clearly in the moonlight, and I erased it, drawing my shoe raspingly along the stone. Then I wandered down to the beach and sprawled out on the sand.

Most of the big shore places were closed now and there were hardly any lights except the shadowy, moving glow of a ferryboat across the Sound. And as the moon rose higher the inessential houses began to melt away until gradually I became aware of the old island here that flowered once for Dutch sailors' eyes—a fresh, green breast of the new world. Its vanished trees, the trees that had made way for Gatsby's house, had once pandered in whispers to the last and greatest of all human dreams; for a transitory enchanted moment man must have held his breath in the presence of this continent, compelled into an æsthetic contemplation he neither understood nor desired, face to face for the last time in history with something commensurate to his capacity for wonder.

And as I sat there brooding on the old, unknown world, I thought of Gatsby's wonder when he first picked out the green light at the end of Daisy's dock. He had come a long way to this blue lawn, and his dream must have seemed so close that he could hardly fail to grasp it. He did not know that it was already behind him, somewhere back in that vast obscurity beyond the city, where the dark fields of the republic rolled on under the night.

Gatsby believed in the green light, the orgastic future that year by year recedes before us. It eluded us then, but that's no matter—tomorrow we will run faster, stretch out our arms farther. . . . And one fine morning——

So we beat on, boats against the current, borne back ceaselessly into the past.

STORIES

THE RICH BOY

B egin with an individual and before you know it you find that you
have created a type; begin with a type, and you find that you have
created—nothing. That is because we are all queer fish, queerer
behind our faces and voices than we want anyone to know or than we
know ourselves. When I hear a man proclaiming himself an "average,
honest, open fellow" I feel pretty sure that he has some definite and
perhaps terrible abnormality which he has agreed to conceal—and
his protestation of being average and honest and open is his way of
reminding himself of his misprision.

There are no types, no plurals. There is a rich boy, and this is his
and not his brothers' story. All my life I have lived among his brothers
but this one has been my friend. Besides, if I wrote about his brothers
I should have to begin by attacking all the lies that the poor have told
about the rich and the rich have told about themselves—such a wild
structure they have erected that when we pick up a book about the
rich, some instinct prepares us for unreality. Even the intelligent and
impassioned reporters of life have made the country of the rich as
unreal as fairyland.

Let me tell you about the very rich. They are different from you and
me. They possess and enjoy early, and it does something to them, makes
them soft where we are hard and cynical where we are trustful, in a way

that, unless you were born rich, it is very difficult to understand. They think, deep in their hearts, that they are better than we are because we had to discover the compensations and refuges of life for ourselves. Even when they enter deep into our world or sink below us, they still think that they are better than we are. They are different. The only way I can describe young Anson Hunter is to approach him as if he were a foreigner and cling stubbornly to my point of view. If I accept his for a moment I am lost—I have nothing to show but a preposterous movie.

II

Anson was the eldest of six children who would some day divide a fortune of fifteen million dollars, and he reached the age of reason—is it seven?—at the beginning of the century when daring young women were already gliding along Fifth Avenue in electric "mobiles." In those days he and his brother had an English governess who spoke the language very clearly and crisply and well, so that the two boys grew to speak as she did—their words and sentences were all crisp and clear and not run together as ours are. They didn't talk exactly like English children but acquired an accent that is peculiar to fashionable people in the city of New York.

In the summer the six children were moved from the house on 71st Street to a big estate in northern Connecticut. It was not a fashionable locality—Anson's father wanted to delay as long as possible his children's knowledge of that side of life. He was a man somewhat superior to his class, which composed New York society, and to his period, which was the snobbish and formalized vulgarity of the Gilded Age, and he wanted his sons to learn habits of concentration and have sound constitutions and grow up into right-living and successful men. He and his wife kept an eye on them as well as they were able until the two older boys went away to school, but in huge establishments this is difficult—it was much simpler in the series of small and medium-sized houses in which my own youth was spent—I was never far out of the reach of my mother's voice, of the sense of her presence, her approval or disapproval.

Anson's first sense of his superiority came to him when he real-ized the half-grudging American deference that was paid to him in the Connecticut village. The parents of the boys he played with always inquired after his father and mother, and were vaguely excited when their own children were asked to the Hunters' house. He accepted this as the natural state of things, and a sort of impatience with all groups of which he was not the center—in money, in position, in authority—remained with him for the rest of his life. He disdained to struggle with other boys for precedence—he expected it to be given him freely and when it wasn't he withdrew into his family. His family was sufficient, for in the East money is still a somewhat feudal thing, a clan-forming thing. In the snobbish West, money separates families to form "sets."

At eighteen, when he went to New Haven, Anson was tall and thick-set with a clear complexion and a healthy color from the ordered life he had led in school. His hair was yellow and grew in a funny way on his head, his nose was beaked—these two things kept him from being handsome—but he had a confident charm and a certain brusque style, and the upper-class men who passed him on the street knew without being told that he was a rich boy and had gone to one of the best schools. Nevertheless his very superiority kept him from being a success in college—the independence was mistaken for egotism, and the refusal to accept Yale standards with the proper awe seemed to belittle all those who had. So, long before he graduated, he began to shift the center of his life to New York.

He was at home in New York—there was his own house with "the kind of servants you can't get anymore"—and his own family, of which, because of his good humor and a certain ability to make things go, he was rapidly becoming the center, and the debutante parties, and the correct manly world of the men's clubs, and the occasional wild spree with the gallant girls whom New Haven only knew from the fifth row. His aspirations were conventional enough—they included even the irreproachable shadow he would someday marry, but they differed from the aspirations of the majority of young men in that there was no mist over them, none of that quality which is variously known as "idealism" or "illusion." Anson accepted without reservation the world of high finance and high extravagance, of divorce and dissipation, of snobbery and of privilege. Most of our lives end as a compromise—it was as a compromise that his life began.

He and I first met in the late summer of 1917 when he was just out of Yale, and, like the rest of us, was swept up into the systematized hysteria of the war. In the blue-green uniform of the naval aviation he came down to Pensacola, where the hotel orchestras played "I'm Sorry, Dear" and we young officers danced with the girls. Everyone liked him, and though he ran with the drinkers and wasn't an especially good pilot, even the instructors treated him with a certain respect. He was always having long talks with them in his confident, logical voice—talks which ended by his getting himself, or more frequently another officer, out of some impending trouble. He was convivial, bawdy, robustly avid for pleasure, and we were all surprised when he fell in love with a conservative and rather proper girl.

Her name was Paula Legendre, a dark, serious beauty from somewhere in California. Her family kept a winter residence just outside of
town, and in spite of her primness she was enormously popular; there
is a large class of men whose egotism can't endure humor in a woman.
But Anson wasn't that sort, and I couldn't understand the attraction of
her "sincerity"—that was the thing to say about her—for his keen and
somewhat sardonic mind.

Nevertheless, they fell in love—and on her terms. He no longer
joined the twilight gathering at the De Soto bar, and whenever they
were seen together they were engaged in a long, serious dialogue,
which must have gone on several weeks. Long afterward he told me
that it was not about anything in particular but was composed on both
sides of immature and even meaningless statements—the emotional
content that gradually came to fill it grew up not out of the words but
out of its enormous seriousness. It was a sort of hypnosis. Often it
was interrupted, giving way to that emasculated humor we call fun;
when they were alone it was resumed again—solemn, low-keyed, and
pitched so as to give each other a sense of unity in feeling and thought.
They came to resent any interruptions of it, to be unresponsive to
facetiousness about life, even to the mild cynicism of their contempo-
raries. They were only happy when the dialogue was going on and its
seriousness bathed them like the amber glow of an open fire. Toward
the end there came an interruption they did not resent—it began to
be interrupted by passion.

Oddly enough Anson was as engrossed in the dialogue as she was
and as profoundly affected by it, yet at the same time aware that, on
his side, much was insincere and, on hers, much was merely simple.
At first, too, he despised her emotional simplicity as well, but with
his love her nature deepened and blossomed and he could despise it

no longer. He felt that if he could enter into Paula's warm safe life he would be happy. The long preparation of the dialogue removed any constraint—he taught her some of what he had learned from more adventurous women and she responded with a rapt holy intensity. One evening after a dance they agreed to marry and he wrote a long letter about her to his mother. The next day Paula told him that she was rich, that she had a personal fortune of nearly a million dollars.

III

It was exactly as if they could say "Neither of us has anything: we shall be poor together"—just as delightful that they should be rich instead. It gave them the same communion of adventure. Yet when Anson got leave in April and Paula and her mother accompanied him north, she was impressed with the standing of his family in New York and with the scale on which they lived. Alone with Anson for the first time in the rooms where he had played as a boy, she was filled with a comfortable emotion, as though she were preeminently safe and taken care of. The pictures of Anson in a skull cap at his first school, of Anson on horseback with the sweetheart of a mysterious forgotten summer, of Anson in a gay group of ushers and bridesmaids at a wedding, made her jealous of his life apart from her in the past, and so completely did his authoritative person seem to sum up and typify these possessions of his that she was inspired with the idea of being married immediately and returning to Pensacola as his wife.

But an immediate marriage wasn't discussed—even the engagement was to be secret until after the war. When she realized that only two days of his leave remained, her dissatisfaction crystallized in the intention of making him as unwilling to wait as she was. They were driving to the country for dinner and she determined to force the issue that night.

Now a cousin of Paula's was staying with them at the Ritz, a severe bitter girl who loved Paula but was somewhat jealous of her impressive engagement, and as Paula was late in dressing, the cousin, who wasn't going to the party, received Anson in the parlor of the suite.

Anson had met friends at five o'clock and drunk freely and indiscreetly with them for an hour. He left the Yale Club at a proper time, and his mother's chauffeur drove him to the Ritz, but his usual capacity was not in evidence, and the impact of the steam-heated sitting-room made him suddenly dizzy. He knew it, and he was both amused and sorry.

Paula's cousin was twenty-five, but she was exceptionally naive, and at first failed to realize what was up. She had never met Anson before, and she was surprised when he mumbled strange information and nearly fell off his chair, but until Paula appeared it didn't occur to her that what she had taken for the odor of a dry-cleaned uniform was really whiskey. But Paula understood as soon as she appeared; her only thought was to get Anson away before her mother saw him, and at the look in her eyes the cousin understood too.

When Paula and Anson descended to the limousine they found two men inside, both asleep; they were the men with whom he had been drinking at the Yale Club, and they were also going to the party. He had entirely forgotten their presence in the car. On the way to Hempstead they awoke and sang. Some of the songs were rough, and though Paula tried to reconcile herself to the fact that Anson had few verbal inhibitions, her lips tightened with shame and distaste.

Back at the hotel the cousin, confused and agitated, considered the incident, and then walked into Mrs. Legendre's bedroom saying: "Isn't he funny?"

"Who is funny?"

"Why—Mr. Hunter. He seemed so funny."

Mrs. Legendre looked at her sharply.

"How is he funny?"

"Why, he said he was French. I didn't know he was French."

"That's absurd. You must have misunderstood." She smiled: "It was a joke."

The cousin shook her head stubbornly.

"No. He said he was brought up in France. He said he couldn't speak any English and that's why he couldn't talk to me. And he couldn't!"

Mrs. Legendre looked away with impatience just as the cousin added thoughtfully, "Perhaps it was because he was so drunk," and walked out of the room.

This curious report was true. Anson, finding his voice thick and uncontrollable, had taken the unusual refuge of announcing that he spoke no English. Years afterward he used to tell that part of the story, and he invariably communicated the uproarious laughter which the memory aroused in him.

Five times in the next hour Mrs. Legendre tried to get Hempstead on the phone. When she succeeded there was a ten-minute delay before she heard Paula's voice on the wire.

"Cousin Jo told me Anson was intoxicated."

"Oh, no. . . ."

"Oh, yes. Cousin Jo says he was intoxicated. He told her he was French and fell off his chair and behaved as if he was very intoxicated. I don't want you to come home with him."

"Mother, he's all right! Please don't worry about—"

"But I do worry. I think it's dreadful. I want you to promise me not to come home with him."

"I'll take care of it, Mother. . . ."

"I don't want you to come home with him."

"All right, Mother. Good-bye."

"Be sure now, Paula. Ask someone to bring you."

Deliberately Paula took the receiver from her ear and hung it up. Her face was flushed with helpless annoyance. Anson was stretched asleep out in a bedroom upstairs, while the dinner party below was proceeding lamely toward conclusion.

The hour's drive had sobered him somewhat—his arrival was merely hilarious—and Paula hoped that the evening was not spoiled after all, but two imprudent cocktails before dinner completed the disaster. He talked boisterously and somewhat offensively to the party at large for fifteen minutes and then slid silently under the table, like a man in an old print—but, unlike an old print, it was rather horrible without being at all quaint. None of the young girls present remarked upon the incident—it seemed to merit only silence. His uncle and two other men carried him upstairs, and it was just after this that Paula was called to the phone.

An hour later Anson awoke in a fog of nervous agony, through which he perceived after a moment the figure of his Uncle Robert standing by the door.

". . . I said are you better?"

"What?"

"Do you feel better, old man?"

"Terrible," said Anson.

"I'm going to try you on another bromo-seltzer. If you can hold it down, it'll do you good to sleep."

With an effort Anson slid his legs from the bed and stood up.

"I'm all right," he said dully.

"Take it easy."

"I thin' if you gave me a glassbrandy I could go downstairs."

"Oh, no—"

"Yes, that's the only thin'. I'm all right now. . . . I suppose I'm in Dutch dow' there."

"They know you're a little under the weather," said his uncle deprecatingly. "But don't worry about it. Schuyler didn't even get here. He passed away in the locker room over at the Links."

Indifferent to any opinion, except Paula's, Anson was nevertheless determined to save the debris of the evening, but when after a cold bath he made his appearance most of the party had already left. Paula got up immediately to go home.

In the limousine the old serious dialogue began. She had known that he drank, she admitted, but she had never expected anything like this—it seemed to her that perhaps they were not suited to each other, after all. Their ideas about life were too different, and so forth. When she finished speaking, Anson spoke in turn, very soberly. Then Paula said she'd have to think it over; she wouldn't decide tonight; she was not angry but she was terribly sorry. Nor would she let him come into the hotel with her, but just before she got out of the car she leaned and kissed him unhappily on the cheek.

The next afternoon Anson had a long talk with Mrs. Legendre while Paula sat listening in silence. It was agreed that Paula was to brood over the incident for a proper period and then, if mother and daughter thought it best, they would follow Anson to Pensacola. On his part he apologized with sincerity and dignity—that was all; with every card in her hand Mrs. Legendre was unable to establish any advantage over him. He made no promises, showed no humility, only delivered a few serious comments on life which brought him off with rather a moral superiority at the end. When they came south three weeks later, neither Anson in his satisfaction nor Paula in her relief at the reunion realized that the psychological moment had passed forever.

IV

He dominated and attracted her and at the same time filled her with anxiety. Confused by his mixture of solidity and self-indulgence, of sentiment and cynicism—incongruities which her gentle mind was unable to resolve—Paula grew to think of him as two alternating personalities. When she saw him alone, or at a formal party, or with his casual inferiors, she felt a tremendous pride in his strong attractive presence, the paternal, understanding stature of his mind. In other company she became uneasy when what had been a fine imperviousness to mere gentility showed its other face. The other face was gross, humorous, reckless of everything but pleasure. It startled her mind temporarily away from him, even led her into a short covert experiment with an old beau, but it was no use—after four months of Anson's enveloping vitality there was an anaemic pallor in all other men.

In July he was ordered abroad and their tenderness and desire reached a crescendo. Paula considered a last-minute marriage— decided against it only because there were always cocktails on his breath now, but the parting itself made her physically ill with grief. After his departure she wrote him long letters of regret for the days of love they had missed by waiting. In August Anson's plane slipped down into the North Sea. He was pulled onto a destroyer after a night in the water and sent to hospital with pneumonia; the armistice was signed before he was finally sent home.

Then, with every opportunity given back to them, with no material obstacle to overcome, the secret weavings of their temperaments came between them, drying up their kisses and their tears, making their voices less loud to one another, muffling the intimate chatter of their hearts until the old communication was only possible by letters from far away. One afternoon a society reporter waited for two hours in the Hunters' house for a confirmation of their engagement. Anson denied it; nevertheless an early issue carried the report as a leading paragraph—they were "constantly seen together at Southampton, Hot Springs, and Tuxedo Park." But the serious dialogue had turned a corner into a long, sustained quarrel, and the affair was almost played out. Anson got drunk flagrantly and missed an engagement with her, whereupon Paula made certain behavioristic demands. His despair was helpless before his pride and his knowledge of himself: the engagement was definitely broken.

"Dearest," said their letters now, "Dearest, Dearest, when I wake up in the middle of the night and realize that after all it was not to be, I feel that I want to die. I can't go on living anymore. Perhaps when we meet this summer we may talk things over and decide differently—we were so excited and sad that day and I don't feel that I can live all my life without you. You speak of other people. Don't you know there are no other people for me but only you. . . ."

But as Paula drifted here and there around the East she would sometimes mention her gaieties to make him wonder. Anson was too acute to wonder. When he saw a man's name in her letters he felt more sure of her and a little disdainful—he was always superior to such things. But he still hoped that they would someday marry.

Meanwhile he plunged vigorously into all the movement and glitter of post-bellum New York, entering a brokerage house, joining half a dozen clubs, dancing late, and moving in three worlds—his own world, the world of young Yale graduates, and that section of the half-world which rests one end on Broadway. But there was always a thorough and infractible eight hours devoted to his work in Wall Street, where the combination of his influential family connection, his sharp intelligence, and his abundance of sheer physical energy brought him almost immediately forward. He had one of those invaluable minds with partitions in it; sometimes he appeared at his office refreshed by less than an hour's sleep, but such occurrences were rare. So early as 1920 his income in salary and commissions exceeded twelve thousand dollars.

As the Yale tradition slipped into the past he became more and more of a popular figure among his classmates in New York, more popular than he had ever been in college. He lived in a great house and had the means of introducing young men into other great houses. Moreover, his life already seemed secure, while theirs, for the most part, had arrived again at precarious beginnings. They commenced to turn to him for amusement and escape, and Anson responded readily, taking pleasure in helping people and arranging their affairs.

There were no men in Paula's letters now but a note of tenderness ran through them that had not been there before. From several sources he heard that she had "a heavy beau," Lowell Thayer, a Bostonian of wealth and position, and though he was sure she still loved him, it made him uneasy to think that he might lose her after all. Save for one unsatisfactory day she had not been in New York for almost five months, and as the rumors multiplied he became increasingly anxious to see her. In February he took his vacation and went down to Florida.

Palm Beach sprawled plump and opulent between the sparkling sapphire of Lake Worth, flawed here and there by house-boats at anchor, and the great turquoise bar of the Atlantic Ocean. The huge bulks of the Breakers and the Royal Poinciana rose as twin paunches from the bright level of the sand and around them clustered the Dancing Glade, Bradley's House of Chance and a dozen modistes and milliners with goods at triple prices from New York. Upon the trellissed verandah of the Breakers two hundred women stepped right, stepped left, wheeled and slid in that then celebrated calisthenic known as the double-shuffle, while in half-time to the music two thousand bracelets clicked up and down on two hundred arms.

At the Everglades Club after dark Paula and Lowell Thayer and Anson and a casual fourth played bridge with hot cards. It seemed to Anson that her kind serious face was wan and tired—she had been around now for four, five years. He had known her for three.

"Two spades."

"Cigarette? . . . Oh, I beg your pardon. By me."

"By."

"I'll double three spades."

There were a dozen tables of bridge in the room, which was filling up with smoke. Anson's eyes met Paula's, held them persistently even when Thayer's glance fell between them. . . .

"What was bid?" he asked abstractedly.

"Rose of Washington Square"

sang the young people in the corners:

> *"I'm withering there*
> *In basement air—"*

The smoke banked like fog, and the opening of a door filled the room with blown swirls of ectoplasm. Little Bright Eyes streaked past the tables seeking Mr. Conan Doyle among the Englishmen who were posing as Englishmen about the lobby.

"You could cut it with a knife."

". . . cut it with a knife."

". . . a knife."

At the end of the rubber Paula suddenly got up and spoke to Anson in a tense, low voice. With scarcely a glance at Lowell Thayer, they walked out the door and descended a long flight of stone steps—in a moment they were walking hand in hand along the moonlit beach.

"Darling, darling. . . ."They embraced recklessly, passionately, in a shadow. . . .Then Paula drew back her face to let his lips say what she wanted to hear—she could feel the words forming as they kissed again. . . . Again she broke away, listening, but as he pulled her close once more she realized that he had said nothing—only *Darling! Darling!"* in that deep, sad whisper that always made her cry. Humbly, obediently, her emotions yielded to him and the tears streamed down her face, but her heart kept on crying: "Ask me—Oh, Anson, dearest, ask me!"

"Paula. . . . *Paula!"*

The words wrung her heart like hands and Anson feeling her tremble knew that emotion was enough. He need say no more, commit their destinies to no practical enigma. Why should he, when he might hold her so, biding his own time, for another year—forever? He was considering them both, her more than himself. For a moment, when she said suddenly that she must go back to her hotel, he hesitated, thinking first, "This is the moment after all," and then: "No, let it wait—she is mine. . . ."

He had forgotten that Paula too was worn away inside with the strain of three years. Her mood passed forever in the night.

He went back to New York next morning filled with a certain restless dissatisfaction. Late in April, without warning, he received a telegram from Bar Harbor in which Paula told him that she was engaged to Lowell Thayer and that they would be married immediately in Boston. What he never really believed could happen had happened at last.

Anson filled himself with whiskey that morning, and going to the office, carried on his work without a break—rather with a fear of what would happen if he stopped. In the evening he went out as usual, saying nothing of what had occurred; he was cordial, humorous, unabstracted. But one thing he could not help—for three days, in any place, in any company, he would suddenly bend his head into his hands and cry like a child.

V

In 1922 when Anson went abroad with the junior partner to investigate some London loans, the journey intimated that he was to be taken into the firm. He was twenty-seven now, a little heavy without being definitely stout, and with a manner older than his years. Old people and young people liked him and trusted him, and mothers felt safe when their daughters were in his charge, for he had a way, when he came into a room, of putting himself on a footing with the oldest and most conservative people there. "You and I," he seemed to say, "we're solid. We understand."

He had an instinctive and rather charitable knowledge of the weaknesses of men and women, and, like a priest, it made him the more concerned for the maintenance of outward forms. It was typical of him that every Sunday morning he taught in a fashionable Episcopal Sunday school—even though a cold shower and a quick change into a cutaway coat were all that separated him from the wild night before.

After his father's death he was the practical head of his family, and, in effect, guided the destinies of the younger children. Through a complication his authority did not extend to his father's estate, which was administrated by his Uncle Robert, who was the horsey member of the family, a good-natured, hard-drinking member of that set which centers about Wheatley Hills.

Uncle Robert and his wife, Edna, had been great friends of Anson's youth, and the former was disappointed when his nephew's superiority failed to take a horsey form. He backed him for a city club which was the most difficult in America to enter—one could only join if one's family had "helped to build up New York" (or, in other words, were rich before 1880)—and when Anson, after his election, neglected it for the Yale Club, Uncle Robert gave him a little talk on the subject. But when on top of that Anson declined to enter Robert Hunter's own conservative and somewhat neglected brokerage house, his manner grew cooler. Like a primary teacher who has taught all he knew, he slipped out of Anson's life.

There were so many friends in Anson's life—scarcely one for whom he had not done some unusual kindness and scarcely one whom he did not occasionally embarrass by his bursts of rough conversation or his habit of getting drunk whenever and however he liked. It annoyed him when anyone else blundered in that regard—about his own lapses he was always humorous. Odd things happened to him and he told them with infectious laughter.

I was working in New York that spring, and I used to lunch with him at the Yale Club, which my university was sharing until the completion of our own. I had read of Paula's marriage, and one afternoon, when I asked him about her, something moved him to tell me the story. After that he frequently invited me to family dinners at his house and behaved as though there was a special relation between us, as though with his confidence a little of that consuming memory had passed into me.

I found that despite the trusting mothers, his attitude toward girls was not indiscriminately protective. It was up to the girl—if she showed an inclination toward looseness, she must take care of herself, even with him.

"Life," he would explain sometimes, "has made a cynic of me."

By life he meant Paula. Sometimes, especially when he was drinking, it became a little twisted in his mind, and he thought that she had callously thrown him over.

This "cynicism," or rather his realization that naturally fast girls were not worth sparing, led to his affair with Dolly Karger. It wasn't his only affair in those years, but it came nearest to touching him deeply, and it had a profound effect upon his attitude toward life.

Dolly was the daughter of a notorious "publicist" who had married into society. She herself grew up into the Junior League, came out at the Plaza, and went to the Assembly; and only a few old families like the Hunters could question whether or not she "belonged," for her picture was often in the papers, and she had more enviable attention than many girls who undoubtedly did. She was dark-haired with carmine lips and a high lovely color which she concealed under pinkish-grey powder

all through the first year out, because high color was unfashionable—
Victorian-pale was the thing to be. She wore black, severe suits and
stood with her hands in her pockets, leaning a little forward, with
a humorous restraint on her face. She danced exquisitely—better
than anything she liked to dance—better than anything except making love. Since she was ten she had always been in love, and, usually,
with some boy who didn't respond to her. Those who did—and there
were many—bored her after a brief encounter, but for her failures
she reserved the warmest spot in her heart. When she met them she
would always try once more—sometimes she succeeded, more often
she failed.

It never occurred to this gypsy of the unattainable that there was
a certain resemblance in those who refused to love her—they shared
a hard intuition that saw through to her weakness, not a weakness of
emotion but a weakness of rudder. Anson perceived this when he first
met her, less than a month after Paula's marriage. He was drinking
rather heavily, and he pretended for a week that he was falling in love
with her. Then he dropped her abruptly and forgot—immediately he
took up the commanding position in her heart.

Like so many girls of that day Dolly was slackly and indiscreetly
wild. The unconventionality of a slightly older generation had been simply one facet of a post-war movement to discredit obsolete manners—
Dolly's was both older and shabbier, and she saw in Anson the two
extremes which the emotionally shiftless woman seeks, an abandon to
indulgence alternating with a protective strength. In his character she
felt both the sybarite and the solid rock, and these two satisfied every
need of her nature.

She felt that it was going to be difficult, but she mistook the
reason—she thought that Anson and his family expected a more

spectacular marriage, but she guessed immediately that her advantage lay in his tendency to drink.

They met at the large debutante dances, but as her infatuation increased they managed to be more and more together. Like most mothers Mrs. Karger believed that Anson was exceptionally reliable, so she allowed Dolly to go with him to distant country clubs and suburban houses without inquiring closely into their activities or questioning her explanations when they came in late. At first these explanations might have been accurate, but Dolly's worldly ideas of capturing Anson were soon engulfed in the rising sweep of her emotion. Kisses in the back of taxis and motor cars were no longer enough; they did a curious thing:

They dropped out of their world for awhile and made another world just beneath it where Anson's tippling and Dolly's irregular hours would be less noticed and commented on. It was composed, this world, of varying elements—several of Anson's Yale friends and their wives, two or three young brokers and bond salesmen and a handful of unattached men, fresh from college, with money and a propensity to dissipation. What this world lacked in spaciousness and scale it made up for by allowing them a liberty that it scarcely permitted itself. Moreover it centered around them and permitted Dolly the pleasure of a faint condescension—a pleasure which Anson, whose whole life was a condescension from the certitudes of his childhood, was unable to share.

He was not in love with her and in the long feverish winter of their affair he frequently told her so. In the spring he was weary—he wanted to renew his life at some other source—moreover, he saw that either he must break with her now or accept the responsibility of a definite seduction. Her family's encouraging attitude precipitated his decision—one evening when Mr. Karger knocked discreetly at the library door to announce that he had left a bottle of old brandy in the dining room, Anson felt that life was hemming him in. That night he wrote her a short letter in which he told her that he was going on his vacation and that in view of all the circumstances they had better meet no more.

It was June. His family had closed up the house and gone to the country, so he was living temporarily at the Yale Club. I had heard about his affair with Dolly as it developed—accounts salted with humor, for he despised unstable women, and granted them no place in the social edifice in which he believed—and when he told me that night that he was definitely breaking with her I was glad. I had seen Dolly here and there and each time with a feeling of pity at the hopelessness of her struggle, and of shame at knowing so much about her that I had no right to know. She was what is known as "a pretty little thing," but there was a certain recklessness which rather fascinated me. Her dedication to the goddess of waste would have been less obvious had she been less spirited—she would most certainly throw herself away, but I was glad when I heard that the sacrifice would not be consummated in my sight.

Anson was going to leave the letter of farewell at her house next morning. It was one of the few houses left open in the Fifth Avenue district, and he knew that the Kargers, acting upon erroneous information from Dolly, had foregone a trip abroad to give their daughter her chance. As he stepped out the door of the Yale Club into Vanderbilt Avenue the postman passed him, and he followed back inside. The first letter that caught his eye was in Dolly's hand.

He knew what it would be—a lonely and tragic monologue, full of the reproaches he knew, the invoked memories, the "I wonder if's"—all the immemorial intimacies that he had communicated to Paula Legendre in what seemed another age. Thumbing over some bills, he brought it on top again and opened it. To his surprise it was a short, somewhat formal note, which said that Dolly would be unable to go to the country with him for the week-end, because Perry Hull from Chicago had unexpectedly come to town. It added that Anson had brought this on himself: "—if I felt that you loved me as I love you I would go with you at any time any place, but Perry is *so* nice, and he so much wants me to marry him—"

Anson smiled contemptuously—he had had experience with such decoy epistles. Moreover, he knew how Dolly had labored over this plan, probably sent for the faithful Perry and calculated the time of his arrival—even labored over the note so that it would make him jealous without driving him away. Like most compromises it had neither force nor vitality but only a timorous despair.

Suddenly he was angry. He sat down in the lobby and read it again. Then he went to the phone, called Dolly and told her in his clear, compelling voice that he had received her note and would call for her at five o'clock as they had previously planned. Scarcely waiting for the pretended uncertainty of her "Perhaps I can see you for an hour," he hung up the receiver and went down to his office. On the way he tore his own letter into bits and dropped it in the street.

He was not jealous—she meant nothing to him—but at her pathetic ruse everything stubborn and self-indulgent in him came to the surface. It was a presumption from a mental inferior and it could not be overlooked. If she wanted to know to whom she belonged she would see.

He was on the doorstep at quarter past five. Dolly was dressed for the street, and he listened in silence to the paragraph of "I can only see you for an hour," which she had begun on the phone.

"Put on your hat, Dolly," he said, "we'll take a walk."

They strolled up Madison Avenue and over to Fifth while Anson's shirt dampened upon his portly body in the deep heat. He talked little, scolding her, making no love to her, but before they had walked six blocks she was his again, apologizing for the note, offering not to see Perry at all as an atonement, offering anything. She thought that he had come because he was beginning to love her.

"I'm hot," he said when they reached 71st Street. "This is a winter suit. If I stop by the house and change, would you mind waiting for me downstairs? I'll only be a minute."

She was happy; the intimacy of his being hot, of any physical fact about him, thrilled her. When they came to the iron-grated door and Anson took out his key she experienced a sort of delight.

Downstairs it was dark, and after he ascended in the lift Dolly raised a curtain and looked out through opaque lace at the houses over the way. She heard the lift machinery stop and, with the notion of teasing him, pressed the button that brought it down. Then on what was more than an impulse she got into it and sent it up to what she guessed was his floor.

"Anson," she called, laughing a little.

"Just a minute," he answered from his bedroom . . . then after a brief delay: "Now you can come in."

He had changed and was buttoning his vest.

"This is my room," he said lightly. "How do you like it?"

She caught sight of Paula's picture on the wall and stared at it in fascination, just as Paula had stared at the pictures of Anson's child-ish sweethearts five years before. She knew something about Paula—sometimes she tortured herself with fragments of the story.

Suddenly she came close to Anson, raising her arms. They embraced. Outside the area window a soft artificial twilight already hovered, though the sun was still bright on a back roof across the way. In half an hour the room would be quite dark. The uncalculated opportunity overwhelmed them, made them both breathless, and they clung more closely. It was imminent, inevitable. Still holding one another, they raised their heads—their eyes fell together upon Paula's picture, staring down at them from the wall.

Suddenly Anson dropped his arms, and sitting down at his desk tried the drawer with a bunch of keys.

"Like a drink?" he asked in a gruff voice.

"No, Anson."

He poured himself half a tumbler of whiskey, swallowed it and then opened the door into the hall.

"Come on," he said.

Dolly hesitated.

"Anson—I'm going to the country with you tonight, after all. You understand that, don't you?"

"Of course," he answered brusquely.

In Dolly's car they rode out to Long Island, closer in their emotions than they had ever been before. They knew what would happen—not with Paula's face to remind them that something was lacking, but when they were alone in the still hot Long Island night that did not care.

The estate in Port Washington where they were to spend the week-end belonged to a cousin of Anson's who had married a Montana copper operator. An interminable drive began at the lodge and twisted under imported poplar saplings toward a huge, pink, Spanish house. Anson had often visited there before.

After dinner they danced at the Linx Club. About midnight Anson assured himself that his cousins would not leave before two—then he explained that Dolly was tired; he would take her home and return to the dance later. Trembling a little with excitement they got into a borrowed car together and drove to Port Washington. As they reached the lodge he stopped and spoke to the night-watchman.

"When are you making a round, Carl?"

"Right away."

"Then you'll be here till everybody's in?"

"Yes, sir."

"All right. Listen: if any automobile, no matter whose it is, turns in at this gate, I want you to phone the house immediately." He put a five-dollar bill into Carl's hand. "Is that clear?"

"Yes, Mr. Anson." Being of the Old World, he neither winked nor smiled. Yet Dolly sat with her face turned slightly away.

Anson had a key. Once inside he poured a drink for both of them— Dolly left hers untouched—then he ascertained definitely the location of the phone, and found that it was within easy hearing distance of their rooms, both of which were on the first floor.

Five minutes later he knocked at the door of Dolly's room.

"Anson?" He went in, closing the door behind him. She was in bed, leaning up anxiously with elbows on the pillow; sitting beside her he took her in his arms.

"Anson, darling."

He didn't answer.

"Anson. . . . Anson! I love you. . . . Say you love me. Say it now— can't you say it now? Even if you don't mean it?"

He did not listen. Over her head he perceived that the picture of Paula was hanging here upon this wall.

He got up and went close to it. The frame gleamed faintly with thrice-reflected moonlight—within was a blurred shadow of a face that he saw he did not know. Almost sobbing, he turned around and stared with abomination at the little figure on the bed.

"This is all foolishness," he said thickly. "I don't know what I was thinking about. I don't love you and you'd better wait for somebody that loves you. I don't love you a bit, can't you understand?"

His voice broke and he went hurriedly out. Back in the salon he was pouring himself a drink with uneasy fingers, when the front door opened suddenly, and his cousin came in.

"Why, Anson, I hear Dolly's sick," she began solicitously. "I hear she's sick. . . ."

"It was nothing," he interrupted, raising his voice so that it would carry into Dolly's room. "She was a little tired. She went to bed."

For a long time afterwards Anson believed that a protective God sometimes interfered in human affairs. But Dolly Karger, lying awake and staring at the ceiling, never again believed in anything at all.

VI

When Dolly married during the following autumn, Anson was in London on business. Like Paula's marriage, it was sudden, but it affected him in a different way. At first he felt that it was funny and had an inclination to laugh when he thought of it. Later it depressed him—it made him feel old.

There was something repetitive about it—why, Paula and Dolly had belonged to different generations. He had a foretaste of the sensation of a man of forty who hears that the daughter of an old flame has married. He wired congratulations and, as was not the case with Paula, they were sincere—he had never really hoped that Paula would be happy.

When he returned to New York, he was made a partner in the firm, and as his responsibilities increased he had less time on his hands. The refusal of a life-insurance company to issue him a policy made such an impression on him that he stopped drinking for a year and claimed that he felt better physically, though I think he missed the convivial recounting of those Celliniesque adventures which, in his early twenties, had played such a part in his life. But he never abandoned the Yale Club. He was a figure there, a personality, and the tendency of his class, who were now seven years out of college, to drift away to more sober haunts was checked by his presence.

His day was never too full nor his mind too weary to give any sort of aid to anyone who asked it. What had been done at first through pride and superiority had become a habit and a passion. And there was always something—a younger brother in trouble at New Haven, a quarrel to be patched up between a friend and his wife, a position to be found for this man, an investment for that. But his specialty was the solving of problems for young married people. Young married people fascinated him and their apartments were almost sacred to him—he knew the story of their love affair, advised them where to live and how, and remembered their babies' names. Toward young wives his attitude was circumspect: he never abused the trust which their husbands—strangely enough in view of his unconcealed irregularities—invariably reposed in him.

He came to take a vicarious pleasure in happy marriages and to be inspired to an almost equally pleasant melancholy by those that went astray. Not a season passed that he did not witness the collapse of an affair that perhaps he himself had fathered. When Paula was divorced and almost immediately remarried to another Bostonian, he talked about her to me all one afternoon. He would never love anyone as he had loved Paula, but he insisted that he no longer cared.

"I'll never marry," he came to say; "I've seen too much of it, and I know a happy marriage is a very rare thing. Besides, I'm too old."

But he did believe in marriage. Like all men who spring from a happy and successful marriage, he believed in it passionately—nothing he had seen would change his belief, his cynicism dissolved upon it like air. But he did really believe he was too old. At twenty-eight he began to accept with equanimity the prospect of marrying without romantic love; he resolutely chose a New York girl of his own class, pretty, intelligent, congenial, above reproach—and set about falling in love with her. The things he had said to Paula with sincerity, to other girls with grace, he could no longer say at all without smiling, or with the force necessary to convince.

"When I'm forty," he told his friends, "I'll be ripe. I'll fall for some chorus girl like the rest."

Nevertheless he persisted in his attempt. His mother wanted to see him married, and he could now well afford it—he had a seat on the stock exchange, and his earned income came to twenty-five thousand a year. The idea was agreeable: when his friends—he spent most of his time with the set he and Dolly had evolved—closed themselves in behind domestic doors at night, he no longer rejoiced in his freedom. He even wondered if he should have married Dolly. Not even Paula had loved him more, and he was learning the rarity, in a single life, of encountering true emotion.

Just as this mood began to creep over him a disquieting story reached his ear. His Aunt Edna, a woman just this side of forty, was carrying on an open intrigue with a dissolute, hard-drinking young man named Cary Sloane. Everyone knew of it except Anson's Uncle Robert, who for fifteen years had talked long in clubs and taken his wife for granted.

Anson heard the story again and again with increasing annoyance. Something of his old feeling for his uncle came back to him, a feeling that was more than personal, a reversion toward that family solidarity on which he had based his pride. His intuition singled out the essential point of the affair, which was that his uncle shouldn't be hurt. It was his first experiment in unsolicited meddling, but with his knowledge of Edna's character he felt that he could handle the matter better than a district judge, or his uncle.

His uncle was in Hot Springs. Anson traced down the sources of the scandal so that there should be no possibility of mistake and then he called Edna and asked her to lunch with him at the Plaza next day. Something in his tone must have frightened her, for she was reluctant, but he insisted, putting off the date until she had no excuse for refusing.

She met him at the appointed time in the Plaza lobby, a lovely, faded, grey-eyed blonde in a coat of Russian sable. Five great rings, cold with diamonds and emeralds, sparkled on her slender hands. It occurred to Anson that it was his father's intelligence and not his uncle's that had earned the fur and the stones, the rich brilliance that buoyed up her passing beauty.

Though Edna scented his hostility, she was unprepared for the directness of his approach.

"Edna, I'm astonished at the way you've been acting," he said in a strong frank voice. "At first I couldn't believe it."

"Believe what?" she demanded sharply.

"You needn't pretend with me, Edna. I'm talking about Cary Sloane. Aside from any other consideration, I didn't think you could treat Uncle Robert—"

"Now look here, Anson—" she began angrily, but his peremptory voice broke through hers:

"—and your children in such a way. You've been married eighteen years, and you're old enough to know better."

"You can't talk to me like that! You—"

"Yes I can. Uncle Robert has always been my best friend." He was tremendously moved. He felt a real distress about his uncle, about his three young cousins.

Edna stood up, leaving her crab-flake cocktail untasted.

"This is the silliest thing—"

"Very well, if you won't listen to me I'll go to Uncle Robert and tell him the whole story—he's bound to hear it sooner or later. And afterwards I'll go to old Moses Sloane."

Edna faltered back into her chair.

"Don't talk so loud," she begged him. Her eyes blurred with tears. "You have no idea how your voice carries. You might have chosen a less public place to make all these crazy accusations."

He didn't answer.

"Oh, you never liked me, I know," she went on. "You're just taking advantage of some silly gossip to try and break up the only interesting friendship I've ever had. What did I ever do to make you hate me so?"

Still Anson waited. There would be the appeal to his chivalry, then to his pity, finally to his superior sophistication—when he had shouldered his way through all these there would be admissions, and he could come to grips with her. By being silent, by being impervious, by returning constantly to his main weapon, which was his own true emotion, he bullied her into frantic despair as the luncheon hour slipped away. At two o'clock she took out a mirror and a handkerchief, shined away the marks of her tears and powdered the slight hollows where they had lain. She had agreed to meet him at her own house at five.

When he arrived she was stretched on a chaise-longue which was covered with cretonne for the summer, and the tears he had called up at luncheon seemed still to be standing in her eyes. Then he was aware of Cary Sloane's dark anxious presence upon the cold hearth.

"What's this idea of yours?" broke out Sloane immediately. "I understand you invited Edna to lunch and then threatened her on the basis of some cheap scandal."

Anson sat down.

"I have no reason to think it's only scandal."

"I hear you're going to take it to Robert Hunter and to my father."

Anson nodded.

"Either you break it off—or I will," he said.

"What God damned business is it of yours, Hunter?"

"Don't lose your temper, Cary," said Edna nervously. "It's only a question of showing him how absurd—"

"For one thing, it's my name that's being handed around," interrupted Anson. "That's all that concerns you, Cary."

"Edna isn't a member of your family."

"She most certainly is!" His anger mounted. "Why—she owes this house and the rings on her fingers to my father's brains. When Uncle Robert married her she didn't have a penny."

They all looked at the rings as if they had a significant bearing on the situation. Edna made a gesture to take them from her hand.

"I guess they're not the only rings in the world," said Sloane.

"Oh, this is absurd," cried Edna. "Anson, will you listen to me? I've found out how the silly story started. It was a maid I discharged who went right to the Chilicheffs—all these Russians pump things out of their servants and then put a false meaning on them." She brought down her fist angrily on the table: "And after Tom lent them the limousine for a whole month when we were south last winter—"

"Do you see?" demanded Sloane eagerly. "This maid got hold of the wrong end of the thing. She knew that Edna and I were friends, and she carried it to the Chilicheffs. In Russia they assume that if a man and a woman——"

He enlarged the theme to a disquisition upon social relations in the Caucasus.

"If that's the case it better be explained to Uncle Robert," said Anson dryly, "so that when the rumors do reach him he'll know they're not true."

Adopting the method he had followed with Edna at luncheon he let them explain it all away. He knew that they were guilty and that presently they would cross the line from explanation into justification and convict themselves more definitely than he could ever do. By seven they had taken the desperate step of telling him the truth—Robert Hunter's neglect, Edna's empty life, the casual dalliance that had flamed up into passion—but like so many true stories it had the misfortune of being old, and its enfeebled body beat helplessly against the armor of Anson's will. The threat to go to Sloane's father sealed their helplessness, for the latter, a retired cotton broker out of Alabama, was a notorious fundamentalist who controlled his son by a rigid allowance and the promise that at his next vagary the allowance would stop forever.

They dined at a small French restaurant and the discussion continued—at one time Sloane resorted to physical threats, a little later they were both imploring him to give them time. But Anson was obdurate. He saw that Edna was breaking up and that her spirit must not be refreshed by any renewal of their passion.

At two o'clock in a small night-club on 53d Street, Edna's nerves suddenly collapsed and she cried to go home. Sloane had been drinking heavily all evening, and he was faintly maudlin, leaning on the table and weeping a little with his face in his hands. Quickly Anson gave them his terms. Sloane was to leave town for six months, and he must be gone within forty-eight hours. When he returned there was to be no resumption of the affair, but at the end of a year Edna might, if she wished, tell Robert Hunter that she wanted a divorce and go about it in the usual way.

He paused, gaining confidence from their faces for his final word.

"Or there's another thing you can do," he said slowly. "If Edna wants to leave her children, there's nothing I can do to prevent your running off together."

"I want to go home!" cried Edna again. "Oh, haven't you done enough to us for one day?"

Outside it was dark, save for a blurred glow from Sixth Avenue down the street. In that light those two who had been lovers looked for the last time into each other's tragic faces, realizing that between them there was not enough youth and strength to avert their eternal parting. Sloane walked suddenly off down the street and Anson tapped a dozing taxi-driver on the arm.

It was almost four: there was a patient flow of cleaning water along the ghostly pavement of Fifth Avenue, and the shadows of two night women flitted over the dark façade of St. Thomas's church. Then the desolate shrubbery of Central Park where Anson had often played as a child, and the mounting numbers, significant as names, of the marching streets. This was his city, he thought, where his name had flourished through five generations. No change could alter the permanence of its place here, for change itself was the essential substratum by which he and those of his name identified themselves with the spirit of New York. Resourcefulness and a powerful will—for his threats in weaker hands would have been less than nothing—had beaten the gathering dust from his uncle's name, from the name of his family, from even this shivering figure that sat beside him in the car.

Cary Sloane's body was found next morning on the lower shelf of a pillar of Queensboro Bridge. In the darkness and in his excitement he had thought that it was the water flowing black beneath him, but in less than a second it made no possible difference—unless he had planned to think one last thought of Edna, and call out her name as he struggled feebly in the water.

VII

Anson never blamed himself for his part in this affair—the situation which brought it about had not been of his making. But the just suffer with the unjust, and he found that his oldest and somehow his most precious friendship was over. He never knew what distorted story Edna told, but he was welcome in his uncle's house no longer.

Just before Christmas Mrs. Hunter retired to a select Episcopal heaven, and Anson became the responsible head of his family. An unmarried aunt who had lived with them for years ran the house and attempted with helpless inefficiency to chaperone the younger girls. All the children were less self-reliant than Anson, more conventional both in their virtues and in their shortcomings. Mrs. Hunter's death had postponed the debut of one daughter and the wedding of another. Also it had taken something deeply material from all of them, for with her passing the quiet, expensive superiority of the Hunters came to an end.

For one thing, the estate, considerably diminished by two inheritance taxes and soon to be divided among six children, was not a notable fortune anymore. Anson saw a tendency in his youngest sisters to speak rather respectfully of families that hadn't "existed" twenty years ago. His own feeling of precedence was not echoed in them— sometimes they were conventionally snobbish, that was all. For another thing, this was the last summer they would spend on the Connecticut estate; the clamor against it was too loud: "Who wants to waste the best months of the year shut up in that dead old town?" Reluctantly he yielded—the house would go into the market in the fall, and next summer they would rent a smaller place in Westchester County. It was a step down from the expensive simplicity of his father's idea, and, while he sympathized with the revolt, it also annoyed him; during his mother's lifetime he had gone up there at least every other week-end— even in the gayest summers.

Yet he himself was part of this change, and his strong instinct for life had turned him in his twenties from the hollow obsequies of that abortive leisure class. He did not see this clearly—he still felt that there was a norm, a standard of society. But there was no norm, it was doubtful if there had ever been a true norm in New York. The few who still paid and fought to enter a particular set succeeded only to find that as a society it scarcely functioned—or, what was more alarming, that the Bohemia from which they fled sat above them at table.

At twenty-nine Anson's chief concern was his own growing lone-liness. He was sure now that he would never marry. The number of weddings at which he had officiated as best man or usher was past all counting—there was a drawer at home that bulged with the official neckties of this or that wedding-party, neckties standing for romances that had not endured a year, for couples who had passed completely from his life. Scarf-pins, gold pencils, cuff-buttons, presents from a generation of grooms had passed through his jewel-box and been lost— and with every ceremony he was less and less able to imagine himself in the groom's place. Under his hearty good-will toward all those marriages there was despair about his own.

And as he neared thirty he became not a little depressed at the inroads that marriage, especially lately, had made upon his friendships. Groups of people had a disconcerting tendency to dissolve and disappear. The men from his own college—and it was upon them he had expended the most time and affection—were the most elusive of all. Most of them were drawn deep into domesticity, two were dead, one lived abroad, one was in Hollywood writing continuities for pictures that Anson went faithfully to see.

Most of them, however, were permanent commuters with an intricate family life centering around some suburban country club, and it was from these that he felt his estrangement most keenly.

In the early days of their married life they had all needed him; he gave them advice about their slim finances, he exorcised their doubts about the advisability of bringing a baby into two rooms and a bath, especially he stood for the great world outside. But now their financial troubles were in the past and the fearfully expected child had evolved into an absorbing family. They were always glad to see old Anson, but they dressed up for him and tried to impress him with their present importance, and kept their troubles to themselves. They needed him no longer.

A few weeks before his thirtieth birthday the last of his early and intimate friends was married. Anson acted in his usual role of best man, gave his usual silver tea-service, and went down to the usual Homeric to say good-bye. It was a hot Friday afternoon in May, and as he walked from the pier he realized that Saturday closing had begun and he was free until Monday morning.

"Go where?" he asked himself.

TheYale Club, of course; bridge until dinner, then four or five raw cocktails in somebody's room and a pleasant confused evening. He regretted that this afternoon's groom wouldn't be along—they had always been able to cram so much into such nights: they knew how to attach women and how to get rid of them, how much consideration any girl deserved from their intelligent hedonism. A party was an adjusted thing—you took certain girls to certain places and spent just so much on their amusement; you drank a little, not much more than you ought to drink, and at a certain time in the morning you stood up and said you were going home. You avoided college boys, sponges, future engagements, fights, sentiment and indiscretions. That was the way it was done. All the rest was dissipation.

In the morning you were never violently sorry—you made no resolutions, but if you had overdone it and your heart was slightly out of order, you went on the wagon for a few days without saying anything about it, and waited until an accumulation of nervous boredom projected you into another party.

The lobby of theYale Club was unpopulated. In the bar three very young alumni looked up at him, momentarily and without curiosity.

"Hello there, Oscar," he said to the bartender. "Mr. Cahill been around this afternoon?"

"Mr. Cahill's gone to New Haven."

"Oh . . . that so?"

"Gone to the ball game. Lot of men gone up."

Anson looked once again into the lobby, considered for a moment and then walked out and over to Fifth Avenue. From the broad window of one of his clubs—one that he had scarcely visited in five years—a grey man with watery eyes stared down at him. Anson looked quickly away—that figure sitting in vacant resignation, in supercilious solitude, depressed him. He stopped and, retracing his steps, started over 47th Street toward Teak Warden's apartment. Teak and his wife had once been his most familiar friends—it was a household where he and Dolly Karger had been used to go in the days of their affair. But Teak had taken to drink, and his wife had remarked publicly that Anson was a bad influence on him. The remark reached Anson in an exaggerated form—when it was finally cleared up, the delicate spell of intimacy was broken, never to be renewed.

"Is Mr. Warden at home?" he inquired.

"They've gone to the country."

The fact unexpectedly cut at him. They were gone to the country and he hadn't known. Two years before he would have known the date, the hour, come up at the last moment for a final drink and planned his first visit to them. Now they had gone without a word.

Anson looked at his watch and considered a week-end with his family, but the only train was a local that would jolt through the aggressive heat for three hours. And tomorrow in the country, and Sunday—he was in no mood for porch-bridge with polite undergraduates, and dancing after dinner at a rural road-house, a diminutive of gaiety which his father had estimated too well.

"Oh no," he said to himself. . . . "No."

He was a dignified, impressive young man, rather stout now, but otherwise unmarked by dissipation. He could have been cast for a pillar of something—at times you were sure it was not society, at others nothing else—for the law, for the church. He stood for a few minutes motionless on the sidewalk in front of a 47th Street apartment-house; for almost the first time in his life he had nothing whatever to do.

Then he began to walk briskly up Fifth Avenue, as if he had just been reminded of an important engagement there. The necessity of dissimulation is one of the few characteristics that we share with dogs, and I think of Anson on that day as some well-bred specimen who had been disappointed at a familiar back door. He was going to see Nick, once a fashionable bartender in demand at all private dances, and now employed in cooling non-alcoholic champagne among the labyrinthine cellars of the Plaza Hotel.

"Nick," he said, "what's happened to everything?"

"Dead," Nick said.

"Make me a whiskey sour." Anson handed a pint bottle over the counter. "Nick, the girls are different; I had a little girl in Brooklyn and she got married last week without letting me know."

"That a fact? Ha-ha-ha," responded Nick diplomatically. "Slipped it over on you."

"Absolutely," said Anson. "And I was out with her the night before."

"Ha-ha-ha," said Nick, "ha-ha-ha!"

"Do you remember the wedding, Nick, in Hot Springs where I had the waiters and the musicians singing 'God Save the King'?"

"Now where was that, Mr. Hunter?" Nick concentrated doubtfully. "Seems to me that was——"

"Next time they were back for more, and I began to wonder how much I'd paid them," continued Anson.

"——seems to me that was at Mr. Trenholm's wedding."

"Don't know him," said Anson decisively. He was offended that a strange name should intrude upon his reminiscences; Nick perceived this.

"Naw—aw——" he admitted, "I ought to know that. It was one of *your* crowd—Brakins . . . Baker——"

"Bicker Baker," said Anson responsively. "They put me in a hearse after it was over and covered me up with flowers and drove me away."

"Ha-ha-ha," said Nick. "Ha-ha-ha."

Nick's simulation of the old family servant paled presently and Anson went upstairs to the lobby. He looked around—his eyes met the glance of an unfamiliar clerk at the desk, then fell upon a flower from the morning's marriage hesitating in the mouth of a brass cuspidor. He went out and walked slowly toward the blood-red sun over Columbus Circle. Suddenly he turned around and, retracing his steps to the Plaza, immured himself in a telephone-booth.

Later he said that he tried to get me three times that afternoon, that he tried everyone who might be in New York—men and girls he had not seen for years, an artist's model of his college days whose faded number was still in his address book—Central told him that even the exchange existed no longer. At length his quest roved into the country, and he held brief disappointing conversations with emphatic butlers and maids. So-and-so was out, riding, swimming, playing golf, sailed to Europe last week. Who shall I say phoned?

It was intolerable that he should pass the evening alone—the private reckonings, which one plans for a moment of leisure, lose every charm when the solitude is enforced. There were always women of a sort, but the ones he knew had temporarily vanished, and to pass a New York evening in the hired company of a stranger never occurred to him—he would have considered that that was something shameful and secret, the diversion of a traveling salesman in a strange town.

Anson paid the telephone bill—the girl tried unsuccessfully to joke with him about its size—and for the second time that afternoon started to leave the Plaza and go he knew not where. Near the revolving door the figure of a woman, obviously with child, stood sideways to the light—a sheer beige cape fluttered at her shoulders when the door turned and, each time, she looked impatiently toward it as if she were weary of waiting. At the first sight of her a strong nervous thrill of familiarity went over him, but not until he was within five feet of her did he realize that it was Paula.

"Why, Anson Hunter!"

His heart turned over.

"Why, Paula—"

"Why, this is wonderful. I can't believe it, *Anson!*"

She took both his hands and he saw in the freedom of the gesture that the memory of him had lost poignancy to her. But not to him—he felt that old mood that she evoked in him stealing over his brain, that gentleness with which he had always met her optimism as if afraid to mar its surface.

"We're at Rye for the summer. Pete had to come east on business—you know of course I'm Mrs. Peter Hagerty now—so we brought the children and took a house. You've got to come out and see us."

"Can I?" he asked directly. "When?"

"When you like. Here's Pete." The revolving door functioned, giving up a fine tall man of thirty with a tanned face and a trim mustache. His immaculate fitness made a sharp contrast with Anson's increasing bulk, which was obvious under the faintly tight cutaway coat.

"You oughtn't to be standing," said Hagerty to his wife. "Let's sit down here." He indicated lobby chairs but Paula hesitated.

"I've got to go right home," she said. "Anson, why don't you—why don't you come out and have dinner with us tonight? We're just getting settled, but if you can stand that—"

Hagerty confirmed the invitation cordially.

"Come out for the night."

Their car waited in front of the hotel, and Paula with a tired gesture sank back against silk cushions in the corner.

"There's so much I want to talk to you about," she said. "It seems hopeless."

"I want to hear about you."

"Well"—she smiled at Hagerty—"that would take a long time too. I have three children—by my first marriage. The oldest is five, then four, then three." She smiled again. "I didn't waste much time having them, did I?"

"Boys?"

"A boy and two girls. Then—oh, a lot of things happened, and I got a divorce in Paris a year ago and married Pete. That's all—except that I'm awfully happy."

In Rye they drove up to a large house near the beach club, from which there issued presently three dark slim children who broke from an English governess and approached them with an esoteric cry. Abstractedly and with difficulty Paula took each one into her arms, a caress which they accepted stiffly, as they had evidently been told not to bump into Mummy. Even against their fresh faces Paula's skin showed scarcely any weariness—for all her physical languor she seemed younger than when he had last seen her at Palm Beach seven years ago.

At dinner she was preoccupied, and afterwards, during the homage to the radio, she lay with closed eyes on the sofa, until Anson wondered if his presence at this time were not an intrusion. But at nine o'clock, when Hagerty rose and said pleasantly that he was going to leave them by themselves for awhile, she began to talk slowly about herself and the past.

"My first baby," she said—"the one we call Darling, the biggest little girl—I wanted to die when I knew I was going to have her, because

Lowell was like a stranger to me. It didn't seem as though she could be my own. I wrote you a letter and tore it up. Oh, you were *so* bad to me, Anson."

It was the dialogue again, rising and falling. Anson felt a sudden quickening of memory.

"Weren't you engaged once?" she asked—"a girl named Dolly something?"

"I wasn't ever engaged. I tried to be engaged, but I never loved anybody but you, Paula."

"Oh," she said. Then after a moment: "This baby is the first one I ever really wanted. You see, I'm in love now—at last."

He didn't answer, shocked at the treachery of her remembrance. She must have seen that the "at last" bruised him, for she continued:

"I was infatuated with you, Anson—you could make me do anything you liked. But we wouldn't have been happy. I'm not smart enough for you. I don't like things to be complicated like you do." She paused. "You'll never settle down," she said.

The phrase struck at him from behind—it was an accusation that of all accusations he had never merited.

"I could settle down if women were different," he said. "If I didn't understand so much about them, if women didn't spoil you for other women, if they had only a little pride. If I could go to sleep for awhile and wake up into a home that was really mine—why, that's what I'm made for, Paula, that's what women have seen in me and liked in me. It's only that I can't get through the preliminaries anymore."

Hagerty came in a little before eleven; after a whiskey Paula stood up and announced that she was going to bed. She went over and stood by her husband.

"Where did you go, dearest?" she demanded.

"I had a drink with Ed Saunders."

"I was worried. I thought maybe you'd run away."

She rested her head against his coat.

"He's sweet, isn't he, Anson?" she demanded.

"Absolutely," said Anson, laughing.

She raised her face to her husband.

"Well, I'm ready," she said. She turned to Anson: "Do you want to see our family gymnastic stunt?"

"Yes," he said in an interested voice.

"All right. Here we go!"

Hagerty picked her up easily in his arms.

"This is called the family acrobatic stunt," said Paula. "He carries me upstairs. Isn't it sweet of him?"

"Yes," said Anson.

Hagerty bent his head slightly until his face touched Paula's.

"And I love him," she said. "I've just been telling you, haven't I, Anson?"

"Yes," he said.

"He's the dearest thing that ever lived in this world, aren't you, darling? . . . Well, good-night. Here we go. Isn't he strong?"

"Yes," Anson said.

"You'll find a pair of Pete's pajamas laid out for you. Sweet dreams—see you at breakfast."

"Yes," Anson said.

VIII

The older members of the firm insisted that Anson should go abroad for the summer. He had scarcely had a vacation in seven years, they said. He was stale and needed a change. Anson resisted.

"If I go," he declared, "I won't come back anymore."

"That's absurd, old man. You'll be back in three months with all this depression gone. Fit as ever."

"No." He shook his head stubbornly. "If I stop, I won't go back to work. If I stop, that means I've given up—I'm through."

"We'll take a chance on that. Stay six months if you like—we're not afraid you'll leave us. Why, you'd be miserable if you didn't work."

They arranged his passage for him. They liked Anson—everyone liked Anson—and the change that had been coming over him cast a sort of pall over the office. The enthusiasm that had invariably signalled up business, the consideration toward his equals and his inferiors, the lift of his vital presence—within the past four months his intense nervousness had melted down these qualities into the fussy pessimism of a man of forty. On every transaction in which he was involved he acted as a drag and a strain.

"If I go I'll never come back," he said.

Three days before he sailed Paula Legendre Hagerty died in childbirth. I was with him a great deal then, for we were crossing together, but for the first time in our friendship he told me not a word of how he felt, nor did I see the slightest sign of emotion. His chief preoccupation was with the fact that he was thirty years old—he would turn the conversation to the point where he could remind you of it and then fall silent, as if he assumed that the statement would start a chain of thought sufficient to itself. Like his partners I was amazed at the change in him, and I was glad when the *Paris* moved off into the wet space between the worlds, leaving his principality behind.

"How about a drink?" he suggested.

We walked into the bar with that defiant feeling that characterizes the day of departure and ordered four martinis. After one cocktail a change came over him—he suddenly reached across and slapped my knee with the first joviality I had seen him exhibit for months.

"Did you see that girl in the red tam?" he demanded, "the one with the high color who had the two police dogs down to bid her good-bye."

"She's pretty," I agreed.

"I looked her up in the purser's office and found out that she's alone. I'm going down to see the steward in a few minutes. We'll have dinner with her tonight."

After awhile he left me and within an hour he was walking up and down the deck with her, talking to her in his strong, clear voice. Her red tam was a bright spot of color against the steel-green sea, and from time to time she looked up with a flashing bob of her head, and smiled with amusement and interest, and anticipation. At dinner we had champagne, and were very joyous—afterwards Anson ran the pool with infectious gusto, and several people who had seen me with him asked me his name. He and the girl were talking and laughing together on a lounge in the bar when I went to bed.

I saw less of him on the trip than I had hoped. He wanted to arrange a foursome, but there was no one available, so I saw him only at meals. Sometimes, though, he would have a cocktail in the bar, and he told me about the girl in the red tam, and his adventures with her, making them all bizarre and amusing, as he had a way of doing, and I was glad that he was himself again, or at least the self that I knew, and with which I felt at home. I don't think he was ever happy unless someone was in love with him, responding to him like filings to a magnet, helping him to explain himself, promising him something. What it was I do not know. Perhaps they promised that there would always be women in the world who would spend their brightest, freshest, rarest hours to nurse and protect that superiority he cherished in his heart.

WINTER DREAMS

Some of the caddies were poor as sin and lived in one-room houses with a neurasthenic cow in the front yard, but Dexter Green's father owned the second best grocery store in Black Bear—the best one was "The Hub," patronized by the wealthy people from Sherry Island—and Dexter caddied only for pocket-money.

In the fall when the days became crisp and grey and the long Minnesota winter shut down like the white lid of a box, Dexter's skis moved over the snow that hid the fairways of the golf course. At these times the country gave him a feeling of profound melancholy—it offended him that the links should lie in enforced fallowness, haunted by ragged sparrows for the long season. It was dreary, too, that on the tees where the gay colors fluttered in summer there were now only the desolate sand boxes knee-deep in crusted ice. When he crossed the hills the wind blew cold as misery, and if the sun was out he tramped with his eyes squinted up against the hard dimensionless glare.

In April the winter ceased abruptly. The snow ran down into Black Bear Lake scarcely tarrying for the early golfers to brave the season with red and black balls. Without elation, without an interval of moist glory, the cold was gone.

Dexter knew that there was something dismal about this northern spring, just as he knew there was something gorgeous about the
fall. Fall made him clench his hands and tremble and repeat idiotic
sentences to himself and make brisk abrupt gestures of command
to imaginary audiences and armies. October filled him with hope
which November raised to a sort of ecstatic triumph, and in this
mood the fleeting brilliant impressions of the summer at Sherry
Island were ready grist to his mill. He became a golf champion and
defeated Mr. T. A. Hedrick in a marvelous match played a hundred
times over the fairways of his imagination, a match each detail of
which he changed about untiringly—sometimes he won with almost
laughable ease, sometimes he came up magnificently from behind.
Again, stepping from a Pierce-Arrow automobile, like Mr. Mortimer
Jones, he strolled frigidly into the lounge of the Sherry Island Golf
Club—or perhaps, surrounded by an admiring crowd, he gave an
exhibition of fancy diving from the springboard of the club raft. . .
. Among those who watched him in open-mouthed wonder was Mr.
Mortimer Jones.

And one day it came to pass that Mr. Jones—himself and not his
ghost—came up to Dexter with tears in his eyes and said that Dexter
was the —— best caddy in the club and wouldn't he decide not to quit
if Mr. Jones made it worth his while, because every other —— caddy
in the club lost one ball a hole for him—regularly.

"No, sir," said Dexter decisively, "I don't want to caddy anymore."
Then, after a pause: "I'm too old."

"You're not more than fourteen. Why the devil did you decide just
this morning that you wanted to quit? You promised that next week
you'd go over to the state tournament with me."

"I decided I was too old."

Dexter handed in his "A Class" badge, collected what money was due him from the caddy-master and walked home to Black Bear Village.

"The best —— caddy I ever saw," shouted Mr. Mortimer Jones over a drink that afternoon. "Never lost a ball! Willing! Intelligent! Quiet! Honest! Grateful!—"

The little girl who had done this was eleven—beautifully ugly as little girls are apt to be who are destined after a few years to be inexpressibly lovely and bring no end of misery to a great number of men. The spark, however, was perceptible. There was a general ungodliness in the way her lips twisted down at the corners when she smiled and in the—Heaven help us!—in the almost passionate quality of her eyes. Vitality is born early in such women. It was utterly in evidence now, shining through her thin frame in a sort of glow.

She had come eagerly out onto the course at nine o'clock with a white linen nurse and five small new golf clubs in a white canvas bag which the nurse was carrying. When Dexter first saw her she was standing by the caddy house, rather ill at ease and trying to conceal the fact by engaging her nurse in an obviously unnatural conversation graced by startling and irrelevant grimaces from herself.

"Well, it's certainly a nice day, Hilda," Dexter heard her say. She drew down the corners of her mouth, smiled and glanced furtively around, her eyes in transit falling for an instant on Dexter.

Then to the nurse:

"Well, I guess there aren't very many people out here this morning, are there?"

The smile again—radiant, blatantly artificial—convincing.

"I don't know what we're supposed to do now," said the nurse, looking nowhere in particular.

"Oh, that's all right. I'll fix it up."

Dexter stood perfectly still, his mouth slightly ajar. He knew that if he moved forward a step his stare would be in her line of vision—if he moved backward he would lose his full view of her face. For a moment he had not realized how young she was. Now he remembered having seen her several times the year before—in bloomers.

Suddenly, involuntarily, he laughed, a short abrupt laugh—then, startled by himself, he turned and began to walk quickly away.

"Boy!"

Dexter stopped.

"Boy—"

Beyond question he was addressed. Not only that, but he was treated to that absurd smile, that preposterous smile—the memory of which at least a dozen men were to carry into middle age.

"Boy, do you know where the golf teacher is?"

"He's giving a lesson."

"Well, do you know where the caddy-master is?"

"He isn't here yet this morning."

"Oh." For a moment this baffled her. She stood alternately on her right and left foot.

"We'd like to get a caddy," said the nurse. "Mrs. Mortimer Jones sent us out to play golf and we don't know how without we get a caddy."

Here she was stopped by an ominous glance from Miss Jones, followed immediately by the smile.

"There aren't any caddies here except me," said Dexter to the nurse, "and I got to stay here in charge until the caddy-master gets here."

"Oh."

Miss Jones and her retinue now withdrew and at a proper distance from Dexter became involved in a heated conversation, which was concluded by Miss Jones taking one of the clubs and hitting it on the ground with violence. For further emphasis she raised it again and was about to bring it down smartly upon the nurse's bosom, when the nurse seized the club and twisted it from her hands.

"You damn little mean old *thing*!" cried Miss Jones wildly.

Another argument ensued. Realizing that the elements of the comedy were implied in the scene, Dexter several times began to laugh, but each time restrained the laugh before it reached audibility. He could not resist the monstrous conviction that the little girl was justified in beating the nurse.

The situation was resolved by the fortuitous appearance of the caddy-master, who was appealed to immediately by the nurse.

"Miss Jones is to have a little caddy and this one says he can't go."

"Mr. McKenna said I was to wait here till you came," said Dexter quickly.

"Well, he's here now." Miss Jones smiled cheerfully at the caddy-master. Then she dropped her bag and set off at a haughty mince toward the first tee.

"Well?" The caddy-master turned to Dexter. "What you standing there like a dummy for? Go pick up the young lady's clubs."

"I don't think I'll go out today," said Dexter.

"You don't—"

"I think I'll quit."

The enormity of his decision frightened him. He was a favorite caddy and the thirty dollars a month he earned through the summer were not to be made elsewhere around the lake. But he had received a strong emotional shock and his perturbation required a violent and immediate outlet.

It is not so simple as that, either. As so frequently would be the case in the future, Dexter was unconsciously dictated to by his winter dreams.

II

Now, of course, the quality and the seasonability of these winter dreams varied, but the stuff of them remained. They persuaded Dexter several years later to pass up a business course at the state university—his father, prospering now, would have paid his way— for the precarious advantage of attending an older and more famous university in the East, where he was bothered by his scanty funds. But do not get the impression, because his winter dreams happened to be concerned at first with musings on the rich, that there was anything merely snobbish in the boy. He wanted not association with glittering things and glittering people—he wanted the glittering things themselves. Often he reached out for the best without knowing why he wanted it—and sometimes he ran up against the mysterious denials and prohibitions in which life indulges. It is with one of those denials and not with his career as a whole that this story deals.

He made money. It was rather amazing. After college he went to the city from which Black Bear Lake draws its wealthy patrons. When he was only twenty-three and had been there not quite two years, there were already people who liked to say: "Now *there's* a boy—" All about him rich men's sons were peddling bonds precariously, or investing patrimonies precariously, or plodding through the two dozen volumes of the "George Washington Commercial Course," but Dexter borrowed a thousand dollars on his college degree and his confident mouth, and bought a partnership in a laundry.

It was a small laundry when he went into it but Dexter made a specialty of learning how the English washed fine woolen golf-stockings without shrinking them, and within a year he was catering to the trade that wore knickerbockers. Men were insisting that their Shetland hose and sweaters go to his laundry just as they had insisted on a caddy who could find golf balls. A little later he was doing their wives' lingerie as well—and running five branches in different parts of the city. Before he was twenty-seven he owned the largest string of laundries in his section of the country. It was then that he sold out and went to New York. But the part of his story that concerns us goes back to the days when he was making his first big success.

When he was twenty-three Mr. Hart—one of the grey-haired men who liked to say "Now there's a boy"—gave him a guest card to the Sherry Island Golf Club for a week-end. So he signed his name one day on the register, and that afternoon played golf in a foursome with Mr. Hart and Mr. Sandwood and Mr. T. A. Hedrick. He did not consider it necessary to remark that he had once carried Mr. Hart's bag over these same links and that he knew every trap and gully with his eyes shut—but he found himself glancing at the four caddies who trailed them, trying to catch a gleam or gesture that would remind him of himself, that would lessen the gap which lay between his present and his past.

It was a curious day, slashed abruptly with fleeting, familiar impressions. One minute he had the sense of being a trespasser—in the next he was impressed by the tremendous superiority he felt toward Mr. T. A. Hedrick, who was a bore and not even a good golfer anymore.

Then, because of a ball Mr. Hart lost near the fifteenth green, an enormous thing happened. While they were searching the stiff grasses of the rough there was a clear call of "Fore!" from behind a hill in their rear. And as they all turned abruptly from their search a bright new ball sliced abruptly over the hill and caught Mr. T. A. Hedrick in the abdomen.

"By Gad!" cried Mr. T. A. Hedrick, "they ought to put some of these crazy women off the course. It's getting to be outrageous."

A head and a voice came up together over the hill:

"Do you mind if we go through?"

"You hit me in the stomach!" declared Mr. Hedrick wildly.

"Did I?" The girl approached the group of men. "I'm sorry. I yelled 'Fore!'"

Her glance fell casually on each of the men—then scanned the fairway for her ball.

"Did I bounce into the rough?"

It was impossible to determine whether this question was ingenuous or malicious. In a moment, however, she left no doubt, for as her partner came up over the hill she called cheerfully:

"Here I am! I'd have gone on the green except that I hit something."

As she took her stance for a short mashie shot, Dexter looked at her closely. She wore a blue gingham dress, rimmed at throat and shoulders with a white edging that accentuated her tan. The quality of exaggeration, of thinness, which had made her passionate eyes and down-turning mouth absurd at eleven, was gone now. She was arrestingly beautiful. The color in her cheeks was centered like the color in a picture—it was not a "high" color, but a sort of fluctuating and feverish warmth, so shaded that it seemed at any moment it would recede and disappear. This color and the mobility of her mouth gave a continual impression of flux, of intense life, of passionate vitality—balanced only partially by the sad luxury of her eyes.

She swung her mashie impatiently and without interest, pitching the ball into a sandpit on the other side of the green. With a quick insincere smile and a careless "Thank you!" she went on after it.

"That Judy Jones!" remarked Mr. Hedrick on the next tee, as they waited—some moments—for her to play on ahead. "All she needs is to be turned up and spanked for six months and then to be married off to an old-fashioned cavalry captain."

"My God, she's good-looking!" said Mr. Sandwood, who was just over thirty.

"Good-looking!" cried Mr. Hedrick contemptuously. "She always looks as if she wanted to be kissed! Turning those big cow-eyes on every calf in town!"

It was doubtful if Mr. Hedrick intended a reference to the maternal instinct.

"She'd play pretty good golf if she'd try," said Mr. Sandwood.

"She has no form," said Mr. Hedrick solemnly.

"She has a nice figure," said Mr. Sandwood.

"Better thank the Lord she doesn't drive a swifter ball," said Mr. Hart, winking at Dexter.

Later in the afternoon the sun went down with a riotous swirl of gold and varying blues and scarlets, and left the dry rustling night of western summer. Dexter watched from the verandah of the golf club, watched the even overlap of the waters in the little wind, silver molasses under the harvest moon. Then the moon held a finger to her lips and the lake became a clear pool, pale and quiet. Dexter put on his bathing suit and swam out to the farthest raft, where he stretched dripping on the wet canvas of the springboard.

There was a fish jumping and a star shining and the lights around the lake were gleaming. Over on a dark peninsula a piano was playing the songs of last summer and of summers before that—songs from "Chin-Chin" and "The Count of Luxembourg" and "The Chocolate Soldier"—and because the sound of a piano over a stretch of water had always seemed beautiful to Dexter he lay perfectly quiet and listened.

The tune the piano was playing at that moment had been gay and new five years before when Dexter was a sophomore at college. They had played it at a prom once when he could not afford the luxury of proms, and he had stood outside the gymnasium and listened. The sound of the tune precipitated in him a sort of ecstasy and it was with that ecstasy he viewed what happened to him now. It was a mood of intense appreciation, a sense that, for once, he was magnificently attuned to life and that everything about him was radiating a brightness and a glamour he might never know again.

A low pale oblong detached itself suddenly from the darkness of the island, spitting forth the reverberate sound of a racing motorboat. Two white streamers of cleft water rolled themselves out behind it and almost immediately the boat was beside him, drowning out the hot tinkle of the piano in the drone of its spray. Dexter, raising himself on his arms, was aware of a figure standing at the wheel, of two dark eyes regarding him over the lengthening space of water—then the boat had gone by and was sweeping in an immense and purposeless circle of spray round and round in the middle of the lake. With equal eccentricity one of the circles flattened out and headed back toward the raft.

"Who's that?" she called, shutting off her motor. She was so near now that Dexter could see her bathing suit, which consisted apparently of pink rompers.

The nose of the boat bumped the raft, and as the latter tilted rakishly he was precipitated toward her. With different degrees of interest they recognized each other.

"Aren't you one of those men we played through this afternoon?" she demanded.

He was.

"Well, do you know how to drive a motorboat? Because if you do I wish you'd drive this one so I can ride on the surf-board behind. My name is Judy Jones"—she favored him with an absurd smirk—rather, what tried to be a smirk, for, twist her mouth as she might, it was not grotesque, it was merely beautiful—"and I live in a house over there on the island, and in that house there is a man waiting for me. When he drove up at the door I drove out of the dock because he says I'm his ideal."

There was a fish jumping and a star shining and the lights around the lake were gleaming. Dexter sat beside Judy Jones and she explained how her boat was driven. Then she was in the water, swimming to the floating surf-board with a sinuous crawl. Watching her was without effort to the eye, watching a branch waving or a sea-gull flying. Her arms, burned to butternut, moved sinuously among the dull platinum ripples, elbow appearing first, casting the forearm back with a cadence of falling water, then reaching out and down, stabbing a path ahead.

They moved out into the lake; turning, Dexter saw that she was kneeling on the low rear of the now up-tilted surf-board.

"Go faster," she called, "fast as it'll go."

Obediently he jammed the lever forward and the white spray mounted at the bow. When he looked around again the girl was standing up on the rushing board, her arms spread wide, her eyes lifted toward the moon.

"It's awful cold," she shouted. "What's your name?"

He told her.

"Well, why don't you come to dinner tomorrow night?"

His heart turned over like the fly-wheel of the boat, and, for the second time, her casual whim gave a new direction to his life.

III

Next evening while he waited for her to come downstairs, Dexter peopled the soft deep summer room and the sun-porch that opened from it with the men who had already loved Judy Jones. He knew the sort of men they were—the men who when he first went to college had entered from the great prep schools with graceful clothes and the deep tan of healthy summers. He had seen that, in one sense, he was better than these men. He was newer and stronger. Yet in acknowledging to himself that he wished his children to be like them he was admitting that he was but the rough, strong stuff from which they eternally sprang.

When the time had come for him to wear good clothes, he had known who were the best tailors in America, and the best tailors in America had made him the suit he wore this evening. He had acquired that particular reserve peculiar to his university, that set it off from other universities. He recognized the value to him of such a mannerism and he had adopted it; he knew that to be careless in dress and manner required more confidence than to be careful. But carelessness was for his children. His mother's name had been Krimslich. She was a Bohemian of the peasant class and she had talked broken English to the end of her days. Her son must keep to the set patterns.

At a little after seven Judy Jones came downstairs. She wore a blue silk afternoon dress, and he was disappointed at first that she had not put on something more elaborate. This feeling was accentuated when, after a brief greeting, she went to the door of a butler's pantry and pushing it open called: "You can serve dinner, Martha." He had rather expected that a butler would announce dinner, that there would be a cocktail. Then he put these thoughts behind him as they sat down side by side on a lounge and looked at each other.

"Father and Mother won't be here," she said thoughtfully.

He remembered the last time he had seen her father, and he was glad the parents were not to be here tonight—they might wonder who he was. He had been born in Keeble, a Minnesota village fifty miles farther north, and he always gave Keeble as his home instead of Black Bear Village. Country towns were well enough to come from if they weren't inconveniently in sight and used as foot-stools by fashionable lakes.

They talked of his university, which she had visited frequently during the past two years, and of the nearby city which supplied Sherry Island with its patrons, and whither Dexter would return next day to his prospering laundries.

During dinner she slipped into a moody depression which gave Dexter a feeling of uneasiness. Whatever petulance she uttered in her throaty voice worried him. Whatever she smiled at—at him, at a chicken liver, at nothing—it disturbed him that her smile could have no root in mirth, or even in amusement. When the scarlet corners of her lips curved down, it was less a smile than an invitation to a kiss.

Then, after dinner, she led him out on the dark sun-porch and deliberately changed the atmosphere.

"Do you mind if I weep a little?" she said.

"I'm afraid I'm boring you," he responded quickly.

"You're not. I like you. But I've just had a terrible afternoon. There was a man I cared about, and this afternoon he told me out of a clear sky that he was poor as a church-mouse. He'd never even hinted it before. Does this sound horribly mundane?"

"Perhaps he was afraid to tell you."

"Suppose he was," she answered. "He didn't start right. You see, if I'd thought of him as poor—well, I've been mad about loads of poor men, and fully intended to marry them all. But in this case, I hadn't thought of him that way and my interest in him wasn't strong enough to survive the shock. As if a girl calmly informed her fiancé that she was a widow. He might not object to widows, but—"

"Let's start right," she interrupted herself suddenly. "Who are you, anyhow?"

For a moment Dexter hesitated. Then:

"I'm nobody," he announced. "My career is largely a matter of futures."

"Are you poor?"

"No," he said frankly, "I'm probably making more money than any man my age in the Northwest. I know that's an obnoxious remark, but you advised me to start right."

There was a pause. Then she smiled and the corners of her mouth drooped and an almost imperceptible sway brought her closer to him, looking up into his eyes. A lump rose in Dexter's throat, and he waited breathless for the experiment, facing the unpredictable compound that would form mysteriously from the elements of their lips. Then he saw—she communicated her excitement to him, lavishly, deeply, with kisses that were not a promise but a fulfilment. They aroused in him not hunger demanding renewal but surfeit that would demand more surfeit . . . kisses that were like charity, creating want by holding back nothing at all.

It did not take him many hours to decide that he had wanted Judy Jones ever since he was a proud, desirous little boy.

IV

It began like that—and continued, with varying shades of intensity, on such a note right up to the dénouement. Dexter surrendered a part of himself to the most direct and unprincipled personality with which he had ever come in contact. Whatever Judy wanted, she went after with the full pressure of her charm. There was no divergence of method, no jockeying for position or premeditation of effects—there was a very little mental side to any of her affairs. She simply made men conscious to the highest degree of her physical loveliness. Dexter had no desire to change her. Her deficiencies were knit up with a passionate energy that transcended and justified them.

When, as Judy's head lay against his shoulder that first night, she whispered, "I don't know what's the matter with me. Last night I thought I was in love with a man and tonight I think I'm in love with you—" —it seemed to him a beautiful and romantic thing to say. It was the exquisite excitability that for the moment he controlled and owned. But a week later he was compelled to view this same quality in a different light. She took him in her roadster to a picnic supper and after supper she disappeared, likewise in her roadster, with another man. Dexter became enormously upset and was scarcely able to be decently civil to the other people present. When she assured him that she had not kissed the other man, he knew she was lying—yet he was glad that she had taken the trouble to lie to him.

He was, as he found before the summer ended, one of a varying dozen who circulated about her. Each of them had at one time been favored above all others—about half of them still basked in the solace of occasional sentimental revivals. Whenever one showed signs of dropping out through long neglect, she granted him a brief honeyed hour, which encouraged him to tag along for a year or so longer. Judy made these forays upon the helpless and defeated without malice, indeed half unconscious that there was anything mischievous in what she did.

When a new man came to town everyone dropped out—dates were automatically cancelled.

The helpless part of trying to do anything about it was that she did it all herself. She was not a girl who could be "won" in the kinetic sense—she was proof against cleverness, she was proof against charm; if any of these assailed her too strongly she would immediately resolve the affair to a physical basis, and under the magic of her physical splendor the strong as well as the brilliant played her game and not their own. She was entertained only by the gratification of her desires and by the direct exercise of her own charm. Perhaps from so much youthful love, so many youthful lovers, she had come, in self-defense, to nourish herself wholly from within.

Succeeding Dexter's first exhilaration came restlessness and dissatisfaction. The helpless ecstasy of losing himself in her was opiate rather than tonic. It was fortunate for his work during the winter that those moments of ecstasy came infrequently. Early in their acquaintance it had seemed for awhile that there was a deep and spontaneous mutual attraction—that first August, for example—three days of long evenings on her dusky verandah, of strange wan kisses through the late afternoon, in shadowy alcoves or behind the protecting trellises of the garden arbors, of mornings when she was fresh as a dream and almost shy at meeting him in the clarity of the rising day. There was all the ecstasy of an engagement about it, sharpened by his realization that there was no engagement. It was during those three days that, for the first time, he had asked her to marry him. She said "maybe someday," she said "kiss me," she said "I'd like to marry you," she said "I love you"—she said—nothing.

The three days were interrupted by the arrival of a New York man who visited at her house for half September. To Dexter's agony, rumor engaged them. The man was the son of the president of a great trust company. But at the end of a month it was reported that Judy was yawning. At a dance one night she sat all evening in a motorboat with a local beau, while the New Yorker searched the club for her frantically. She told the local beau that she was bored with her visitor and two days later he left. She was seen with him at the station and it was reported that he looked very mournful indeed.

On this note the summer ended. Dexter was twenty-four and he found himself increasingly in a position to do as he wished. He joined two clubs in the city and lived at one of them. Though he was by no means an integral part of the stag-lines at these clubs, he managed to be on hand at dances where Judy Jones was likely to appear. He could have gone out socially as much as he liked—he was an eligible young man, now, and popular with downtown fathers. His confessed devotion to Judy Jones had rather solidified his position. But he had no social aspirations and rather despised the dancing men who were always on tap for the Thursday or Saturday parties and who filled in at dinners with the younger married set. Already he was playing with the idea of going east to New York. He wanted to take Judy Jones with him. No disillusion as to the world in which she had grown up could cure his illusion as to her desirability.

Remember that—for only in the light of it can what he did for her be understood.

Eighteen months after he first met Judy Jones he became engaged to another girl. Her name was Irene Scheerer, and her father was one of the men who had always believed in Dexter. Irene was light-haired and sweet and honorable, and a little stout, and she had two suitors whom she pleasantly relinquished when Dexter formally asked her to marry him.

Summer, fall, winter, spring, another summer, another fall—so much he had given of his active life to the incorrigible lips of Judy Jones. She had treated him with interest, with encouragement, with malice, with indifference, with contempt. She had inflicted on him the innumerable little slights and indignities possible in such a case—as if in revenge for having ever cared for him at all. She had beckoned him and yawned at him and beckoned him again and he had responded often with bitterness and narrowed eyes. She had brought him ecstatic happiness and intolerable agony of spirit. She had caused him untold inconvenience and not a little trouble. She had insulted him and she had ridden over him and she had played his interest in her against his interest in his work—for fun. She had done everything to him except to criticize him—this she had not done—it seemed to him only because it might have sullied the utter indifference she manifested and sincerely felt toward him.

When autumn had come and gone again it occurred to him that he could not have Judy Jones. He had to beat this into his mind but he convinced himself at last. He lay awake at night for awhile and argued it over. He told himself the trouble and the pain she had caused him, he enumerated her glaring deficiencies as a wife. Then he said to himself that he loved her, and after awhile he fell asleep. For a week, lest he imagined her husky voice over the telephone or her eyes opposite him at lunch, he worked hard and late and at night he went to his office and plotted out his years.

At the end of a week he went to a dance and cut in on her once. For almost the first time since they had met he did not ask her to sit out with him or tell her that she was lovely. It hurt him that she did not miss these things—that was all. He was not jealous when he saw that there was a new man tonight. He had been hardened against jealousy long before.

He stayed late at the dance. He sat for an hour with Irene Scheerer and talked about books and about music. He knew very little about either. But he was beginning to be master of his own time now, and he had a rather priggish notion that he—the young and already fabulously successful Dexter Green—should know more about such things.

That was in October when he was twenty-five. In January, Dexter and Irene became engaged. It was to be announced in June and they were to be married three months later.

The Minnesota winter prolonged itself interminably, and it was almost May when the winds came soft and the snow ran down into Black Bear Lake at last. For the first time in over a year Dexter was enjoying a certain tranquillity of spirit. Judy Jones had been in Florida and afterwards in Hot Springs and somewhere she had been engaged and somewhere she had broken it off. At first, when Dexter had definitely given her up, it had made him sad that people still linked them together and asked for news of her, but when he began to be placed at dinner next to Irene Scheerer people didn't ask him about her anymore—they told him about her. He ceased to be an authority on her.

May at last. Dexter walked the streets at night when the darkness was damp as rain, wondering that so soon, with so little done, so much of ecstasy had gone from him. May one year back had been marked by Judy's poignant, unforgivable, yet forgiven turbulence—it had been one of those rare times when he fancied she had grown to care for him. That old penny's worth of happiness he had spent for this bushel of content. He knew that Irene would be no more than a curtain spread behind him, a hand moving among gleaming tea cups, a voice calling to children . . . fire and loveliness were gone, the magic of nights and the wonder of the varying hours and seasons . . . slender lips, down-turning, dropping to his lips and bearing him up into a heaven of eyes. . . . The thing was deep in him. He was too strong and alive for it to die lightly.

In the middle of May when the weather balanced for a few days on the thin bridge that led to deep summer he turned in one night at Irene's house. Their engagement was to be announced in a week now—no one would be surprised at it. And tonight they would sit together on the lounge at the University Club and look on for an hour at the dancers. It gave him a sense of solidity to go with her—she was so sturdily popular, so intensely "great."

He mounted the steps of the brownstone house and stepped inside.

"Irene," he called.

Mrs. Scheerer came out of the living room to meet him.

"Dexter," she said, "Irene's gone upstairs with a splitting headache. She wanted to go with you but I made her go to bed."

"Nothing serious, I—"

"Oh, no. She's going to play golf with you in the morning. You can spare her for just one night, can't you, Dexter?"

Her smile was kind. She and Dexter liked each other. In the living room he talked for a moment before he said good-night.

Returning to the University Club, where he had rooms, he stood in the doorway for a moment and watched the dancers. He leaned against the doorpost, nodded at a man or two—yawned.

"Hello, darling."

The familiar voice at his elbow startled him. Judy Jones had left a man and crossed the room to him—Judy Jones, a slender enamelled doll in cloth of gold: gold in a band at her head, gold in two slipper points at her dress's hem. The fragile glow of her face seemed to blossom as she smiled at him. A breeze of warmth and light blew through the room. His hands in the pockets of his dinner jacket tightened spasmodically. He was filled with a sudden excitement.

"When did you get back?" he asked casually.

"Come here and I'll tell you about it."

She turned and he followed her. She had been away—he could have wept at the wonder of her return. She had passed through enchanted streets, doing things that were like provocative music. All mysterious happenings, all fresh and quickening hopes, had gone away with her, come back with her now.

She turned in the doorway.

"Have you a car here? If you haven't, I have."

"I have a coupé."

In then, with a rustle of golden cloth. He slammed the door. Into so many cars she had stepped—like this—like that—her back against the leather, so—her elbow resting on the door—waiting. She would have been soiled long since had there been anything to soil her—except herself—but this was her own self outpouring.

With an effort he forced himself to start the car and back into the street. This was nothing, he must remember. She had done this before and he had put her behind him, as he would have crossed a bad account from his books.

He drove slowly downtown and, affecting abstraction, traversed the deserted streets of the business section, peopled here and there where a movie was giving out its crowd or where consumptive or pugilistic youth lounged in front of pool halls. The clink of glasses and the slap of hands on the bars issued from saloons, cloisters of glazed glass and dirty yellow light.

She was watching him closely and the silence was embarrassing, yet in this crisis he could find no casual word with which to profane the hour. At a convenient turning he began to zig-zag back toward the University Club.

"Have you missed me?" she asked suddenly.

"Everybody missed you."

He wondered if she knew of Irene Scheerer. She had been back only a day—her absence had been almost contemporaneous with his engagement.

"What a remark!" Judy laughed sadly—without sadness. She looked at him searchingly. He became absorbed in the dashboard.

"You're handsomer than you used to be," she said thoughtfully. "Dexter, you have the most rememberable eyes."

He could have laughed at this, but he did not laugh. It was the sort of thing that was said to sophomores. Yet it stabbed at him.

"I'm awfully tired of everything, darling." She called everyone darling, endowing the endearment with careless, individual camaraderie. "I wish you'd marry me."

The directness of this confused him. He should have told her now that he was going to marry another girl, but he could not tell her. He could as easily have sworn that he had never loved her.

"I think we'd get along," she continued, on the same note, "unless probably you've forgotten me and fallen in love with another girl."

Her confidence was obviously enormous. She had said, in effect, that she found such a thing impossible to believe, that if it were true he had merely committed a childish indiscretion—and probably to show off. She would forgive him, because it was not a matter of any moment but rather something to be brushed aside lightly.

"Of course you could never love anybody but me," she continued. "I like the way you love me. Oh, Dexter, have you forgotten last year?"

"No, I haven't forgotten."

"Neither have I!"

Was she sincerely moved—or was she carried along by the wave of her own acting?

"I wish we could be like that again," she said, and he forced himself to answer:

"I don't think we can."

"I suppose not. . . . I hear you're giving Irene Scheerer a violent rush."

There was not the faintest emphasis on the name, yet Dexter was suddenly ashamed.

"Oh, take me home," cried Judy suddenly; "I don't want to go back to that idiotic dance—with those children."

Then, as he turned up the street that led to the residence district, Judy began to cry quietly to herself. He had never seen her cry before.

The dark street lightened, the dwellings of the rich loomed up around them, he stopped his coupé in front of the great white bulk of the Mortimer Jones house, somnolent, gorgeous, drenched with the splendor of the damp moonlight. Its solidity startled him. The strong walls, the steel of the girders, the breadth and beam and pomp of it were there only to bring out the contrast with the young beauty beside him. It was sturdy to accentuate her slightness—as if to show what a breeze could be generated by a butterfly's wing.

He sat perfectly quiet, his nerves in wild clamor, afraid that if he moved he would find her irresistibly in his arms. Two tears had rolled down her wet face and trembled on her upper lip.

"I'm more beautiful than anybody else," she said brokenly. "Why can't I be happy?" Her moist eyes tore at his stability—her mouth turned slowly downward with an exquisite sadness: "I'd like to marry you if you'll have me, Dexter. I suppose you think I'm not worth having, but I'll be so beautiful for you, Dexter."

A million phrases of anger, pride, passion, hatred, tenderness fought on his lips. Then a perfect wave of emotion washed over him, carrying off with it a sediment of wisdom, of convention, of doubt, of honor. This was his girl who was speaking, his own, his beautiful, his pride.

"Won't you come in?" He heard her draw in her breath sharply.

Waiting.

"All right," his voice was trembling, "I'll come in."

V

It was strange that neither when it was over nor a long time afterward did he regret that night. Looking at it from the perspective of ten years, the fact that Judy's flare for him endured just one month seemed of little importance. Nor did it matter that by his yielding he subjected himself to a deeper agony in the end and gave serious hurt to Irene

Scheerer and to Irene's parents, who had befriended him. There was nothing sufficiently pictorial about Irene's grief to stamp itself on his mind.

Dexter was at bottom hard-minded. The attitude of the city on his action was of no importance to him, not because he was going to leave the city, but because any outside attitude on the situation seemed superficial. He was completely indifferent to popular opinion. Nor, when he had seen that it was no use, that he did not possess in himself the power to move fundamentally or to hold Judy Jones, did he bear any malice toward her. He loved her and he would love her until the day he was too old for loving—but he could not have her. So he tasted the deep pain that is reserved only for the strong, just as he had tasted for a little while the deep happiness.

Even the ultimate falsity of the grounds upon which Judy terminated the engagement, that she did not want to "take him away" from Irene—Judy, who had wanted nothing else—did not revolt him. He was beyond any revulsion or any amusement.

He went east in February with the intention of selling out his laundries and settling in New York—but the war came to America in March and changed his plans. He returned to the West, handed over the management of the business to his partner, and went into the first officers' training-camp in late April. He was one of those young thousands who greeted the war with a certain amount of relief, welcoming the liberation from webs of tangled emotion.

VI

This story is not his biography, remember, although things creep into it which have nothing to do with those dreams he had when he was young. We are almost done with them and with him now. There is only one more incident to be related here, and it happens seven years farther on.

It took place in New York, where he had done well—so well that there were no barriers too high for him. He was thirty-two years old, and, except for one flying trip immediately after the war, he had not been west in seven years. A man named Devlin from Detroit came into his office to see him in a business way, and then and there this incident occurred, and closed out, so to speak, this particular side of his life.

"So you're from the Middle West," said the man Devlin with careless curiosity. "That's funny—I thought men like you were probably born and raised on Wall Street. You know—wife of one of my best friends in Detroit came from your city. I was an usher at the wedding."

Dexter waited with no apprehension of what was coming.

"Judy Simms," said Devlin with no particular interest; "Judy Jones she was once."

"Yes, I knew her." A dull impatience spread over him. He had heard, of course, that she was married—perhaps deliberately he had heard no more.

"Awfully nice girl," brooded Devlin meaninglessly. "I'm sort of sorry for her."

"Why?" Something in Dexter was alert, receptive, at once.

"Oh, Lud Simms has gone to pieces in a way. I don't mean he ill-uses her, but he drinks and runs around—"

"Doesn't she run around?"

"No. Stays at home with her kids."

"Oh."

"She's a little too old for him," said Devlin.

"Too old!" cried Dexter. "Why, man, she's only twenty-seven."

He was possessed with a wild notion of rushing out into the streets and taking a train to Detroit. He rose to his feet spasmodically.

"I guess you're busy," Devlin apologized quickly. "I didn't realize—"

"No, I'm not busy," said Dexter, steadying his voice. "I'm not busy at all. Not busy at all. Did you say she was—twenty-seven? No, I said she was twenty-seven."

"Yes, you did," agreed Devlin dryly.

"Go on, then. Go on."

"What do you mean?"

"About Judy Jones."

Devlin looked at him helplessly.

"Well, that's—I told you all there is to it. He treats her like the devil. Oh, they're not going to get divorced or anything. When he's particularly outrageous she forgives him. In fact, I'm inclined to think she loves him. She was a pretty girl when she first came to Detroit."

A pretty girl! The phrase struck Dexter as ludicrous.

"Isn't she—a pretty girl, anymore?"

"Oh, she's all right."

"Look here," said Dexter, sitting down suddenly, "I don't understand. You say she was a 'pretty girl' and now you say she's 'all right.' I don't understand what you mean—Judy Jones wasn't a pretty girl, at all. She was a great beauty. Why, I knew her, I knew her. She was—"

Devlin laughed pleasantly.

"I'm not trying to start a row," he said. "I think Judy's a nice girl and I like her. I can't understand how a man like Lud Simms could fall madly in love with her, but he did." Then he added: "Most of the women like her."

Dexter looked closely at Devlin, thinking wildly that there must be a reason for this, some insensitivity in the man or some private malice.

"Lots of women fade just like *that*," Devlin snapped his fingers. "You must have seen it happen. Perhaps I've forgotten how pretty she was at her wedding. I've seen her so much since then, you see. She has nice eyes."

A sort of dullness settled down upon Dexter. For the first time in his life he felt like getting very drunk. He knew that he was laughing loudly at something Devlin had said, but he did not know what it was or why it was funny. When, in a few minutes, Devlin went he lay down on his lounge and looked out the window at the New York skyline into which the sun was sinking in dull lovely shades of pink and gold.

He had thought that having nothing else to lose he was invulnerable at last—but he knew that he had just lost something more, as surely as if he had married Judy Jones and seen her fade away before his eyes.

The dream was gone. Something had been taken from him. In a sort of panic he pushed the palms of his hands into his eyes and tried to bring up a picture of the waters lapping on Sherry Island and the moonlit verandah, and gingham on the golf links and the dry sun and the gold color of her neck's soft down. And her mouth damp to his kisses and her eyes plaintive with melancholy and her freshness like new fine linen in the morning. Why, these things were no longer in the world! They had existed and they existed no longer.

For the first time in years the tears were streaming down his face. But they were for himself now. He did not care about mouth and eyes and moving hands. He wanted to care and he could not care. For he had gone away and he could never go back anymore. The gates were closed, the sun was gone down and there was no beauty but the grey beauty of steel that withstands all time. Even the grief he could have borne was left behind in the country of illusion, of youth, of the richness of life, where his winter dreams had flourished.

"Long ago," he said, "long ago, there was something in me, but now that thing is gone. Now that thing is gone, that thing is gone. I cannot cry. I cannot care. That thing will come back no more."

ABSOLUTION

There was once a priest with cold, watery eyes, who, in the still of the night, wept cold tears. He wept because the afternoons were warm and long, and he was unable to attain a complete mystical union with our Lord. Sometimes, near four o'clock, there was a rustle of Swede girls along the path by his window, and in their shrill laughter he found a terrible dissonance that made him pray aloud for the twilight to come. At twilight the laughter and the voices were quieter, but several times he had walked past Romberg's Drug Store when it was dusk and the yellow lights shone inside and the nickel taps of the soda fountain were gleaming, and he had found the scent of cheap toilet soap desperately sweet upon the air. He passed that way when he returned from hearing confessions on Saturday nights, and he grew careful to walk on the other side of the street so that the smell of the soap would float upward before it reached his nostrils as it drifted, rather like incense, toward the summer moon.

But there was no escape from the hot madness of four o'clock. From his window, as far as he could see, the Dakota wheat thronged the valley of the Red River. The wheat was terrible to look upon and the carpet pattern to which in agony he bent his eyes sent his thoughts brooding through grotesque labyrinths, open always to the unavoidable sun.

One afternoon when he had reached the point where the mind runs down like an old clock, his housekeeper brought into his study a beautiful, intense little boy of eleven named Rudolph Miller. The little boy sat down in a patch of sunshine and the priest, at his walnut desk, pretended to be very busy. This was to conceal his relief that someone had come into his haunted room.

Presently he turned around and found himself staring into two enormous, staccato eyes, lit with gleaming points of cobalt light. For a moment their expression startled him—then he saw that his visitor was in a state of abject fear.

"Your mouth is trembling," said Father Schwartz, in a haggard voice.

The little boy covered his quivering mouth with his hand.

"Are you in trouble?" asked Father Schwartz, sharply. "Take your hand away from your mouth and tell me what's the matter."

The boy—Father Schwartz recognized him now as the son of a parishioner, Mr. Miller, the freight agent—moved his hand reluctantly off his mouth and became articulate in a despairing whisper.

"Father Schwartz—I've committed a terrible sin."

"A sin against purity?"

"No, Father . . . worse."

Father Schwartz's body jerked sharply.

"Have you killed somebody?"

"No—but I'm afraid—" the voice rose to a shrill whimper.

"Do you want to go to confession?"

The little boy shook his head miserably. Father Schwartz cleared his throat so that he could make his voice soft and say some quiet, kind thing. In this moment he should forget his own agony and try to act like God. He repeated to himself a devotional phrase, hoping that in return God would help him to act correctly.

"Tell me what you've done," said his new soft voice.

The little boy looked at him through his tears and was reassured by the impression of moral resiliency which the distraught priest had created. Abandoning as much of himself as he was able to this man, Rudolph Miller began to tell his story.

"On Saturday, three days ago, my father he said I had to go to confession, because I hadn't been for a month, and the family they go every week, and I hadn't been. So I just as leave go, I didn't care. So I put it off till after supper because I was playing with a bunch of kids and Father asked me if I went and I said 'no,' and he took me by the neck and he said 'You go now,' so I said 'All right,' so I went over to church. And he yelled after me: 'Don't come back till you go.' . . ."

II
"On Saturday, Three Days Ago"

The plush curtain of the confessional rearranged its dismal creases, leaving exposed only the bottom of an old man's old shoe. Behind the curtain an immortal soul was alone with God and the Reverend Adolphus Schwartz, priest of the parish. Sound began, a labored whispering, sibilant and discreet, broken at intervals by the voice of the priest in audible question.

Rudolph Miller knelt in the pew beside the confessional and waited, straining nervously to hear and yet not to hear what was being said within. The fact that the priest was audible alarmed him. His own turn came next, and the three or four others who waited might listen unscrupulously while he admitted his violations of the Sixth and Ninth Commandments.

Rudolph had never committed adultery, not even coveted his neighbor's wife—but it was the confession of the associate sins that was particularly hard to contemplate. In comparison he relished the less shameful fallings away—they formed a greyish background which relieved the ebony mark of sexual offenses upon his soul.

He had been covering his ears with his hands, hoping that his refusal to hear would be noticed, and a like courtesy rendered to him in turn, when a sharp movement of the penitent in the confessional made him sink his face precipitately into the crook of his elbow. Fear assumed solid form and pressed out a lodging between his heart and his lungs. He must try now with all his might to be sorry for his sins—not because he was afraid, but because he had offended God. He must convince God that he was sorry and to do so he must first convince himself. After a tense emotional struggle he achieved a tremulous self-pity, and decided that he was now ready. If, by allowing no other thought to enter his head, he could preserve this state of emotion unimpaired until he went into that large coffin set on end, he would have survived another crisis in his religious life.

For some time, however, a demoniac notion had partially possessed him. He could go home now, before his turn came, and tell his mother that he had arrived too late and found the priest gone. This, unfortunately, involved the risk of being caught in a lie. As an alternative he could say that he *had* gone to confession, but this meant that he must avoid communion next day, for communion taken upon an uncleansed soul would turn to poison in his mouth, and he would crumple limp and damned from the altar rail.

Again Father Schwartz's voice became audible.

"And for your—"

The words blurred to a husky mumble and Rudolph got excitedly to his feet. He felt that it was impossible for him to go to confession this afternoon. He hesitated tensely. Then from the confessional came a tap, a creak and a sustained rustle. The slide had fallen and the plush curtain trembled. Temptation had come to him too late. . . .

"Bless me, Father, for I have sinned. . . . I confess to Almighty God and to you, Father, that I have sinned. . . . Since my last confession it has been one month and three days. . . . I accuse myself of—taking the Name of the Lord in vain. . . ."

This was an easy sin. His curses had been but bravado—telling of them was little less than a brag.

". . . of being mean to an old lady."

The wan shadow moved a little on the latticed slat.

"How, my child?"

"Old lady Swenson," Rudolph's murmur soared jubilantly. "She got our baseball that we knocked in her window, and she wouldn't give it back, so we yelled 'Twenty-three Skidoo' at her all afternoon. Then about five o'clock she had a fit and they had to have the doctor."

"Go on, my child."

"Of—of not believing I was the son of my parents."

"What?"

The interrogator was distinctly startled.

"Of not believing that I was the son of my parents."

"Why not?"

"Oh, just pride," answered the penitent airily.

"You mean you thought you were too good to be the son of your parents?"

"Yes, Father." On a less jubilant note.

"Go on."

"Of being disobedient and calling my mother names. Of slandering people behind my back. Of smoking—"

Rudolph had now exhausted the minor offenses and was approaching the sins it was agony to tell. He held his fingers against his face like bars as if to press out between them the shame in his heart.

"Of dirty words and immodest thoughts and desires," he whispered very low.

"How often?"

"I don't know."

"Once a week? Twice a week?"

"Twice a week."

"Did you yield to these desires?"

"No, Father."

"Were you alone when you had them?"

"No, Father. I was with two boys and a girl."

"Don't you know, my child, that you should avoid the occasions of sin as well as the sin itself? Evil companionship leads to evil desires and evil desires to evil actions. Where were you when this happened?"

"In a barn in back of—"

"I don't want to hear any names," interrupted the priest sharply.

"Well, it was up in the loft of this barn and this girl and—a fella, they were saying things—saying immodest things, and I stayed."

"You should have gone—you should have told the girl to go."

He should have gone! He could not tell Father Schwartz how his pulse had bumped in his wrist, how a strange, romantic excitement had possessed him when those curious things had been said. Perhaps in the houses of delinquency among the dull and hard-eyed incorrigible girls can be found those for whom has burned the whitest fire.

"Have you anything else to tell me?"

"I don't think so, Father."

Rudolph felt a great relief. Perspiration had broken out under his tight-pressed fingers.

"Have you told any lies?"

The question startled him. Like all those who habitually and instinctively lie, he had an enormous respect and awe for the truth. Something almost exterior to himself dictated a quick, hurt answer.

"Oh, no, Father, I never tell lies."

For a moment, like the commoner in the king's chair, he tasted the pride of the situation. Then as the priest began to murmur conventional admonitions he realized that in heroically denying he had told lies, he had committed a terrible sin—he had told a lie in confession.

In automatic response to Father Schwartz's "Make an act of contrition," he began to repeat aloud meaninglessly:

"Oh, my God, I am heartily sorry for having offended Thee. . . ."

He must fix this now—it was a bad mistake—but as his teeth shut on the last words of his prayer there was a sharp sound, and the slat was closed.

A minute later when he emerged into the twilight the relief in coming from the muggy church into an open world of wheat and sky postponed the full realization of what he had done. Instead of worrying he took a deep breath of the crisp air and began to say over and over to himself the words "Blatchford Sarnemington, Blatchford Sarnemington!"

Blatchford Sarnemington was himself, and these words were in effect a lyric. When he became Blatchford Sarnemington a suave nobility flowed from him. Blatchford Sarnemington lived in great sweeping triumphs. When Rudolph half closed his eyes it meant that Blatchford had established dominance over him and, as he went by, there were envious mutters in the air: "Blatchford Sarnemington! There goes Blatchford Sarnemington."

He was Blatchford now for awhile as he strutted homeward along the staggering road, but when the road braced itself in macadam in order to become the main street of Ludwig, Rudolph's exhilaration faded out and his mind cooled and he felt the horror of his lie. God, of course, already knew of it—but Rudolph reserved a corner of his mind where he was safe from God, where he prepared the subterfuges with which he often tricked God. Hiding now in this corner he considered how he could best avoid the consequences of his misstatement.

At all costs he must avoid communion next day. The risk of angering God to such an extent was too great. He would have to drink water "by accident" in the morning and thus, in accordance with a church law, render himself unfit to receive communion that day. In spite of its flimsiness this subterfuge was the most feasible that occurred to him. He accepted its risks and was concentrating on how best to put it into effect, as he turned the corner by Romberg's Drug Store and came in sight of his father's house.

III

Rudolph's father, the local freight agent, had floated with the second wave of German and Irish stock to the Minnesota-Dakota country. Theoretically, great opportunities lay ahead of a young man of energy in that day and place, but Carl Miller had been incapable of establishing either with his superiors or his subordinates the reputation for approximate immutability which is essential to success in a hierarchic industry. Somewhat gross, he was, nevertheless, insufficiently hard-headed and unable to take fundamental relationships for granted, and this inability made him suspicious, unrestful and continually dismayed.

His two bonds with the colorful life were his faith in the Roman Catholic Church and his mystical worship of the Empire Builder, James J. Hill. Hill was the apotheosis of that quality in which Miller himself was deficient—the sense of things, the feel of things, the hint of rain in the wind on the cheek. Miller's mind worked late on the old decisions of other men, and he had never in his life felt the balance of any single thing in his hands. His weary, sprightly, undersized body was growing old in Hill's gigantic shadow. For twenty years he had lived alone with Hill's name and God.

On Sunday morning Carl Miller awoke in the dustless quiet of six o'clock. Kneeling by the side of the bed he bent his yellow-grey hair and the full dapple bangs of his mustache into the pillow, and prayed for several minutes. Then he drew off his night-shirt—like the rest of his generation he had never been able to endure pajamas—and clothed his thin, white, hairless body in woollen underwear.

He shaved. Silence in the other bedroom where his wife lay nervously asleep. Silence from the screened-off corner of the hall where his son's cot stood, and his son slept among his Alger books, his collection of cigar-bands, his mothy pennants—"Cornell," "Hamline," and "Greetings from Pueblo, New Mexico"—and the other possessions of his private life. From outside Miller could hear the shrill birds and the whirring movement of the poultry and, as an undertone, the low, swelling click-a-tick of the six-fifteen through-train for Montana and the green coast beyond. Then as the cold water dripped from the washrag in his hand he raised his head suddenly—he had heard a furtive sound from the kitchen below.

He dried his razor hastily, slipped his dangling suspenders to his shoulders, and listened. Someone was walking in the kitchen, and he knew by the light foot-fall that it was not his wife. With his mouth faintly ajar he ran quickly down the stairs and opened the kitchen door.

Standing by the sink, with one hand on the still dripping faucet and the other clutching a full glass of water, stood his son. The boy's eyes, still heavy with sleep, met his father's with a frightened, reproachful beauty. He was barefooted and his pajamas were rolled up at the knees and sleeves.

For a moment they both remained motionless—Carl Miller's brow went down and his son's went up, as though they were striking a balance between the extremes of emotion which filled them. Then the bangs of the parent's mustache descended portentously until they obscured his mouth, and he gave a short glance around to see if anything had been disturbed.

The kitchen was garnished with sunlight which beat on the pans and made the smooth boards of the floor and table yellow and clean as wheat. It was the center of the house where the fire burned and the tins fitted into tins like toys, and the steam whistled all day on a thin pastel note. Nothing was moved, nothing touched—except the faucet where beads of water still formed and dripped with a white flash into the sink below.

"What are you doing?"

"I got awful thirsty, so I thought I'd just come down and get—"

"I thought you were going to communion."

A look of vehement astonishment spread over his son's face.

"I forgot all about it."

"Have you drunk any water?"

"No—"

As the word left his mouth Rudolph knew it was the wrong answer, but the faded indignant eyes facing him had signalled up the truth before the boy's will could act. He realized, too, that he should never have come downstairs; some vague necessity for verisimilitude had made him want to leave a wet glass as evidence by the sink; the honesty of his imagination had betrayed him.

"Pour it out," commanded his father, "that water!"

Rudolph despairingly inverted the tumbler.

"What's the matter with you, anyways?" demanded Miller angrily.

"Nothing."

"Did you go to confession yesterday?"

"Yes."

"Then why were you going to drink water?"

"I don't know—I forgot."

"Maybe you care more about being a little bit thirsty than you do about your religion."

"I forgot." Rudolph could feel the tears straining in his eyes.

"That's no answer."

"Well, I did."

"You better look out!" His father held to a high, persistent, inquisitory note: "If you're so forgetful that you can't remember your religion something better be done about it."

Rudolph filled a sharp pause with:

"I can remember it all right."

"First you begin to neglect your religion," cried his father, fanning his own fierceness, "the next thing you'll begin to lie and steal, and the *next* thing is the *reform* school!"

Not even this familiar threat could deepen the abyss that Rudolph saw before him. He must either tell all now, offering his body for what he knew would be a ferocious beating, or else tempt the thunderbolts by receiving the Body and Blood of Christ with sacrilege upon his soul.

And of the two the former seemed more terrible—it was not so much the beating he dreaded as the savage ferocity, outlet of the ineffectual man, which would lie behind it.

"Put down that glass and go upstairs and dress!" his father ordered. "And when we get to church, before you go to communion, you better kneel down and ask God to forgive you for your carelessness."

Some accidental emphasis in the phrasing of this command acted like a catalytic agent on the confusion and terror of Rudolph's mind. A wild, proud anger rose in him, and he dashed the tumbler passionately into the sink.

His father uttered a strained, husky sound, and sprang for him. Rudolph dodged to the side, tipped over a chair, and tried to get beyond the kitchen table. He cried out sharply when a hand grasped his pajama shoulder, then he felt the dull impact of a fist against the side of his head and glancing blows on the upper part of his body. As he slipped here and there in his father's grasp, dragged or lifted when he clung instinctively to an arm, aware of sharp smarts and strains, he made no sound except that he laughed hysterically several times. Then in less than a minute the blows abruptly ceased. After a lull during which Rudolph was tightly held and during which they both trembled violently and uttered strange, truncated words, Carl Miller half dragged, half threatened his son upstairs.

"Put on your clothes!"

Rudolph was now both hysterical and cold. His head hurt him, and there was a long, shallow scratch on his neck from his father's fingernail, and he sobbed and trembled as he dressed. He was aware of his mother standing at the doorway in a wrapper, her wrinkled face compressing and squeezing and opening out into a new series of wrinkles which floated and eddied from neck to brow. Despising her nervous ineffectuality and avoiding her rudely when she tried to touch his neck with witch-hazel, he made a hasty, choking toilet. Then he followed his father out of the house and along the road toward the Catholic church.

IV

They walked without speaking except when Carl Miller acknowledged automatically the existence of passers-by. Rudolph's uneven breathing alone ruffled the hot Sunday silence.

His father stopped decisively at the door of the church.

"I've decided you'd better go to confession again. Go in and tell Father Schwartz what you did and ask God's pardon."

"You lost your temper, too!" said Rudolph quickly.

Carl Miller took a step toward his son, who moved cautiously backward.

"All right, I'll go."

"Are you going to do what I say?" cried his father in a hoarse whisper.

"All right."

Rudolph walked into the church and for the second time in two days entered the confessional and knelt down. The slat went up almost at once.

"I accuse myself of missing my morning prayers."

"Is that all?"

"That's all."

A maudlin exultation filled him. Not easily ever again would he be able to put an abstraction before the necessities of his ease and pride. An invisible line had been crossed and he had become aware of his isolation—aware that it applied not only to those moments when he was Blatchford Sarnemington but that it applied to all his inner life. Hitherto such phenomena as "crazy" ambitions and petty shames and fears had been but private reservations, unacknowledged before the throne of his official soul. Now he realized unconsciously that his private reservations were himself—and all the rest a garnished front and a conventional flag. The pressure of his environment had driven him into the lonely secret road of adolescence.

He knelt in the pew beside his father. Mass began. Rudolph knelt up—when he was alone he slumped his posterior back against the seat—and tasted the consciousness of a sharp, subtle revenge. Beside him his father prayed that God would forgive Rudolph, and asked also that his own outbreak of temper would be pardoned. He glanced sidewise at this son and was relieved to see that the strained, wild look had gone from his face and that he had ceased sobbing. The Grace of God, inherent in the Sacrament, would do the rest, and perhaps after Mass everything would be better. He was proud of Rudolph in his heart and beginning to be truly as well as formally sorry for what he had done.

Usually, the passing of the collection box was a significant point for Rudolph in the services. If, as was often the case, he had no money to drop in he would be furiously ashamed and bow his head and pretend not to see the box, lest Jeanne Brady in the pew behind should take notice and suspect an acute family poverty. But today he glanced coldly into it as it skimmed under his eyes, noting with casual interest the large number of pennies it contained.

When the bell rang for communion, however, he quivered. There was no reason why God should not stop his heart. During the past twelve hours he had committed a series of mortal sins increasing in gravity, and he was now to crown them all with a blasphemous sacrilege.

"*Dómini, non sum dignus, ut intres sub tectum meum: sed tantum dic verbo, et sănábitur ánima mea. . . .*"

There was a rustle in the pews and the communicants worked their ways into the aisle with downcast eyes and joined hands. Those of larger piety pressed together their fingertips to form steeples. Among these latter was Carl Miller. Rudolph followed him toward the altar rail and knelt down, automatically taking up the napkin under his chin. The bell rang sharply, and the priest turned from the altar with the white Host held above the chalice:

"*Corpus Dómini nostri Jesu Christi custódiat ánimam meam in vitam ætérnam.*"

A cold sweat broke out on Rudolph's forehead as the communion began. Along the line Father Schwartz moved, and with gathering nausea Rudolph felt his heart-valves weakening at the will of God. It seemed to him that the church was darker and that a great quiet had fallen, broken only by the inarticulate mumble which announced the approach of the Creator of Heaven and Earth. He dropped his head down between his shoulders and waited for the blow.

Then he felt a sharp nudge in his side. His father was poking him to sit up, not to slump against the rail; the priest was only two places away.

"*Corpus Dómini nostri Jesu Christi custódiat ánimam meam in vitam ætérnam.*"

Rudolph opened his mouth. He felt the sticky wax taste of the wafer on his tongue. He remained motionless for what seemed an interminable period of time, his head still raised, the wafer undissolved in his mouth. Then again he started at the pressure of his father's elbow, and saw that the people were falling away from the altar like leaves and turning with blind downcast eyes to their pews, alone with God.

Rudolph was alone with himself, drenched with perspiration and deep in mortal sin. As he walked back to his pew the sharp taps of his cloven hoofs were loud upon the floor, and he knew that it was a dark poison he carried in his heart.

V

"Sagitta Volante in Die"

The beautiful little boy with eyes like blue stones, and lashes that sprayed open from them like flower-petals, had finished telling his sin to Father Schwartz—and the square of sunshine in which he sat had moved forward half an hour into the room. Rudolph had become less frightened now; once eased of the story a reaction had set in. He knew that as long as he was in the room with this priest God would not stop his heart, so he sighed and sat quietly, waiting for the priest to speak.

Father Schwartz's cold watery eyes were fixed upon the carpet pattern on which the sun had brought out the swastikas and the flat bloomless vines and the pale echoes of flowers. The hall clock ticked insistently toward sunset, and from the ugly room and from the afternoon outside the window arose a stiff monotony, shattered now and then by the reverberate clapping of a far-away hammer on the dry air. The priest's nerves were strung thin and the beads of his rosary were crawling and squirming like snakes upon the green felt of his table top. He could not remember now what it was he should say.

Of all the things in this lost Swede town he was most aware of this little boy's eyes—the beautiful eyes, with lashes that left them reluctantly and curved back as though to meet them once more.

For a moment longer the silence persisted while Rudolph waited, and the priest struggled to remember something that was slipping farther and farther away from him, and the clock ticked in the broken house. Then Father Schwartz stared hard at the little boy and remarked in a peculiar voice—

"When a lot of people get together in the best places things go glimmering."

Rudolph started and looked quickly at Father Schwartz's face.

"I said—" began the priest, and paused, listening. "Do you hear the hammer and the clock ticking and the bees? Well, that's no good. The thing is to have a lot of people in the center of the world, wherever that happens to be. Then"—his watery eyes widened knowingly—"things go glimmering."

"Yes, Father," agreed Rudolph, feeling a little frightened.

"What are you going to be when you grow up?"

"Well, I was going to be a baseball player for awhile," answered Rudolph nervously, "but I don't think that's a very good ambition, so I think I'll be an actor or a navy officer."

Again the priest stared at him.

"I see *exactly* what you mean," he said, with a fierce air.

Rudolph had not meant anything in particular, and at the implication that he had, he became more uneasy.

"This man is crazy," he thought, "and I'm scared of him. He wants me to help him out some way, and I don't want to."

"You look as if things went glimmering," cried Father Schwartz wildly. "Did you ever go to a party?"

"Yes, Father."

"And did you notice that everybody was properly dressed? That's what I mean. Just as you went into the party there was a moment when everybody was properly dressed. Maybe two little girls were standing by the door and some boys were leaning over the banisters, and there were bowls around full of flowers."

"I've been to a lot of parties," said Rudolph, rather relieved that the conversation had taken this turn.

"Of course," continued Father Schwartz triumphantly, "I knew you'd agree with me. But my theory is that when a whole lot of people get together in the best places things go glimmering all the time."

Rudolph found himself thinking of Blatchford Sarnemington.

"Please listen to me!" commanded the priest impatiently. "Stop worrying about last Saturday. Apostasy implies an absolute damnation only on the supposition of a previous perfect faith. Does that fix it?"

Rudolph had not the faintest idea what Father Schwartz was talking about, but he nodded and the priest nodded back at him and returned to his mysterious preoccupation.

"Why," he cried, "they have lights now as big as stars—do you realize that? I heard of one light they had in Paris or somewhere that was as big as a star. A lot of people had it—a lot of gay people. They have all sorts of things now that you never dreamed of.

"Look here—" He came nearer to Rudolph, but the boy drew away, so Father Schwartz went back and sat down in his chair, his eyes dried out and hot.

"Did you ever see an amusement park?"

"No, Father."

"Well, go and see an amusement park." The priest waved his hand vaguely. "It's a thing like a fair, only much more glittering. Go to one at night and stand a little way off from it in a dark place—under dark trees. You'll see a big wheel made of lights turning in the air and a long slide shooting boats down into the water. A band playing somewhere and a smell of peanuts—and everything will twinkle. But it won't remind you of anything, you see. It will all just hang out there in the night like a colored balloon—like a big yellow lantern on a pole."

Father Schwartz frowned as he suddenly thought of something.

"But don't get up close," he warned Rudolph, "because if you do you'll only feel the heat and the sweat and the life."

All this talking seemed particularly strange and awful to Rudolph, because this man was a priest. He sat there, half terrified, his beautiful eyes open wide and staring at Father Schwartz. But underneath his terror he felt that his own inner convictions were confirmed. There was something ineffably gorgeous somewhere that had nothing to do with God. He no longer thought that God was angry at him about the original lie, because He must have understood that Rudolph had done it to make things finer in the confessional, brightening up the dinginess of his admissions by saying a thing radiant and proud. At the moment when he had affirmed immaculate honor a silver pennon had flapped out into the breeze somewhere and there had been the crunch of leather and the shine of silver spurs and a troop of horsemen waiting for dawn on a low green hill. The sun had made stars of light on their breastplates like the picture at home of the German cuirassiers at Sedan.

But now the priest was muttering inarticulate and heartbroken words, and the boy became wildly afraid. Horror entered suddenly in at the open window, and the atmosphere of the room changed. Father

Schwartz collapsed precipitously down on his knees and let his body settle back against a chair.

"Oh, my God!" he cried out, in a strange voice, and wilted to the floor.

Then a human oppression rose from the priest's worn clothes and mingled with the faint smell of old food in the corners. Rudolph gave a sharp cry and ran in a panic from the house—while the collapsed man lay there quite still, filling his room, filling it with voices and faces until it was crowded with echolalia, and rang loud with a steady, shrill note of laughter.

◆

Outside the window the blue sirocco trembled over the wheat, and girls with yellow hair walked sensuously along roads that bounded the fields, calling innocent, exciting things to the young men who were working in the lines between the grain. Legs were shaped under starchless gingham, and rims of the necks of dresses were warm and damp. For five hours now hot fertile life had burned in the afternoon. It would be night in three hours, and all along the land there would be these blonde northern girls and the tall young men from the farms lying out beside the wheat, under the moon.

RAGS MARTIN-JONES
and THE PR-NCE OF W-LES

T he *Majestic* came gliding into New York harbor on an April morning. She sniffed at the tug-boats and turtle-gaited ferries, winked
at a gaudy young yacht, and ordered a cattle-boat out of her way
with a snarling whistle of steam. Then she parked at her private dock
with all the fuss of a stout lady sitting down, and announced compla-
cently that she had just come from Cherbourg and Southampton with
a cargo of the very best people in the world.

The very best people in the world stood on the deck and waved idiotically to their poor relations who were waiting on the dock for gloves
from Paris. Before long a great toboggan had connected the *Majestic*
with the North American continent and the ship began to disgorge
these very best people in the world—who turned out to be Gloria
Swanson, two buyers from Lord & Taylor, the financial minister from
Graustark with a proposal for funding the debt, and an African king
who had been trying to land somewhere all winter and was feeling
violently seasick.

The photographers worked passionately as the stream of passengers
flowed onto the dock. There was a burst of cheering at the appearance
of a pair of stretchers laden with two middle-westerners who had
drunk themselves delirious on the last night out.

The deck gradually emptied but when the last bottle of Benedictine had reached shore the photographers still remained at their posts. And the officer in charge of debarkation still stood at the foot of the gang-way, glancing first at his watch and then at the deck as if some important part of the cargo was still on board. At last from the watchers on the pier there arose a long-drawn "Ah-h-h!" as a final entourage began to stream down from deck B.

First came two French maids, carrying small, purple dogs, and followed by a squad of porters, blind and invisible under innumerable bunches and bouquets of fresh flowers. Another maid followed, leading a sad-eyed orphan child of a French flavor, and close upon its heels walked the second officer pulling along three neurasthenic wolfhounds, much to their reluctance and his own.

A pause. Then the captain, Sir Howard George Witchcraft, appeared at the rail, with something that might have been a pile of gorgeous silver fox fur standing by his side—

Rags Martin-Jones, after five years in the capitals of Europe, was returning to her native land!

Rags Martin-Jones was not a dog. She was half a girl and half a flower and as she shook hands with Captain Sir Howard George Witchcraft she smiled as if someone had told her the newest, freshest joke in the world. All the people who had not already left the pier felt that smile trembling on the April air and turned around to see.

She came slowly down the gang-way. Her hat, an expensive, inscrutable experiment, was crushed under her arm so that her scant boy's hair, convict's hair, tried unsuccessfully to toss and flop a little in the harbor wind. Her face was like seven o'clock on a wedding morning save where she had slipped a preposterous monocle into an eye of clear childish blue. At every few steps her long lashes would tilt out the monocle and she would laugh, a bored, happy laugh, and replace the supercilious spectacle in the other eye.

Tap! Her one hundred and five pounds reached the pier and it seemed to sway and bend from the shock of her beauty. A few porters fainted. A large, sentimental shark which had followed the ship across made a despairing leap to see her once more, and then dove, broken-hearted, back into the deep sea. Rags Martin-Jones had come home.

There was no member of her family there to meet her for the simple reason that she was the only member of her family left alive. In 1912 her parents had gone down on the *Titanic* together rather than be separated in this world, and so the Martin-Jones fortune of seventy-five millions had been inherited by a very little girl on her tenth birthday. It was what the consumer always refers to as a "shame."

Rags Martin-Jones (everybody had forgotten her real name long ago) was now photographed from all sides. The monocle persistently fell out and she kept laughing and yawning and replacing it, so no very clear picture of her was taken—except by the motion-picture camera. All the photographs, however, included a flustered, handsome young man, with an almost ferocious love-light burning in his eyes, who had met her on the dock. His name was John M. Chestnut, he had already written the story of his success for the "American Magazine" and he had been hopelessly in love with Rags ever since the time when she, like the tides, had come under the influence of the summer moon.

When Rags became really aware of his presence they were walking down the pier, and she looked at him blankly as though she had never seen him before in this world.

"Rags," he began, "Rags—"

"John M. Chestnut?" she inquired, inspecting him with great interest.

"Of course!" he exclaimed angrily. "Are you trying to pretend you don't know me? That you didn't write me to meet you here?"

She laughed. A chauffeur appeared at her elbow and she twisted out of her coat, revealing a dress made in great splashy checks of sea-blue and grey. She shook herself like a wet bird.

"I've got a lot of junk to declare," she remarked absently.

"So have I," said Chestnut anxiously, "and the first thing I want to declare is that I've loved you, Rags, every minute since you've been away."

She stopped him with a groan.

"Please! There were some young Americans on the boat. The subject has become a bore."

"My God!" cried Chestnut. "Do you mean to say that you class *my* love with what was said to you on a *boat*?"

His voice had risen and several people in the vicinity turned to hear.

"Sh!" she warned him. "I'm not giving a circus. If you want me to even see you while I'm here you'll have to be less violent."

But John M. Chestnut seemed unable to control his voice.

"Do you mean to say"—it trembled to a carrying pitch—"that you've forgotten what you said on this very pier five years ago last Thursday?"

Half the passengers from the ship were now watching the scene on the dock and another little eddy drifted out of the customs house to see.

"John"—her displeasure was increasing—"if you raise your voice again I'll arrange it so you'll have plenty of chance to cool off. I'm going to the Ritz. Come and see me there this afternoon."

"But, Rags—!" he protested hoarsely. "Listen to me. Five years ago—"

Then the watchers on the dock were treated to a curious sight. A beautiful lady in a checkered dress of sea-blue and grey took a brisk step forward so that her hands came into contact with an excited young man by her side. The young man retreating instinctively reached back with his foot, but, finding nothing, relapsed gently off the thirty-foot dock and plopped, after a not ungraceful revolution, into the Hudson River.

A shout of alarm went up and there was a rush to the edge just as his head appeared above water. He was swimming easily and, perceiving this, the young lady who had apparently been the cause of the accident leaned over the pier and made a megaphone of her hands.

"I'll be in at half past four," she cried.

And with a cheerful wave of her hand, which the engulfed gentleman was unable to return, she adjusted her monocle, threw one haughty glance at the gathered crowd and walked leisurely from the scene.

II

The five dogs, the three maids and the French orphan were installed in the largest suite at the Ritz and Rags tumbled lazily into a steaming bath, fragrant with herbs, where she dozed for the greater part of an hour. At the end of that time she received business calls from a masseuse, a manicure and finally a Parisian hair-dresser, who restored her hair-cut to criminal's length. When John M. Chestnut arrived at four he found half a dozen lawyers and bankers, the administrators of the Martin-Jones trust fund, waiting in the hall. They had been there since half past one and were now in a state of considerable agitation.

After one of the maids had subjected him to a severe scrutiny, possibly to be sure that he was thoroughly dry, John was conducted immediately into the presence of M'selle. M'selle was in her bedroom reclining on the chaise longue among two dozen silk pillows that had accompanied her from the other side. John came into the room somewhat stiffly and greeted her with a formal bow.

"You look better," she said, raising herself from her pillows and staring at him appraisingly. "It gave you a color."

He thanked her coldly for the compliment.

"You ought to go in every morning." And then she added irrelevantly, "I'm going back to Paris tomorrow."

John Chestnut gasped.

"I wrote you that I didn't intend to stay more than a week anyhow," she added.

"But, Rags——"

"Why should I? There isn't an amusing man in New York."

"But listen, Rags, won't you give me a chance? Won't you stay for, say, ten days and get to know me a little?"

"Know you!" Her tone implied that he was already a far too open book. "I want a man who's capable of a gallant gesture."

"Do you mean you want me to express myself entirely in pantomime?"

Rags uttered a disgusted sigh.

"I mean you haven't any imagination," she explained patiently. "No Americans have any imagination. Paris is the only large city where a civilized woman can breathe."

"Don't you care for me at all anymore?"

"I wouldn't have crossed the Atlantic to see you if I didn't. But as soon as I looked over the Americans on the boat I knew I couldn't marry one. I'd just hate you, John, and the only fun I'd have out of it would be the fun of breaking your heart."

She began to twist herself down among the cushions until she almost disappeared from view.

"I've lost my monocle," she explained.

After an unsuccessful search in the silken depths she discovered the elusive glass hanging down the back of her neck.

"I'd love to be in love," she went on, replacing the monocle in her childish eye. "Last spring in Sorrento I almost eloped with an Indian rajah, but he was half a shade too dark, and I took an intense dislike to one of his other wives."

"Don't talk that rubbish!" cried John, sinking his face into his hands.

"Well, I didn't marry him," she protested. "But in one way he had a lot to offer. He was the third richest subject of the British Empire. That's another thing—are you rich?"

"Not as rich as you."

"There you are. What have you to offer me?"

"Love."

"Love!" She disappeared again among the cushions. "Listen, John. Life to me is a series of glistening bazaars with a merchant in front of each one rubbing his hands together and saying 'Patronize this place here. Best bazaar in the world.' So I go in with my purse full of beauty and money and youth, all prepared to buy. 'What have you got for sale?' I ask him, and he rubs his hands together and says: 'Well, Mademoiselle, today we have some perfectly be-*oo*-tiful love.' Sometimes he hasn't even got that in stock but he sends out for it when he finds I have so much money to spend. Oh, he always gives me love before I go—and for nothing. That's the one revenge I have."

John Chestnut rose despairingly to his feet and took a step toward the window.

"Don't throw yourself out," Rags exclaimed quickly.

"All right." He tossed his cigarette down into Madison Avenue.

"It isn't just you," she said in a softer voice. "Dull and uninspired as you are, I care for you more than I can say. But life's so endless here. Nothing ever comes off."

"Loads of things come off," he insisted. "Why, today there was an intellectual murder in Hoboken and a suicide by proxy in Maine. A bill to sterilize agnostics is before Congress——"

"I have no interest in humor," she objected, "but I have an almost archaic predilection for romance. Why, John, last month I sat at a dinner table while two men flipped a coin for the kingdom of Schwartzberg-Rhineminster. In Paris I knew a man named Blutchdak who really started the war, and has a new one planned for year after next."

"Well, just for a rest you come out with me tonight," he said doggedly.

"Where to?" demanded Rags with scorn. "Do you think I still thrill at a night-club and a bottle of sugary mousseux? I prefer my own gaudy dreams."

"I'll take you to the most highly strung place in the city."

"What'll happen? You've got to tell me what'll happen."

John Chestnut suddenly drew a long breath and looked cautiously around as if he were afraid of being overheard.

"Well, to tell you the truth," he said in a low worried tone, "if everything was known, something pretty awful would be liable to happen to *me*."

She sat upright and the pillows tumbled about her like leaves.

"Do you mean to imply that there's anything shady in your life?" she cried, with laughter in her voice. "Do you expect me to believe that? No, John, you'll have your fun by plugging ahead on the beaten path—just plugging ahead."

Her mouth, a small insolent rose, dropped the words on him like thorns. John took his hat and coat from the chair and picked up his cane.

"For the last time—will you come along with me tonight and see what you will see?"

"See what? See who? Is there anything in this country worth seeing?"

"Well," he said, in a matter-of-fact tone, "for one thing you'll see the Prince of Wales."

"What?" She left the chaise longue at a bound. "Is he back in New York?"

"He will be tonight. Would you care to see him?"

"Would I? I've never seen him. I've missed him everywhere. I'd give a year of my life to see him for an hour." Her voice trembled with excitement.

"He's been in Canada. He's down here incognito for the big prize fight this afternoon. And I happen to know where he's going to be tonight."

Rags gave a sharp ecstatic cry:

"Dominic! Louise! Germaine!"

The three maids came running. The room filled suddenly with vibrations of wild, startled light.

"Dominic, the car!" cried Rags in French. "St. Raphael, my gold dress and the slippers with the real gold heels. The big pearls too—all the pearls, and the egg diamond and the stockings with the sapphire clocks. Germaine—send for a beauty-parlor on the run. My bath again—ice cold and half full of almond cream. Dominic—Tiffany's, like lightning, before they close! Find me a brooch, a pendant, a tiara, anything—it doesn't matter—with the arms of the House of Windsor."

She was fumbling at the buttons of her dress—and as John turned quickly to go it was already sliding from her shoulders.

"Orchids!" she called after him, "orchids, for the love of heaven! Four dozen, so I can choose four."

And then maids flew here and there about the room like frightened birds. "Perfume, St. Raphael, open the perfume trunk, and my rose-colored sables, and my diamond garters, and the sweet-oil for my hands! Here, take these things! This too—and this—Ouch!—and this!"

With becoming modesty John Chestnut closed the outside door. The six trustees in various postures of fatigue, of ennui, of resignation, of despair, were still cluttering up the outer hall.

"Gentlemen," announced John Chestnut, "I fear that Miss Martin-Jones is much too weary from her trip to talk to you this afternoon."

III

"This place, for no particular reason, is called the Hole in the Sky."

Rags looked around her. They were on a roof garden wide open to the April night. Overhead the true stars winked cold and there was a lunar sliver of ice in the dark west. But where they stood it was warm as June, and the couples dining or dancing on the opaque glass floor were unconcerned with the forbidding sky.

"What makes it so warm?" she whispered as they moved toward a table.

"It's some new invention that keeps the warm air from rising. I don't know the principle of the thing, but I know that they can keep it open like this even in the middle of winter—"

"Where's the Prince of Wales?" she demanded tensely.

John looked around.

"He hasn't arrived yet. He won't be here for about half an hour."

She sighed profoundly.

"It's the first time I've been excited in four years."

Four years—one year less than he had loved her. He wondered if when she was sixteen, a wild lovely child, sitting up all night in restaurants with officers who were to leave for Brest next day, losing the glamour of life too soon in the old, sad, poignant days of the war, she had ever been so lovely as under these amber lights and this dark sky. From her excited eyes to her tiny slipper heels, which were striped with layers of real silver and gold, she was like one of those amazing ships that are carved complete in a bottle. She was finished with that delicacy, with that care, as though the long lifetime of some worker in fragility had been used to make her so. John Chestnut wanted to take her up in his hands, turn her this way and that, examine the tip of a slipper or the tip of an ear or squint closely at the fairy stuff from which her lashes were made.

"Who's that?" She pointed suddenly to a handsome Latin at a table over the way.

"That's Roderigo Minerlino, the movie and face-cream star. Perhaps he'll dance after while."

Rags became suddenly aware of the sound of violins and drums but the music seemed to come from far away, seemed to float over the crisp night and on to the floor with the added remoteness of a dream.

"The orchestra's on another roof," explained John. "It's a new idea— Look, the entertainment's beginning."

A negro girl, thin as a reed, emerged suddenly from a masked entrance into a circle of harsh barbaric light, startled the music to a wild minor and commenced to sing a rhythmic, tragic song. The pipe of her body broke abruptly and she began a slow incessant step, without progress and without hope, like the failure of a savage insufficient dream. She had lost Papa Jack, she cried over and over with a hysterical monotony at once despairing and unreconciled. One by one the loud horns tried to force her from the steady beat of madness but she listened only to the mutter of the drums which were isolating her in some lost place in time, among many thousand forgotten years. After the failure of the piccolo, she made herself again into a thin brown line, wailed once with a sharp and terrible intensity, then vanished into sudden darkness.

"If you lived in New York you wouldn't need to be told who she is," said John when the amber light flashed on. "The next fella is Sheik B. Smith, a comedian of the fatuous, garrulous sort—"

He broke off. Just as the lights went down for the second number Rags had given a long sigh and leaned forward tensely in her chair. Her eyes were rigid like the eyes of a pointer dog, and John saw that they were fixed on a party that had come through a side entrance and were arranging themselves around a table in the half darkness.

The table was shielded with palms and Rags at first made out only three dim forms. Then she distinguished a fourth who seemed to be placed well behind the other three—a pale oval of a face topped with a glimmer of dark yellow hair.

"Hello!" ejaculated John. "There's his majesty now."

Her breath seemed to die murmurously in her throat. She was dimly aware that the comedian was now standing in a glow of white light on the dancing floor, that he had been talking for some moments, and that there was a constant ripple of laughter in the air. But her eyes remained motionless, enchanted. She saw one of the party bend and whisper to another, and, after the low glitter of a match, the bright button of a cigarette end gleamed in the background. How long it was before she moved she did not know. Then something seemed to happen to her eyes, something white, something terribly urgent, and she wrenched about sharply to find herself full in the center of a baby spotlight from above. She became aware that words were being said to her from somewhere and that a quick trail of laughter was circling the roof, but the light blinded her and instinctively she made a half movement from her chair.

"Sit still!" John was whispering across the table. "He picks somebody out for this every night."

Then she realized—it was the comedian, Sheik B. Smith. He was talking to her, arguing with her—about something that seemed incredibly funny to everyone else, but came to her ears only as a blur of muddled sound. Instinctively she had composed her face at the first shock of the light and now she smiled.[1] It was a gesture of rare self-possession. Into this smile she insinuated a vast impersonality, as if she were unconscious of the light, unconscious of his attempt to play upon her loveliness—but amused at an infinitely removed *him*, whose darts might have been thrown just as successfully at the moon. She was no longer a "lady"—a lady would have been harsh or pitiful or absurd; Rags stripped her attitude to a sheer consciousness of her own impervious beauty, sat there glittering until the comedian began to feel alone as he had never felt alone before. At a signal from him the spotlight was switched suddenly out. The moment was over.

The moment was over, the comedian left the floor and the faraway music began. John leaned toward her.

"I'm sorry. There really wasn't anything to do. You were wonderful."

She dismissed the incident with a casual laugh—then she started, there were now only two men sitting at the table across the floor.

"He's gone!" she exclaimed in quick distress.

"Don't worry—he'll be back. He's got to be awfully careful, you see, so he's probably waiting outside with one of his aides until it gets dark again."

"Why has he got to be careful?"

"Because he's not supposed to be in New York. He's even under one of his second-string names."

The lights dimmed again and almost immediately a tall man appeared out of the darkness and approached their table.

"May I introduce myself?" he said rapidly to John in a supercilious British voice. "Lord Charles Este, of Baron Marchbanks' party." He glanced at John closely as if to be sure that he appreciated the significance of the name.

John nodded.

"That is between ourselves, you understand."

"Of course."

Rags groped on the table for her untouched champagne and tipped the glassful down her throat.

"Baron Marchbanks requests that your companion will join his party during this number."

Both men looked at Rags. There was a moment's pause.

"Very well," she said, and glanced back again interrogatively at John. Again he nodded. She rose and with her heart beating wildly threaded the tables, making the half circuit of the room; then melted, a slim figure in shimmering gold, into the table set in half darkness.

IV

The number drew to a close and John Chestnut sat alone at his table, stirring auxiliary bubbles in his glass of champagne. Just before the lights went on there was a soft rasp of gold cloth and Rags, flushed and breathing quickly, sank into her chair. Her eyes were shining with tears.

John looked at her moodily.

"Well, what did he say?"

"He was very quiet."

"Didn't he say a word?"

Her hand trembled as she took up her glass of champagne.

"He just looked at me while it was dark. And he said a few conventional things. He was like his pictures, only he looks very bored and tired. He didn't even ask my name."

"Is he leaving New York tonight?"

"In half an hour. He and his aides have a car outside, and they expect to be over the border before dawn."

"Did you find him—fascinating?"

She hesitated and then slowly nodded her head.

"That's what everybody says," admitted John glumly. "Do they expect you back there?"

"I don't know." She looked uncertainly across the floor but the celebrated personage had again withdrawn from his table to some retreat outside. As she turned back an utterly strange young man who had been standing for a moment in the main entrance came toward them hurriedly. He was a deathly pale person in a dishevelled and inappropriate business suit, and he laid a trembling hand on John Chestnut's shoulder.

"Monte!" exclaimed John, starting up so suddenly that he upset his champagne. "What is it? What's the matter?"

"They've picked up the trail!" said the young man in a shaken whisper. He looked around. "I've got to speak to you alone."

John Chestnut jumped to his feet, and Rags noticed that his face too had become white as the napkin in his hand. He excused himself and they retreated to an unoccupied table a few feet away. Rags watched them curiously for a moment, then she resumed her scrutiny of the table across the floor. Would she be asked to come back? The prince had simply risen and bowed and gone outside. Perhaps she should have waited until he returned, but though she was still tense with excitement she had, to some extent, become Rags Martin-Jones again. Her curiosity was satisfied—any new urge must come from him. She wondered if she had really felt an intrinsic charm—she wondered especially if he had in any marked way responded to her beauty.

The pale person called Monte disappeared and John returned to the table. Rags was startled to find that a tremendous change had come over him. He lurched into his chair like a drunken man.

"John! What's the matter?"

Instead of answering he reached for the champagne bottle, but his fingers were trembling so that the splattered wine made a wet yellow ring around his glass.

"Are you sick?"

"Rags," he said unsteadily, "I'm all through."

"What do you mean?"

"I'm all through, I tell you." He managed a sickly smile. "There's been a warrant out for me for over an hour."

"What have you done?" she demanded in a frightened voice. "What's the warrant for?"

The lights went out for the next number and he collapsed suddenly over the table.

"What is it?" she insisted, with rising apprehension. She leaned forward—his answer was barely audible.

"Murder?" She could feel her body grow cold as ice.

He nodded. She took hold of both arms and tried to shake him upright, as one shakes a coat into place. His eyes were rolling in his head.

"Is it true? Have they got proof?"

Again he nodded drunkenly.

"Then you've got to get out of the country now! Do you understand, John? You've got to get out *now*, before they come looking for you here!"

He loosed a wild glance of terror toward the entrance.

"Oh, God!" cried Rags, "why don't you do something?" Her eyes strayed here and there in desperation, became suddenly fixed. She drew in her breath sharply, hesitated and then whispered fiercely into his ear.

"If I arrange it, will you go to Canada tonight?"

"How?"

"I'll arrange it—if you'll pull yourself together a little. This is Rags talking to you, don't you understand, John? I want you to sit here and not move until I come back!"

A minute later she had crossed the room under cover of the darkness.

"Baron Marchbanks," she whispered softly, standing just behind his chair.

He motioned her to sit down.

"Have you room in your car for two more passengers tonight?"

One of the aides turned around abruptly.

"His lordship's car is full," he said shortly.

"It's terribly urgent." Her voice was trembling.

"Well," said the prince hesitantly, "I don't know."

Lord Charles Este looked at the prince and shook his head.

"I don't think it's advisable. This is a ticklish business anyhow with contrary orders from home. You know we agreed there'd be no complications."

The prince frowned.

"This isn't a complication," he objected.

Este turned frankly to Rags.

"Why is it urgent?"

Rags hesitated.

"Why"—she flushed suddenly—"it's a runaway marriage."

The prince laughed.

"Good!" he exclaimed. "That settles it. Este is just being official. Bring him over right away. We're leaving shortly, what?"

Este looked at his watch.

"Right now!"

Rags rushed away. She wanted to move the whole party from the roof while the lights were still down.

"Hurry!" she cried in John's ear. "We're going over the border—with the Prince of Wales. You'll be safe by morning."

He looked up at her with dazed eyes. She hurriedly paid the check, and seizing his arm piloted him as inconspicuously as possible to the other table, where she introduced him with a word. The prince acknowledged his presence by shaking hands—the aides nodded, only faintly concealing their displeasure.

"We'd better start," said Este, looking impatiently at his watch.

They were on their feet when suddenly an exclamation broke from all of them—two policemen and a redhaired man in plain clothes had come in at the main door.

"Out we go," breathed Este, impelling the party toward the side entrance. "There's going to be some kind of riot here." He swore—two more bluecoats barred the exit there. They paused uncertainly. The plain-clothes man was beginning a careful inspection of the people at the tables.

Este looked sharply at Rags and then at John, who shrank back behind the palms.

"Is that one of your revenue fellas out there?" demanded Este.

"No," whispered Rags. "There's going to be trouble. Can't we get out this entrance?"

The prince with rising impatience sat down again in his chair.

"Let me know when you chaps are ready to go." He smiled at Rags. "Now just suppose we all get in trouble just for that jolly face of yours."

Then suddenly the lights went up. The plain-clothes man whirled around quickly and sprang to the middle of the cabaret floor.

"Nobody try to leave this room!" he shouted. "Sit down, that party behind the palms! Is John M. Chestnut in this room?"

Rags gave a short involuntary cry.

"Here!" cried the detective to the policeman behind him. "Take a look at that funny bunch over there. Hands up, you men!"

"My God!" whispered Este, "we've got to get out of here!" He turned to the prince. "This won't do, Ted. You can't be seen here. I'll stall them off while you get down to the car."

He took a step toward the side entrance.

"Hands up, there!" shouted the plain-clothes man. "And when I say hands up I mean it! Which one of you's Chestnut?"

"You're mad!" cried Este. "We're British subjects. We're not involved in this affair in any way!"

A woman screamed somewhere and there was a general movement toward the elevator, a movement which stopped short before the muzzles of two automatic pistols. A girl next to Rags collapsed in a dead faint to the floor, and at the same moment the music on the other roof began to play.

"Stop that music!" bellowed the plain-clothes man. "And get some earrings on that whole bunch—quick!"

Two policemen advanced toward the party, and simultaneously Este and the other aides drew their revolvers, and, shielding the prince as they best could, began to edge toward the side. A shot rang out and then another, followed by a crash of silver and china as half a dozen diners overturned their tables and dropped quickly behind.

The panic became general. There were three shots in quick succession and then a fusillade. Rags saw Este firing coolly at the eight amber lights above, and a thick fume of grey smoke began to fill the air. As a strange undertone to the shouting and screaming came the incessant clamor of the distant jazz band.

Then in a moment it was all over. A shrill whistle rang out over the roof, and through the smoke Rags saw John Chestnut advancing toward the plain-clothes man, his hands held out in a gesture of surrender. There was a last nervous cry, a chill clatter as someone inadvertently stepped into a pile of dishes, and then a heavy silence fell on the roof— even the band seemed to have died away.

"It's all over!" John Chestnut's voice rang out wildly on the night air. "The party's over. Everybody who wants to can go home!"

Still there was silence—Rags knew it was the silence of awe—the strain of guilt had driven John Chestnut insane.

"It was a great performance," he was shouting. "I want to thank you one and all. If you can find any tables still standing, champagne will be served as long as you care to stay."

It seemed to Rags that the roof and the high stars suddenly began to swim round and round. She saw John take the detective's hand and shake it heartily, and she watched the detective grin and pocket his gun. The music had recommenced, and the girl who had fainted was suddenly dancing with Lord Charles Este in the corner. John was running here and there patting people on the back, and laughing and shaking hands. Then he was coming toward her, fresh and innocent as a child.

"Wasn't it wonderful?" he cried.

Rags felt a faintness stealing over her. She groped backward with her hand toward a chair.

"What was it?" she cried dazedly. "Am I dreaming?"

"Of course not! You're wide awake. I made it up, Rags, don't you see? I made up the whole thing for you. I had it invented! The only thing real about it was my name!"

She collapsed suddenly against his coat, clung to his lapels and would have wilted to the floor if he had not caught her quickly in his arms.

"Some champagne—quick!" he called, and then he shouted at the Prince of Wales, who stood nearby. "Order my car quick, you! Miss Martin-Jones has fainted from excitement."

V

The skyscraper rose bulkily through thirty tiers of windows before it attenuated itself to a graceful sugar-loaf of shining white. Then it darted up again another hundred feet, thinned to a mere oblong tower in its last fragile aspiration toward the sky. At the highest of its high windows Rags Martin-Jones stood full in the stiff breeze, gazing down at the city.

"Mr. Chestnut wants to know if you'll come right in to his private office."

Obediently her slim feet moved along the carpet into a high cool chamber overlooking the harbor and the wide sea.

John Chestnut sat at his desk, waiting, and Rags walked to him and put her arms around his shoulder.

"Are you sure *you*'re real?" she asked anxiously. "Are you absolutely *sure*?"

"You only wrote me a week before you came," he protested modestly, "or I could have arranged a revolution."

"Was the whole thing just *mine*?" she demanded. "Was it a perfectly useless, gorgeous thing, just for me?"

"Useless?" He considered. "Well, it started out to be. At the last minute I invited a big restaurant man to be there, and while you were at the other table I sold him the whole idea of the night-club."

He looked at his watch.

"I've got one more thing to do—and then we've got just time to be married before lunch." He picked up his telephone. "Jackson? . . . Send a triplicated cable to Paris, Berlin and Budapest and have those two bogus dukes who tossed up for Schwartzberg-Rhineminster chased over the Polish border. If the Duchy won't act, lower the rate of exchange to point triple zero naught two. Also, that idiot Blutchdak is in the Balkans again, trying to start a new war. Put him on the first boat for New York or else throw him in a Greek jail."

He rang off, turned to the startled cosmopolite with a laugh.

"The next stop is the City Hall. Then if you like we'll run over to Paris."

"John," she asked him intently, "who was the Prince of Wales?"

He waited till they were in the elevator, dropping twenty floors at a swoop. Then he leaned forward and tapped the lift boy on the shoulder.

"Not so fast, Cedric. This lady isn't used to falls from high places."

The elevator boy turned around, smiled. His face was pale, oval, framed in yellow hair. Rags blushed like fire.

"Cedric's from Wessex," explained John. "The resemblance is, to say the least, amazing. Princes are not particularly discreet, and I suspect Cedric of being a Guelph in some left-handed way."

Rags took the monocle from around her neck and threw the ribbon over Cedric's head.

"Thank you," she said simply, "for the second greatest thrill of my life."

John Chestnut began rubbing his hands together in a commercial gesture.

"Patronize this place, lady," he besought her. "Best bazaar in the city!"

"What have you got for sale?"

"Well, M'selle, today we have some perfectly bee-*oo*-tiful love."

"Wrap it up, Mr. Merchant," cried Rags Martin-Jones. "It looks like a bargain to me."

LETTERS

c. April 10, 1924   *Long Island, New York*

Great Neck.

Dear Max:

A few words more relative to our conversation this afternoon. While I have every hope + plan of finishing my novel in June you know how those things often come out. And even it takes me 10 times that long I cannot let it go out unless it has the very best I'm capable of in it or even as I feel sometimes, something better than I'm capable of. Much of what I wrote last summer was good but it was so interrupted that it was ragged + in approaching it from a new angle I've had to discard a lot of it—in one case 18,000 words (part of which will appear in the Mercury as a short story). It is only in the last four months that I've realized how much I've—well, almost <u>deteriorated</u> in the three years since I finished the Beautiful and Damned. The last four months of course I've worked but in the two years—over two years—before that, I produced exactly <u>one</u> play, <u>half a dozen</u> short stories and three or four articles—an average of about <u>one</u> <u>hundred</u> words a day. If I'd spent this time reading or travelling or doing anything—even staying healthy—it'd be different but I spent it uselessly, niether in study nor in contemplation but only in drinking and raising hell generally. If I'd written the B. & D. at the rate of 100 words a day it would have taken me <u>4 years</u> so you can imagine the moral effect the whole chasm had on me.

What I'm trying to say is just that I'll have to ask you to have patience about the book and trust me that at last, or at least for the

1st time in years, I'm doing the best I can. I've gotten in dozens of bad habits that I'm trying to get rid of

1. Laziness
2. Referring everything to Zelda—a terrible habit, nothing ought to be referred to anybody until its finished
3. Word consciousness—self doubt

ect. ect. ect. ect.

I feel I have an enormous power in me now, more than I've ever had in a way but it works so fitfully and with so many bogeys because I've <u>talked so much</u> and not lived enough within myself to delelop the nessessary self reliance. Also I don't know anyone who has used up so [torn]sonel experience as I have at 27. Copperfield + Pendennis were written at past forty while This Side of Paradise was three books + the B. + D. was two. So in my new novel I'm thrown directly on purely creative work—not trashy imaginings as in my stories but the sustained imagination of a sincere and yet radiant world. So I tread slowly and carefully + at times in considerable distress. This book will be a consciously artistic achievment + must depend on that as the 1st books did not.

If I ever win the right to any liesure again I will assuredly not waste it as I wasted this past time. Please believe me when I say that now I'm doing the best I can.

Yours Ever

Scott F————

Villa Marie, Valescure
St Raphael, France

Dear Max:

(1) The novel will be done next week. That doesn't mean however that it'll reach America before October 1st. as Zelda + I are contemplating a careful revision after a weeks complete rest.

(2) The clippings have never arrived.

(3) Seldes has been with me and he thinks "For the Grimalkins" is a wonderful title for Rings book. Also I've got great ideas about "My Life and Loves" which I'll tell Ring when comes over in September.

(4) How many copies has his short stories sold?

(5) Your bookkeeper never did send me my royalty report for Aug 1st.

(6) For Christs sake don't give anyone that jacket you're saving for me. I've written it into the book.

(7) I think my novel is about the best American novel ever written. It is rough stuff in places, runs only to about 50,000 words, and I hope you won't shy at it

(8) Its been a fair summer. I've been unhappy but my work hasn't suffered from it. I am grown at last.

(9) What books are being talked about? I don't mean best sellers. Hergeshiemers novel in the Post seems vile to me.

(10) I hope you're reading Gertrude Stiens novel in The <u>Transatlantic Review</u>.

(11) Raymond Radiguets last book (he is the young man who wrote "<u>Le deable au Corps</u>" at sixteen [untranslatable]) is a great hit here. He wrote it at 18. Its called "<u>Le Bal de Compte Orgel</u>" + though I'm only half through it I'd get an opinion on it if I were you. Its cosmopolitan rather than French and my instinct tells me that in a good translation it might make an enormous hit in America where everyone is yearning for Paris. Do look it up + get at least one opinion of it. The preface is by the da-dist Jean Cocteau but the book is not da-da at all.

(12) Did you get hold of Rings other books?

(13) We're liable to leave here by Oct 1st so after the 15th of Sept I wish you'd send everything care of Guarantee Trust Co. Paris

(14) Please ask the bookstore, if you have time, to send me Havelock Ellis "Dance of Life" + charge to my account

(15) I asked Struthers Burt to dinner but his baby was sick.

(16) Be <u>sure</u> and answer <u>every</u> question, Max.

I miss seeing you like the devil.

<u>Scott</u>

Villa Marie,

Valescure

St Raphael, France

Dear Max:

The royalty was better than I'd expected. This is to tell you about a young man named Ernest Hemmingway, who lives in Paris, (an American) writes for the transatlantic Review + has a brilliant future. Ezra Pount published a a collection of his short pieces in Paris, at some place like the Egotist Press. I havn't it hear now but its remarkable + I'd look him up right away. He's the real thing.

My novel goes to you with a long letter within five days. Ring arrives in a week. This is just a hurried scrawl as I'm working like a dog. I thought Stalling's book was disappointingly rotten. It takes a genius to whine appealingly. Have tried to see Struthers Burt but he's been on the move. More later.

Scott

[. . . .]

October 27th, 1924
Villa Marie, Valescure
St. Raphael, France
(After Nov. 3d Care of
American Express Co, Rome Italy)

Dear Max:

Under separate cover I'm sending you my third novel:

The Great Gatsby

(I think that at last I've done something really my own), but how good "my own" is remains to be seen.

I should suggest the following contract.

15% up to 50,000
20% after 50,000

The book is only a little over fifty thousand words long but I believe, as you know, that Whitney Darrow has the wrong psychology about prices (and about what class constitute the bookbuying public now that the lowbrows go to the movies) and I'm anxious to charge two dollars for it and have it a <u>full size book</u>.

Of course I want the binding to be absolutely uniform with my other books—the stamping too—and the jacket we discussed before. This time I don't want any signed blurbs on the jacket—not Mencken's or Lewis' or Howard's or anyone's. I'm tired of being the author of <u>This Side of Paradise</u> and I want to start over.

About serialization. I am bound under contract to show it to Hearsts but I am asking a prohibitive price, Long hates me and its not a very serialized book. If they should take it—they won't—it would put of publication in the fall. Otherwise you can publish it in the spring. When Hearst turns it down I'm going to offer it to Liberty for $15,000 on condition that they'll publish it in ten weekly installments before April 15th. If they don't want it I shan't serialize. <u>I am absolutely positive Long won't want it</u>.

I have an alternative title:

<u>Gold-hatted Gatsby</u>

After you've read the book let me know what you think about the title. Naturally I won't get a nights sleep until I hear from you but do tell me the absolute truth, <u>your first impression of the book</u> + tell me anything that bothers you in it.

As Ever
Scott

I'd rather you wouldn't call Reynolds as he might try to act as my agent. Would you send me the N.Y. World with accounts of Harvard-Princeton and Yale-Princeton games?

FROM: Maxwell Perkins

Nov. 18, 1924

Dear Scott:

I think the novel is a wonder. I'm taking it home to read again and shall then write my impressions in full;—but it has vitality to an extraordinary degree, and <u>glamour</u>, and a great deal of underlying thought of unusual quality. It has a kind of mystic atmosphere at times that you infused into parts of "Paradise" and have not since used. It is a marvelous fusion, into a unity of presentation, of the extraordinary incongruities of life today. And as for sheer writing, it's astonishing.

Now deal with this question: various gentlemen here don't like the title,—in fact none like it but me. To me, the strange incongruity of the words in it sound the note of the book. But the objectors are more practical men than I. Consider as quickly as you can the question of a change.

But if you do not change, you will have to leave that note off the wrap. Its presence would injure it too much;—and good as the wrap always seemed, it now seems a masterpiece for this book. So judge of the value of the title when it stands alone and write or cable your decision the instant you can.

> With congratulations, I am,
> Yours,
> [Max]

FROM: Maxwell Perkins

November 20, 1924

Dear Scott:

I think you have every kind of right to be proud of this book. It is an extraordinary book, suggestive of all sorts of thoughts and moods. You adopted exactly the right method of telling it, that of employing a narrator who is more of a spectator than an actor: this puts the reader upon a point of observation on a higher level than that on which the characters stand and at a distance that gives perspective. In no other way could your irony have been so immensely effective, nor the reader have been enabled so strongly to feel at times the strangeness of human circumstance in a vast heedless universe. In the eyes of Dr. Eckleberg various readers will see different significances; but their presence gives a superb touch to the whole thing: great unblinking eyes, expressionless, looking down upon the human scene. It's magnificent!

I could go on praising the book and speculating on its various elements, and meanings, but points of criticism are more important now. I think you are right in feeling a certain slight sagging in chapters six and seven, and I don't know how to suggest a remedy. I hardly doubt that you will find one and I am only writing to say that I think it does need something to hold up here to the pace set, and ensuing. I have only two actual criticisms:—

One is that among a set of characters marvelously palpable and vital—I would know Tom Buchanan if I met him on the street and would avoid him—Gatsby is somewhat vague. The reader's eyes can never quite focus upon him, his outlines are dim. Now everything about Gatsby is more or less a mystery i.e. more or less vague, and this may be somewhat of an artistic intention, but I think it is mistaken. Couldn't <u>he</u> be physically described as distinctly as the others, and couldn't you add one or two characteristics like the use of that phrase "old sport",—not verbal, but physical ones, perhaps. I think that for some reason or other a reader—this was true of Mr. Scribner and of Louise—gets an idea that Gatsby is a much older man than he is, although you have the writer say that he is little older than himself. But this would be avoided if on his first appearance he was seen as vividly as Daisy and Tom are, for instance;—and I do not think your scheme would be impaired if you made him so.

The other point is also about Gatsby: his career must remain mysterious, of course. But in the end you make it pretty clear that his wealth came through his connection with Wolfshiem. You also suggest this much earlier. Now almost all readers numerically are going to be puzzled by his having all this wealth and are going to feel entitled to an explanation. To give a distinct and definite one would be, of course, utterly absurd. It did occur to me though, that you might here and there interpolate some phrases, and possibly incidents, little touches of various kinds, that would suggest that he was in some active way mysteriously engaged. You do have him called on the telephone, but couldn't he be seen once or twice consulting at his parties with people of some sort of mysterious significance, from the political, the gambling, the sporting world, or whatever it may be. I know I am floundering, but that fact may help you to see what I mean. The <u>total</u> lack of an explanation through so large a part of the story does seem to me a defect;—or not of an explanation, but of the suggestion of an explanation. I wish you were here so I could talk about it to you for then I know I could at least make you understand what I mean. What Gatsby did ought never to be definitely imparted, even if it could be.

Whether he was an innocent tool in the hands of somebody else, or to what degree he was this, ought not to be explained. But if some sort of business activity of his were simply adumbrated, it would lend further probability to that part of the story.

There is one other point: in giving deliberately Gatsby's biography when he gives it to the narrator you do depart from the method of the narrative in some degree, for otherwise almost everything is told, and beautifully told, in the regular flow of it,—in the succession of events or in accompaniment with them. But you can't avoid the biography altogether. I thought you might find ways to let the truth of some of his claims like "Oxford" and his army career come out bit by bit in the course of actual narrative. I mention the point anyway for consideration in this interval before I send the proofs.

The general brilliant quality of the book makes me ashamed to make even these criticisms. The amount of meaning you get into a sentence, the dimensions and intensity of the impression you make a paragraph carry, are most extraordinary. The manuscript is full of phrases which make a scene blaze with life. If one enjoyed a rapid railroad journey I would compare the number and vividness of pictures your living words suggest, to the living scenes disclosed in that way. It seems in reading a much shorter book than it is, but it carries the mind through a series of experiences that one would think would require a book of three times its length.

The presentation of Tom, his place, Daisy and Jordan, and the unfolding of their characters is unequalled so far as I know. The description of the valley of ashes adjacent to the lovely country, the conversation and the action in Myrtle's apartment, the marvelous catalogue of those who came to Gatsby's house,—these are such things as make a man famous. And all these things, the whole pathetic episode, you have given a place in time and space, for with the help of T. J. Eckleberg and by an occasional glance at the sky, or the sea, or the city, you have imparted a sort of sense of eternity. You once told me you were not a <u>natural</u> writer—my God! You have plainly mastered the craft, of course; but you needed far more than craftsmanship for this.

As ever,

[Max]

P.S. Why do you ask for a lower royalty on this than you had on the last book where it changed from 15% to 17½% after 20,000 and to 20% after 40,000? Did you do it in order to give us a better margin for advertising? We shall advertise very energetically anyhow and if you stick to the old terms you will sooner overcome the advance. Naturally we should like the ones you suggest better, but there is no reason you should get less on this than you did on the other.

Hotel des Princes
Piazza di Spagna
Rome, Italy

Dear Max:

Your wire + your letters made me feel like a million dollars—I'm sorry I could make no better response than a telegram whining for money. But the long siege of the novel winded me a little + I've been slow on starting the stories on which I must live.

I think all your critisisms are true

(a) About the title. I'll try my best but I don't know what I can do. Maybe simply "Trimalchio" or "Gatsby." In the former case I don't see why the note shouldn't go on the back.

(a) Chapters VI + VII I know how to fix

(b) Gatsby's business affairs I can fix. I get your point about them.

(c) His vagueness I can repair by <u>making more pointed</u>—this doesn't sound good but wait and see. It'll make him clear

(d) But his long narrative in Chap VIII will be difficult to split up. Zelda also thought I was a little out of key but it is good writing and I don't think I could bear to sacrifice any of it

(e) I have 1000 minor corrections which I will make on the proof + several more large ones which you didn't mention.

Your critisisms were excellent + most helpful + you picked out all my favorite spots in the book to praise as high spots. Except you didn't mention my favorite of all—the chapter where Gatsby + Daisy meet.

Two more things. Zelda's been reading me the cowboy book aloud to spare my mind + I love it—tho I think he learned the American language from Ring rather than from his own ear.

Another point—in Chap. II of my book when Tom + Myrte go into the bedroom while Carraway reads Simon called Peter—is that raw? Let me know. I think its pretty nessessary.

I made the royalty smaller because I wanted to make up for all the money you've advanced these two years by letting it pay a sort of interest on it. But I see by calculating I made it too small—a difference of 2000 dollars. Let us call it 15% up to 40,000 and 20% after that. That's a good fair contract all around.

[. . . .]

Anyhow thanks + thanks + thanks for your letters. I'd rather have you + Bunny like it than anyone I know. And I'd rather have you like it than Bunny. If its as good as you say, when I finish with the proof it'll be perfect.

Remember, by the way, to put by some cloth for the cover uniform with my other books.

As soon as I can think about the title I'll write or wire a decision. Thank Louise for me, for liking it. Best Regards to Mr. Scribner. Tell him Galsworthy is here in Rome.

As Ever,
Scott

c. December 20, 1924

Hotel des Princes, Piazza de Spagna, Rome.

Dear Max:

I'm a bit (not very—not dangerously) stewed tonight + I'll probably write you a long letter. We're living in a small, unfashionable but most comfortable hotel at $525.00 a month including tips, meals ect. Rome does <u>not</u> particularly interest me but its a big year here, and early in the spring we're going to Paris. There's no use telling you my plans because they're usually just about as unsuccessful as to work as a religious prognosticaters are as to the End of the World. I've got a new novel to write—title and all, that'll take about a year. Meanwhile, I don't want to start it until this is out + meanwhile I'll do short stories for money (I now get $2000.00 a story but I hate worse than hell to do them) and there's the never dying lure of another play.

Now! Thanks enormously for making up the $5000.00. I know I don't technically deserve it considering I've had $3000.00 or $4000.00 for as long as I can remember. But since you force it on me (inexecrable [or is it execrable] joke) I will accept it. I hope to Christ you get 10 times it back on Gatsby——and I think perhaps you will.

For:

I can now make it perfect but the proof (I will soon get the immemorial letter with the statement "We now have the book in hand and will soon begin to send you proof" [what is 'in hand'—I have a vague picture of everyone in the office holding the book in the right and and reading it]) will be one of the most expensive affairs since Madame Bovary. <u>Please</u> charge it to my account. If its possible to send a second proof over here I'd love to have it. Count on 12 days each way—four days here on first proof + two on the second. I hope there are other good books in the spring because I think now the public interest in <u>books</u> per se rises when there seems to be a group of them as in 1920 (spring + fall), 1921 (fall), 1922 (spring). Ring's + Tom's (first) books, Willa Cathers <u>Lost Lady</u> + in an inferior, cheap way Edna Ferber's are the only American fiction in over two years that had a really excellent press (say, since Babbit).

With the aid you've given me I can make "Gatsby" perfect. The chapter VII (the hotel scene) will never quite be up to mark—I've worried about it too long + I can't quite place Daisy's reaction. But I can improve it a lot. It isn't imaginative energy thats lacking—its because I'm automaticly prevented from thinking it out over again <u>because I must get all those characters to New York</u> in order to have the catastrophe on the road going back + I must have it pretty much that way. So there's no chance of bringing the freshness to it that a new free conception sometimes gives.

The rest is easy and I see my way so clear that I even see the mental quirks that queered it before. Strange to say my notion of Gatsby's vagueness was O.K. What you and Louise + Mr. Charles Scribner found wanting was that:

<u>I myself didn't know what Gatsby looked like or was engaged in</u> + you felt it. If I'd known + kept it from you you'd have been <u>too impressed with my knowledge to protest</u>. This is a complicated idea but I'm sure you'll understand. But I know now—and as a penalty for not having known first, in other words to make sure I'm going to tell more.

It seems of almost mystical significance to me that you thot he was older—the man I had in mind, half unconsciously, <u>was</u> older (a specific individual) and evidently, without so much as a definate word, I conveyed the fact.—or rather, I must qualify this Shaw-Desmond-trash by saying, that I conveyed it without a word that I can at present and for the life of me, trace. (I think Shaw Desmond was one of your bad bets—I was the other)

Anyhow after careful searching of the files (of a man's mind here) for the Fuller Magee case + after having had Zelda draw pictures until her fingers ache I know Gatsby better than I know my own child. My first instinct after your letter was to let him go + have Tom Buchanan dominate the book (I suppose he's the best character I've ever done—I think he and the brother in "Salt" + Hurstwood in "Sister Carrie" are the three best characters in American fiction in the last twenty years, perhaps and perhaps not) but Gatsby sticks in my heart. I had him for awhile then lost him + now I know I have him again. I'm sorry Myrtle is better than Daisy. Jordan of course was a great idea (perhaps you know its Edith Cummings) but she fades out. Its Chap VII thats the trouble with Daisy + it may hurt the book's popularity that its <u>a man's book</u>.

Anyhow I think (for the first time since The Vegetable failed) that I'm a wonderful writer + its your always wonderful letters that help me to go on believing in myself.

Now some practical, very important questions. Please answer every one.

(1) Montenegro has an order called <u>The Order of Danilo</u>. Is there any possible way you could find out for me there what it would look like—whether a courtesy decoration given to an American would bear an English inscription—or anything to give versimilitude to the medal which sounds horribly amateurish.

②   Please have <u>no blurbs of any kind on the jacket</u>!!! No
    Mencken or Lewis or Sid Howard or anything. I don't
    believe in them <u>one bit</u> any more.

③   Don't forget to change name of book in list of works

④   Please shift exclamation point from end of 3d line to end of
    4th line in title page. <u>Please!</u> Important!

⑤   I thought that the whole episode (2 paragraphs) about their
    playing the Jazz History of the world at Gatsby's first party
    was rotten. Did you? Tell me frank <u>reaction</u>—<u>personal</u>.
    Don't <u>think</u>! We can all think!

[. . . .]

I still owe the store almost $700 on my Encyclopedia but I'll pay
them on about Jan 10th—all in a lump as I expect my finances will
then be on a firm footing. Will you ask them to send me Ernest Boyd's
book? Unless it has about my drinking in it that would reach my family.
However, I guess it'd worry me more if I hadn't seen it than if I had.
If my book is a big success or a great failure (financial—no other sort
can be imagined, I hope) <u>I don't</u> want to publish stories in the fall. If
it goes between 25,000 and 50,000 I have an excellent collection for
you. This is the longest letter I've written in three or four years. Please
thank Mr. Scribner for me for his exceeding kindness.

Always yours

Scott Fitz———

TO: Maxwell Perkins
c. January 15, 1925

American Express Co.

Rome.

Dear Max:

Proof hasn't arrived yet. Have been in bed for a week with grippe but I'm ready to attack it violently. Here are two important things.

1. In the scene in Myrtes appartment—in the place where <u>Tom + Myrtle dissapear for awhile</u> noticeably raw. Does it stick out enough so that the censor might get it. Its the only place in the book I'm in doubt about on that score. Please let me know right away

2. Please have <u>no quotations from any critics whatsoever on the jacket</u>—simply your own blurb on the back and don't give away too much of the idea—especially don't connect Daisy + Gatsby (I need the quality of surprise there) Please be <u>very general</u>.

These points are both very important. Do drop me a line about them. Wish I could see your new house. I havn't your faith in Will James—I feel its old material without too much feeling or too new a touch.

As Ever,

Scott

Jan. 20, 1925

Dear Scott:

I am terribly rushed for time so I am answering your letter as briefly and rapidly as I can,—but I will have a chance to write to tell you the news, etc. etc., soon.

First as to the jazz history of the world:—that did jar on me unfavorably. And yet in a way it pleased me as a tour de force, but one not completely successful. Upon the whole, I should probably have objected to it in the first place except that I felt you needed something there in the way of incident, something special. But if you have something else, I would take it out.

You are beginning to get me worried about the scene in Myrtle's apartment for you have spoken of it several times. It never occurred to me to think there was any objection to it. I am sure there is none. No censor could make an issue on that,—nor I think on anything else in the book.

I will be sure not to use any quotations and I will make it very general indeed, because I realize that not much ought to be said about the story. I have not thought what to say, but we might say something very brief which gave the impression that nothing need any longer be said.

I certainly hope the proofs have got to you and that you have been at work on them for some time. If not you had better cable. They were sent first-class mail. The first lot on December 27th and the second lot on December 30th.

Yours,

[Max]

P.S. The mysterious hand referred to in the immemorial phrase is that of the typesetter.

Hotel des Princes

Rome, Italy

January 24. 1925

(But address the American Express Co.

because its damn cold here and we may leave any day.

Dear Max:

This is a most important letter so I'm having it typed. Guard it as your life.

1) Under a separate cover I'm sending the first part of the proof. While I agreed with the general suggestions in your first letters I differ with you in others. I <u>want</u> Myrtle Wilson's breast ripped off—its exactly the thing, I think, and I don't want to chop up the good scenes by too much tinkering. When Wolfshiem says "sid" for "said", it's deliberate. "Orgastic" is the adjective from "orgasm" and it expresses exactly the intended ecstasy. It's not a bit dirty. I'm much more worried about the disappearance of Tom and Myrtle on galley 9—I think it's all right but I'm not sure. If it isn't please wire and I'll send correction.

2) Now about the page proof—under certain conditions never mind sending them (unless, of course, there's loads of time, which I suppose there isn't. I'm keen for late March or early April publication)

<u>The conditions are two.</u>

a)   That someone reads it <u>very carefully twice</u> to see that every one of my inserts are put in correctly. There are so many of them that I'm in terror of a mistake.

b)   That no changes <u>whatsoever</u> are made in it except in the case of a misprint so glaring as to be certain, and that only by you.

If there's some time left but not enough for the double mail send them to me and I'll simply wire O.K. which will save two weeks. However don't postpone for that. In any case send me the page proof as usual just to see.

3)   Now, many thanks for the deposit. Two days after wiring you I had a cable from Reynolds that he'd sold two stories of mine for a total of $3,750. but before that I was in debt to him and after turning down the ten thousand dollars from College Humor I was afraid to borrow more from him until he'd made a sale. I won't ask for any more from you until the book has earned it. My guess is that it will sell about 80,000 copies but I may be wrong. Please thank Mr. Charles Scribner for me. I bet he thinks he's caught another John Fox now for sure. Thank God for John Fox. It would have been awful to have had no predecessor.

4)   This is very important. Be sure not to give away <u>any</u> of my plot in the blurb. Don't give away that Gatsby <u>dies</u> or is a <u>parvenu</u> or <u>crook</u> or anything. It's a part of the suspense of the book that all these things are in doubt until the end. You'll watch this won't you? And remember about having no quotations from critics on the jacket—<u>not even about my other books</u>!

5) This is just a list of small things.
   a) What's Ring's title for his spring book?
   b) Did O'Brien star my story Absolution or any of my others on his trash-album?
   c) I wish your bookkeeping department would send me an account on Feb. 1st. Not that it gives me pleasure to see how much in debt I am but that I like to keep a yearly record of the sales of all my books.

Do answer every question and keep this letter until the proof comes. Let me know how you like the changes. I miss seeing you, Max, more than I can say.

As ever,
Scott

P.S. I'm returning the proof of the title page ect. It's O.K. but my heart tells me I should have named it Trimalchio. However against all the advice I suppose it would have been stupid and stubborn of me. Trimalchio in West Egg was only a compromise. Gatsby is too much like Babbit and The Great Gatsby is weak because there's no emphasis even ironically on his greatness or lack of it. However let it pass.

TO: *Maxwell Perkins*
c. February 18, 1925

New Address ⎰ Hotel Tiberio
⎱ Capri

Dear Max:

After six weeks of uninterrupted work the proof is finished and the last of it goes to you this afternoon. On the whole its been very successful labor

(1.) I've brought Gatsby to life

(2.) I've accounted for his money

(3.) I've fixed up the two weak chapers (VI and VII)

(4.) I've improved his first party

(5.) I've broken up his long narrative in Chap. VIII

This morning I wired you to <u>hold up the galley of Chap 40</u>. The correction—and God! its important because in my other revision I made Gatsby look too mean—is enclosed herewith. Also some corrections for the page proof.

We're moving to Capri. We hate Rome, I'm behind financially and have to write three short stories. Then I try another play, and by June, I hope, begin my new novel.

Had long interesting letters from Ring and John Bishop. Do tell me if all corrections have been recieved. I'm worried

Scott

I hope you're setting publication date at first possible moment.

Dear Scott:

I congratulate you on resisting the $10,000. I don't see how you managed it. But it delighted us, for otherwise book publication would have been deferred until too late in the spring. . . . Those [changes] you have made do wonders for Gatsby,—in making him visible and palpable. You're right about the danger of meddling with the high spots—instinct is the best guide there. I'll have the proofs read twice, once by Dunn and once by Roger, and shall allow no change unless it is certain the printer has blundered. I know the whole book so well myself that I could hardly decide wrongly. But I won't decide anything if there is ground for doubt.

Ring Lardner came back last week from Nassau looking brown and well, with the page proof of his new book—"What of It". I'll send you a copy soon. That and "How to Write Short Stories," "Alibi Ike," "The Big Town," and "Gullible's Travels," with new prefaces, constitute the set. I simply could not get Ring to pay enough attention to it to reorganize the material as we might have done. I tried to work out a book to contain "Symptoms of Being 35" and some of the shorter things; but without the war material—which, good as it was, seems dreadfully old now—there was not enough. And the subscription agents wanted to retain the familiar titles for their canvassing. "How to Write Short Stories" has sold 16,500 copies and it continues steadily to sell: the new book and the old books in new forms and wrappers, in the trade, will give it new impetus. We'll have a wonderful Ring Lardner window when we get all these books out.

As for Hemingway: I finally got his "In our time" which accumulates a fearful effect through a series of brief episodes, presented with economy, strength and vitality. A remarkable, tight, complete expression of the scene, in our time, as it looks to Hemingway. I have written him that we wish he would write us about his plans and if possible send a ms.; but I must say I have little hope that he will get the letter,—so hard was it for me to get his book. Do you know his address?

[. . . .]

As ever,

[Max]

CHRONOLOGY
NOTE ON THE TEXTS
NOTES

CHRONOLOGY

1896   Born September 24 at his parents' home at 481 Laurel Avenue, in St. Paul, Minnesota, first surviving child of Mollie McQuillan Fitzgerald and Edward Fitzgerald. Named Francis Scott Key Fitzgerald after the author of "The Star-Spangled Banner," his father's second cousin three times removed. Mother, born 1860 in St. Paul, is the eldest of five children of successful grocery wholesaler who at his death in 1877 left an estate of more than $250,000 and a large Victorian home on Summit Avenue, St. Paul's most fashionable street. Father, born in 1853 in Rockville, Maryland, is a furniture manufacturer. They had two daughters who died, aged three and one, earlier in 1896.

1898   When furniture business fails, family moves to Buffalo, New York, where father takes a job as a wholesale grocery salesman for Procter & Gamble.

1901   Father transferred by Procter & Gamble to Syracuse, New York, and family moves in January. Sister Annabel born in July.

1902   Enrolls in Miss Goodyear's School in September.

1903   Family moves back to Buffalo. Attends school at Holy Angels Convent.

1905   Transfers to Miss Nardin's private Catholic school. Reads *The Scottish Chiefs*, *Ivanhoe*, and the adventure novels of G. A. Henty.

1908   Father loses his job at Procter & Gamble in March and in July family moves back to St. Paul, where at first they live with the McQuillans and then in a series of rented homes, eventually settling at 599 Summit Avenue. Enters St. Paul Academy in September.

1909   Publishes first story, "The Mystery of the Raymond Mortgage," in *Now and Then*, the St. Paul Academy school paper, in October.

1910   Publishes two more stories in *Now and Then*, "Reade, Substitute Right Half" (February) and "A Debt of Honor" (March).

1911   Publishes story "The Room with the Green Blinds" in the June *Now and Then*. In August, writes and plays the lead in a play, *The Girl from Lazy J*, for the Elizabethan Dramatic Club, local amateur theatrical group. Because of poor grades at St. Paul Academy, is sent in September to boarding school at the Newman School in Hackensack, New Jersey, where his boastful and domineering personality makes him unpopular. Takes frequent trips to New York City and attends theater often, seeing Ina Claire in *The Quaker Girl* and Gertrude Bryant in *Little Boy Blue*. Publishes poem "Football" in Christmas issue of the school magazine, the *Newman News*.

1912–13   Writes another play, *The Captured Shadow*, which is produced by the Elizabethan Dramatic Club in the summer of 1912. Publishes three stories in the *Newman News* during the 1912–13 school year. Meets Father Cyril Sigourney Webster Fay, prominent Catholic priest, who becomes a mentor. During a visit to Father Fay in Washington, meets Henry Adams and Anglo-Irish writer Shane Leslie. Despite failing four courses in two years at the Newman School, Fitzgerald takes entrance examination for Princeton University in May 1913. Writes play *Coward* for Elizabethan Dramatic Club in July. Grandmother McQuillan dies in August, leaving his mother enough money for his college tuition. Enters Princeton in September as member of Class of 1917.

1914   Meets John Peale Bishop and Edmund Wilson, fellow students at Princeton. In January his book and lyrics for *Fie! Fie! Fi-Fi!* win the competition for the 1914–15 Triangle Club show. Contributes to the *Princeton Tiger*, the college humor magazine. Reads and admires the social reform writings of H. G. Wells and George Bernard Shaw and Compton Mackenzie's novel *Sinister Street*. Writes fourth and last play for the Elizabethan Dramatic Club, *Assorted Spirits*, during summer. Returns to Princeton in September but is ineligible for extracurricular activities because of poor grades and cannot act in *Fie! Fie! Fi-Fi!* during the fall semester.

1915   Meets Ginevra King, sixteen-year-old from socially prominent Lake Forest, Illinois, family, while home for Christmas vacation. Falls in love with her and writes to her almost daily after he returns to Princeton. Elected secretary of the Triangle Club in February after his grades improve; later in the term is selected for the Cottage Club and for the editorial board of the *Tiger*. Story "Shadow Laurels" is published in the *Nassau Literary Magazine* (the *Lit*) in April, followed in June by "The Ordeal." Writes the lyrics (Edmund Wilson writes the book) for *The Evil Eye*, the 1915–16 Triangle Club show. Takes Ginevra King to the Princeton prom in June. In the fall, his low grades again make him ineligible for campus activities. Takes French literature course taught by Christian Gauss and begins lifelong friendship with Gauss, who later becomes Dean of the College. Continues to write for the *Tiger*. In November, falls ill and leaves college for the remainder of the semester to recuperate (illness is diagnosed as malaria, but may have been mild case of tuberculosis).

1916　　Spends the spring in St. Paul on a leave of absence from Princeton; publishes poem "To My Unused Greek Book" in the *Lit*. Continues courtship of Ginevra King, whom he visits in Lake Forest in August. Returns to Princeton in September to repeat his junior year and writes the lyrics for the Triangle Club show, *Safety First,* in which he is again ineligible to perform. Attends Princeton–Yale football game with King in November.

1917　　Courtship of Ginevra King ends in January. Publishes play "The Debutante," whose title character is modeled on King, in the *Lit*. During spring semester, his writing appears another twelve times in the *Lit* (four stories, three poems, and five reviews of books by Shane Leslie, E. F. Benson, H. G. Wells, and Booth Tarkington). In May, a month after the U.S. enters World War I, signs up for three weeks of intensive military training and takes exam for infantry commission. During summer in St. Paul, reads William James, Schopenhauer, and Bergson. While waiting for his commission, returns to Princeton in September and rooms with John Biggs, Jr., editor of the *Tiger,* and continues to contribute to both the *Tiger* and the *Lit*. Receives commission as second lieutenant in the infantry and in November reports for training to Fort Leavenworth, Kansas. Expecting that he will eventually be killed in combat, begins writing a novel.

1918　　On leave from the army in February, finishes novel, "The Romantic Egotist," at the Cottage Club in Princeton and sends it to Shane Leslie, who has agreed to recommend it to his publisher, Charles Scribner's Sons. Reports in March to 45th Infantry Regiment at Camp Zachary Taylor, near Louisville; in April, regiment is transferred to Camp

Gordon in Georgia, and in June, to Camp Sheridan, outside Montgomery, Alabama. In July, at a dance at the Country Club of Montgomery, meets Zelda Sayre, eighteen-year-old daughter of a justice of the Alabama Supreme Court. Scribner's rejects "The Romantic Egotist" in August; Fitzgerald submits a revised version, which is rejected in October. War ends on November 11, as Fitzgerald is waiting to embark for France with his regiment. Continues courtship of Zelda Sayre, who is reluctant to commit to marriage because of his lack of income and prospects.

1919 Father Fay dies on January 10. Fitzgerald is discharged from the army, moves to New York in February, and takes job at Barron Collier advertising agency writing trolley-car ads. Writes fiction and poetry at night, accumulating 112 rejection slips. *The Smart Set* accepts "Babes in the Woods," revised version of story published in 1917 issue of the *Lit,* paying him $30 (story appears in September). Sends Zelda his mother's engagement ring in March, but cannot convince her to marry him during visits to Montgomery, April–June. During his last visit, Zelda breaks off the engagement. Quits job and returns to parents' house in St. Paul, determined to rewrite novel and have it accepted for publication. Sends novel, now titled *This Side of Paradise,* to editor Maxwell Perkins at Scribner's in September. Perkins writes on September 16 that firm has accepted it: "The book is so different that it is hard to prophesy how it will sell but we are all for taking a chance and supporting it with vigor." Revises several of his rejected stories; four are accepted by *The Smart Set,* two by *Scribner's Magazine,* and one by *The Saturday Evening Post.* Earns $879 from his writing by the end of the year. During a trip to New York in November, engages Harold Ober as his agent. Visits Zelda in Montgomery.

1920 With Harold Ober's assistance, begins to sell stories regularly to *The Saturday Evening Post,* which pays $400 each for them; by February, they have bought six. Reads Samuel Butler's *Note-Books* and H. L. Mencken's essays. Spends January in New Orleans writing stories and reading proofs of his novel, then moves back to New York in February. Sells story "Head and Shoulders" to Metro Films for $2,500. *This Side of Paradise* is published March 26; it sells three thousand copies in three days, and makes its author a celebrity. Marries Zelda in vestry of New York's St. Patrick's Cathedral on April 3. Develops friendships with Mencken and George Jean Nathan, editors of *The Smart Set.* Reads Mark Twain. In

May, *Metropolitan Magazine* takes option on his stories at $900 per story and, eventually, publishes four. Rents house in Westport, Connecticut, and in July takes car trip to Montgomery. Scribner's publishes *Flappers and Philosophers,* collection of eight stories, September 10. Rents apartment on West 59th Street in New York in October and works on second novel.

1921   Zelda discovers she is pregnant in February. In May, they sail for Europe, visiting England (where they have tea with John Galsworthy), Paris, Venice, Florence, and Rome, returning in July to the U.S., where they live in St. Paul. Second novel, *The Beautiful and Damned*, begins to run serially in *Metropolitan Magazine* in September. Daughter Frances Scott (Scottie) Fitzgerald is born on October 26.

1922   *The Beautiful and Damned* published by Scribner's March 4; it receives mixed reviews and sells forty thousand copies in a year. Begins work on play. Moves to Great Neck, Long Island, where he begins close friendships with Ring Lardner and John Dos Passos. *Tales of the Jazz Age,* short-story collection, published by Scribner's on September 22. Reads Dostoevsky and Dickens.

1923   Sells first option on his stories to Hearst organization for $1,500 per story. Receives $10,000 for film rights to *This Side of Paradise.* Play *The Vegetable* is published by Scribner's on April 27. Begins work on third novel. *The Vegetable* opens for pre-Broadway tryout in Atlantic City, New Jersey, on November 19, is received badly, and closes almost immediately, leaving its author in debt. Starts selling stories to *The Saturday Evening Post* for $1,250 each. Earns $28,759.78 from his writing for the year, but spends more.

1924   Sails for France in May to complete novel, settling on the Riviera. Zelda becomes romantically involved with French naval aviator Edouard Jozan in July; although the relationship ends quickly, Fitzgerald later writes, "I knew something had happened that could never be repaired." Meets Gerald and Sara Murphy during the summer. In October, recommends the work of Ernest Hemingway to Perkins and Scribner's. After sending manuscript of new novel to Scribner's in late October, goes to Rome and Capri for winter. Drinks heavily and quarrels constantly with Zelda.

1925   Extensively revises novel in galley proof in January and February, changing title to *The Great Gatsby.* Moves to Paris in April. *The Great*

Gatsby is published by Scribner's on April 10, receives mostly favorable reviews, but sales are disappointing. Meets Hemingway for first time at the Dingo bar in Montparnasse and subsequently takes trip to Lyon with him. Has tea with Edith Wharton at her home outside Paris in July. Through Hemingway, meets Gertrude Stein, Robert McAlmon (founder of Contact Editions publishers), and Sylvia Beach (owner of Shakespeare & Co. bookstore in Paris). Spends part of summer ("1000 parties and no work") on the Riviera, where his friends include writers Dos Passos, Max Eastman, Archibald MacLeish, and Floyd Dell and movie star Rudolph Valentino. Returns to Paris in September and spends a great deal of time with Hemingway.

1926 *All the Sad Young Men*, short-story collection, is published by Scribner's on February 26. Returns to the Riviera in March and begins work on new novel. Encourages Scribner's to publish Hemingway's novels *The Torrents of Spring* and *The Sun Also Rises*. Reads draft of *The Sun Also Rises* in July and convinces Hemingway to eliminate the first two chapters. Returns to U.S. in December, spending Christmas in Montgomery.

1927 Spends first two months of year in Hollywood, under contract to United Artists to write flapper comedy for Constance Talmadge; script, "Lipstick," is eventually rejected. Meets and is infatuated with seventeen-year-old Hollywood starlet Lois Moran; also meets producer Irving Thalberg, Lillian Gish, John Barrymore, and Richard Barthelmess. With help of Princeton roommate John Biggs, Jr., rents Ellerslie, Greek Revival–style mansion outside Wilmington, Delaware. Zelda begins ballet lessons with director of Philadelphia Opera Ballet and also writes magazine articles. Fitzgerald's income from writing for year totals $29,757.87, a new high.

1928 Goes to Paris for the summer in April. Zelda continues ballet studies there with Lubov Egorova. Writes nine Basil Duke Lee stories for *The Saturday Evening Post*, which earn him $31,500. Meets James Joyce at dinner given by Sylvia Beach in June. Later in summer, meets Thornton Wilder and heavyweight boxing champion Gene Tunney, who are on a walking tour of Europe together. Returns to U.S. in October and resumes work on novel. Attends Princeton–Yale football game in Princeton on November 19 with Hemingway and his wife, Pauline.

1929 Gives up lease on Ellerslie in spring and returns to Europe, renting apartment in Paris in April. Zelda resumes ballet lessons with Egorova and also publishes series of short stories in *College Humor*. Fitzgerald reads typescript of Hemingway's novel *A Farewell to Arms* in June and offers suggestions for revisions, all of which Hemingway ridicules but some of which he takes. Rents villa in Cannes from July to September. Now is paid $4,000 per story by *The Saturday Evening Post*. Returns to Paris in October and lives in rented apartment. Works on novel, while Zelda continues her ballet lessons and writing.

1930   Travels with Zelda to North Africa in February. Her behavior shows signs of extreme stress, and on April 23, she enters Malmaison clinic outside Paris. Discharges herself on May 11 to resume ballet lessons, then attempts suicide and enters Val-Mont clinic in Glion, Switzerland, on May 22. After being diagnosed as schizophrenic by Dr. Oscar Forel, she is transferred in June to Forel's Les Rives de Prangins clinic on Lake Geneva. Fitzgerald spends summer traveling between Paris and Switzerland. Meets Thomas Wolfe in Paris and later spends time with him in Switzerland. In order to pay for Zelda's treatment, writes and sells stories to *The Saturday Evening Post,* earning $32,000 for the year from eight stories, among them "Babylon Revisited," published in December. Spends fall at Hotel de la Paix in Lausanne and has brief affair with Englishwoman Bijou O'Conor.

1931   Father dies in January in Washington and Fitzgerald goes home for funeral. After visits to Montgomery and New York, returns to Europe and finds Zelda's condition improved; she becomes an outpatient and is allowed to take trips to Paris and the Austrian Tyrol, then is discharged from Prangins on September 15. Sails for U.S. with Zelda on September 19, and settles in Montgomery. Goes to Hollywood in November after being offered $1,200 a week by M-G-M to work on a Jean Harlow movie, leaving Zelda in Montgomery to be with her ailing father, who dies on November 17. Returns to Montgomery for Christmas.

1932   Takes Zelda in January on vacation to Florida and she works on a novel. Zelda has relapse on trip back to Montgomery, and enters Henry Phipps Psychiatric Clinic in Baltimore on February 12. Fitzgerald remains in Montgomery to work on his novel. Zelda finishes her novel while at the Phipps Clinic and, after Fitzgerald comes to Baltimore to help her revise it, Scribner's accepts it. Rents La Paix, Victorian-style house on the Turnbull estate in Towson, just outside Baltimore, in May. Zelda is discharged from Phipps on June 26. In August, Fitzgerald spends time at Johns Hopkins Hospital with what is diagnosed as typhoid fever (will eventually be hospitalized there eight more times from 1933 to 1937 for alcoholism and chronic inactive fibroid tuberculosis). Zelda's novel *Save Me the Waltz* is published October 7; it receives bad reviews and sells very poorly. Resumes serious work on his novel, while Zelda paints and writes play, *Scandalabra.*

1933   *Scandalabra* is produced by the Junior Vagabonds, Baltimore amateur little theater, in the spring. In September, Ring Lardner dies and Fitzgerald writes tribute for *The New Republic.* Sends new novel, *Tender Is the Night,* to Scribner's in late October.

1934   *Tender Is the Night* serialized in *Scribner's Magazine,* January–April, and is published on April 12, receiving largely favorable reviews and selling well. While working on revising the book in New York in January and February, spends time with John O'Hara and with Dorothy Parker. Zelda reenters Phipps Clinic on February 12 and later is transferred to Craig House in Beacon, New York ("I left my capacity for hoping on the little roads that led to Zelda's sanitarium"). Fitzgerald arranges showing of her paintings at art gallery in New York in March and April, and she is permitted to attend opening. When her condition deteriorates, Zelda is admitted to the Sheppard and Enoch Pratt Hospital outside Baltimore on May 19. Fitzgerald begins to sell stories and articles to recently established magazine *Esquire,* which pays $250 per piece.

1935   Travels to Tryon, North Carolina, in February in attempt to improve his health. *Taps at Reveille,* short-story collection, published by Scribner's on March 10. Spends summer in Asheville, North Carolina, at the Grove Park Inn, where he has affair with Beatrice Dance, who is married. Returns to Baltimore in September and lives in rented apartment. Spends winter in Hendersonville, North Carolina.

1936   Writes three confessional articles, "The Crack-Up," "Pasting It Together," and "Handle With Care," which appear in *Esquire,* February–April, and arouse considerable consternation among his friends. Zelda is transferred to Highland Hospital in Asheville on April 6, and Fitzgerald spends summer at Grove Park Inn to be near her. Mother dies in August, but Fitzgerald is unable to attend funeral. Daughter enters Ethel Walker School in Simsbury, Connecticut, in September. On his fortieth birthday in September is interviewed by Michel Mok of the New York *Post.* Subsequent article is headlined "Scott Fitzgerald, 40, Engulfed in Despair"; after it appears, Fitzgerald attempts suicide with overdose of morphine. Through Perkins, meets Marjorie Kinnan Rawlings when she comes to Asheville. Spends Christmas holidays in Johns Hopkins Hospital recovering from influenza and heavy drinking.

1937   Spends first months of year at Oak Hall Hotel in Tryon, North Carolina. Has great difficulty selling stories; his debts exceed $40,000, with $12,000 owed to his agent, Harold Ober. Hired as a screenwriter by M-G-M in July for six months at $1,000 per week. Rents small apartment at Garden of Allah, 8152 Sunset Boulevard, in Hollywood. Meets Sheilah Graham, twenty-eight-year-old Englishwoman who writes a Hollywood gossip column, at a party soon after his arrival, and they begin an affair. Works on film adaptation of Erich Maria Remarque's novel *Three Comrades*. Though it is extensively altered by producer Joseph Mankiewicz, his work on it contributes to renewal of his M-G-M contract (will be only screenplay for which he receives on-screen credit).

1938   Visits Zelda in January and takes her to Florida and Montgomery. Returns to Hollywood, and works from February to May on "Infidelity," movie for Joan Crawford, which is never produced. During daughter's spring vacation, takes her and Zelda to Virginia Beach and Norfolk, Virginia, but gets drunk and behaves badly. Moves to house at 114 Malibu Beach in April. Daughter is accepted at Vassar College. Fitzgerald works from May to October on screenplay of Claire Booth Luce's play *The Women* but is eventually replaced. Moves to Encino in November and rents small house on Belly Acres estate of actor Edward Everett Horton. Hires Frances Kroll as his secretary. Plans educational curriculum, "College of One," for Sheilah Graham, a two-year course in the arts and humanities that he participates in by tutoring her as well as assigning readings. Begins work in November on *Madame Curie,* film for Greta Garbo.

1939   Plans for *Madame Curie* are shelved in January, and after he is loaned to David O. Selznick to work very briefly on *Gone With the Wind,* Fitzgerald learns that M-G-M is dropping its option after eighteen months. Becomes freelance screenwriter and socializes in Hollywood with, among others, Nathanael West and S. J. Perelman. Hired by producer Walter Wanger of United Artists to collaborate with recent Dartmouth graduate Budd Schulberg on screenplay of *Winter Carnival*; they take a disastrous trip to Dartmouth College in February, during which Fitzgerald is drunk the entire time, and they are both fired. Goes on trip to Cuba with Zelda in April, and is so drunk and ill that she has to take him to New York, where he is hospitalized before returning to California. Begins work on a novel about Hollywood, with main character, Monroe Stahr, based on Irving Thalberg (never completed, it is edited by Edmund Wilson and published posthumously in 1941 as *The Last Tycoon*). Receives intermittent but brief screenwriting assignments but falls deeper in debt, eventually severing ties with longtime agent Harold Ober because Ober refuses to lend him any more money; becomes his own agent.

1940   Begins to publish series of stories in *Esquire* about Pat Hobby, a hack Hollywood writer, for which he receives $250 per story; ultimately, *Esquire* publishes seventeen Pat Hobby stories, one in each monthly number from January 1940 to July 1941. Writes "Cosmopolitan," screen adaptation of his story "Babylon Revisited," but it is never used. Moves in May to apartment at 1403 Laurel Avenue in Hollywood, a block from Sheilah Graham's apartment, and works intensively on his novel through the summer and fall. Suffers heart attack in late November and is ordered to rest in bed. Moves to Sheilah Graham's apartment, where he dies, apparently of a second heart attack, on December 21. With Zelda's approval, decision is made to bury Fitzgerald with his father's family in Rockville, Maryland, but he is refused burial at St. Mary's Church cemetery because he was not a practicing Catholic at his death. Buried December 27 at Rockville Union Cemetery.

NOTE ON THE TEXTS

This volume brings together F. Scott Fitzgerald's third novel, *The Great Gatsby* (1925); four stories from his third collection, *All the Sad Young Men* (1926)—"The Rich Boy," "Winter Dreams," "Absolution," and "Rags Martin-Jones and the Pr-nce of W-les"—that were written around the time Fitzgerald was working on *The Great Gatsby* and exploring similar themes; and a selection of thirteen letters between Fitzgerald and Maxwell Perkins, his editor at Scribner's, concerning the composition, editing, and publication of his novel. New, corrected texts of *The Great Gatsby* and the selected stories—which appear in the order Fitzgerald arranged them in for *All the Sad Young Men*—have been prepared for Library of America by James L. W. West III. The texts for all selections are described below.

In the late spring of 1922, while living at the resort town of White Bear Lake, near his hometown of St. Paul, Minnesota, Fitzgerald began work on the novel that was to become *The Great Gatsby*. He had recently finished correcting the proofs of *Tales of the Jazz Age*, his second collection of short stories, and was keen to get to work on a new book. In a letter dated June 20, 1922, he wrote to Maxwell Perkins, informing him that the novel would have a "catholic element" and would be set in "the middle west and New York of 1885." Four months later, Fitzgerald moved his family to Great Neck, Long Island, where he worked sporadically on the manuscript during the next year and a half. His progress was interrupted by other creative projects—first by the writing and production of his play, *The Vegetable*, and then, after its pre-Broadway flop in November 1923, by the composition of magazine stories to get himself out of debt.

In the early spring of 1924, Fitzgerald reconceived the novel, changing its omniscient narration to Nick Carraway's not always reliable first-person reminiscences and placing most of the action in a fictionalized version of contemporary Great Neck. He drafted three chapters in March and April. The following month, he and his wife and daughter sailed to France for an extended stay. They settled on the French Riviera, where Fitzgerald continued to work on the novel through the summer and early fall of that year. He composed in longhand on sheets of foolscap and worked with stenographers, through two or three drafts, to produce a type-script setting copy of the novel. This document he sent to Perkins via transatlantic mail on October 27, 1924.

In a long letter of November 20, 1924, to Fitzgerald, Perkins lavished praise on the new novel but offered suggestions about how to bring Jay Gatsby's character and physical appearance into sharper focus. Perkins's advice prompted Fitzgerald to revise his novel heavily. The text was now in galley proofs, two sets of which had been sent to him in late December. Fitzgerald supplied more information about the early years of Jay Gatsby's life and the origins of his money, but he went far beyond addressing Perkins's criticisms, almost rewriting the novel. He made Nick into a more sympathetic character, moved material about, reordered chapters, deleted long sections of exposition, provided fresh passages of description and dialogue, and polished the prose throughout. And Fitzgerald seemed to settle at last on *The Great Gatsby* as the title. He had previously tried out several possibilities, including "Among the Ash Heaps and Millionaires," "Gold-Hatted Gatsby," "Trimalchio," "Trimalchio in West Egg," "The High-Bouncing Lover," "On the Road to West Egg," and "Gatsby." In December 1924, Fitzgerald and Perkins agreed to contractual terms, though there was never any doubt that Fitzgerald would publish the novel with Scribner's, which had published all of his books.

In January and February 1925, Fitzgerald sent a final set of galleys bearing his handwritten revisions to Perkins (the other set, his working galleys, he kept for himself). He was now living in Italy, and there was not enough time for the publisher to send another round of proofs. Three weeks before publication, he cabled his editor: "CRAZY ABOUT TITLE UNDER THE RED WHITE AND BLUE STOP WHART WOULD DELAY BE." Perkins cabled back on the following day: "Advertised and sold for April tenth publication. Change suggested would mean some weeks delay, very great psychological damage. Think irony is far more effective under less leading title. Everyone likes present title. Urge we keep it." Fitzgerald conceded in a March 22 cable: "YOURE RIGHT." Fitzgerald continued to send revisions to Perkins, by letter and cable, until almost the day of publication.

The job of incorporating Fitzgerald's revisions into the text and seeing the novel through the press fell to Perkins. The novel was published on schedule by Scribner's, with few textual errors, on April 10, 1925.

The Great Gatsby had an initial print run of 20,870 copies; a second printing of 3,000 copies followed in August 1925. Reviews were generally favorable, but sales were modest, disappointing the expectations of both author and publisher. Harold Ober, Fitzgerald's literary agent, sold the subsidiary rights for both a stage adaptation and a movie version of the novel. Fitzgerald's share was $26,000, but the 1926 Broadway play and the silent movie of the same year failed to boost book sales. Fitzgerald felt that *The Great Gatsby* had not succeeded commercially because, as he explained to Perkins in a letter of late April 1925, the title was "only fair" and because the novel lacked any important female characters. In 1926, Chatto & Windus published the novel in London, using duplicate plates cast in the Scribner's printing plant.

This volume presents the text of the first printing of the 1925 Scribner's edition of *The Great Gatsby*, emended to account for typographical errors and other obvious mistakes that require correction, for Fitzgerald's preferred American spellings, and for subsequent alterations authorized by Fitzgerald. The first printing has been collated with Fitzgerald's composite manuscript, his working galleys, and his personal reading copy of the novel as well as all printings of the novel in the author's lifetime. Additionally, Fitzgerald's correspondence with Perkins has been consulted. The typescript setting copy is not known to be extant, nor is the set of galleys that Fitzgerald sent back to Scribner's (which evidently contained revisions not entered on his working galleys and may have omitted some he had previously made on those galleys). These materials were likely discarded soon after the novel's publication.

It was Scribner's practice up until the 1930s to impose British spelling on the texts of its American authors. Fitzgerald was not an exception in this regard, nor was Scribner's unique among American publishers in this practice, intended to encourage British publishers to purchase sheets from American publishers or to use their plates for a fee. Instances of this British orthography in *The Great Gatsby* include "defence," "centre," and "criticising." This volume restores Fitzgerald's preferred American spellings, with a few exceptions (for example, "theatre"), in deference to Fitzgerald's own long-standing habit. Hyphenated spellings introduced by Fitzgerald's editors (for example, "to-day" and "week-end") have been replaced by the unhyphenated spellings found in the author's manuscripts.

As evidenced by Fitzgerald's manuscript and the extensive revisions he made to the working galleys, he tended to punctuate more lightly than his editors; however, with the exception of the correction of typographical errors, no attempt has been made to restore the punctuation in the composite manuscript, which constitutes a working draft of the novel, not a fair copy.

Fitzgerald sometimes mispunctuated split speech in dialogue, and his pointing was inconsistently corrected by his typists or by the copyeditors at Scribner's. For example, in Chapter I, the 1925 Scribner's text reads as follows:

"I'm stiff," she complained, "I've been lying on that sofa for as long as I can remember."

In this edition, the comma following the verb has been emended to a period in this and other similar instances. Where necessary, the first word of the second clause has been capitalized.

Six alterations were introduced into the plates for the second printing of *The Great Gatsby* in August 1925. Four of these revisions are changes authorized by Fitzgerald; the other two are corrections of typographical errors. All six plate changes have been adopted for the present edition. These emendations are found in the 1926 Chatto & Windus printing. A single additional emendation appears in the British text; that emendation has been adopted ("self-absorbtion" has been corrected to "self-absorption"). In black pencil, Fitzgerald marked about three dozen revisions into the text of his personal reading copy of *The Great Gatsby* (a first impression of the 1925 Scribner's text), including corrections in spelling, capitalization, and punctuation as well as substantive alterations. These altered readings from the marked copy are incorporated into the present edition. Tom Buchanan's "God Damn" and "God Damned," from the manuscript and galleys, are adopted for this edition instead of the milder "God damned" of the first edition. An alternative reading adopted from an April 10, 1925, letter from Fitzgerald to Perkins has been adopted for this edition and is noted in the list of emendations.

Within a few weeks after the publication of *The Great Gatsby*, Fitzgerald—now living in Paris—began to assemble and edit the nine stories that comprise *All the Sad Young Men*. All the stories had been previously published in magazines, but Fitzgerald now heavily reworked them for book publication. Given the scope of his revisions, he likely submitted new typescripts rather than marked-up tearsheets to Scribner's. In the case of "Winter Dreams," he wrote several new passages of descriptive prose and substituted them for passages he had incorporated into *The Great Gatsby*. This was a common practice for Fitzgerald; he identified passages of good description and dialogue from his stories, copied them into his notebooks, and often used them again in his novels. In a letter of June 1925 to Perkins, Fitzgerald reported that the setting copy "will reach you by July 15th." In the same letter, he proposed language for the flap copy of the jacket: the collection shows the "transition from his early exuberant stories of youth which created a new type of American girl and the later and more serious mood which produced *The Great Gatsby* and marked him as one of the half dozen masters of English prose now writing in America."

Based on Fitzgerald's reported progress, Perkins scheduled *All the Sad Young Men* for publication in the fall of 1925, but Fitzgerald did not mail the setting copy until late August. And there was another problem: Harold Ober had sold "The Rich Boy" to *Red Book* magazine for publication in two parts, and the editors at *Red Book* were unable to clear the necessary space in the monthly magazine until January and February 1926. *Red Book* had paid $3,500 for "The Rich Boy," a high price at the time, and insisted the collection not be released until after the publication of the February issue. Fitzgerald had originally agreed not to see galleys of the book so that it might pass quickly into print and be available for the Christmas bookselling season, but the postponement in publication now made it possible for galleys to be mailed to him in mid-October. He corrected the galleys and sent them back to Perkins by the end of November. Scribner's published *All the Sad Young Men* on February 26, 1926, to favorable reviews. An initial printing of 10,100 copies was soon followed by two smaller printings of 3,020 and 3,050 copies, in March and May 1926.

For "The Rich Boy," "Winter Dreams," "Absolution," and "Rags Martin-Jones and the Pr-nce of W-les," this volume presents the text of the first printing of the 1926 Scribner's edition of *All the Sad Young Men*, emended in consultation with the published magazine versions of the stories and, when they exist, with typescripts, to account for Fitzgerald's preferred American spellings, typographical errors, and other mistakes requiring correction. No copy of the printed book bearing revisions by Fitzgerald is known to survive, nor are any galleys extant. No plate changes were introduced into subsequent printings of the collection. There was no British printing of the collection during the author's lifetime. Details of the first publication of the four stories selected for this volume are given below.

The Rich Boy. *The Red Book Magazine*, January and February 1926.

Winter Dreams. *Metropolitan Magazine*, December 1922.

Absolution. *The American Mercury*, June 1924.

Rags Martin-Jones and the Pr-nce of W-les, *McCall's*, July 1924.

The letters between Fitzgerald and Perkins selected for this volume are printed in *F. Scott Fitzgerald: A Life in Letters* (Scribner's, 1994), ed. by Matthew Bruccoli, with the following three exceptions. Fitzgerald's letter of January 15, 1925, to Perkins, and Perkins's letters of January 20, 1925, and February 24, 1925, to Fitzgerald have been newly transcribed by James L. W. West from scans of the originals or from carbon copies, and they are given here as Fitzgerald and Perkins wrote them, in keeping with the textual policies guiding Bruccoli's transcriptions in *F. Scott Fitzgerald: A Life in Letters*. Misspellings and other irregularities are preserved in all the selections. In a handful of stipulated cases, words dropped from the letters have been supplied in brackets. Some material not concerning *The Great Gatsby* has been omitted from the present volume; these omissions are signaled in the texts by four ellipsis points. Fitzgerald's letters were typically handwritten, and in the rarer instances in which they were typed Fitzgerald had them prepared by a professional secretary. Perkins's letters, typewritten from his dictation to his secretary, survive in carbon copies. Their correspondence reveals the close working relationship between author and editor and more particularly Perkins's influence on revisions to *The Great Gatsby*. All these letters—Fitzgerald's originals and Perkins's carbons—are preserved in the Archives of Charles Scribner's Sons, Department of Rare Books and Special Collections, Princeton University Library.

The texts presented in this volume reproduce those of the selected sources, altered only in the ways described above. Substantive alterations to *The Great Gatsby* and selected stories from *All the Sad Young Men* are indicated in the list of emendations below. The two lists record, by page and line number, the changes incorporated into the respective texts. A key to the abbreviations used to indicate the source of a particular reading precedes the list of emendations for each text.

THE GREAT GATSBY

MS   *The Great Gatsby*, composite manuscript, March–September 1924, F. Scott Fitzgerald Papers, Department of Rare Books and Special Collections, Princeton University Library.

G   Fitzgerald's working galleys, January–February 1925, F. Scott Fitzgerald Papers, Department of Rare Books and Special Collections, Princeton University Library.

Ai   *The Great Gatsby*. New York: Scribner's, 1925. Copy-text.

Ai2   *The Great Gatsby*, second printing (August 1925). New York: Scribner's, 1925.

Aib   *The Great Gatsby*. London: Chatto & Windus, 1926.

FC   Fitzgerald's marked copy of *The Great Gatsby* (first printing).

L   Letter from Fitzgerald to Perkins, April 10, 1925, Archives of Charles Scribner's Sons, Department of Rare Books and Special Collections, Princeton University Library.

ed   Editor.

8.29   confusion] FC; wonder

9.1   arresting] FC; interesting

14.4   Damn] MS; damned

18.15   said] FC; began

19.8   startlingly] MS; startingly

24.11   been at] ed; been

25.8   men] FC; ash-gray men

26.7–8   restaurants] FC; cafés

27.17   surplus flesh] FC; flesh

30.1   so warm] FC; warm

30.2   afternoon that I] FC; afternoon. I

31.9   disappeared] FC; both disappeared

36.14   had played no part in her past] FC; expected no affection

36.18   out." She looked to see who was listening. "'Oh] FC; out: 'Oh

37.3–4   was him] FC; saw him

41.11   shorn] FC; bobbed

42.10   amusement parks] FC; an amusement park

45.3   sometime] MS; sometimes

47.27   Third] FC; First

48.1   Ninth Machine-Gun Battalion] FC; Twenty-eighth Infantry

48.2   Seventh Infantry] FC; Sixteenth

48.25   external] FC; eternal

50.7   echolalia] Ai2; chatter

50.9   Vladimir] ed; Vladmir

50.14   Vladimir] ed; Vladmir

50.28–29   formed with] MS; formed for

55.19   them little] MS; them a little

57.12   five] FC; lined five

57.16   outlined] FC; made

57.16   gestures] FC; circles

63.3   work or rigid sitting] FC; work

65.6   two machine-gun detachments] FC; the remains of my machine-gun battalion

68.29   asked Gatsby] MS; asked

74.20   Seelbach] FC; Muhlbach

76.17   Victoria] MS; victoria

77.16   he's a regular] FC; he's regular

80.12   looked] FC; looked down

86.17   occasionally willing] FC; willing, even eager,

86.23   a large] FC; the large

89.9   Adam] ed; Adam's

93.22   will store] FC; can store

96.24   self-absorption] Aib; self-absorbtion

97.7   southern] Ai2; northern

117.11–13   expectantly. ¶"Pardon me?" ¶"Have] G; expectantly. ¶"Have

118.12   stop] MS; spot

125.2   added, as if she might have sounded irreverent,] FC; added,

128.23   God Damned] G; God damned

133.14   Michaelis] FC; Mavromichaelis

134.20   its] Ai2; it's

134.29   ripped] FC; ripped a little

135.4   away.] Ai2; away

135.17   wire] FC; metal

135.23   disarranged] MS; deranged

137.19   him, seized] ed; him seized

137.19   him] MS; him,

138.26   God Damn] MS; God damned

139.10   moonlit] MS; moonlight

146.18   finger] MS; fingers

152.2   Central] ed; central

152.3   Long Distance] ed; long distance

157.3   thereabouts] MS; thereabout

158.19   compass] L; transit

161.5   as] FC; though

161.5   unmoved] FC; shocked

166.14   sickantired] Ai2; sick in tired

166.17   at me all] MS; at me

166.19   Wolfshiem] MS; Wolfsheim

171.6   Owl Eyes] ed; Owl-eyes

171.16   Union Station] Ai2; Union Street station

FROM ALL THE SAD YOUNG MEN

MS   Early holograph manuscript for "Rags Martin-Jones and the Pr-nce of W-les," December 1923, F. Scott Fitzgerald Papers, Department of Rare Books and Special Collections, Princeton University Library.

TS   Typescript for "The Rich Boy" from Harold Ober files, bearing Fitzgerald's final revisions for serial publication, August 1925, F. Scott Fitzgerald Papers, Department of Rare Books and Special Collections, Princeton University Library.

Ai   *All the Sad Young Men*. New York: Scribner's, 1926. Copy-text.

ed   Editor.

185.9   De Soto] ed; De Sota

186.19   bridesmaids] TS; bridesmaid

201.22   Vanderbilt] ed; Madison

203.29   imminent] ed; eminent

204.14   out] TS; on

204.16   that] TS; they

207.21   in] TS; of

235.19   these] ed; this

259.20   thoughts] ed; thought

263.22   interrogator] ed; interrogation

267.21   Hamline] ed; Hamlin

267.29   shoulders] ed; shoulder

274.7   *Die*] ed; *Dei*

281.10   1912] ed; 1913

285.7   elusive] ed; illusive

289.24   after] MS; after a

290.6   with a] MS; with

293.26   laid] MS; had laid

297.20   bunch over] MS; bunch across over

NOTES

In the notes below, the reference numbers denote page and line of this volume (the line count includes chapter headings). For biographical information not contained in the Chronology, see David S. Brown, *Paradise Lost: A Life of F. Scott Fitzgerald* (Cambridge, MA: Belknap Press, 2017); Matthew J. Bruccoli, *Some Sort of Epic Grandeur: The Life of F. Scott Fitzgerald*, 1981, second revised edition (Columbia: University of South Carolina Press, 2002); Scott Donaldson, *Fool for Love: A Biography of F. Scott Fitzgerald*, 1983, revised edition (Minneapolis: University of Minnesota Press, 2012); André Le Vot, *F. Scott Fitzgerald: A Biography*, translated by William Byron (Garden City, NY: Doubleday, 1983); James R. Mellow, *Invented Lives: F. Scott and Zelda Fitzgerald* (Boston: Houghton Mifflin, 1984); Arthur Mizener, *The Far Side of Paradise: A Biography of F. Scott Fitzgerald*, 1951, revised edition (Boston: Houghton Mifflin, 1965); Andrew Turnbull, *Scott Fitzgerald* (New York: Scribner's, 1962). For a history of the early versions of *The Great Gatsby* see the texts published in The Cambridge Edition of the Works of F. Scott Fitzgerald, 18 vols. (1991–2019): *Trimalchio: An Early Version of The Great Gatsby*, ed. James L. W. West III (New York: Cambridge University Press, 2000) and *The Great Gatsby: An Edition of the Manuscript*, ed. James L. W. West III and Don C. Skemer (New York: Cambridge University Press, 2018). A detailed account of the making of *The Great Gatsby* and a history of its publication are included in the final volume of The Cambridge Edition of the Works of F. Scott Fitzgerald: *The Great Gatsby: A Variorum Edition*, ed. James L. W. West III (New York: Cambridge University Press, 2019).

THE GREAT GATSBY

1.4–8   *Then wear . . .* THOMAS PARKE D'INVILLIERS.] Epigraph composed by Fitzgerald. D'Invilliers is a character in *This Side of Paradise*, a literary man and one of Amory Blaine's best friends at Princeton. Fitzgerald based D'Invilliers on American poet John Peale Bishop (1892–1944).

NOTES

3.1–3   ONCE AGAIN TO ZELDA] Fitzgerald had previously dedicated his second book, *Flappers and Philosophers* (1920), to his wife, Zelda Sayre Fitzgerald.

6.25–26   the Dukes of Buccleuch] Ducal house of the Scotts of Buccleuch, granted land by King James II of Scotland in the fifteenth century. The title "Duke of Buccleuch" was created for James Scott, Duke of Monmouth (1649–1685).

7.1   sent a substitute . . . Civil War] The Enrollment Act of 1863 allowed men in the Northern states who were eligible for conscription to avoid service in the Civil War by hiring a substitute.

7.5   New Haven] Yale University, located in New Haven, Connecticut.

7.21   eighty a month] In 1922, the year in which *The Great Gatsby* is set, eighty dollars would have had the approximate buying power of thirteen hundred dollars in 2022.

7.24   an old Dodge] The Dodge Brothers Company of Hamtramck, Michigan, began making cars in 1914. Their Model 30, a four-cylinder passenger vehicle, was meant to compete with the Ford Model T.

8.11–12   Midas and Morgan and Maecenas] Midas, in Greek and Roman mythology, a king of Phrygia, who was granted his wish that everything he touched be turned to gold. John Pierpont Morgan (1837–1913), American financier and banker of the Gilded Age. Gaius Macenas (c. 70–8 B.C.E.), Roman statesman, friend and confidant of Augustus, and great literary patron of the "golden" Augustan era who fostered the careers of both Horace and Vergil.

8.27   the egg in the Columbus story] Apocryphal story concerning Christopher Columbus. Columbus is said to have challenged detractors of his discovery of the "New World" to stand an egg on its end. After they all had failed in the attempt, Columbus smashed one end of the egg against the table.

9.3   West Egg . . . less fashionable of the two] East Egg and West Egg suggest, respectively, Manhasset Neck (old money) and Great Neck (new money) on Long Island. In the manuscript version of the novel, Jordan gives Tom this description of West Egg: "Most expensive town on Long Island. Full of moving picture people, playrites, singers and cartoonists and kept women. You'd love it." From October 1922 until April 1924, Fitzgerald and his wife and daughter lived in a rented house on Great Neck.

10.1   Lake Forest.] A suburb of Chicago on the North Shore of Lake Michigan. Ginevra King, Fitzgerald's first serious romantic interest, lived in Lake Forest for much of the summer season. Her father, Charles Garfield King, was a successful stockbroker; he kept a string of polo ponies and played in matches at Onwentsia, a country club for the wealthy near Lake Forest.

12.24   Miss Baker's] Before World War I, young men and women of the haute bourgeoisie addressed each other as "Mr." and "Miss"—at least until they became friends. These customs began to fade after the war, but Nick still observes them in the novel.

13.19   She's three years old.] The Buchanans were married in June 1919; according to Jordan, their daughter was born ten months later, in April 1920. The child must therefore be two years old when this scene takes place in June 1922. The reading "three years old" originated in the manuscript, where the action of the novel was set at a later date and "three years old" was correct. Fitzgerald failed to adjust the child's age when he shifted the year to 1922.

16.15–16   'The Rise of the Colored Empires' by . . . Goddard?"] Tom misremembers the title and author of *The Rising Tide of Color against White World-Supremacy* (1920), by the American historian and white supremacist Lothrop Stoddard (1883–1950). According to Stoddard's thesis, a racial world war was inevitable if Africans and Asians were not prevented from migrating to Western nations.

19.4   Cunard or White Star Line.] The two major British transatlantic passenger lines of Fitzgerald's era. (In 1934, the two rivals merged to form the Cunard–White Star Line.) The Cunard liners included the *Mauretania*, the *Aquitania*, and the *Berengaria*; the White Star liners, which were known for their black-topped funnels, included the *Olympic*, the *Britannic*, and the ill-fated *Titanic*.

20.11–12   I woke up . . . ether] During the 1920s, halogenated ether was a commonly used anesthetic. Daisy would have been unconscious during childbirth.

21.2–3   the Saturday Evening Post—] The most popular middle-class magazine of the period and Fitzgerald's most dependable market for short fiction during the peak years of his career.

21.17   Jordan Baker."] Jordan Baker's name combines the titles of two early automobile manufacturers. Both produced vehicles aimed at female buyers. The Jordan Motor Car Company (1916–1931) in Cleveland was known for its stylish runabouts; the Baker Motor Vehicle Company (1899–1914), also based in Cleveland, specialized in electric two-seaters, ideal for use in town.

21.19   rotogravure pictures] Rotogravure was a printing process using intaglio cylinders on a rotary press. Here, "rotogravure" refers to the illustrated supplement found in most Sunday newspapers of the day, featuring printed images of celebrities, society people, stage and movie stars, and sports figures.

21.20   Asheville and Hot Springs and Palm Beach.] Luxury resorts known for their golf courses, in North Carolina, Arkansas, and Florida.

25.14–15   the eyes . . . T. J. Eckleburg.] Likely suggested by a painting, a gouache on paper by the illustrator Francis Cugat, that Fitzgerald saw in the Scribner's offices before departing for France in May 1924. In late August, while at work on the manuscript of the novel, he wrote to Maxwell Perkins: "For Christs sake don't give anyone that jacket you're saving for me. I've written it into the book." Cugat's painting, which depicts a woman's eyes hovering over an amusement-park scene, was used on the front panel of the first-edition dust jacket.

28.22   Town Tattle] A fictional magazine. Cf. *Town Topics,* a New York gossip rag known for printing scandalous stories about the rich and celebrated, published from 1885 to 1937.

29.4   John D. Rockefeller] American business magnate and wealthiest American of the twentieth century (1839–1937), known for his philanthropy and for his Social Darwinist beliefs. He founded the Standard Oil Company in 1870.

30.26   "Simon Called Peter,"] Scandalous best-selling novel of 1921 by British author Robert Keable (1887–1927). The protagonist is an army chaplain who loses his morals and ideals while serving on the front during World War I. In letters to Maxwell Perkins, Fitzgerald expressed nervousness about the reference.

34.4   Kaiser Wilhelm's.] Kaiser Wilhelm II (1859–1941), the last German emperor, who abdicated in November 1918 at the end of World War I after losing the support of the German army. He spent the rest of his life in exile in the Netherlands.

39.9   the morning Tribune] The *New-York Tribune*, founded by Horace Greeley in 1841, the leading Republican newspaper in the country and the chief rival of *The New York Times.* The *Tribune* merged with the *New York Herald* in 1924 to form the *New York Herald-Tribune.*

40.7   aquaplanes] Aquaplaning was a water sport popular before the advent of waterskiing. The participant, either standing or kneeling, rode a flat board towed behind a motorboat.

41.28–29   moving her hands like Frisco] In the dancing style of Joe Frisco (1889–1958), a comedian popular during the 1920s. Frisco was famous for a soft-shoe shuffle, of his own invention, called the "Frisco Dance." Beginning in 1918, he was featured in *The Midnight Frolic*, a late-night floor show staged by the impresario Florenz Ziegfeld (1867–1932) on the rooftop of Broadway's New Amsterdam Theatre. He performed also in *Vanities*, a Broadway girly-leggy variety show produced by Earl Carroll (1893–1948).

42.2–3   Gilda Gray's understudy from the Follies.] Gilda Gray (1901–1959), born Marianna Michalska, was a Polish American dancer and cabaret singer who popularized the "shimmy" in the 1920s when she performed in the Ziegfeld Follies, a Broadway revue with revealing costumery and elaborate sets. The shimmy was characterized by movement of the shoulders and hips ("I'm shaking my shimmy, that's what I'm doing," Gray explained).

46.16   "Stoddard Lectures."] John L. Stoddard (1850–1931), an American author and popular performer on the lecture circuit. He was among the first to use the stereopticon in his presentations. His travelogues, comprising ten volumes and five supplements, were issued in a uniform edition beginning in 1897.

46.18   a regular Belasco] David Belasco (1853–1931), a Broadway dramatist and producer, was known for creating lifelike illusions onstage. Among his best-known productions were *Lord Chumley* in 1888 and *The Girl of the Golden West* in 1905.

46.19–20   didn't cut the pages.] In the early twentieth century, some books were still issued with untrimmed edges. Progressing through the book, the reader separated the leaves from one another with a paper knife or letter-opener.

48.6   hydroplane] Here, a fixed-wing aircraft that could take off and land on water.

50.9–10   Mr. Vladimir Tostoff's . . . Carnegie Hall] The Russian jazz musician Vladimir Tostoff is a fictional invention. George Gershwin's *Rhapsody in Blue* (1923) and other works of serious jazz made their world premieres at New York's Carnegie Hall.

54.6   a long duster] A lightweight overcoat worn by drivers and passengers for protection against engine exhaust and dirt from the roads.

56.18   the Yale Club—] A private New York club for graduates and faculty of Yale University. It was located at the corner of Vanderbilt and East 44th Street.

56.23   the old Murray Hill Hotel] Late Victorian New York hotel that was razed in 1947. The Murray Hill Hotel had one entrance on Park Avenue opposite Grand Central Station and another entrance on 40th Street. According to one 1920s guidebook, the atmosphere inside was "heavily gracious."

60.7   Von Hindenburg] Paul von Hindenburg (1847–1934), field marshal of the German armed forces during World War I. After the war he served as president of the Weimar Republic (1925–1934).

63.1   the dashboard] Narrow platform fixed beneath each car door. Later, it was called a "running-board."

65.2   the Bois de Boulogne] Wooded area of over two thousand acres, lying just west of Paris, originally designated by Napoleon III in the 1850s as a recreational space for the upper classes. By the early 1900s "Le Bois" had been transformed into a public park for the bourgeoisie, with areas for rowing, riding, and picnicking.

65.5   Argonne Forest] Forest in northeastern France, 135 miles east of Paris, through which American troops pushed in the final offensive of World War I, known as the Meuse-Argonne Offensive, which lasted from September 26, 1918, until the Armistice on November 11, 1918. American troops sustained more than 110,000 casualties.

65.6–10   so far forward . . . of dead.] Gatsby's exploits are based on the story of the "Lost Battalion," a unit of the 77th Division that advanced well beyond its flank support during the Meuse-Argonne Offensive. The battalion held its ground but at a heavy cost. Of some 554 men, there were only 194 survivors. The Lewis gun, a standard weapon in most American units, was a one-man air-cooled machine gun with a circular cartridge drum.

65.14–15   Montenegro's troubled history] Montenegro was among the Allied Powers during the First World War. After the Treaty of Versailles, it was absorbed by Yugoslavia as part of a newly unified Montenegro and Serbia; however, the unification was contested by the exiled king of Montenegro and his supporters.

65.28   Trinity Quad—] Trinity College, Oxford, founded in 1555, is one of the constituent colleges of the University of Oxford. On his first trip to Europe, during the spring of 1921, Fitzgerald and his wife, Zelda, visited Trinity.

66.6   the Grand Canal] A major waterway through the city of Venice, lined with opulent palaces belonging to the wealthiest Venetian families.

NOTES

68.20 "Highballs?"] A whiskey drink, usually mixed with soda water or ginger ale, and served with ice in a tall glass.

69.2–7 "The old Metropole . . . outside.] Fitzgerald based Wolfshiem's recollections on the murder of the gangster and bookmaker Herman Rosenthal. The shooting took place on July 16, 1912, in New York, at the Metropole Hotel, 147 West 43rd Street, near Times Square. Accounts of the killing stayed on the front pages of metropolitan newspapers for the rest of the summer.

72.2 the man who fixed the World's Series] Racketeer Arnold Rothstein (1882–1928), on whom Wolfshiem is based, is said to have fixed the 1919 World's Series in the infamous "Black Sox" scandal. Rothstein got wind of a plan by several players on the Chicago White Sox team to throw the series; he therefore bet heavily on the Cincinnati Reds, their opponents. The White Sox lost the series, and Rothstein won more than $300,000. Rothstein was never formally charged with involvement in the swindle, but eight members of the Chicago White Sox, including star outfielder "Shoeless Joe" Jackson and pitcher Eddie Cicotte, were banned for lifetime from baseball for their participation.

73.3 the Plaza Hotel] The Plaza, among the most fashionable of the New York caravansaries, stands across from the southeast corner of Central Park at Fifth Avenue and 59th Street.

74.16 the armistice] The agreement that ended hostilities between the Allies and Germany in World War I specified that fighting should cease on November 11, 1918, at 11:00 A.M.—the eleventh hour of the eleventh day of the eleventh month (Matthew 20:1–16). Here, "after the armistice" means "after the war."

74.20 the Seelbach Hotel] A grand hotel in downtown Louisville, designed in the opulent European style, that was operated by immigrant brothers from Bavaria named Louis and Otto Seelbach.

76.17 a Victoria] A low, light, horse-drawn carriage that had a calash top and, in front, a perch for the driver.

76.21–24 "I'm the Sheik . . . I'll creep—"] Lyrics from "The Sheik of Araby," a hit tune in 1921, with words by Harry B. Smith and Francis Wheeler and music by Ted Snyder. Contemporary readers might also have been reminded of *The Sheik*, a silent movie of 1921 starring Rudolph Valentino (1895–1926), the first "Latin lover" screen idol. During the early 1920s, romantic young men were often called "sheiks."

82.10   The Journal.] The *New York Evening Journal*, a Hearst newspaper known for its racy, sensationalist reporting. It carried a daily comic-strip page and sold for one cent in 1922. Columnists included O. O. McIntyre and Nellie Bly, with society news provided by Maury Henry Biddle Paul (a.k.a. "Cholly Knickerbocker").

82.20   Clay's "Economics,"] *Economics: An Introduction for the General Reader* (1916) by British economist and lecturer Henry Clay (1883–1954). Among Clay's concerns was the redistribution of wealth for the public good.

83.16   Castle Rackrent.] The ancestral home of the Irish Rackrent family in the novel of the same name by Anglo-Irish novelist Maria Edgeworth (1767–1849). *Castle Rackrent* recounts the adventures of three generations of Rackrents. They squander their wealth and eventually lose their tumbledown castle.

86.10–11   like Kant at his church steeple] The German philosopher Immanuel Kant (1724–1804) was said to gaze at a church steeple visible from the window of his writing room in Königsberg.

88.28–89.1   "the Merton College Library"] Merton College, which dates from 1264, was among the first colleges to be founded at Oxford. Its library is considered one of the most beautiful at the university. The library at Cottage Club (Fitzgerald's club at Princeton) is modelled on the Merton College Library.

89.9   an Adam study] The "Adam style" was a neoclassical furniture style developed by the Scottish brothers Robert and James Adam, an ornate choice for a man of Gatsby's age during the 1920s.

91.15   "The pompadour!] A hairstyle in which the hair is swept upward from the sides and forehead and fixed in place with hair oil or gel. The pompadour was popular during the 1910s but would have been passé by 1922.

92.25   "The Love Nest"] Popular song from the 1920 Broadway musical comedy *Mary*, with music by Louis A. Hirsch (1887–1924) and lyrics by Otto Harbach (1873–1963). The lyrics read in part: "Just a love nest, / Cozy with charm, / Like a dove nest, / Down on a farm . . . Better than a palace with a gilded dome, / Is a love nest / You can call home."

93.1–12   "In the morning . . . in between time—"] The seven lines are from "Ain't We Got Fun?" (1921), with music by Richard A. Whiting (1891–1938) and lyrics by Gus Kahn (1886–1941) and Raymond B. Egan (1890–1952). In the third-from-last line, Klipspringer sings the variant "children" for "poorer."

95.15   "underground pipe-line to Canada"] Illegal alcohol entered the U.S. from Canada, but a popular myth of the Prohibition era held that liquor flowed southward across the border through an underground pipeline.

97.7   Lutheran college of St. Olaf's] St. Olaf College in Northfield, Minnesota, founded in 1874 by Norwegian Lutherans.

97.20   Madame de Maintenon] Françoise d'Aubigné (1635–1719), known as Madame de Maintenon, who was secretly married in 1683 to Louis XIV, king of France. She was said to be pious and narrow-minded; she exercised much influence over the king during the last years of his reign.

106.26   "Three o'Clock in the Morning,"] Popular song of the 1920s with music by Julián Robledo (1887–1940) and lyrics by Dorothy Terriss (1883–1953). An instrumental version by Paul Whiteman's orchestra was released on the Victor label in 1922 and sold more than three million copies.

110.4   Trimalchio] A wealthy freed slave in the *Satyricon,* a Latin fiction likely written by the Roman author Petronius (c. 27–66 C.E.). Trimalchio, who appears in a section of the work called "Trimalchio's Feast," throws ostentatious parties for his guests. The narrator of the *Satyricon* is a layabout named Encolpius. Fitzgerald considered "Trimalchio" and "Trimalchio in West Egg" as possible titles for *The Great Gatsby*.

111.23   National Biscuit Company] A sprawling Nabisco plant located in Long Island City in the borough of Queens.

115.3   gin rickeys] A hot-weather drink made with gin, lime juice, fruit syrup or sugar, and seltzer water. It is served over ice, usually with a wedge of lime, in a lowball glass.

118.12–13   You can . . . drug-store nowadays."] During Prohibition some drugstores were fronts for bootlegging, the suggestion by Tom being that Gatsby is a bootlegger.

120.1   both brakes] During the 1920s most automobiles were equipped with two mechanisms for stopping: hand brakes, which acted on the rear wheels, and pedal-operated brakes, which acted on the transmission shaft.

124.20–21   Mendelssohn's Wedding March] Fitzgerald refers to the march from the incidental music for *A Midsummer Night's Dream* (1842), by Felix Mendelssohn (1809–1847), usually played as a recessional at weddings. The ceremony downstairs appears to be beginning; the music one might expect to hear would be the "Bridal Chorus" ("Here comes the bride . . .") from *Lohengrin*, by Richard Wagner (1813–1883).

124.27   Biloxi, Tennessee."] Biloxi is a city in Harrison County, Mississippi, on the Gulf Coast. Daisy is perhaps confused.

126.5–6   New Haven."] See note 7.5.

129.18   Kapiolani?"] A three hundred–acre park in Honolulu, Hawaii.

129.22   the Punch Bowl] Extinct volcano crater in Honolulu.

146.21   the Argonne battles] See note 65.5.

147.9–10   "Beale Street Blues"] Early blues tune by American songwriter and pianist W. C. Handy (1873–1958), first published in 1917.

152.2   an exasperated Central] Telephones during the early 1920s were not equipped with mechanisms for dialing. An operator at a central office placed the call through a switchboard. For long-distance calls the line had to be cleared in advance through several interchanges.

164.15   James J. Hill.] A Canadian American railroad executive and financier (1838–1916) whose base of operations was in St. Paul, Minnesota, Fitzgerald's hometown. A self-made man, Hill was a hero to many midwestern boys. His thirty-two-room mansion, which contains a ballroom and an art gallery, still stands on Summit Avenue in St. Paul.

166.3   "The Rosary,"] Popular sentimental tune written by American composer and pianist Ethelbert Nevin (1862–1901), with words by Robert Cameron Rogers (1862–1912): "The hours I spent with thee, dear heart, / Are as a string of pearls to me; / I count them over, every one apart, / My rosary, my rosary!"

168.28–29   "Hopalong Cassidy."] One in a series of novels and stories by American writer Clarence E. Mulford (1883–1956) that featured the rough-talking but upright cowboy of the same name. The novel is an anachronism, since Jimmy Gatz's list is dated September 12, 1906—and the book was not published until 1910.

171.4   "Blessed are the dead . . . falls on,"] Paraphrase of a line from "Rain" (1916), by the British war poet Edward Thomas (1878–1917), killed on the Western Front during World War I.

172.23   El Greco] Doménikos Theotokópoulos (1541–1614), a Greek painter and sculptor.

STORIES

183.21   New Haven] See note 7.5.

184.21   Pensacola] Pensacola, Florida, the location of the U.S. Naval Air Station during World War I. There, trainees learned to fly seaplanes, dirigibles, and kite balloons.

184.21–22   "I'm Sorry, Dear"] A war song with music by N. J. Clesi (1880–1950) and lyrics by Harry Tobias (1895–1994), popularized by Fats Waller in a 1918 recording. "I'm sorry dear, so sorry dear, / I'm sorry I made you cry. / Won't you forget, won't you forgive, / Don't let us say goodbye."

187.3   The Ritz] The Ritz-Carlton Hotel, located in the 1920s at Madison and 46th Street, famous for its elegantly appointed Palm Room.

189.26   bromo-seltzer] Bromo-Seltzer, a bromide. The granules were mixed with water before ingesting.

190.4–5   in Dutch] In trouble.

190.8   the Links."] Exclusive New York club located on East 62nd Street, about a block from Central Park.

194.2   the Breakers and the Royal Poinciana] Gilded Age luxury hotels built by American oil, real estate, and railroad tycoon Henry Flagler. The two hotels occupied the same property in Palm Beach.

194.7   the double-shuffle] A three-step dance—a variation on the polka, with extra steps interpolated for syncopated music. By convention, dancers performing the double-shuffle moved counterclockwise around the floor.

194.10   the Everglades Club] Exclusive Palm Beach club that opened in 1919.

194.22–25   "*Rose of Washington Square . . . basement air*—"] Three lines from the popular 1920 song "Rose of Washington Square," with music by the vaudeville accompanist James F. Hanley (1892–1942) and lyrics by Princeton alumnus Ballard MacDonald (1882–1935). The song has two versions, one serious and the other comic. The lyrics here are from the comic rendition: "Rose of Washington Square, she's withering there; / In basement air she's fading . . . / She's got those Broadway vampires lashed to the mast; / She's got no future, but oh! What a past; / She's Rose of Washington Square."

195.3   Mr. Conan Doyle] Sir Arthur Conan Doyle (1859–1930), British author of the Sherlock Holmes detective stories.

197.5–6   a cutaway coat] A coat with the front cut back to curve toward the tails, worn with striped trousers, vest, winged collar, and ascot. The ensemble was worn for formal daytime occasions, such as weddings and Sunday morning churchgoing.

197.12   Wheatley Hills.] Exclusive club on Long Island, in East Williston, New York.

198.24–25   Junior League . . . the Plaza . . . the Assembly] The Junior League and the Assembly, social organizations for women of wealth who wanted to do civic good works and help the indigent and poor. Dolly's debutante ball was held at New York's Plaza Hotel (see also note 73.3).

207.1   Celliniesque] Resembling the extravagant escapades of the Florentine goldsmith and writer Benvenuto Cellini (1500–1571), recounted in *The Auto-biography of Benvenuto Cellini* (English translation 1791).

213.21   St. Thomas's church.] Protestant Episcopal church at 53rd Street and Fifth Avenue. Its congregation was drawn from the ranks of the rich and socially prominent. One of the ornaments above its "marriage door," situated to the left of the main entrance, resembles a dollar sign—a matter for joking among some of the parishioners.

216.9   continuities for pictures] In the motion-picture business, a "continuity" is a written plan, set down in advance of filming. It details the order and connection of the scenes.

216.25   Homeric] Big, formal send-off.

219.19   'God Save the King'?"] British national anthem, adopted in 1745 during the reign of George II.

220.14–15   the exchange existed no longer.] Telephone numbers of the time were preceded by lettered prefixes that stood for exchanges or central of-fices—Plaza or Rhinelander, for example. Certain exchanges were more pres-tigious than others. See also note 152.2.

226.1   the *Paris*] Luxury transatlantic French liner that entered service in 1921. It was decorated in a combination of Art Deco, Art Nouveau, and Moorish styles. The Fitzgeralds traveled to France on the *Paris* in April 1928.

229.18–19   Black Bear Lake] Cf. White Bear Lake, a town on the lake of the same name, near Fitzgerald's hometown of St. Paul, Minnesota. As a youth

Fitzgerald attended dances at the White Bear Yacht Club; after their marriage, he and Zelda lived at the lake in August 1921 and again during the summer of 1922.

230.13   Pierce-Arrow] Large luxury automobile with a powerful thirteen-liter engine. It was the most elegant car of the period.

236.19   mashie shot] The mashie, a standard club for most golfers. It had the approximate loft of a five-iron and was used for medium-length shots.

238.2–3   "Chin-Chin" and "The Count of Luxembourg" and "The Chocolate Soldier"—] "Chin-Chin Chinaman," a comic song from the 1896 musical *The Geisha*, by Sidney Jones (which enjoyed a Broadway revival in 1913). *The Count of Luxembourg* (1912), a two-act Broadway operetta with English lyrics and libretto by Basil Hood and Adrian Ross, adapted from Austro-Hungarian composer Franz Lehár's three-act operetta *Der Graf von Luxembourg* (1909). *The Chocolate Soldier* (1909), an English-language adaptation of an operetta by Viennese composer Oscar Straus, based on George Bernard Shaw's play *Arms and the Man* (1894). Prior to the manufacture of high-quality record discs and phonographs, hits from Broadway shows circulated as sheet music.

247.15   when he was twenty-five.] The only date provided in the story is February 1917, just before Dexter enters the war. Here, Dexter should be twenty-six, not twenty-five.

253.19   the war came to America in March] U.S. diplomatic relations with Germany ceased in February 1917, and entrance into World War I seemed certain by March. On April 6, 1917, the United States formally declared war on Germany and its allies.

261.25–26   the Sixth and Ninth Commandments.] As numbered by the Roman Catholic Church, the commandments, respectively, against adultery and the coveting of one's neighbor's wife.

263.17   'Twenty-three Skidoo'] Slang term (early twentieth century) of uncertain origin, meaning "Beat it!" or "Scram!"

267.4–5   James J. Hill] See note 164.15.

267.20   Alger books] American author Horatio Alger, Jr. (1832–1899), wrote *Ragged Dick* (1868) and numerous other rags-to-riches stories extolling honesty, hard work, and perseverance.

267.21   "Hamline,"] Hamline University, a small Methodist institution in Fitzgerald's native St. Paul.

273.3–4   *"Dómini, non sum dignus . . . ánima mea . . ."*] From the Ordinary of the Roman Catholic Mass (c. 1910): "Lord, I am not worthy that Thou shouldst come under my roof; but only say the word, and my soul will be healed."

273.12–13   *"Corpus Dómini . . . vitam ætérnam"*] "May the Body of our Lord Jesus Christ preserve (my/your) soul unto life everlasting." See note 273.3–4.

274.8   *"Sagitta Volante in Die"*] Latin: Flies by day. See Psalms 90:5–7 (the Douay version, 1914): "His truth shall compass thee with a shield: thou shalt not be afraid of the terror of the night. / Of the arrow that flieth in the day, of the business that walketh about in the dark: of invasion, or of the noonday devil."

277.25   the German cuirassiers at Sedan.] During the Franco-Prussian War, Sedan, on the Meuse River in northeastern France, was the site of a battle on September 1–2, 1870, that resulted in the capture of Napoleon III and the effective defeat of the French. The Prussian cuirassiers, a unit of heavy cavalry, wore breastplates and plumed or spiked helmets.

279.3   The *Majestic*] Luxurious White Star liner that began life as the partly built German liner *Bismarck*. Under the reparations agreements in the Treaty of Versailles, the ship was awarded to the British as compensation for the sinking of the *Britannic* by a German mine. The *Majestic* was completed in 1921 and worked the transatlantic service between New York and Southampton.

279.14–16   Gloria Swanson . . . Lord & Taylor . . . Graustark] Gloria Swanson (1899–1983), American actress who became famous in the 1920s while under contract with Paramount Pictures. Lord & Taylor, the department store chain, whose New York flagship store and headquarters had moved in 1914 from Broadway and 20th Street in the "Ladies' Mile" to a new building at Fifth Avenue and 38th Street. Graustark, a fictional Balkan kingdom that is the setting of several novels by popular American writer George Barr McCutcheon (1866–1928), including *Graustark* (1901), *Beverly of Graustark* (1904), and *The Prince of Graustark* (1914)—all adapted for the screen as silent films.

281.21–22   "American Magazine"] *The American Magazine* (1906–1956), a monthly magazine that began as a vehicle for muckraking journalism. Under the editorship of John M. Siddall (1915–23), the magazine expanded its market by focusing on female readers.

282.27   the Ritz] See note 187.3.

287.10–12   See who? . . . the Prince of Wales."] Edward, Prince of Wales (1894–1972), toured the U.S. and Canada during the summer and fall of 1919.

The press regarded him as the world's most eligible bachelor. While in New York City, he was given a ticker-tape parade and attended the Ziegfeld Follies.

301.9–11 Wessex . . . a Guelph] Wessex, an Anglo-Saxon kingdom in southern England, famous as the setting for many of Thomas Hardy's novels. The Guelphs, a European (and primarily German) dynasty from which the British House of Hanover was descended.

LETTERS

305.13 in the Mercury as a short story] "Absolution," first published in *The American Mercury* 2 (June 1924) and collected in *All the Sad Young Men* (1926). It is included in the present volume.

305.15 the Beautiful and Damned.] Fitzgerald's second novel, published by Scribner's in March 1922.

306.12 Copperfield + Pendennis] *David Copperfield* (1850) by Charles Dickens (1812–1870), and *Pendennis* (1849–50) by W. M. Thackeray (1811–1863).

306.13 This Side of Paradise] Fitzgerald's first novel, published by Scribner's in March 1920.

307.11–12 Seldes . . . Ring's book.] Gilbert Seldes (1893–1970) was an editor, book reviewer, and cultural critic. He published two reviews of *The Great Gatsby*, both highly favorable: "New York Chronicle," *New Criterion* 4 (January 1926); and "Spring Flight," *The Dial* 79 (August 1925). Fitzgerald's friend Ring Lardner (1885–1933), a humorist, playwright, and short-story writer, eventually settled on *What of It?* as the title of his 1925 collection of stories.

307.13 "My Life and Loves"] Sexually explicit memoir by Irish American writer Frank Harris (1856–1931), published privately from 1922 to 1927.

307.18–19 that jacket . . . written it into the book.] Before departing with his wife and daughter for an extended stay in Europe, Fitzgerald had seen in the Scribner's offices a gouache on paper by the Cuban American artist Francis Cugat (1893–1981). He asked that the image be reserved for the dust jacket of his novel in progress. The painting, which depicts a woman's eyes hovering over an amusement-park scene, was used on the first-edition jacket of *The Great Gatsby*.

307.26 Hergeshiemers novel] *Basiland* (1924) by American novelist Joseph Hergesheimer (1880–1954). First serialized in *The Saturday Evening Post*, it would soon be published in book form by A. A. Knopf.

308.1–2   Gertrude Stiens novel in the Transatlantic Review.] Excerpts from *The Making of Americans*—a novel of encyclopedic scope by Gertrude Stein (1874–1946)—began appearing in 1924 in Ford Madox Ford's *The Transatlantic Review*. In 1925 a limited edition of the novel would be published in Paris by Contact Press.

308.3–11   Raymond Radiguets last book . . . Jean Cocteau] During his brief literary career, French writer Raymond Radiguet (1903–1923) wrote two novels. *Le Diable au corps* (1923), about a married woman who has an affair with a sixteen-year-old boy while her husband is away fighting the Germans on the Western Front, was a *succèss de scandale*. *Le bal du Comte d'Orgel* (1924) appeared after the author's death from typhoid fever, its preface supplied by his friend and mentor Jean Cocteau (1889–1963).

308.18   Havelock Ellis "Dance of Life"] *The Dance of Life* (1923), by the English physician, writer, and eugenicist Havelock Ellis (1859–1939), advocates self-development through a variety of activities, including meditation, writing, and dance.

308.19   Struthers Burt] Maxwell Struthers Burt (1882–1954), American poet and fiction writer, and fellow Princetonian and friend of Fitzgerald. Burt's first novel, *The Interpreter's House*, was published by Scribner's in 1924.

309.8–12   Hemingway . . . the real thing.] American novelist and short-story writer Ernest Hemingway (1899–1961) was then living in Paris with his wife, Hadley Richardson Hemingway, and their newborn son, John Hadley Nicanor Hemingway. Ezra Pound (1885–1972) had published six prose vignettes by Hemingway in the Spring 1923 issue of *The Little Review*. By the date of this letter Fitzgerald would have seen Hemingway's two small-press books published in Paris: *Three Stories and Ten Poems* (1923) and *in our time* (1924), the former published by Robert McAlmon's Contact Publishing and the latter part of Ezra Pound's "Inquest" series (an "Inquest into the state of contemporary English prose") for William Bird's Three Mountains Press.

309.15–16   Stalling's book . . . whine appealingly.] The autobiographical novel *Plumes* (1924) by the American author Lawrence Stallings (1894–1968) depicts the physical and mental anguish of a wounded World War I veteran. The book was the basis for King Vidor's 1925 film *The Big Parade*.

310.16   Whitney Darrow] Head of the sales department at Scribner's.

310.22–23 Mencken's or Lewis' or Howard's] H. L. Mencken (1880–1956), American journalist and critic; Sinclair Lewis (1885–1951), American novelist; Sidney Howard (1891–1939), American playwright and screenwriter.

310.25–26 About serialization. . . . Hearsts . . . Long] In January 1923 Fitzgerald signed a contract with the Hearst organization giving them an option on all the short stories he would produce that year. The contract also granted Hearst first refusal on the serial rights for Fitzgerald's next novel. Ray Long (1878–1935) was the editor of *Cosmopolitan*, a Hearst magazine.

311.3 Liberty] An American weekly illustrated magazine, founded earlier in 1924, that competed with *The Saturday Evening Post*. It was promoted as "A Weekly Periodical for Everyone."

311.15 Reynolds] Paul Revere Reynolds (1864–1944), head of Paul R. Reynolds and Son, the literary agency that handled Fitzgerald's magazine fiction until 1929, when Fitzgerald followed Harold Ober after he left Reynolds to open his own agency.

312.8 "Paradise"] *This Side of Paradise* (1920), Fitzgerald's first novel.

312.11–17 the title . . . the wrap.] Perkins refers to "Trimalchio in West Egg," one of several provisional titles for *The Great Gatsby*. The title alludes to a character in Petronius's *Satyricon*—a freed slave known for his lavish parties. If published under that title, an explanatory note in the jacket copy would have been necessary. See also note 110.4.

314.5–6 Mr. Scribner and of Louise—] Charles Scribner II (1854–1930), president of the publishing firm bearing his father's name, and Louise Saunders Perkins (1887–1965), wife of Maxwell Perkins.

316.9–15 P.S. Why . . . lower royalty . . . the other.] The eventual contract between Fitzgerald and Scribner's for *The Great Gatsby*, dated December 22, 1924, gave the author a royalty of 15 percent of the retail price for the first 40,000 copies sold and 20 percent thereafter. No mention is made in the contract of subsidiary rights; by custom these were divided equally between author and publisher.

318.1 the cowboy book] *Cowboys North and South* (1924) by Canadian American writer Will James (1892–1942). It was the first of many books by James about the American West that Scribner's would publish.

318.5 Simon called Peter—] See note 30.26.

318.14   Bunny] Nickname for Fitzgerald's Princeton friend Edmund Wilson
(1895–1972), now a young journalist and book critic. At Fitzgerald's request,
Wilson had previously read the manuscript of *The Beautiful and Damned*, giving
him advice about language and style in the novel.

318.21   Galsworthy] John Galsworthy (1867–1933), English novelist whose
books were published in the U.S. by Scribner's. Fitzgerald and Zelda had met
Galsworthy in the spring of 1921 on their first trip to England.

319.11–12   new novel] Fitzgerald would begin work in the spring of 1925 on
a novel of matricide, set on the French Riviera. Among his working titles: "Our
Type," "The Boy Who Shot His Mother," and "The World's Fair." The novel would
eventually be published by Scribner's in 1934 as *Tender Is the Night*.

319.16–20   Thanks enormously . . . on Gatsby] Fitzgerald refers to his advance
against royalties for *The Great Gatsby*.

319.26–27   most expensive affairs since Madame Bovary.] Gustave Flaubert
(1821–1880) was a compulsive reviser of his own writing. His revisions in proof
for *Madame Bovary* (1857) were especially heavy. Fitzgerald did in fact make major revisions to *The Great Gatsby* in galley proofs.

320.5–8   Ring's + Tom's . . . since Babbit] Fitzgerald refers to Ring Lardner's
How to Write Short Stories (1924), Thomas Boyd's *Through the Wheat* (1923), Willa
Cather's *A Lost Lady* (1923), Edna Ferber's *So Big* (1924), and Sinclair Lewis's
Babbitt (1922).

320.29   the man I had in mind] Likely newspaperman Herbert Bayard Swope
(1882–1958), who was living in a rented mansion on East Shore Road in Great
Neck, near Ring Lardner's residence, during the period in which Fitzgerald was
renting a cottage on Long Island and working on the early chapters of *The Great
Gatsby*. Fitzgerald attended elaborate parties at Swope's mansion, which had fifteen bedrooms, a seven-car garage, and a guest house.

321.2–5   Shaw-Desmond-trash . . . bad bets] The Irish novelist and playwright
Shaw Desmond (1887–1960) was a proponent of spiritualism and a student of
fairy lore and the occult. Scribner's published Desmond's *The Drama of Sinn Fein*
in 1923.

321.7   Fuller Magee case] High-profile criminal trial of 1923 in which the New
York stockbrokers Edward W. Fuller and William F. McGee pled guilty to using
their firm as a "bucket shop"—a brokerage that permits gambling on the rise
and fall of stocks without purchasing or selling any shares. The racketeer Arnold

Rothstein (1882–1928), the model for Meyer Wolfshiem in *The Great Gatsby*, was believed to have been involved in the machinations.

321.11   the brother in "Salt" + Hurstwood in "Sister Carrie"] Leslie Wagstaff, half brother to Griffith Adams, in *Salt; or the Education of Griffith Adams* (1919), by Charles G. Norris (1881–1945), and George Hurstwood in *Sister Carrie* (1900), by Theodore Dreiser (1871–1945).

321.16   Edith Cummings] Cummings (1899–1984) was a Chicago socialite and friend of Ginevra King, Fitzgerald's first serious sweetheart. Cummings was a talented golfer; she won the U.S. Women's Amateur tournament in 1923 and was known as the "Fairway Flapper." Her photograph appeared on the cover of the August 25, 1924, issue of *Time* magazine.

321.19   The Vegetable failed] Fitzgerald's satirical play *The Vegetable: or from President to Postman*, which he wrote in 1921 and 1922, opened in Atlantic City on November 19, 1923. The play was a flop. It never made it to Broadway and left Fitzgerald in serious debt. Scribner's published *The Vegetable* in 1923.

321.24   The Order of Danilo.] Award given by Montenegro since 1853. In chapter IV of *The Great Gatsby*, Gatsby—who received the award for service during the First World War—shows his medal to Nick Carraway (see p. 63).

322.12   I still owe . . . my Encyclopedia] Scribner's was the American publisher of the *Encyclopedia Britannica*. Fitzgerald had purchased the multivolume set from his publisher on credit.

322.14–15   Ernest Boyd's book?] Fitzgerald is asking for a copy of *Portraits: Real and Imaginary* (1924) by the Irish journalist and literary critic Ernest Boyd (1887–1946). Published in the U.S. by Doran, the book contains a personality sketch of Fitzgerald.

323.19–21   Will James] See note 318.1.

324.6–11   the jazz history of the world . . . take it out.] Perkins refers to a passage in the version of his novel—then titled *Trimalchio*—that Fitzgerald had first submitted to his editor. Fitzgerald would cut his narrator's account of the "Jazz History of the World" in revision. The passage survives in the galleys of the novel and is reproduced in the Cambridge edition of *Trimalchio* (2000).

324.26–27   mysterious hand . . . the typesetter.] Perkins refers to Fitzgerald's query about his manuscript being "in hand," this from Fitzgerald's letter c. December 20, 1924. See p. 319.

326.12   Reynolds] See note 311.15.

326.14–15   turning down . . . College Humor] Fitzgerald had rejected an offer from *College Humor* for serial rights to *The Great Gatsby*. He feared that the appearance of *The Great Gatsby* in a magazine of light humor and satire would damage both his literary reputation and the reception of the book version.

326.19–21   John Fox . . . no predecessor.] American journalist and novelist John Fox Jr. (1862–1919) published several novels with Scribner's, including the bestsellers *The Little Shepherd of Kingdom Come* (1903) and *The Trail of the Lonesome Pine* (1908), historical romances set in the Appalachian Mountains of Kentucky and Virginia. Fox had borrowed large amounts of money from Scribner's during his career.

327.2   Ring's title for his spring book?] Forthcoming from Scribner's in the spring of 1925, Lardner's short story collection was titled *What of It?*

327.3–4   Did O'Brien . . . his trash-album?] Fitzgerald refers to the annual Best Short Stories series, edited by anthologist Edward J. O'Brien (1890–1941). Each year O'Brien made his selections from American periodicals, having previously chosen Fitzgerald's "Two for a Cent" for the 1922 volume ("Babylon Revisited" would be reprinted in the 1931 volume). At the back of each volume, O'Brien awarded stars to worthy stories not included in his roundup. "Absolution" received three stars in *The Best Short Stories of 1923*. Though Fitzgerald was disdainful of the series, he made a note in his personal ledger whenever one of his stories was starred.

328.21   John Bishop.] John Peale Bishop (1892–1944), American poet and critic. A friend of Fitzgerald from his Princeton years, Bishop is the model for the character Thomas Parke D'Invilliers in *This Side of Paradise*.

329.9   Dunn and . . . Roger] Charles Dunn and Roger Burlingame, members of the editorial department at Scribner's.

329.14–17   "What of It" . . . the set.] In 1925 Scribner's reissued *You Know Me Al*, *The Big Town*, and *Gullible's Travels*—previously published by other firms—as part of a five-volume set that included *What of It?* and *How to Write Short Stories*.

329.19   "Symptoms of Being 35"] Perkins refers to Ring Lardner's article "General Symptoms of Being 35—Which Is What I Am," published in *American Magazine* (May 1921). It would later be included in an augmented third printing of *What of It?*

330.1   finally got his "In our time"] Perkins refers to Hemingway's *in our time* (1924), published in Paris in a limited edition by Three Mountains Press. The book would have been difficult for Perkins to find: approximately 130 copies of the 300-copy print run were spoiled by the printer, leaving only about 170 copies for sale. The expanded *In Our Time* (1925), Hemingway's first commercial book, would be published in October 1925 by Boni & Liveright.

◆

The text in this book is set in 12 point Perpetua, a serif typeface designed by the British sculptor Eric Gill and, after seven years of development, released in 1932 by the Monotype Corporation. Influenced by Gill's experience with lettering for monuments, the type was named for the third-century Christian martyr Vibia Perpetua; its italic complement was initially named Felicity after her companion, who was also slain. The chapter heads are set in Carat, a serif face designed by Dieter Hofrichter in 2012, and the part titles and drop caps are in Ayer Poster, a version of a condensed typeface originally designed by Miguel Reyes for a fashion magazine and released commercially in 2019.

The paper is an acid-free Forest Stewardship Council–certified stock that exceeds the requirements for permanence of the American National Standards Institute. Text design and composition by Neuwirth & Associates, New York, New York. Printing and binding by McNaughton & Gunn, Saline, Michigan.